DOUBLE HELIX

DOUBLE HELIX

a novel by

Sigmund
Brouwer

WORD PUBLISHING

Dallas London Vancouver Melbourne

PUBLISHED BY WORD PUBLISHING,
DALLAS, TEXAS

Book Design by Mark McGarry
Set in Electra

LIBRARY OF CONGRESS CATALOGING-IN-PUBLICATION DATA

Brouwer, Sigmund, 1959–
Double Helix / Sigmund Brouwer.
p. cm.
ISBN 0–8499–1215–6
I. Title.
PS3552.R6825D68   1995
813'.54—dc20   95–10690
CIP

5 6 7 8 9 0   RRD   6 5 4 3 2 1

PRINTED IN THE UNITED STATES OF AMERICA

To Lana,

for encouragement, support, and friendship.
This book would not be here without your help.
Thank you.

ACKNOWLEDGMENTS

For generous advice on genetics and genetics technology, thank you to Dr. Paul Mains at the University of Calgary. Any errors are mine; much of what is accurate is his.

Thank you to Nancy, Joey, and Kip at Word. I hope you've had as much fun with this project as I have.

Prologue

THREE PEOPLE occupied the room on the sixth floor of the Institute—a tall man in a lab coat and a short, dark-skinned woman hovered near the operating table in the center of the room. A second woman, on her back on that table, screamed through the pains of labor.

The woman's screams abated briefly.

The tall man examined the white translucent rubber of his gloved hands against the light above the operating table. "Velma," he said. "How much longer must I tolerate this?"

Velma lifted the sheet draped over the screaming woman's belly. "Soon it will arrive," she said in her broken, lilting accent. "That I can plainly see."

"Not soon enough," the man said. He absently pulled at the rubber on his right index finger then released it with a snap lost in the screaming. "Roll up a towel and stuff it in her mouth."

Velma nodded. The black skin of her broad face glistened with sweat brought by the heat of the light and the exertion of holding the woman down.

As Velma reached for the towel on a cart near the table, the woman screamed again. And again. With enough agony to bring her into a half-sitting position.

The man brought his hand back in a threat to slap her, but she was far beyond noticing.

She screamed and writhed, pulling at the sheet that covered her lower body.

"Velma!" the man shouted to be heard above the woman's screams.

Velma had already dropped the half-rolled towel and had her hands on the woman's shoulders, trying to push her down. But the woman was frantic with pain and shook off Velma's strong hands.

Her screams somehow grew in volume. Quickened in pace. Her body lurched and shuddered, and she managed to rip away the covering sheet.

They all saw the gleaming dark wetness of the top of the baby's head.

Now the man did slap the woman, then he pushed her back and threw the sheet into place again. He leaned his weight onto her, feeling her struggle like a fish pulled from water.

Velma positioned herself between the woman's legs. She placed a hand below the sheet on the woman's belly to feel for the rhythm of her contractions.

Slowly, scream by scream, the baby's head emerged.

Velma eased the baby's movement, ready to assist, to turn the baby's shoulders during the next contraction.

The woman screamed with shorter, stronger bursts, matching her short, strong pushes of agony.

When Velma felt the baby's shoulders emerge, she lifted her eyes to the tall man. That's all it had taken for her to know—contact with the baby's shoulders.

The tall man had been watching, waiting for Velma's reaction.

She shook her head no to his silent question as a final contraction pushed the baby into her hands.

The tall man turned his head to the side and spit disgust onto the floor.

In that moment of distraction, the woman rose to her elbows, ripped at the sheet, and saw, for the first time, the baby she had brought dead into the world.

She tried to scream again, but the shock of what she saw robbed her of breath.

They were all three frozen for that single moment. The tall man at the side of the table. The short woman at the end of the table. And the woman on the table unable to comprehend.

The moment ended as the woman's body finally delivered air to her lungs, and she screamed with a different sound, a primal, piercing cry of horror.

The tall man turned from the table and exited the room on the sixth floor of the Institute. He slammed the door shut and angrily strode down the wide corridor.

Behind him came the heavy thumping of leather soles.

The tall man turned. He frowned at the sight of a giant sprinting down the hall toward him.

Why would Zwaan be running?

The tall man put up a hand to stop Zwaan. "Listen," the tall man said. "Velma is in the birthing room. The woman with her cannot be permitted to return to the ward."

"Josef," the giant said. His voice came out as a strained whisper, made more eerie by his efforts to control his hard breathing.

"Understand, Zwaan. Do not let the woman live. She saw too much."

"Josef!"

"Yes, Zwaan." Josef Van Klees knew well that Zwaan had an urgent message. But the Institute's master never showed concern, not even to Zwaan.

"It is not good," Zwaan said. "There has been an escape."

One

Tuesday, May 14

SLATER ELLIS SLAMMED on his brakes, throwing chunks of gravel as he fought his 4 x 4 to a sliding stop. At first he'd figured the shiny red spots reflected at that height to be the eyes of a deer, mesmerized by his headlights. A second later, no. Not with white reflected in the halogen glare; too much white for any animal that size. The white of human skin. It had been a boy, naked, held motionless for the final seconds before impact, startled into forward flight by the grinding roar of skidding gravel as Slater had finally believed the message delivered to his eyes.

A boy? Here in the canyon?

Slater took a deep breath, reached into the glove compartment for a flashlight, stepped into the night, and left his truck idling in the center of the road, headlights now bouncing off dust that settled like fog. It'd be good if another vehicle came this way, was forced to stop and park behind him. Give him another set of eyes to search for the boy—if he could get anyone to believe him about the boy.

Yet there it was, where the gravel gave way to sand on the shoulder of the road. The print of a bare foot, small, its edge softening as grains of sand trickled inward.

Bare feet?

"Son!" he called into the brush beside the road. "You all right?"

No answer. Chittering of insects. Droning of an airplane. Ticking of the truck's engine. But no answer from the boy.

"Son! It's okay! I can take you to your home!"

Again no answer. Slater shook his head. Home? What could possibly be home for a boy lost here in New Mexico's canyons? Cuba was the closest town to the west, twelve miles ahead, ten of it this narrow gravel and sand that wound through the mountains. Yet wouldn't it be in the news if one of the town boys were missing in these canyons?

No tourists in this area. Not exactly the beaten path for runaways to Los Angeles either. And the boy's skin had been too pale. This was no Navajo kid on some sort of manhood ritual, and anyway the edge of the Jemez reserve was a half-hour south, over mountains as the crow flies, where the mountain wall dropped abruptly to the desert flats.

"Son!" Slater drew breath to shout more, but stopped. The kid still had to be in hearing range. Why didn't he answer?

Okay. If he hadn't answered by now, he didn't want to be found. Frightened maybe? Dropped off or escaped from some loony who thought this part of New Mexico was remote enough for whatever he'd planned to do with the boy?

Maybe the boy was hurt, too hurt to reply.

But Slater would have sworn his front bumper had missed the kid. Still, it had happened quickly. Best, Slater decided, to follow the footprints.

Slater pushed into darkness, letting his flashlight probe the ground. A few steps later he found another print. Way ahead, the next. The kid had been running some kind of fast to stretch them apart like this. But through brush at night—did the kid have headlights for eyes?

Slater checked the ground for blood. Nothing. Sand. Wiry grass like thin shadow dancers in the beam of his flashlight. Dry grass. Dry brush. Skinny trunks of ponderosa pines. Nothing that gleamed black-red. Because that was how blood appeared at night, Slater knew. Dark glittering jewels more expensive than any ruby. And not nearly as rare.

Slater continued to follow the footprints. How stupid was this? At least two hundred yards into the tangled wildness of brush and snake-filled gullies that normally he wouldn't attempt in daylight.

"Come on kid," he tried again at a half-yell. "This is crazy. You need help. I'll take you straight to town."

"Uvilla strodum nodi! Va go! Va go!"

Slater froze, almost as startled by the sound as by the fact that the kid had finally responded. The voice had come from the deep darkness to his right. Maybe fifty yards away. Had the kid spoken Spanish?

"Español?" Slater called. He struggled to find words in that language and briefly cussed himself for the lack. In New Mexico for four years now, and pressed like this, he couldn't even say hello in Spanish. Would have to do something about that. But for now, there was some kid out there who needed to know Slater could help. *"Español?"* Slater called again.

"Uvilla strodum nodi! Va go! Va go!" Accurate or not, it's what the words sounded like to Slater.

Slater took a half-dozen steps toward the voice. Something whizzed nearby in the darkness, clipped a branch.

"Kid, it's just me. One of the good guys." *Right,* Slater told himself with a shake of his head. A *forty-year-old runaway, and you're calling yourself one of the good guys, when maybe the best you could say about yourself is that you haven't let yourself run to fat, you have no debts, and you've managed to live here in the canyons for nine months without intruding or being intruded on.* The next rock caught Slater just above the wrist and knocked the flashlight loose. It felt like he'd been hit by a baseball bat. Slater grunted, swore, danced, picked up the flashlight, and examined his wrist to find a deep gash, blood gleaming black-red. Slater decide a second later that the flashlight was a dumb idea. Nothing like giving the kid a target. He was not prepared to believe that last rock had been lucky.

He shut off the flashlight. "You win, kid! I'm out of here."

Slater began his retreat, feeling his way back, glad that his eyes had begun to adjust to the new darkness. If it weren't for the clearness of the night sky and the light that came from the moon . . .

A snap of broken branch nearby and behind him.

He felt his first chill of fear. The kid had moved on him. Why was the kid following him after throwing rocks at him?

More rustling. Now closer. Then, incredibly, ahead of him even though he'd picked up his pace. How'd the kid do it?

His fear became a slick sheen of cold sweat. Slater fought the urge to sprint ahead, barely held himself from crashing through the brush like a wounded animal. Slater told himself, commanded himself, to relax. What was the kid going to do? Jump him? Jump an adult three times his size? Hardly.

Slater heard himself breathing, and despite his fierce warnings to himself, he broke into a half-run. Branches tore at his arms. His face.

A high keening sound came from beside him. Too close.

This kid was crazy.

And in full pursuit.

Slater could no longer push it away. Irrational panic. As if a deep instinct was overloading him with the sense of his own violent death.

He snapped on his flashlight and began to sprint, running away in desperation from a kid he knew had barely stood higher than his headlights. *What was this screaming fear that possessed him so completely?*

Slater ducked what branches he saw, ripped through brush he couldn't avoid. He finally reached the last gully before the road and scrambled upward.

Almost to the truck, he made the mistake of turning his head. Like he was trying to convince himself he had a reason to run from some kid here in the middle of the desert night.

He had time to blink. But that was it. What he saw was a shadow hurtling through the air. Slater wasn't conscious to hear how the chunk of wood bounced off his head like a heavy marble against a melon. And he certainly wasn't able to hear the sigh that left his mouth in a whispered gush, nor did he hear the thump of his own body topple onto the sand shoulder of the road.

Two time zones east, in the cloying sweet humidity of a Florida summer night, Paige Stephens, too, lay alone and motionless on her back. But it was with the forced composure of someone who did not expect the relief of sleep. Beneath the silk sheets, she unclenched the fists at her sides and crossed her hands, resting them palms down on her lower ribs, as if she were in a coffin.

That thought crossed her mind, and she nearly laughed bitterly into the darkness. The red negligee, straps now cutting into her shoulders, had cost two hundred plus tax; another sixty dollars for the Paloma Picasso because maybe he just didn't notice the other perfumes anymore; eighty for the champagne that she imagined she could hear fizzing into deadness from the half-empty flute glasses; and two thousand a year, plus endless hours of sweat—no, *perspiration*—for the workouts that kept enough sags out of her thirty-six-year-old body, so that it shouldn't have been too ridiculous, in the strip-me-now negligee, to arch her back and stretch against the doorway and invite him from his office into the low light of bedroom candles and background Kenny G on the saxophone.

But, as usual, she could have been in a coffin for all that he'd responded.

Sleepless, in the terrible long minutes of self-doubt, Paige finally dared ask herself the question she knew she had been avoiding for months, a question she decided wives probably avoided for as long as possible in the face of overwhelming evidence.

Who was the other woman?

Paige Stephens wanted to step to the window, throw it open regardless of how much air-conditioned coolness it cost the room, and scream that question across the clipped sawgrass lawn, past their docked thirty-six-foot SeaRay that rocked slightly with the swells of the canal beyond the lawn. *Who are you?*

Paige knew it was another woman. What else could explain what Darby had become over the last few months? Edgy. Secretive. Subject to long, late work nights. Too many weekends on business trips. Unromantic. Definitely unromantic.

Who are you?

Auburn hair too? My height? Or had Darby's taste changed with his obvious disinterest? Was it his secretary, a clichéd suspicion only clichéd because it too often did happen that way?

So what hurts worse, Paige asked herself, *that he has another woman, or that he won't even bother with me anymore?*

The phone rang. A half-ring. Darby in his home office down the hall had snatched it up quickly, as if that could convince her the phone had not rung at all, that the damage had not been done.

But the damage had been done. Unless it was an emergency, none of their friends would call at this hour. She'd really have to practice self-deception to believe it was a business call, that her husband-in-name, the head accountant for International World Relief Committee, was responding to yet another funding crisis.

Paige sat up and hugged her knees as she wondered what to do about the telephone.

Today, she now told herself, had been the first day of competition. Her careful choice of negligee, the long bubble bath, all of it had been a subconscious plan to fight back for what she had lost. Her husband. She'd been fighting the unknown, yes, even at that point, the unadmitted enemy.

Until now. The choice was here to be made. Fight on. Or retreat.

She pivoted to set her feet on the floor and sat on the edge of the bed. She worked a finger beneath the handset of the extension telephone and pressed the release button, holding the pressure so that she could lift the handset to her ear. She eased the pressure slowly, hoped the connecting click would not be obvious to Darby.

"...you think I care you're upset I called you at home?"

Paige nearly gasped with surprised pleasure to discover the enemy's voice was low and male. Raspy, rough, strained. Not female, throaty, husky, purring as she'd feared.

"You've been making yourself scarce. Not returning calls."

"I'm tired of it." Darby's voice was barely more than a whisper. "Ends don't justify the means."

"Cut the philosophical crap. You're in too deep. And you know it."

"I want out."

"With a guarantee of silence?"

"Of course."

"Impossible to guarantee." It seemed the man was straining to speak. "Especially with what you did, Darby. We know it was you. Who else would have done it? Air vents, right?"

"I want out. I can't sleep. When I close my eyes, all I see is that room with the jars and..."

"You get paid, what, a half-million a year?"

"That's for time and expertise. Not my conscience."

"Spare me, Darby. You had a good idea of what this was about when you set it up."

There was a long pause. Breathing. Paige wanted to hang up. This explained enough. She still had her husband. But was it a husband she knew? She pressed the phone harder against her ear and strained to listen.

"Darby, you don't actually believe we would let this go unpunished."

"You will. You won't get to me. Nobody will."

"Anywhere in the world, we'll get you."

"Not where I'm going."

"If not you, how about your wife? She is beautiful, isn't she? Your wife?"

"She's protected. From the beginning I set that up," Darby said. "You won't dare touch her. I've got computer disks that show all the numbers. All the corporations. Names, too, right into D.C. Anything happens to her, everything is released to the media."

"Redhead, right?" the raspy voice continued. "Long legs that reach at least to her neck and—"

Paige winced at the slamming of the phone.

Silence. No dial tone.

"Darby?" The male voice laughed cruelly. "Darby?"

Paige realized the disconnection had not happened because she still held the extension to her ear. She set the handset back into place.

Five minutes later, she heard Darby's office door shut. She listened to his progress as he padded down the hallway. She already knew what she would do once he got into bed. Ease his strain, hold him close, comfort him, not ask questions, just let him know she cared about him, loved him even through his periods of silence and noncommunication.

The bedroom door did not open as expected.

Instead, his footsteps continued down the hall to the guest bedroom.

That had been another habit that until tonight had bothered her. He often readied himself in the guest bathroom. Taking a shower to rid himself of perfume, she'd always thought without letting herself think it. Well, she no longer needed to worry about that. Whatever was distracting him, it wasn't another woman.

She relaxed in her world of darkness. It did not upset her now to be staring at the ceiling. Whatever was bothering Darby could be fixed. It wasn't the nightmare of infidelity. Whatever it was, she could deal with it.

The sharp, sudden loudness echoed for several heartbeats before she recognized what she had heard.

A gunshot. From down the hallway. From the guest bathroom.

A single gunshot. With the horror of silence after.

Behind his smile—a winning, engaging smile he knew and used accordingly—Josef Van Klees enjoyed a set of thoughts that ran parallel to the dinner conversation. With only half the meal finished, the parallel thoughts were the only way he could contemplate getting through the boredom ahead.

"Have more wine, please," he said to Simon Curzio with that winning, engaging smile. But Josef's thoughts were on that distasteful yet fascinating documentary he'd once seen showing men with spiked clubs killing baby seals on the ice floes off the northern Atlantic Coast.

To further enjoy the workings of his brain, Josef Van Klees decided to test himself while pouring the red wine for the graduate student in front of him.

"You see, your work sparkles as does a good wine," Dr. Van Klees said in the smooth voice. *Retrieve data ... northern Atlantic Coast. Off Labrador, a section of the Canadian province of Newfoundland, approximate area 285,000 square kilometers. Latitude, then: 54 degrees latitude, 58 degrees longitude.... Aren't wonderful minds good and good minds wonderful?* "Yes, Simon, my friend. I may call you friend? Like a good wine, Simon, your graduate work has been so powerful it is almost intoxicatingly delightful at times."

Van Klees chose not to bestow upon Simon another winning, engaging smile and instead leaned forward slightly to set his elbows down on the white linen tablecloth, furrowing his brow to indicate sincere seriousness.

Van Klees gave Simon a full-voltage intense stare and gauged his subject.

Simon Curzio. Twenty-seven, no immediate family, no girlfriend, but, as Van Klees already knew from Zwaan's report, he had a habit of visiting peep shows most Friday nights. Little income, $35,000 in outstanding student loans. Also, as was now obvious, awkward, skinny, with a straggly goatee, smudge of garlic butter on a red polyester tie—polyester!—much too wide and much too short and much too red, faded as it was, for the green-brown of his worn suit jacket.

Curzio responded as if salivating to a bell. "Well, Dr. Van Klees..."

Good. No "Josef" in return. The fool at least recognizes his inferiority. It is always so tiring to endure chummy familiarity.

"...the limitation of the restriction enzymes, it seemed, was that the bacteria are so determined to destroy foreign invading viruses. It started off as intuition, but I thought if I could find a different way to biofacture these genes into becoming more precise scalpels, the recombinant factor—"

"Simon, Simon." Van Klees interrupted with a benevolent chuckle. Anything, not to have to listen to a four-year-old explain the ABCs. "Look around us Simon. Chicago's most elegant restaurant. Surely, we can leave the laboratory behind for a single evening!"

Curzio dropped his head, actually dropped his head as if reprimanded, and nervously rubbed his goatee with his left hand. Fingernails, naturally, chewed to stubs.

Now lift him up again.

"Simon," Van Klees said gently, "I can only give you such advice because I was just like you. My mind was always on work. It took many difficult years to finally understand I could improve my work by resting on occasion. A pause to sharpen the ax, so to speak. If you realize that, why, you will outshine me as the sun outshines the stars."

Curzio looked up again. Grinned. Shyly. Admiration, even adoration in his eyes. And why not? Josef knew the picture he painted as he strode back and forth in the university lecture hall. Tall, with sleek emphasis given to his height by the elegant cut of his European tailored suits, an even-featured face, hair graying at the temples and trimmed twice weekly, the hint of a dimple in the cleft of his chin when he smiled. No, mirrors do not lie. He always checked himself carefully before facing his students. His wonderful appearance reflected his mind, as they all knew. But what they didn't know—and it was impossible, of course, for any of the sheep to understand—was how inadequately his cultured appearance reflected the supreme greatness of his mind. Who else could juggle what he did in his mind, so superbly continue with business as usual, and not betray a single hint of worry for the escape in New Mexico or the matters in Florida?

"Dr. Van Klees..."

Josef waived away any hint at a compliment.

"Simon, you have probably guessed this is no ordinary evening. Yes, with your brilliance, you probably even realize the purpose of our time together."

"I can only hope..."

Because his brain worked so much faster than those of ordinary humans, Josef knew he could process whatever thoughts he chose to use as a welcome distraction and still return to the conversation before Curzio stammered further.

Like clubbing the hapless baby seals, he mused. Deception is so easy. People are so stupid, so transparent. Their transparency allows you to see clearly what they want, and their stupidity causes them to believe your illusions. The more powerful, the easier the deception, for their wants are far grander and the urge to believe accordingly greater. What better proof of this than the laboratory for which he was now successfully wooing this candidate?

At that thought, Dr. Van Klees almost coughed laughter into his red wine. He refrained, however. Common as the wine was, it was still excellent. Van Klees prided himself on not being such a snob that he might refuse excellence simply because it was common. Only someone vastly cruder than he would cough and spew traces of body fluids into the wonders of a fermented cabernet sauvignon grape. Besides, he didn't want to startle the little fish before him into jumping off the hook.

"Your hope is, of course, close to the mark, Simon. I know of a corporation that is determined to put you in their employ."

Simon's pocked face brightened more, if that were possible. Then dimmed. "Grunt work, I suppose," he said softly, muted in disappointment. "For just one more Ph.D. lab assistant in a pharmaceutical company."

The fool didn't even ask why a corporate spokesman was not here to make the pitch. Although there was an answer prepared for that.

"Tut-tut." Van Klees swept his arm to indicate the restaurant settings. "Would they be putting all of this on a corporate voucher for ordinary recruitment? They know there are dozens of Ph.D.'s desperate for work in their field. A meal like this is redundant alongside any job offer."

Simon went back to rubbing his goatee.

Remember this, Van Klees told himself, a nervous mannerism to let you look into his mind.

"No, Simon, you will head designated projects." Designated by himself, naturally, the one with a brilliant mind capable of the insight to find new directions. After all, Simon Curzio had not been chosen because of his initiative—as the fool was so willing to believe—but rather for his steady lab work and distinct ability to absorb new information instead of questioning it. "Simon, the laboratory is the most modern that money can buy. The taxes alone on your first year's salary will be more than you've earned in the last five years."

Simon laughed. "There's got to be a catch somewhere."

"Only if you dislike seventy-hour work weeks and total focus on the pursuit of knowledge."

"You don't get a Ph.D. without either, do you?"

Van Klees gave the benevolent smile, as if that last statement had actually been profound, then he returned to more serious sincerity. This little fish had the hook deep in his throat. Give him slightly more line to see if he was ready to swallow hard.

"You'll have to move from Chicago," Van Klees said. "Throughout the year, four weeks on-site, five days off. The site has every amenity you could possibly need, including, shall we say . . . entertainment that is warm and willing."

For the first time since sitting opposite Van Klees, Simon Curzio frowned. His fingers worked faster on the goatee. "Site? Sounds like a military base."

Had this little fish tasted steel beneath the bait?

"Military? Not precisely."

"My apologies, sir, but even close to military . . . I would need to know more."

Fine then, my little fool, I shall present you the bait of your life. Swallow the hook. Or disgorge.

"The site is private," Van Klees said. "To maintain privacy, it does have practical aspects copied from the military. The inconvenience is more than compensated for by the luxury of working on projects that certain sectors of the more fanatical public might hinder."

Curzio's frown deepened.

He is spitting out the hook. I know it already.

"Unfortunately, Dr. Van Klees, that makes me more nervous." Greasy fingers through greasy beard. How repugnant. "Genetics is an area that I, well, I don't want to sound naive, but I'm in it because I want to have influence on the direction it takes. The ethics, that stuff."

Van Klees clapped with glee, an action so unexpected that Curzio dropped his hand from his goatee.

"Well done, Simon!" Van Klees poured more red wine into both of their glasses. "You have successfully passed this corporation's biggest test!"

"I don't understand."

"Had you agreed to exploring some of the less savory boundaries, young man, I would have smiled and nodded and finished the meal and recommended against you. This corporation, too, realizes that genetics is a two-edged sword. It does not wish to employ scientists who have no scruples."

Simon sat back and grinned in triumphant understanding.

Van Klees permitted his smile to broaden as well, using it to hide seething fury. How could Zwaan have missed this? Bleeding-heart idealism. The illusions of a high moral cause. Zwaan knew, absolutely knew, it was standard procedure to discover whether the candidates put pure science above all.

Van Klees continued to smile outwardly. Then he let it grow inwardly. Zwaan was arriving tomorrow. Zwaan had caused this problem; Zwaan would fix it.

"Yes, a toast," Van Klees said as he raised his glass. Against the light of a chandelier, it shimmered blood red. "Next week, Simon, corporate officials will contact you with more details."

Details of your accidental death, you stupid little fish.

Simon accepted the toast and tossed back half the glass.

Behind his smile—the winning, engaging smile—Josef Van Klees returned to enjoying his thoughts.

Deception is so easy.

Two

CONSCIOUSNESS was not a pleasant return for Slater Ellis. Not when his first sensation was a tickling along his jawline below his left ear.

He groaned, wiped at the tickling, stared in disbelief at the tiny ants mired and struggling in the blood that smeared his hand.

"What the—"

He pushed to sit upright, sudden movement that brought him to curses at the drums of throbbing pain in his skull.

Ants! Their tiny shapes, like a moving alphabet barely visible atop the sand at the edge of the road, formed a line of army precision that disappeared in the grass beyond.

Slater tottered to his feet. He slapped at the skin of his chest and stomach and legs, sending the dust of the sand and the clinging ants in all directions. That's when it hit him—he was slapping at skin, not clothing.

All he wore was a pair of boxer shorts. No shirt. No pants. No shoes. Just boxer shorts. Purple-paisley boxer shorts.

He saw no humor in it.

Slater wobbled as he started putting it together. He'd been hit on the side of the head. The skin just above his ear must have split wide. His ear felt plugged. Blood of course. He'd have to get to Los Alamos, the closest town with a hospital.

He wiped again, tentatively. The blood was almost crusty, and there was lots of it. He didn't need the crustiness of the blood to tell him how long he'd been unconscious. The mountain edges showed clearly against a pale sky of early dawn. But how long had he been ant food?

At least the truck was still in the center of the road where he'd left it idling. Except now it was silent.

Another thing to cuss. Unless his attacker had kindly turned off the ignition—and kindness didn't seem to be a likely characteristic, given his current condition—the last of the tank had burned. Just one more stupid thing; he'd forgotten to fill the gas tank.

Slater took a ginger step toward the vehicle, reluctant to leave the sand shoulder and walk barefoot on the gravel between him and the truck. Thin air at this altitude held no heat at night, and the ache of his movement made him realize how chilled he'd become. There was a blanket inside the truck; he'd wrap it around himself before walking the last half-mile home, not for modesty, but for warmth. Traffic was sparse on this road, and he expected no passersby now at the break of dawn.

Each step brought pain. Not only from his head—he felt warmth on his neck as fresh blood trickled downward—but also from the soles of his feet as sharp pieces of gravel bit into his unprotected skin.

He cursed each step. Then cussed more as he swung open the driver's side door.

The little brat had been inside.

The truck's glove compartment was open, as were the console storage areas. Everything was scattered, as if the kid had been determined to rip the truck apart for anything of value.

Slater squeezed his eyes shut and opened them again, hoping he hadn't seen right the first time.

He had. The grocery bags in the backseat were torn, contents dumped everywhere. At the far back of the interior, carpet uplifted, tool kit apart.

He groaned. Without getting inside, he leaned against the door frame and shivered. It had taken that much out of him to move this far.

A new thought galvanized him.

His wallet. Whenever he drove, he placed it in the console between the bucket seats of the 4 x 4 because he didn't like the pressure of it digging into him as he sat behind the wheel. Slater preferred not to use credit cards; the wallet held at least five hundred in cash.

Slater leaned across the cold leather of the driver's seat and pushed through the papers and odd junk that filled the console.

Incredibly, there it was. Fat, unprotected, and safe. Cash intact.

Slater frowned, puzzled.

The radar detector was still attached with suction cups to the inside of the windshield. His cellular phone still on the passenger seat. All of his cassettes still in the box on the floor mat of the same side. And his wallet, too, was still here?

But the brat had taken the blanket, about half his tools, and his tire jack. Plus the bread, apples, jugs of orange juice, and wrapped meat from his grocery bags. Almost as if the kid had been loading up for survival here in the mountains.

Why not the electronics? Why not the wallet? Or at least the cash?

And for that matter, why hadn't the kid taken more of the groceries? All of the canned goods remained, strewn across the backseat and floor.

Slater squinted and rubbed his face. Even thinking hurt.

The brat could have even taken the 4 x 4. Run it up one of the trails deep into the mountains. It wouldn't be found for weeks.

Slater tried to puzzle it through but came up with no answers that made any sense. He'd been attacked by a superhuman kid, one who had no hesitation to steal but was too stupid to steal what mattered.

He took the wallet and locked the truck. He thought of the remaining half mile he'd have to walk to his house at Seven Springs. He thought of his bare feet.

Slater sighed. Not a great way to start a day. Bloodied, throbbing head. Purple-paisley boxer shorts, without pockets, of course. So, wallet in one hand and keys in the other. And a half-mile hike in this condition. Sure he'd cut his feet on the way. But regardless of the pain, he decided that if a car or truck did happen to pass by at this unlikely hour, he'd be behind some trees, not out on the road hitchhiking.

He lost his sardonic humor in a matter of seconds. That's how long it took to retrace his steps to where he had lain through the night.

Scattered tracks were obvious in the soft sand of the road's shoulder. Any tracker could read most of what had happened in the beam of his headlights the night before.

Slater's bootprints—toes pointed away from the 4 x 4—led in long strides to the grass at the edge of the road. He'd been in a hurry at that point but not frantic enough to run.

Another set of bootprints—toes pointed toward the 4 x 4—led from the grass a couple dozen yards up from the truck. He'd been running then. Scared, with a fear he could still taste if he chose to remember his feelings before the chunk of wood had struck him.

Smaller footprints, the boy's, led to and from the truck, evidence of the looting that had taken place during Slater's unconsciousness.

Almost to the truck, there were the irregular depressions that blurred the tire tracks from traffic that had passed by earlier. These showed how his body had been dragged to and fro as the boy had worked his clothing loose. Small, barefoot tracks, some smudged, some clear, remained where the boy had walked around his body.

There was, too, a deeper depression in the sand, where Slater had lain undisturbed after the boy had finally finished removing his clothing. This resting place was made obvious by the clumped and dark sand from the blood that had leaked from his head during the night hours.

What disturbed Slater was what he learned from the dew on the tracks, for most of them showed tiny beads of moisture. These were the older tracks, made before the air's moisture condensed.

It didn't take much more than a glance at the ground to see the obviousness of his more recent tracks, his staggered barefoot prints. These tracks were much paler, where his weight had pushed through the surface sand to reach the dry sand below.

Trouble was, Slater's barefoot prints weren't the only ones fresher than the dew. Around the depression where his body had lain, he saw several fresh sets of his own bootprints. As if the boy, wearing Slater's boots, had returned more than once to stare down at his body.

Slater could guess at what the boy had been considering.

Resting in the sand, very near the dried blood where his head had been, was a rock the size of a cantaloupe. Slater wondered how long that rock had been poised above his head and why the boy had finally decided not to crush his skull.

"Oh, dear Lord. Hasn't enough already happened?"

Paige Stephens wasn't aware that she'd spoken aloud to the silent house, her words barely more than a trembling moan. Not with what faced her as she stepped from the white glare of Florida heat into the air-conditioned dimness of her front hall.

The first half of the day had stretched into a continuing nightmare, a blur of numbness. Cops. Lawyers. Friends. Faces that loomed in and out of her vision as she staggered like a zombie through the day. And with every conscious thought, she grappled with the incomprehensible: Darby was gone. A single piece of lead had torn out the back of his skull, a single piece of lead triggered by his own hand.

Going through the details at the funeral home had been an event her body mechanically attended and her mind dimly registered but nothing she grasped as reality. Friends had offered to return home with her, but she'd declined. Nothing mattered. Conversation and condolences would be as empty as she felt.

And now this. She'd only been gone a couple of hours. Is this what should happen as you pick out a coffin for your husband, that your house gets ripped apart?

Step by slow, disbelieving step she moved down the hallway. Her high heels barely clicked on the floor tiles. She was forced to step around paintings that had been thrown down, canvas slashed and frames splintered. Clothing from the front hall closet lay scattered in all directions.

A few more steps brought the living room into view. She couldn't find the energy to gasp.

All the cushions from the couch had been ripped apart. Stuffing covered the floor like snow. The television screen had been kicked in. The television lay on its back. All the paintings had been thrown from the walls, each suffering the same fate as the ones in the front hallway.

A thought occurred to her, one that should have been frightening but wasn't because she did not have the capacity to care. *Am I alone in the house? Or is someone lurking in another room?*

With no haste, she turned back to the front hallway and step by slow, disbelieving step, she walked back into the sunshine, toward the cellular phone in her BMW. She didn't bother closing the door behind her.

The cop's name was Robert. She knew because she could see it clearly on the nametag pinned to the chest pocket of his blue uniform.

Robert sat on one of the kitchen chairs, its padding and upholstery as shredded as the chair Paige used. He sat so close that Paige could not only clearly read the white letters of his nametag but could also smell stale sweat past the mint gum Robert chewed as he leaned toward her.

He took her right hand in his meaty fingers and rolled Paige's index finger across ink on a square glass plate then lifted her hand and pressed the finger on a standard form. He squeezed her index finger and held it a fraction of a second longer than necessary before releasing it to take the next finger.

She could hear the other police moving through the house.

"The rest of the boys should be gone real quick." He popped his gum. "We'll be comparing your prints with any that the boys pick up around here. You'll find our fingerprint dust everywhere, but compared to the rest of the mess..." He shrugged.

The rest of the mess was as thorough as the damage in the living room. Here in the kitchen, all the cupboards had been emptied. Jam scooped out of the jam jars, dishwasher detergent powder splashed across the linoleum, cereal scattered from the cereal box. In the bedroom, the mattress had been savaged with a butcher knife. Drawers had been pulled open, clothes thrown in all directions. The bathrooms had received the same treatment. Toilet lids shattered, towels strewn, medicine cabinets trashed. Even all the cans of shaving foam had been sprayed empty.

Robert rolled two more of her fingers. With each one, the squeeze became more pronounced, the suggestiveness more obvious.

"You should think of a hotel," he told her. He gave her a leer that might let her misinterpret his suggestion. He let that hang there, then, just enough of a pause so she couldn't claim it had been anything but professional advice. He continued, "They managed to bypass your security system. If they didn't find what they were looking for, they might be back."

"Looking for?" Paige didn't have the strength to be anything but a weak echo. From her BMW in the driveway, she'd dialed 911 and given her address, then waited with the same numbness that had been draining her since Darby's death.

"Looking for," Robert repeated. "Thieves don't do this kind of damage. Vandals aren't smart enough to get past a security system. They were obviously looking for something."

Paige thought of the conversation she had overheard. Darby had mentioned protection. Disks. Had they been hidden in the house? Had the disks been taken? And if her protection was gone ...but why was she in need of protection?

The cop took her other hand and squeezed slightly before rolling the first finger through the ink.

She frowned at another thought. "You were here before, weren't you? Last night?"

He nodded and gave her that dirty smile. "A long shift, lady. I could use a hotel myself."

She placed his voice from the jumble of voices that had surrounded her as cops and ambulance attendants had crowded in and out of the bathroom where Darby's body had left a blood smear as it had fallen against the side of the bathtub.

One cop had been asking her in the living room if she'd found a note, if she'd been cheating on him, if Darby'd been cheating on her. The other voice, Robert's, had floated clearly from the bedroom where that champagne still fizzled. *Why would anyone want to check out of a pad like this, 'specially when it had a broad with her kind of legs?*

He squeezed her next finger, rubbed the sides of it, leered faintly.

Paige had heard others describe how they felt violated after a break-in, hated the creepiness of knowing a stranger had been through their belongings. She had no such feelings. This, to Paige, was no longer her house. Sure mortgage insurance would give her clear title to the house, but in her heart it was no longer hers. She had already decided she was moving out as soon as possible to rid herself of the ugly memory of the blood-smeared bathtub. This destruction bothered her little. Once she stepped out of the house today, she would never return. New wardrobe, new furniture—everything within the walls of this house was disposable. Someone else could come in and clean it and absolve her of the situation. That's how little she cared, and that's why she felt no sense of violation.

But something finally stirred inside her at Robert's leer and at hearing in her mind again the words he'd spoken even as Darby's body cooled. "A broad with her kind of legs..."

Anger.

Darby had been running from something. Something he could only escape through death. She could be angry at that.

Their marriage—and her love for him—had slowly been dying because of it. She could be angry at that.

Someone had ripped her house apart, choosing to wait until she was arranging Darby's funeral to do it. She could be angry at that.

And this sweating, mouth-breathing cop kept trying to look down her top as he leaned forward and caressed her fingers. That's where the anger could start.

She waited until he'd finished taking all her prints. Before Robert rose from his chair, she stood, moved to the kitchen table where the bottle of fingerprint ink rested, lid beside it. Politely, she reached for it and began to hand it to Robert.

"Oops," she said as it tilted from her fingers and fell into his lap. The ink spread in a huge wet circle on his pants.

"What a mess," she said. "I hope it doesn't get on my floor."

She smiled sweetly. As revenge, it ranked at the effectiveness and maturity level of a kindergarten student. But it was a start. Next she had to find the man who'd spoken with Darby during his final conversation on earth. Paige was quite certain it would take a little more than spilled ink to satisfy her anger then.

"Let me get this straight, mister. A naked boy? Running across the road? What was your name again?"

Slater took a deep breath, a sound that seemed magnified in the phone booth just outside the Los Alamos hospital. He'd expected the disbelief and suspicion he now heard in the trooper's voice.

"The name's Clive Stewart," Slater said without hesitation. "Look, some poor kid is lost. In the canyons up near Fenton State Park," Slater said. "Cut north on 126 from Highway 4—"

"I know Fenton State Park," the voice said curtly.

"About two miles after the pavement ends is where I saw him." No need to mention Seven Springs specifically. Not if he was pretending to be a tourist who had taken an errant shortcut down the road that led to his house.

"And?"

"And I'm reporting it. You've probably already heard from his parents, and I imagine they're worried sick. I thought this might help you in your search."

"You'll have to stop by the sheriff's office here in Los Alamos. We need a full statement in person."

Along with my name, address, and a host of other things I'd rather keep to myself, Slater thought. *Which is exactly why I'm using this pay phone.*

"I'm clear on the other side of the mountains." Slater spoke slowly, confident with the story he had rehearsed. "I drove as fast as I could to the first pay phone to call this in. But I'm heading north on 44 and in a hurry to get home. Family emergency. I don't have the time it'll take to get back to Los Alamos. Especially not back on that road. Last time I try that shortcut."

The trooper's voice suddenly softened. "Sir, we have a great deal of difficulty acting on just a phone call. If..."

"Nobody's been reported missing?" Slater asked.

"If you would sign a statement, sir, we could begin a search."

Slater shook his head. The trooper, of course, saw neither the movement nor Slater's grimace of pain along with it. The gash had taken twenty-seven stitches, each one obvious on the shiny patch of skull where the nurse had so carefully shaved around the wound. "No statement," Slater said. "I'm just trying to help out with this call."

There was a pause.

"Certainly, sir. I appreciate that. Why don't you give me as much information as you have. We'll do our best from there."

Something about the trooper's sudden change in attitude bothered Slater. Suspicion first, understandable. But now friendly chumminess? As if the trooper was settling in for a long conversation?

Slater hung up.

Maybe he was being paranoid. Still, how long would a trace to this line take? Then for a patrol car to cruise up while he was still talking? But the last thing he wanted was any public knowledge of his whereabouts. If he ended up at the sheriff's office, there'd be phone calls from journalists, headlines. He didn't have anything to hide. Not from the state patrol. Not about this. But the other stuff...

Slater turned from the pay phone, cut across the parking lot of the hospital, and climbed into the 4 x 4.

He could call again, from a pay phone outside of Los Alamos. Far enough away that, if traced, he'd be clear before a patrol car could arrive. After all, some kid—brat or not—was alone in the mountains. But along with his worries for the kid, he had to look out for himself too.

"You heard me. I was doing the best I could. But he's gone, Del. Hung up."

Trooper Juan Martinez let the phone receiver dangle in his hand. The dial tone clearly supported his statement.

Del Silverton nodded but showed no happiness in his agreement. He reached across the trooper's desk and grabbed the radio mike to speak to the dispatched patrol car. "Jim, you'll find the phone booth empty. When you get there, stay put. Don't let anyone inside until someone stops by to dust the phone. Got that?"

Del waited for affirmation, then set the mike back in its place.

"All right," he told Martinez. "Send someone out there to dust and then get that call on paper."

"Paper?"

"Transcribed. Tape was rolling wasn't it? I want everything he said typed and on my desk by this afternoon."

"Sure it was taped. Like everything that comes in. But..."

Del didn't owe Martinez an explanation. At six foot five and so wide his olive-colored police uniform had to be tailor made, Del Silverton was not a weak man. He avoided the political correctness garbage that came down in directives, phrases like *shared responsibility, horizontal authority,* and *management skills.* Del didn't believe in management, not when his size and temperament gave him the tools to remain a dictator.

This time, however, it would be much better if Del headed off any questions the rookie trooper might have. After all, once Del had heard Martinez say "naked boy," he'd moved to stand beside the desk, then written instructions on a notepad: STALL HIM.

All local calls that came in showed the number and location of the caller. This one was from a pay phone near the hospital. Del had hurried, actually hurried—and no one could remember the last time Del had moved faster than a walk—to a nearby office to dispatch a car to the phone booth. Then he'd hurried back to Martinez, getting there just as the caller had hung up.

All in all, it was an unusual enough event that if Juan Martinez didn't vocalize his curiosity, it'd be there anyway.

"I heard rumors in Sante Fe about some weirdo getting kicks this way." Del said in a clipped voice. "Trying to send cops out on a wild goose chase."

Martinez pursed his lips. "He sure sounded sincere."

Del gave him a dark look. Was Martinez actually doubting him? Del followed that with a shake of his massive head. "Any kids been reported missing?"

"No."

"So it'd be nice to nail this jerk." Del didn't elaborate further. Elaboration would be out of character and might cause the same questions he didn't want asked in the first place.

Besides, there was a number he needed to call.

Del went into his office and closed the door behind him. Although he had never been forced to call the number before, he had it well memorized. Del had no intention of making the slightest mistake.

He punched it in. He made a mental bet with himself that he wouldn't have to wait more than one ring. Not with the organization on the other end.

"Five, eight, three, four." Answered in one ring. The confirmation of the last four digits that Del had dialed. The strained whisper continued. "Who is it?"

"Nine, nine, two, three." Dale gave the last four digits of his own number.

"Yes?"

Del speculated on the man's location, as if maybe that would give him a clue to the identity of the spook. Since the connection was fuzzy, it couldn't be anything but a cellular phone on the other end. Where was the man now? Restaurant in Washington? Walking the streets of London?

"There's been a sighting," Del reported.

Silence.

"Over in the Seven Springs area," Del said into the slight hiss of cellular vacuum between them. He thought he heard a message being paged in the background. Was the man in a hotel lobby, at a convention, maybe in an airport?

"Well, then," the voice rasped after a short pause, "You have your instructions."

Wind off Lake Michigan and across Lake Shore Drive blew light spray from Buckingham Fountain into their faces. No matter. Josef Van Klees and Peter Zwaan stood close together; the noise of the fountain's splattering streams masked their conversation, and that was what truly mattered to both.

Late spring had been terrible in Chicago, and this day was no exception. Hunched against the chill of the wind, Van Klees had his hands in the pockets of his coat. Because Van Klees had to look up to make eye contact during conversation—something with his tall, elegant height he was rarely forced to do—most of the Sears Tower filled his vision over Zwaan's shoulders.

Peter Zwaan, however was not attempting to make eye contact in return. He was, in fact, almost squirming with discomfort— something *he* was rarely forced to do.

"Nothing," Van Klees repeated, spitting low anger. "You found nothing."

It wasn't Zwaan's size that most menaced people or the hideous patch of waxlike skin that stretched tight from his lower-left jaw almost to his eye and the puckered baldness of his skull, the result of a boyhood prank when a gasoline bomb had ignited fractionally too soon. What most menaced people were Zwaan's eyes. Flat yellow-gray as expressionless and dangerous as tiger eyes. When he spoke, some even backed away without realizing they were doing it. Breathing in fire adds scar tissue to vocal cords, and Zwaan's voice in normal conversation was a strained raspiness that seemed to promise violence.

Zwaan continued to squirm. "We even sonar-bounced the walls. Nothing. His office disks were filled with nothing but normal business garbage."

"This has not been a good week."

"Maybe Darby was bluffing. Maybe he had nothing."

"Nothing?" Van Klees raised his voice slightly. "Then explain why his desk was stripped clean of his backup computer disks. Who did he leave them with, Zwaan? You find that out. Nothing could be more important right now. Especially with the situation in the mountains."

"I only suggested . . ."

"You also suggested she might have overheard your call."

"He slammed the phone down," Zwaan defended himself. "Yet I heard no dial tone for several seconds."

"So you will not take chances, then." Van Klees waited. Zwaan said nothing. "I thought not."

"I have made arrangements," Zwaan said. "She can be killed any time."

"Not until I say. We've been through this. Too little time has passed since her husband died. I do not want any official attention in that area of our operation."

"Until then, her phones are tapped, her mail will be searched. She will be watched." Zwaan stared at the ground. "If there is a package, it will not reach her."

Van Klees grunted. Despite his show of disapproval, he knew if Zwaan couldn't do it, it couldn't be done.

"And our military shipments?" Van Klees asked.

"It would be helpful to make another flight. Rwanda appears to be a promising area. If you could make arrangements..."

Van Klees pondered, but only briefly. "Friday," he announced after flicking through his mental daytimer. "I should be able to get to D.C. by Friday. Prowse needs his liver soon, and the good general is in no position to refuse us. Is there a day next week that suits you more than any other?"

Zwaan shrugged.

Time to soften, Van Klees told himself. "You look tired, my friend. I speak of endless travel for you. Yet I know crisscrossing the continent takes its toll. I should show more appreciation for your efforts."

Zwaan did not, as Van Klees expected, lift his head.

What does this mean? My servant is more troubled than he should be?

"Yes?" Van Klees asked.

Zwaan did not answer immediately. Even with wind blowing off the lake, the roar of traffic as it stopped and started at the lights of Congress Parkway penetrated the fountain's background screen of noise.

"Yes?" Van Klees repeated.

"While I was in the airport—in Tampa—I received a call."

Van Klees stiffened. Zwaan had a pocket cellular phone with a D.C. number; calls were forwarded to wherever he traveled. No ringer, but a vibration buzzer to alert him, for there were occasions when a ringing phone would be inconvenient for Zwaan. Few people had that number, and of those few, only one might have reason to call this week.

"New Mexico." Van Klees said it as a statement.

Zwaan nodded.

"What is it?" No effort to hide his impatience.

"Silverton said there's been a sighting."

"Sighting. As in alive?"

Zwaan nodded again.

The expected anger arrived. "Impossible," Van Klees exploded. "Not after a week."

"Worse," Zwaan told him. "One has made it over the mountain."

Van Klees spun on his heel. Walked away. Returned.

"Silverton knows what to do?" Van Klees demanded.

"Silverton knows what to do."

"And the person who made the sighting?"

"Silverton knows what to do." Zwaan lost no patience. Not around Van Klees.

"There can be no leaks."

"Silverton knows what to do."

Van Klees let out a deep breath. He reminded himself that if Zwaan couldn't do it, it couldn't be done.

"Next time, don't delay to tell me."

Zwaan finally looked Van Klees directly in the eye. "It was either call you or catch my flight. How many ears might hear if I called you during my flight?"

"Of course, of course," Van Klees said. "*Next* time."

Zwaan took the undeserved rebuke without protest.

"Anything else?" he asked. "You did tell me to expect an overnight stay here in Chicago."

An old lady walking a poodle approached. Van Klees resisted the urge to kick the poodle into the waters of the fountain. Intellectual pride or not, he understood the value of venting emotion and had no trouble indulging himself, when convenient.

"Only for the night," Van Klees told him after allowing the lady and poodle to pass. "Tomorrow, New Mexico. I'd like you to meet with two of our scientists. Dr. Kurt needs a refresher course on motivation. Dr. Enrico, I'm afraid, didn't learn his previous lesson and must be dealt with."

Zwaan, for the first time during the conversation, smiled. The prospect of inflicting pain did that for him. The smile was less than saintly, and it pulled the scarred skin on his face into an inhuman mask.

"And it won't hurt to have you nearby if Silverton is less than . . . perfect," Van Klees continued. "As well, when everything is cleaned up, you may consider Silverton a possible leak."

Zwaan's smile widened.

Van Klees withdrew his right hand from his coat pocket. He shook his forefinger at Zwaan as if admonishing a naughty boy.

"Zwaan," he said, "you were sloppy. And that is the reason for your overnight stay here."

Zwaan's smile disappeared.

"Your little friend Simon Curzio. He was not a suitable recruit."

Van Klees smiled quickly to show he carried no real anger. "Not to worry Zwaan, sometimes the moral fiber cannot be detected until it is too late. I do not hold you to blame."

Van Klees stuffed his hand back into his pocket. The wind rushing up his sleeve was chilly, and he preferred to avoid any creature discomforts, no matter how slight.

"Yet, blame or no blame, it was a mistake. So take care of it, Zwaan."

Van Klees knew he did not have to warn Zwaan to make it look like an accident. All of them looked like accidents. Peter Zwaan had little imagination, except when it came to death.

Three

Thursday, May 16

Caller: Hello. My name is Clive Stewart. I'd like to report something you might think is strange, but this is no crank call. I nearly ran over a boy last night. He did not appear to be wearing any clothing.

Martinez: No clothing at all. This boy was naked?

Caller: I believe so. I don't think I hit him. But I'm worried for the kid because he kept running. And he might still be in the mountains.

Martinez: Let me get this straight, mister. A naked boy? Running across the road? What was your name again?

Caller: The name's Clive Stewart. Look, some poor kid is lost. In the canyons up near Fenton State Park. Cut north on 126 from Highway 4.

Martinez: I know Fenton State Park.

Caller: About two miles after the pavement ends is where I saw him.

Martinez: And?

Caller: And I'm reporting it. You've probably already heard from his parents, and I imagine they're worried sick. I thought this might help you in your search.

Martinez: You'll have to stop by the sheriff's office here in Los Alamos. We need a full statement in person.

Caller: I'm clear on the other side of the mountains. I drove as fast as I could to the first pay phone to call this in. But I'm heading north on 44 and in a hurry to get home. Family emergency. I don't have the time it'll take to get back to Los Alamos. Especially not back on that road. Last time I try that shortcut.

Martinez: Sir, we have a great deal of difficulty acting on just a phone call. If . . .

Caller: Nobody's been reported missing?

Martinez: If you would sign a statement, sir. We could begin a search.

Caller: No statement. I'm just trying to help out with this call.

Martinez: Certainly, sir. I appreciate that. Why don't you give me as much information as you have. We'll do our best from there.

Del Silverton, seated and hunched forward over the transcript, rubbed his face without lifting his elbows from his desk. He ignored his 8:00 A.M. coffee.

First of all, he should be calling Martinez in and reaming him for yesterday's sloppy work. He wouldn't, though. Not when it seemed Martinez had forgotten all about the call. Still, it was there in black type on white paper. A person didn't even need to hear the voice inflections on the tape to see how sloppy Martinez had been. Calling him "mister," then going to "sir." Demanding a visit to the sheriff's office, then making a 180 degree turn to be as obliging as possible. That'd be enough to get the warning bells at full clang if anybody had anything to hide.

Which begged the question.

Silverton stared at the transcript as if it could give him the answer. *What did this Clive Stewart have to hide?*

Did the call come from someone in the spooksville organization? Del suspected—no, he *knew* with certainty that someone from the organization would have plenty to hide. These had to be some kind of deep-cover spooks, deeper, darker than a deep-cover arm of the CIA, and he'd even considered they might be foreign spooks. But if they were trying to cover something, any calls from that side would go directly to the top. Not to him.

Someone outside of the organization then. But why not come in and report it if you didn't have something to hide?

Del read the transcript through again. The excuse not to come in sounded good, real good. If it weren't for the automatic trace they now used on every incoming call, Del would have fully believed it was some tourist in too much of a hurry to return to Los Alamos. As it was now, the one obvious lie about the location of the phone booth threw the rest into doubt. The caller's name probably wasn't Clive Stewart. Maybe all that was true was the sighting. And, of course, the boy.

So what would a concerned citizen have that was so important to hide he wouldn't come in to the office from a phone booth not even a half mile away and report a naked boy in the canyon? Did private citizen Clive Stewart, or whatever his name was, have something interesting to hide from the law?

Del straightened at a new thought.

If Del had to pin it to something—this hunch that he knew was a direct hit—it would be the way Stewart had spoken. All you had to do was look at the transcript to know Stewart was white-collar, over thirty. No slang. Well-structured sentences. *You've probably already heard from his parents, and I imagine they're worried sick.* Not *they gotta be worried sick.*

Del knew the stats and hated the media liberals who thought cops were too quick to find blame anywhere but in the strata of the white and sleek. Sure he'd arrested his share of WASPs. Some of them were sicker and nastier than the worst scum he found away from suburban households. But going with the numbers, it was low odds that someone who spoke like this actually had anything to

hide from the cops. Not only that, but even if Stewart had something to hide, he could be almost certain that showing up with a
straight haircut and a clean shirt and ironed tie would be enough
to not face any hassles anyway.

Assume then Stewart didn't have anything to hide from the law.
That's why Del had straightened at his sudden hunch. Maybe that
brought all of this back full circle. Maybe Stewart was someone in
the organization, trying to get this public, while hiding from
spooksville—trying to have the cake and the icing. A good hunch,
especially since the call's origin was Los Alamos, the town where
two out of every three jobs was government.

Del grinned at his thoughts.

Simple. Stewart wasn't hiding from the cops. Stewart was hiding
from the organization. And more specifically and understandably,
Stewart was hiding from the freak who Del himself had found
frightening during their quiet ten-minute discussion one evening
the previous summer.

The conversation had taken place at Del's house, barely more
than a cabin. It was perched at the edge of the Pajarito Plateau to
give him a breathtaking view across the Rio Grande valley from his
veranda. Around the sides and back, ponderosa pines, deep and
thick, were broken only by the short gravel road that led in from
the highway.

His wife worked shifts at the hospital, and during her evening
shifts, Del liked to sit on his front veranda, thinking as little as possible and tilting back longnecks that he kept chilled beside him in
a galvanized steel bucket filled with as much ice as beer.

At a certain time of the evening—the time he liked best
because the sun's light softened as the valley filled with shadow
and the far side of the desert walls became a blend of rose hues—a
car pulled into his driveway.

Del watched without rising as the car stopped and the dust
around it settled. When the car door opened, he raised his eyebrows in surprise at the bulk of the driver. Three-piece suit or not,
this was no banker. Some kind of big, the way he unfolded from

the car. The file folder he carried in his right hand seemed to be the size of a postage stamp in comparison to the rest of him.

Still, Del made no move to stand. That might show interest, politeness, or weakness, none of them habits Del encouraged in himself.

The driver approached.

At first, Del figured it was tricks of the sun in high-altitude air— something that happened often enough here in the land of enchantment. But as the driver stepped onto the veranda, Del saw clearly he'd been wrong. The light bouncing off this monster's face had truly been reflecting a hideous stretching of the skin across one side and the puckered skin of his bald scalp.

By force of habit, Del didn't blink or show any other surprise. Del didn't offer the guy a beer either.

The freak spoke first as he tossed the file folder onto Del's lap.

"Look through this." A raspy, strained voice. Maybe whatever accident caused the massive scarring had also done something to the guy's vocal cords.

"Why?" Del didn't glance down at the weight in his lap.

"Because then you'll understand why you're about to accept a hundred-thousand-a-year retainer fee."

"I've already got a job," Del said. But he felt his first chill of fear. A small chill, but it was there, and he was man enough to admit it to himself. The chill didn't feel good. Del hadn't been afraid of anything since Nam. Not afraid of another man, armed or not. Not afraid of bankers. Not afraid of job security. Not afraid of his wife. But now something in this guy's voice told him he should pay attention, real close attention.

"Sheriff, Los Alamos County. That's your job," came the rasping reply. "And now you have another job. Consider it moonlighting. Except your hundred grand a year doesn't involve any extra hours of work."

Del had a bad feeling about the file folder growing heavier in his lap.

The scarred man reached into his vest pocket.

Del fought the urge to bolt. Then he told himself if the guy was pulling a gun, there was nothing he could do anyway.

What came out, though, was much more harmful. A stack of hundreds—neat, tidy, and compactly wrapped with rubber bands.

"First six months up front," the guy said in his eerie whisper. He tossed that on top of the file folder that Del had yet to open. "If you don't hear from us by the end of that six months, don't worry. The next payment will find you."

"Us?" Del asked.

"No questions," the guy said, managing to sound patient through the straining of his vocal cords. "That's rule one of your job description. No questions, ever."

About then, Del realized he was gripping his longneck bottle so hard it hurt the bones of his hand.

"There's only one other part of the job description." The guy didn't even pause to savor his words. That made it scarier. No enjoyment of power, but instead a casual delivery, as if threatening a U.S. sheriff was hardly worth more attention than picking at his teeth. "Rule two is you do whatever we tell you."

The guy turned and left. Del didn't even have a chance to argue. Not that he would have been inclined. The freak threw fear into him, even though Del guessed they were about the same size. To have him announce with certainty that Del would do whatever they told him, without bothering to say what that whatever was and without bothering to wait for an answer—that was more than bluff. That was power so big it was frightening.

Plus, there was the file folder in Del's lap.

His fingers trembled as he opened it. But he didn't have to see the photographs to understand two things. He would do whatever they asked. And these spooks had pull and connections in the military far beyond what was available even to the president of the United States.

When she reached the Courtney Campbell Causeway to cross the bay from Clearwater to Tampa, Paige had no reason to suspect a gray late-model car had been following her from the aging motel where she'd spent the night at Clearwater Beach.

Once on the causeway, Paige had less reason to suspect the car was following her. The causeway was barely more than a hump of paved ribbon that cut across the flat green waters of Old Tampa Bay. Only occasional strips of sparsely grassed beach on either side of the road broke the monotony of the next half-dozen miles that remained until the Tampa side. Although the entire distance had finally been built to four lanes, traffic was still bumper to bumper, almost too busy at this hour for cars to jockey for position by passing. The gray car, now securely wedged four cars back in the snake of traffic crossing the water, would be with her until she reached land again.

More to the advantage of her followers, at this early hour the sun glared directly into Paige's face and made it difficult for her to squint at anything beyond the bumper of the car ahead. An ocean-going freighter, finally nearing the port after days at sea, cast a dark silhouette against the rays of the rising sun. Paige noticed these boats as little as she did the gray car. Even without the distraction of the sun or the lulling monotony of the drive, she had the distraction of her thoughts to keep her from observing much around her.

As a result, when she reach the mainland, passed the airport, and took the first exit south to the headquarters of the International World Relief Committee, the vehicle remained invisible behind her.

"Mrs. Stephens, how unexpected to see you. And, of course, how pleasant." The brittle cheerfulness of the secretary's voice said otherwise. As did the smile that did not reach her eyes. "In these circumstances, I would have thought you might be . . . resting."

Paige took a deep breath. In better days, she would have thought of something snappy to wipe the unwrinkled smile from this red-nailed bimbette, ten years her younger, who had never hidden her glossy interest in Darby.

"I thought I would clear Darby's things from his desk," Paige said. Her grief was like a fog around her, and she had neither the spirit nor energy to play games. "I probably won't be long."

Paige moved past the secretary's desk and closed the door as she stepped into the office that Darby had occupied for nearly a decade.

Her view was simple. A computer screen and telephone on a large, uncluttered desk, swivel chair behind. Filing cabinet to the right. Floor-to-ceiling window as a backdrop. Five stories up, she had a clear view of airport runways and of the corner of the bay, where scattered boats drew white lines in the water.

How many times had Darby swiveled to contemplate this view, she wondered, bitten the tip of his pencil as he always did when distracted, and stared absently out the window?

Paige tried to push away her memories, like trying to flap a clearing in heavy fog.

Concentrate, she told herself, *use the search as a way to numb yourself.*

Paige set her purse on the floor and settled in Darby's chair. She tried not to imagine she could still smell his aftershave.

Paige leaned over and reached into her purse. On motel stationery, she'd done some scribbling the night before, during her sleepless hours. She smoothed the paper and placed it on Darby's desk. She reread what she'd written to the best of her memory.

Weird voice: I don't care about calling you at home, we have something to discuss.

Darby: I'm tired of it. Ends don't justify the means. I want out.

voice: Not with what you did. We know it was you. Who else would have done it? Air vents, right?

Darby: I can't sleep. When I close my eyes, all I see is that room with the jars.

voice: You get paid, what, a half-million a year?

Darby: For my expertise. Not my conscience.

voice: You had a good idea of what this was about when you set it up. You don't actually believe we would let you go unpunished.

Darby: You can't get to me. Nobody will.

voice: How about your wife?

Darby: She's protected. From the beginning I set that up. With computer disks that show all the corporations. You won't dare touch her. I've got computer disks that show all the numbers. All the corporations. Names, too, right into D.C. Anything happens to her, everything is released to the media.

Four times, maybe more, Paige had broken into tears as she transcribed her memory of that final phone call. It was so strange, trying to remove herself from her feelings, to be so cold and objective. Each time the tears came, it had taken anger to force her to begin again. Each time the anger had arrived, she'd felt fractionally better, and her focus moved from grief toward determination to find out what had driven Darby to his desperate act of ultimate earthly escape. *You can't get to me. Nobody will.*

After satisfying herself that she had done her best in recalling the strange conversation, Paige had stared at the page for another sleepless hour. Then she'd jotted down some questions at the bottom of the page.

What was Darby in, if not IWRC?

- If Darby was getting a half-million a year, where was the money?
- Why couldn't Darby get out?
- What did Darby do with air vents? Where?
- What jars?
- What was the information on computer disks, and where are the disks?

All the questions bothered her. Each one implied that Darby had been hiding something not only from her but also from the people here at the International World Relief Committee, and indeed from the world.

But what? Darby had been trained to be an accountant. What could he know outside of his background that would be worth a half-million a year to someone else? Would she find any clues in his desk?

Would she like what she found? She wanted to preserve memories of their early love, didn't want to face her nagging doubts of the last cold six months.

She pulled open the top drawer on her left: Rolodex, paper clip tray, phone book, two candy bars.

What was she looking for anyway? Something unusual that might help her make sense of the jottings on the paper.

Paige took another deep breath. She'd never sat behind Darby's desk, let alone snooped through it before. How could she know what was unusual in it without first knowing what was usual?

The next drawer down held two long empty plastic trays. Paige knew little about computers, but guessed the trays were designed to hold disks like the ones Darby occasionally pulled from his briefcase to use in his home office. Empty. She hadn't expected this to be easy.

The bottom drawer held a visitor's guide to Los Alamos, New Mexico. She frowned. When had Darby been in New Mexico? He'd never mentioned it as one of his business trips.

A knock on the door interrupted her thoughts.

Bimbette stuck her head inside without waiting for an answer.

"Mrs. Stephens, I hope you don't mind. Mr. Hammond happened to be here this morning, so I let him know this was a good chance to visit with you. He's requested that you stop by the boardroom."

Paige smiled a smile she didn't feel. Not with Bimbette leaning around the door's edge at an angle that showed too much ease with making announcements in this manner and conveniently displaying too much cleavage. She felt stirrings of anger again. How often had Bimbette done this for Darby's eyes?

"I'll get there soon," Paige said. No smile.

"I'm sorry, Mrs. Stephens, but Mr. Hammond is on a tight schedule." Bimbette smirked to show who was in charge. "He doesn't fly through Tampa often. He requested you stop by immediately."

"Fine."

Paige smoothed her dress as she rose. Refolding her notes, she reached for her purse, tucked the paper in, and headed for the hallway. Almost out of the reception area, she turned back and paused.

"You wore that dress when I was here before, didn't you?" Paige asked. "Of course, it looks so good, I can see why you'd want to wear it as much as possible."

Paige strode on before Bimbette could reply. She felt vaguely ashamed of her cattiness—twice now in two days if you included dumping ink on the cop—but she also enjoyed the sensation of any emotion besides grief and confusion.

She'd heard the John Hammond legend many times from Darby and others at the occasional social functions that drew the executives and their wives together.

John Hammond. Reclusive millionaire, maybe billionaire by now. Funding charity for charity's sake, not for profile or tax deductions.

As the story went, he'd taken money from his profitable New York real estate development firm and seeded the beginnings of the International World Relief Committee. Most of the seed money had gone into hiring the best people from the private sector. John Hammond believed that volunteers did no better than volunteer-quality work, and although IWRC was a not-for-profit organization, he insisted his people be better paid than any other executives at the same level in any corporation, including IBM and General Motors. As a result, IWRC outperformed any similar relief group, which in turn helped it outmarket and outfundraise that same competition. Combined with Hammond's almost genius organizational skills, these capable people ensured Hammond's first money seeds matured into a self-supporting, rapidly growing, nondenominational, worldwide organization that flew food and medical supplies into areas torn apart by war, natural disasters, or famine.

Nearly five hundred IWRC people now worked for John Hammond. Few had met him. While hundreds of millions had heard of and contributed to IWRC, none had seen him, either by photo or television screen.

Paige was unprepared, then, for the man who greeted her at the boardroom door. This was no white-haired gnome with a twinkle of charity in his eyes. Definitely no Santa Claus. Paige, often conscious of her height, felt petite, protected as she took his hand.

"Paige," he said in a cultured voice. "I'm here, too, because of Darby. It is so sad we meet in these circumstances."

He meant it, too, as his eyes searched hers. Blue eyes, she noted, then felt a stab of guilt as she realized she was noting his eyes.

John Hammond was midforties, maybe a couple of years more, but he obviously exercised and found time to get sun in his schedule, and that made it difficult for Paige to decide any closer his exact age. Tall, lean face. Crinkles, not wrinkles when he smiled. Dressed elegantly in two-piece brown for boardroom discussions, but not overbearingly formal in a navy power suit, which so many insecure executives chose as a way to belong to the pack.

"You're here because of Darby . . . ?" She left it as a question.

"Unfortunately," he said with a smile of apology, "we need to find someone to replace him."

He finally let go of her hand and gestured her inside the boardroom. "Your husband was an excellent man. We're only now discovering how indispensable he was. A lesser man would not have been missed for a month, maybe two, and we could have been more decent in waiting to find someone else. His qualities, however, place more pressure on us to immediately review a list of candidates."

Paige took the chair he indicated. He sat opposite her at the large, long oval table. With the boardroom door closed, they were in complete silence except for a slight hiss of air-conditioning.

"It would be inane," he said moments later, "to tritely inquire of your well-being. I cannot imagine the pain you might be facing. If there is anything I or the company can do to help . . ."

Paige shook her head. Tears threatened. This was much worse than dueling with bimbo secretaries. There she could at least lash out as a way of relief. Here, the sadness and confusion just settled heavier.

"This is indelicate," he began again. "Yet too often I've found people ignore finances when it is so crucial not to have another reason to worry. Are you well taken care of?"

Paige nodded. Almost smiled. There was the feeling of protection again.

Hammond gave her a gentle look. "I understand this was completely unexpected."

Paige nodded again. She hadn't told anyone of the final words she'd heard her husband speak on the other phone extension. She hadn't told the police the night of his death—there would be enough questions to cloud Darby's reputation without relaying a conversation that made no sense and implied so much. In fact, until her sleepless musings, she'd tried to block it out of her mind, as if by ignoring it she could find some normalcy in the suicide of her bright, young husband.

"Yes." She answered slowly. "His death was unexpected."

Then she spoke a question before consciously realizing it had entered her mind. She spoke it suspecting she had as little reason to trust John Hammond as anyone else in her mixed-up world.

"Mr. Hammond," she said, "how well do you know everything that happens at all levels here at IWRC?"

Although Slater needed to reload on groceries after the attack, he hadn't found the energy to return to Los Alamos until Thursday morning. Upon his return at noon to Seven Springs, the last thing Slater had expected to find was a neighbor armed with a shotgun at his front door.

By then, Slater had regained an internal equilibrium. Much of that resulted from the drive itself. Westward from Los Alamos, the highway cut into the pines of the Jemez Mountains and wound around and over the first crest, then descended to Valle Grande, where the pines opened to show the massive bowl of an ancient crater, softened now into a giant grassy meadow. Once around the edges of the valley, the road ducked back into mountains and tree shadows, and eventually met the turnoff to Seven Springs. Smooth, wide pavement continued up the turnoff for only a few miles, up and over another crest, then abruptly the road became pitted gravel that followed the fold of a canyon base.

Slater enjoyed the drive. Always did. Most often, he had the road to himself. The sky never failed to fascinate him: its blue on cloudless days an azure in the clean mountain air he'd seen nowhere else, its occasional storms a rapidly darkening drama of menace.

During the entire drive, he'd forced himself to concentrate on the breathtaking views and the peacefulness of the mountains, and in so doing had avoided pondering the strangeness of his fright of a boy who seemed to have supernatural abilities, the rock that had been dropped beside his head instead of on it, and his paranoia about the police tracking him down.

Not even rumbling through the dust at the spot where he'd seen the boy broke him from his mood. There was nothing left to show that anything unusual had happened Tuesday evening.

A half-mile later, he'd reached Seven Springs, announced by hand-painted letters on a weather-beaten plank crookedly nailed to a post at the side of the road.

Seven Springs, merely a collection of cabins, stood among screening pines at the base of a narrow canyon. A creek ran alongside the road, passing by each of the cabins. Some of the buildings were shacks, retreats for stream fishermen who simply wanted a roof to keep out rain and bugs at night. Others, more recent, were chalets as comfortable as any house. Few were year-round buildings, for when winter's snow filled the canyon, it became nearly impossible to reach Seven Springs with anything less than a 4 x 4 truck, and indeed just beyond Seven Springs, the road was closed during the winter months, making passage impossible out of the mountains into the town of Cuba and the desert plains.

Seven Springs was not a town—the reason Slater had chosen it. Its cabins and houses were isolated from each other. It had no general store, no streets. Just a winding gravel road, with houses and cabins set back among the trees. Slater had been there since the previous fall and had yet to meet any of his neighbors. It hadn't taken much work to keep it that way either.

Until now.

Slater recognized the man waiting on his front porch. Had seen him maybe a half-dozen times, usually on weekends, usually in a station wagon with his fat wife, driving into or out of a trail that led to a cabin at least five minutes' walk from the small creek. He was a middle-aged, balding, chunky man, distinctive by the rim of red, wiry hair that rimmed his big, round head. Now he wore a checked flannel shirt tucked into jeans—a weekend camper feeling like Kit Carson. Especially with a shotgun in the crook of his right arm.

Slater wondered briefly if he should hit reverse. Stupid move, he quickly decided. If the guy was actually here to shoot him, he'd have hidden in ambush. Besides, the driveway was so narrow Slater knew he'd lose any race against shotgun pellets blasted from a full-bore barrel. And even if he did get away, how would he know when it was safe to return?

Slater sighed at the tension that tightened his stomach muscles. He shut down the ignition and stepped into the sunshine.

"Good morning," Slater said evenly as he shut the door.

"Maybe," his visitor wheezed. "Depends on how our discussion goes."

Slater became aware of all the sounds around him. Faint warbling of birds. Creaking of insects warming up with the midmorning sun. The ticking of his cooling engine. And the total lack of any sound to suggest any other human beings nearby. No passing cars. No radio. Nothing but the anger of a chunky balding man armed with a shotgun.

"This your boot?" the man asked before Slater could think of something suitable to say in a social situation of this kind.

The man kicked a mud-caked boot from the porch onto the ground near Slater's feet.

"Don't deny it isn't," he said to Slater's silence. The man stepped closer, almost off the porch. "I checked it against the other ones on your back steps. Same, identical size."

Slater had seen the boot, all right. But did he feel like explaining how it had been stolen from him sometime earlier in the week?

"My wife seen you, skulking down the road almost buck naked yesterday morning," the man continued, wheeze more pronounced. "Is that how you get your kicks, running naked in the early hours and stealing women's underwear?"

The man raised his shotgun. "Answer me."

"Sure," Slater said. Sudden anger gave him strength. "How's this for an answer? I figure you're already good for two years in jail."

"Huh?"

"The right to bear arms doesn't include the right to threaten me on my own property. I'm sure the judge will see it that way too."

The shotgun faltered.

Slater pressed. "Unless you set it aside and discuss this in a civilized way, it'll get worse. I'll toss you off my porch, or you'll end up shooting to stop me. Either way, you'll get no more answers."

For a moment, Slater wondered if he'd pushed too hard. The sides of the man's jaws bulged as he bit back his own anger. The gun lifted, as if of its own accord, then faltered again.

"Course," Slater said, realizing this man now had no way to back down without losing pride, "if I were you, I'd tell a judge I was out to hunt some pesky crows, and when I discovered I had wandered off my own property, I stopped by my neighbor's, hoping for some beer and good conversation."

The bulge on the jaw eased. The wrinkles of suspicion on the fat man's face didn't.

"And being the good neighbor," Slater said, "I'd be happy to offer beer and conversation. Why don't you set the gun aside?"

The man shook his head in self-disgust as he laid the shotgun along the top railing of the porch. "Joyce told me to take it along, being as you weren't exactly small, and if it was you stealing underwear, you were probably already crazy. And I didn't disagree with her, not with the nearest sheriff a half-hour away. And you do keep to yourself, so I didn't know what might happen and—"

"Lemonade do if I'm out of beer?" Slater asked. "I'm not sure what I've got in the fridge."

The man nodded.

When Slater returned with two glasses, the man took the offered glass with his left hand and extended his right hand to introduce himself. "Josh Burns," he said. "Manage the service department at a car dealership out of Sante Fe."

"Slater Ellis." Slater didn't elaborate. Just took the man's hand and shook it firm and friendly.

Josh nodded.

"Why don't we trade stories?" Slater asked. He pointed at cane chairs in the shade of the porch. "Out of the sun."

Each sat.

"Mind telling me where you found that boot?" Slater asked. "It's been missing, and I'm curious about it."

Josh pressed the cool glass against his forehead. "Last night, my wife hung some clothes out to dry. Woke up this morning and found them all gone."

"All her clothes. Not just her underwear?"

"All," Josh confirmed. He had the grace to stare down at his feet. "She figured you'd taken them all so we wouldn't guess the real reason was you wanted her underwear."

Slater nearly grinned at about a dozen smart-alec thoughts. Like did the thief need an emergency tent and her undies seemed about the right size?

Slater gulped lemonade instead, hoping it would hide his thoughts.

"Anyway," Josh said. "She'd seen you skulking—that *was* you wasn't it?"

"Maybe she saw me jogging," Slater said. He'd lied to the county sheriff yesterday morning. Might as well add another lie to the list, mainly because the truth was so difficult to believe. "I was trying to beat the heat by getting out early. Even then, a shirt feels hot. If she's squeamish about bare skin though, I'll keep that in mind."

"Sounds sensible to me, but Joyce said it looked like you was sneaking from tree to tree."

"Crouched?" Slater asked. He'd tried to be cautious upon nearing the houses. "Ducking around like I was playing games, trying to sneak up on a deer I'd seen?"

"Yeah. She went on and on about it." Josh grinned. "Sounds funny, now that I hear your end of it."

Slater nodded, grateful that the baseball cap he wore hid his stitches and prevented more questions. "How'd the missing clothes lead to my boot?"

"Bootprints," Josh answered. "She seen bootprints right below the clothesline, bootprints dug in the sand. She sent me out after the bootprints, told me not to come back until I had her underwear. I stayed with them prints until I got to the creek. Reached some mud along the bank, and there the boot was. Stuck but good. So I pulled it loose and brought it back to Joyce. Maybe she watches too many soaps, but after seeing you on your jog and making the mistake of figuring you was some pervert, she figured it had to be your boot, and she sent me here next."

Josh shook his head. "Teaches me right for running out here half-cocked. Should have known there was a good explanation for this. Your boots was stolen, too, just like her clothes." He frowned. "But that don't explain who done it, or the whyfores, do it?"

"No," Slater said. "It surely does not."

Four

JUST PAST BREAKFAST, Peter Zwaan knocked on an already open door of one of the lab rooms on the fourth floor.

"It's almost at the sixteen-cell stage. This is not a convenient time." A bearded man on a stool spoke almost into his chest as he peered into a microscope. "Go away."

Zwaan smiled. While he did not like people, he liked rude people less. Therefore he enjoyed his work more with rude people.

"I'm afraid it is a necessity, Dr. Kurt."

Zwaan's raspy voice brought the man to attention. Dr. Kurt squinted in the direction of the doorway. Zwaan filled most of it. Dr. Kurt fumbled around his bench with his left hand for his glasses and pushed them on in a hurry.

"I do not recognize you." Kurt was of medium build, thin-faced. A big greasy nose that looked almost false beneath his thick horn-rimmed glasses, combined with a bushy dark mustache, made Dr. Kurt a caricature of one of the Marx brothers in disguise.

Dr. Kurt continued to study Zwaan through the new focus of his glasses.

Better yet, Zwaan thought. The doctor had not flinched in fear as most did when they saw his face and skull. Brave people made Zwaan's music play the longest. Rude and brave was a wonderful combination.

"I am a troubleshooter," Zwaan said quietly. "And it has been brought to my attention you are trouble to the Institute."

Dr. Kurt reddened. Indignation or rage or fear, it did not matter. Zwaan had been given his instructions.

"I will not tolerate impertinence," Dr. Kurt finally squeezed out. "Have you any idea of my importance here?"

Zwaan nodded. He reached for the letters inside his suit jacket and tossed them on the floor in front of Dr. Kurt. "You are important, Dr. Kurt. Which is why you shouldn't persist in trying to tell the world of that importance. The single most crucial part of your agreement with the Institute was one of noncommunication."

The doctor stared at the letters at his feet. The red in his face drained to white. Dr. Kurt recognized his own handwriting on the scattered papers.

Zwaan smiled again. A smile not of satisfaction, but a cognitive aha. White, then, was the color of the doctor's fear. White would sweeten the music.

"Dr. Kurt," Zwaan said, "you will pick up your letters and follow me down to the sixth floor."

"*Sixth* floor? I was unaware..."

"Sixth floor. I hope what you learn there saves your life."

It took them more than a simple walk down the hallway and an elevator ride to reach the sixth floor. Because the Institute was in the shape of an H, they had to leave the north section and cross through the connecting corridor to the south section. Entering the corridor required a retina check by an electronic sensor. Leaving the corridor to join the other section of the H required the same.

During the entire walk, Zwaan said nothing. He noted with mild pleasure that Dr. Kurt had no need to babble to fill their silence.

Once inside the elevator, Zwaan used a key to open the service panel. With a second key, he turned a recessed lock. The indicator lights for floor level did not change, but the elevator continued to hum with movement.

When the doors opened, Zwaan gestured like a doorman and spoke with deliberate, heavy irony. "Sixth floor."

Ahead of them was a metal detector, halfway down a short hallway leading to a vault door. Beyond the metal detector, a keypad and another retina sensor.

Zwaan pushed Dr. Kurt ahead, chuckled when the metal detector rang alarms at his own gun tucked in his shoulder holster, and kept a firm grip on the doctor's elbow as he punched a seven-digit number into the keypad. Zwaan spent few seconds leaning his face into the retina sensor, then straightened as the vault door swung inward.

"You know much about the Institute," Zwaan said, "and your letters openly wonder about its true purpose. While the existence of this level confirms reason for suspicion, I hope to convince you to keep this secret to yourself."

He pushed the doctor ahead in the wide hallway beyond the vault door.

"I am a doctor, respected worldwide," Dr. Kurt said, breaking his long, stubborn silence.

Zwaan caught and enjoyed the undercurrent of nervousness. A distant strain of music teased Zwaan, like the glimpse of a leaf swirling on the current.

"I am also forty-eight years old," Kurt continued. "A grown man, an independent scientist. You had no right to intercept my mail."

"You are wrong, Dr. Kurt. You signed an agreement of total secrecy before taking this job. Follow me."

Zwaan walked ahead without looking back. The vault door had

already closed; the doctor had no place to run. It was ludicrous to think that Kurt might attack him from behind, and Zwaan moved with confidence to a door farther down on his right.

The door was not locked.

Zwaan gestured for Dr. Kurt to step inside ahead of him. Zwaan wanted Kurt to have no distractions as he viewed the room's contents.

"What you see are not used for experiments," Zwaan said to Kurt's back, "but instead are my assistants."

Kurt's head moved in a slow half-circle as he surveyed the small aquariums, each set on a low table. Some were heated by infrared lamps, some merely by bright light bulbs. Others by no special light. But each was covered with a flat sheet of glass. The room, barely more than a large office, held seven of these aquariums. Waterless. But not empty.

"Yes, assistants," Zwaan said. "Creatures who assist me in my tasks. And at this moment, you are one of my tasks."

Kurt grew measurably still. He was beginning to understand.

"Immediately to your right," Zwaan explained, "you might notice the egg cocoon in the twigs of the lower corner. It should contain three hundred to five hundred eggs of the black widow spider."

"Black widow?"

"*Latrodectus mactans*, if your scientific mind prefers the Latin, which I cannot resist showing off." Zwaan was aware that his voice had a tendency to seem stronger the quieter he whispered. So he dropped his voice further.

"As you can see, I also have timber rattlesnakes, very mature specimens. Some coral snakes. And of course, my rats. Rats do very interesting things under certain conditions. Conditions like you strapped on your back, and the rats trapped on your stomach beneath an overturned basket. It usually takes two days for them to get hungry enough to eat their way out through your stomach."

White showed again on the doctor's face. In his mind, Zwaan heard the first of sweet violin strings.

"Yet for you, Dr. Kurt," Zwaan said as he smiled to his private music, "I believe I reserve assistants from the next glass cage. Do you see them half-buried in the sand? If not, step closer."

Kurt remained rigid.

"*Centruoides sculpturatus*," Zwaan whispered. "You may find it of interest that while their pincers look formidable, they do not hurt. Rather, my assistants sting. Their tails end in very sharp tips, driven into flesh with a springlike flick. Very effective, our little scorpion friends, for the puncture wounds are tiny, and once the poison is injected beneath the skin, treatment is difficult.

"The beauty of having such assistants is that your death will not seem unnatural, only unfortunate. I will place you in a sleeping bag, funnel a dozen of my little friends inside, and pull the drawstring tight. Won't that be interesting, to feel them crawling on your naked body, wondering when the first will sting?"

"Enough," Kurt said. His shoulders were ramrod straight, and he did not turn to address Zwaan.

"I'm afraid you will listen. For if you listen well, my assistants may not be required." Zwaan paused. "You will listen?"

Kurt nodded the slightest of movements.

Zwaan did enjoy this, but he also knew the fear he was inspiring served a practical purpose. Perhaps Kurt actually would listen, and the Institute would not lose a skilled researcher.

"Once stung—and I would set at least a dozen to crawl on your naked body—you will feel intense pain at the site of the stings, but there will be little inflammation or swelling. You will soon become restless. At that point, you will be unbound, but, of course, not permitted to leave whichever room I choose for your execution."

Zwaan listened and watched for reaction, but Kurt disappointed him. The violin music in Zwaan's mind began to fade.

"Shortly after this restlessness, your abdominal muscles will become rigid, and your arms and legs will begin to contract. You will start drooling as your body produces excess saliva, and your heart rate will increase. You can expect feverish body temperatures. Blue skin, too, which you as a doctor know as cyanosis. Breathing will become more difficult as you approach the end.

Eventually it is exhaustion that kills you. But not before you experience the indignity of involuntary urination and defecation."

Dr. Kurt finally turned. "Monstrous. You are totally monstrous."

Zwaan smiled inside as the music swelled again.

"Fear is good, Dr. Kurt. It may keep you alive. Please follow me."

Dr. Kurt stumbled out of the room behind Zwaan, who marched down the corridor and stopped in front of another door.

"Open please," Zwaan said. "It is one of the few unlocked doors on this floor."

This room, twice the size of a janitor's closet, held two chairs facing each other. And a sledgehammer in the corner. Nothing else.

"Please sit," Zwaan said as he shut the door behind them.

Dr. Kurt did as directed.

Zwaan sat opposite. He knew he gave the impression of filling the entire room. A psychological tactic that had never failed.

"This is intimate," Zwaan said in his raspy whisper, "however, perhaps sharing death is the ultimate intimacy."

Zwaan listened for the music that came with his rapture. A symphony of wonder that absorbed him more fully as he dealt more pain. And death created the crescendo.

"I am a world-renowned scientist. You cannot—"

Zwaan reached across the small space between them and with his thumb and index finger, tenderly squeezed the doctor's lips shut. He was interfering with the music.

"*Listen*, remember?" Zwaan released his hold on the man's lips. "You see, Dr. Kurt, every detail of your death has been planned. From the first day you began work here, I have prepared for its possible necessity."

Zwaan leaned back and crossed his legs. The bizarreness of such casual body language in the midst of such a deadly discussion was much more crippling than yelling or striking.

"You have not been outside of this building for an entire year. Where is the Institute located?"

Dr. Kurt blinked at the sudden change in the conversation's direction.

"Where?" Zwaan repeated quietly.

"Redmond, Oregon."

Zwaan nodded. "Yes, you did mention that in your letters. Do you recall your first day at the Institute?"

Again, Dr. Kurt blinked. His eyelashes were comically huge behind the thick lenses. Zwaan thought briefly of the jars and all the music they had provided him.

"Your first day was actually your first two days," Zwaan said. He didn't alter his tone in the slightest during his explanation. "Yes, you entered a military compound in the forest outside Redmond. But as you slept, you were drugged. By inhalation. You slept through the night, the next day, and the next night. Enough time for us to move you here. Think of it, doctor. Thirty-six hours of unconsciousness. You could be anywhere in the world."

Dr. Kurt opened his mouth to protest.

"Tut-tut. Listen. Since your arrival, I have been sending occasional postcards to your sister in St. Paul. She's the only one out there who might care if you disappeared. You'd be surprised at how well our forgeries seem like your handwriting. Marge is convinced you have spent the last year at a laboratory in Australia."

Zwaan sighed. "You could be dead for years, but as long as the postcards continue, she won't know otherwise, will she?"

Kurt grew visibly smaller, as if he were hugging himself without using his arms to do so.

"In short, Doctor, you signed a letter of agreement that included total secrecy and devotion to the Institute. In return, you were provided with almost unlimited research resources. We have not taken away those privileges. Thus you have no reason to fail your end of the deal. Please don't try to contact your former colleagues again. And it would be healthy for you to abstain from speculating about the remainder of the sixth floor."

Zwaan stood and stretched. Yawned and took his time doing it.

"You may consider this conversation a warning," Zwaan said.

"The threat of death is real, and if you try anything stupid again, you will die in the manner promised. However, continue with your research as agreed—research I know you enjoy—and I will not visit you again."

Dr. Kurt's shoulders sagged in relief.

"You find me cold, Dr. Kurt; don't deny it. When I am gone, you will have second thoughts about the Institute. You may even wonder whether you will be permitted to leave at the end of your research. That fear may affect your work for us, so please remember it is an unnecessary fear. For you do not know the location of the Institute."

Kurt tried a tentative smile. He allowed hope to enter his eyes.

Zwaan continued his lie. Otherwise Kurt's work *would* suffer badly. "That was done for your protection as well as ours, Dr. Kurt. When your obsession for research no longer compels you to remain with us, we can safely take you back to Oregon, knowing that our location will remain hidden. And because you cannot harm the Institute by divulging its location, you in turn do not face harm."

Kurt closed his eyes and let a deep breath escape him.

"There is one small, final matter, Dr. Kurt."

"Yes?"

"Take off your right shoe. Then the sock."

"But I don't understand."

"There is a sledgehammer in the corner. Surely you saw it as you entered."

Dr. Kurt tightened once more. Zwaan's music began to rise in volume. Violin strings. Then the sweetness of clarinets. All of this was a nice prelude to the scheduled meeting with Dr. Roberto Enrico, who had not learned from the lesson Zwaan was about to give Dr. Kurt.

"You see, Doctor, although you will live to continue research, I cannot let you go unpunished. Once your foot is bare, I intend to break your little toe."

"This...is...barbarous!"

"Not particularly. Even if the toe doesn't heal properly, it will not disable you. A knee on the other hand..." Zwaan shrugged.

"I will not."

"There is a condition." Zwaan continued as if he hadn't heard Kurt's protest. "You must not pull your foot back as I swing downward. In fact, I will break one extra toe for each time you try to avoid your punishment. I suggest, then, you keep your eyes closed during the first swing. My experience shows it simplifies matters greatly."

Zwaan watched Kurt carefully.

Zwaan had found this to be a good test—the litmus paper of a man's spirit, so to speak. If the foot was offered and the eyes closed, the man's spirit had been successfully crushed and Zwaan rarely had a need to return. If there was still resistance, however, it never bothered Zwaan to take extra pleasure in his work.

Kurt trembled. Tears trickled from his eyes.

Zwaan smiled. "If you prefer the left foot over the right foot, I will not prove disagreeable. But decide quickly. Let me assure you the stupidity of forcing me to remove your shoe for you."

More tears fell. The symphony filled Zwaan. At this point, always, he began to feel a form of love at what the two of them would share.

Kurt began to unlace his right shoe. By the time he had removed his sock, he was weeping openly.

Match the spooks—secret for dark secret. Gut instinct told Del that's all it would take to be his own man again. Whatever Clive Stewart was hiding was more than enough to cover the file of photographs spooksville held over him like a piano suspended by thread. Del was prepared to use whatever method it took, from bribery to torture, to get Clive Stewart to spill.

Which left one simple problem.

Find Clive Stewart.

As he mulled through his thoughts, Del resisted an urge to stand and pace away his frustration in the hospital nurses station.

Instead, he focused his attention downward and pretended interest in the Eskimos and dogsleds on page 32 of a six-year-old *National Geographic*. He'd never seemed impatient here in the hospital before; it wouldn't do to start now. Who knew where the spooks had eyes in this government town? Del had told himself to make every move as if he were watched—to the point where he wasn't even putting in an official inquiry for hospital records. If the spooks caught the faintest trace of what he was doing, he was dead. Within hours.

Del, big as he was, shivered, actually shivered, at the thought of how death might arrive at the hands of the scar-faced, bald spook with a raspy voice and lifeless eyes. He searched for another thought.

Where was Louise anyway? Three nurses had come and gone in the last five minutes—someone had to be here by now to take over her shift.

Del reminded himself to look calm. Louise was sharp. Taking her to lunch was enough out of the ordinary in their relationship. She'd worry plenty if she discovered him nervous for the first time in their three years of marriage.

Del gazed, out of focus, at the glossy dogsleds in his hands. He tried to reassure himself that his reasoning was correct.

First of all, there was no doubt the caller had seen a boy, probably exactly where claimed. It had been more than a week after Del had been put on alert—and a week's travel could have put the boy where Clive Stewart claimed to have seen him. Still that was some tough kid. The terrain was brutal on grown men in combat clothing.

Figure the sighting then to be that far west, almost out of the mountains and into the desert. But this Clive Stewart made the call here in Los Alamos at 8:45 A.M., when it would take nearly an hour to get in from the Seven Springs area. Why not make the call from there? Why come all the way into Los Alamos to make it?

More important, what was the significance of the location of the pay phone that Stewart used? There were easily a dozen phone booths more accessible than the one outside the hospital where they'd traced the call to. What had brought Stewart in from the Seven Springs area to the hospital?

Del knew it had to be one of two things. Either Stewart worked here, or he had come in for medical attention. Both choices were logical.

From what Del could guess about the spooksville operation, it had some medical aspects. It could fit that Stewart had an association with the hospital.

On the other hand, from the warning Del had received after the escape, it was just as likely Stewart had come in for medical attention.

Del knew what to do, all right. Check the employee records and see if anyone on the hospital payroll lived west, in the mountains. Check the emergency-room records for the same thing. And start first with the emergency records for that morning—probably the shortest list.

Only he'd have to recruit Louise to help him. Tell her it was a drug situation, needed to be hushed and off the record because it might involve the hospital director and Del didn't want to give any warning. It would take longer because she couldn't just march in and pull the records, but it would be worth the extra caution.

Yes sir, Del told himself, if he could find Clive Stewart, by whatever name Stewart normally used, it would leave some pretty good options. Keep Clive Stewart to himself, alive. Or deliver him dead to spooksville.

Slater had just finished cleaning away his supper dishes when, through the screened window above his kitchen sink, he heard the crunch of tires over gravel.

It crossed his mind that maybe, somehow, the police had traced him from call from the phone booth. He immediately told himself he was being ridiculous—more than two days had passed since the call, and besides, there'd been no radio, television, or newspaper reports about a missing boy, which in itself had been another worry.

Slight as the odds were of police, Slater fought butterflies of fear as he set down his dishtowel. Unexpected visitors were unwelcome visitors, and he never expected visitors. Not here in Seven Springs.

He reached the front door as heavy footsteps thumped onto the porch.

"Ellis," a voice called.

Slater relaxed as he placed the voice. It was the booming geniality of the half-bald redhead, Jeremy—no, Josh—Burns.

"Good evening," Slater said, opening the door to see a wide smile on the man's pumpkin face.

"Evening. Joyce and me—" Josh broke off to point at the shiny-faced woman in the station wagon behind him. "Well, actually it was Joyce's idea. We wanted to bring over a pie, as a sort of peace offering, what with yesterday's misunderstanding and all."

Slater did not see any pie in Josh's hands.

"It's not necessary," Slater said, "but thanks, it's much appreciated."

Josh half-turned to face the station wagon and pumped his heavy head up and down.

Joyce creaked the door open and began to maneuver her body out of the station wagon.

Too late, Slater realized the station wagon's engine had been shut off. Obviously this peace offering included a self-invitation.

Slater forced a smile. "You want coffee along with your pie?"

"Hey, great!" Josh pumped his head up and down for Slater's benefit. "You'll love the pie. Joyce cooks great."

Slater glanced at the station wagon to measure Joyce's progress. She had finally made it out of the car and was bending through the rear door into the backseat. To Slater, it looked like a tight squeeze, and her pink dress could have been a curtain coming down on a play. He fought any conjecture about her underwear billowing on the clothesline like a mainsail.

"Make yourself comfortable out here," Slater said. "I'll get the coffee started and grab an extra chair."

"Don't go to so much trouble," Josh said, "we'll just follow you inside."

"Too hot in there," Slater said. He'd caught Josh craning for a better look in the house and was beginning to wonder about the authenticity of the pie as a peace offering. "You just hang tight."

Before Josh could protest, Slater had pushed him toward one of the two chairs on the porch. Slater made sure the door shut behind him and returned within seconds with a third chair. Joyce was still struggling to pull herself from the backseat of the car. Slater assumed when she finally did, she'd be holding a pie.

"Tell Joyce to make herself comfortable too," Slater told Josh. "The coffee won't take but a second."

From the kitchen, as he measured the coffee grounds, Slater saw movement at the screen of his front door. He shook his head in mild amusement. The woman did make plenty of shadow. And she wasn't shy with her curiosity either. Her face was almost pressed into the screen.

"How you doing?" Slater called. "Give me a second, I'll come introduce myself."

When he reached the porch, he discovered she was tall too. Nearly as tall as he was. Poorly dyed blonde hair and greasy skin gave Slater a whole new sympathy for the blustering Josh Burns. Slater figured he would probably have listened, too, if Joyce had told him to go visiting with a shotgun.

"Slater Ellis." He extended his hand. "Pleased to make your acquaintance."

She examined him, squinting suspicion as she did, a movement that tightened her cheeks into fat balls.

"Slater Ellis," she repeated as if doubting him.

"My wife Joyce," Josh said with an nervous half-chuckle.

Slater drew a deep breath. The next half hour, or however long it took for his uninvited guests to leave, promised to be awkward. Long ago, he'd learned a way to deal with such circumstances: pretend he was an invisible observer and find amusement in the entire situation. After all, if this were happening to someone else, it would be plenty funny.

Joyce didn't take long to cut to the chase. She grunted as

she lowered herself onto a chair, took a breath, and spoke to Slater.

"Josh here tells me you had your boots stolen."

"Sure did."

"Well, I been talking to folks up and down the road, and it appears we ain't the only ones to have things missing. The Oxfords lost stuff from their clothesline too. Shirley right next door to the Oxfords swears she was one bag of groceries short by the time she finished unloading—takes her five or six trips from the car to the house, she says. The Byrnes allowed that some of their garden tools are pretty scarce."

Slater nodded.

"Any idea what's happening?" Her question came out like she was backing him against the wall.

Slater shook his head.

"Let me catch whoever's doing it, and they'll be sorry."

"I'm sure they will." Slater kept a straight face.

The fat woman glared at him, unsure how to take it.

"Coffee's probably ready," Slater said.

He returned a minute later with a tray of cups, plates, forks, and knives and cream and sugar. As he stepped onto the porch, Joyce abruptly ended a whispered conversation with her husband.

They watched in silence as he cut slices of pie.

"Cherry," Josh finally said. "Joyce here does a mean cherry pie."

Joyce hardly waited for her first forkful of pie to begin again. "Where'd you tell Josh you were from?"

Slater realized this fat woman had probably been asking and speculating about him while discussing the mysterious thefts with others in the neighborhood. Slater discarded most of the answers that came to mind, and finally, politely said, "I never got around to it."

Her chin jutted forward. "You weren't here last summer."

"No, ma'am. It sure is nice here, too, isn't it? I haven't regretted a day." Slater would take pleasure in making her work to satisfy her curiosity.

"Where you from then?"

Slater had misjudged. It didn't bother her the slightest to be pushing in areas anyone else would understand he was trying to avoid.

"Out east."

"Where out east?"

Slater realized if he didn't answer, it would give her more ammunition during her next speculations with the neighbors. On the other hand, he'd worked hard to disappear here in Seven Springs.

"Boston," he lied.

"You can't be retired."

Slater shrugged, knowing it wouldn't unimpale him from her dark mean eyes.

"Josh says he seen computers and stuff through your window when he was waiting for you the other day. Is that what you do?"

"Integrated software products," Slater said. He hid a smile, knowing how he'd deal with her now. "Take the computer in the corner. Color screen. Hard drive storage at 540 megabytes. Added a card to get 16 meg of RAM. With a modem, I can tap into any main across the world, process those bytes at about—"

"You married?" she interrupted. "I ain't seen a woman around here."

Tough crowd, Slater thought. *I'm down three nothing and fading fast.*

"Why, you got someone in mind for me?" he tried a light-hearted change of subject.

"Or maybe you don't prefer women," she said, not to be deflected.

Josh, at least, had the grace to wince.

"Ma'am, last time I tried to tell the story, I broke down and cried halfway through. She was a good woman, and I'm doing my best to forget, if you don't mind."

That snapped her mouth shut, and the story was close enough to the truth too.

"How about this cherry pie?" Josh asked.

"Love it," Slater said. "Glad you stopped by."

Joyce was a marvel to watch. Silent, she became an eating machine. She finished her first helping of pie within seconds and was reaching for the pie plate as Slater stepped back inside to get more coffee.

Halfway to the kitchen, he stopped at his computer and flicked on the power switch. He continued to the kitchen, grabbed the coffeepot, and stopped by the computer on his way back. It had booted up by then, and he spent less than thirty seconds in front of it, coffeepot in his left hand, computer mouse rapidly moving in his right hand. His last adjustment was to move the volume of the computer as high as possible.

Satisfied with his work, he resumed his trip out to the porch.

"Nice night, huh?" Slater said.

Josh nodded. Joyce concentrated on her pie.

Slater delayed pouring more coffee. The computer should be—

Bing. Bing. Bing. Bing.

"Nuts," Slater said, "looks like I've got some incoming e-mail. I've been waiting for it all day. You don't mind if I..."

"By all means," Josh said. "We ain't in no hurry."

Slater shook his head. "This will take a couple of hours, I'm afraid. Maybe some other evening?"

"Sure," Josh said.

"I really wish I could walk you out to the car."

Joyce was trying to push herself up from the chair.

"Just leave the dishes on the porch," Slater said. "I'll get them later."

Slater backed away, nodding and smiling as he did so. Once inside, he shut the screen door and immediately approached the computer. *Fat lady,* he thought, *will probably take one final glance inside the house.*

He studied the computer screen, reading the message that accompanied the warning bings. CAN'T FIND PRINTER. MAKE SURE CONNECTION IS IN PLACE. That had been simple, commanding a document to print but not turning on the printer.

After a minute Slater shut down the computer, but his movements were automatic and absentminded, for he could not as easily shut down his growing concern for the obviously abandoned kid.

The boy was still out there, staying in the area, scavenging like a coyote. Yet it appeared the authorities and media had no interest and no one else knew about him.

Was the boy a runaway who needed help? If so, why was he determined to remain feral? And why was he afraid to seek help? If the boy was a delinquent, why hadn't he stolen Slater's truck or the wallet and expensive electronic toys inside?

All of this spelled weird.

There was only one way to get an explanation. But first he had to successfully answer another question: How did a person go about trapping another human being?

"I had no idea when I left New York yesterday that I would enjoy the end of my week so much," John Hammond said. "I'm truly sorry, however, that we had to meet under these circumstances."

Paige smiled, uncertain how else to respond. After their meeting the day before, Hammond had flown to Houston for a meeting. He rebooked his return flight to bring him back through Tampa before going on to New York. He had insisted on taking her for this early supper and had treated her with kindness and respect—not unbearable sympathy and cloying flattery. Dessert and coffee was about to arrive. The last hour had flown in minutes. She had yet to broach some of the questions she decided would justify spending time with this single man, and she felt deep guilt for having enjoyed the quiet meal in dim light; grieving widows should not dally with attractive millionaires.

Unless the grieving widow had a good reason, she firmly told herself. With that resolve, she spoke.

"John, can you tell me about the structure of IWRC?"

He smiled in return. "You've been very patient."

"I beg your pardon?"

"Yesterday you asked me basically the same question, and on impulse, I suggested this restaurant for tonight. You've been gracious to wait this long to pursue your reason for agreeing to join me."

Paige blushed. "It's just that..."

John interrupted. "Don't explain yourself. I'm a big boy. I fully intended to answer. As I said yesterday I had too many meetings that I couldn't cancel. And I didn't want you shuffled off to the PR. department. Answering your questions as well as possible was the price I expected to pay for this pleasant break in my grinding schedule."

With smooth, silent efficiency, their waiter placed white china cups between them and disappeared again. John lifted his cup from his saucer and, holding the coffee, just below his nose, inhaled deeply.

"It never fails to amaze me," he said, "the joys of life that come without a price tag. The aroma of this coffee for example. No amount of money could buy the ability to smell it, enjoy it. Our five senses come free at birth."

He pointed at her cup. "Come on. Smell it as if smelling coffee for the first time. Taste it and concentrate on the taste."

John smiled as she followed instructions. Paige had to agree that the coffee did taste much better when she gave it some attention.

"I find it ironic," John said, "as my wealth accumulates—and once you get to a certain point, it grows as if it has a mind of its own—I tend to search for ways to enjoy life without it. Night skies, sunsets, the satisfaction of hard exercise. Nobody needs money for those. All of it's there for the taking. And no matter how much one person takes, there's enough for everyone else."

Paige nodded an encouraging smile, something she had been doing frequently in John's presence. If he's for real, she thought, he would be a terrific catch for someone. Considerate, thoughtful, attractive, and well off. Again, a stab of guilt. Then anger. *Darby,* she told him silently, *if you hadn't run out on me and your problems, I wouldn't be here . . .*

". . . a roundabout way to tell you about starting IWRC," John was saying, "from a philosophy that once you have enough money for what you need, your money should go to other people's needs."

"We're just asking for your leftovers . . ." Paige said.

John grinned back. ". . . only for the crumbs from your table. Not a bad slogan, huh? It's served us well over the years, brought in millions in donations." His grin continued. "Unfortunately, I can't take credit for it. Some whiz kid at a New York ad agency picked my brain for an hour, then wrapped it up in that slogan," the grin became wry, "and charged me a grand."

He paused to sip more coffee. "I'm not sure what you know about the beginning of IWRC. When you hear the truth, please don't be too disillusioned."

Darby's voice came back to Paige. *I'm tired of it. The ends don't justify the means.*

"You see, I began by registering it as a nonprofit organization. I lent it five million dollars, the amount I figured necessary for two things: a year's budget for extensive national advertising to solicit donations and a year's worth of salaries for a team of the best executives I could find. I had decided if it wasn't bringing in enough donations to cover expenses by the end of the first year, I would pull the plug."

John shrugged. "As you might be able to guess, it was these executives who put together what it took for IWRC to continue. Again, I can't take credit."

Paige let out a breath she hadn't realized she'd been holding. *"That* should disillusion me?"

"Contrary to what most people believe, I didn't give IWRC any money at all. I simply advanced a loan. It's still on the books. I can get my five million back at any time now. In fact, I've used the outstanding loan as an asset to leverage more than one development deal over the last couple of years. "

"But if the concept hadn't worked, you would have lost that five million."

He shook his head. "No illusions. It would have given me some hefty tax breaks. And New York real estate was booming so much at the time, I actually needed as much tax relief as possible."

Paige forced herself to concentrate on the crumpled stationery in her purse. How, with the muted conversations of other diners in the background, with an elegant, handsome man across from her, how could it be real that some dark secret had driven her husband to kill himself only days earlier? This seemed more like part of a dream world. Suddenly, she felt ridiculous.

"Do you mind if I excuse myself?" she asked.

"Certainly not." If her abruptness bothered John Hammond, he gave no sign.

In the ladies restroom, Paige followed her routine without thought. She applied lipstick, powdered her cheeks, smoothed her dress. All automatically. Her mind was so much on the notes in her purse that she finally pulled them out and reread them. Slowly, the horror came back to her. The horror of the sound of a single gunshot, the disbelief of opening the door to see him slumped in his own blood.

She returned to the restaurant table with new resolve.

Blueberry marbled cheesecake, fresh from the pastry chef's kitchen, awaited her. She took one bite, didn't taste it as she swallowed, and returned to her questions.

"Structure, John. You're at the top?"

"Symbolically. I overview some of the major decisions, sign all checks over fifty-thousand dollars, visit once a month."

"You know the structure?"

He was amused. "I did supervise the setup. Why?"

"Darby never said much about what he did. And I never cared much, except that his paychecks arrived on time. Can you tell me how IWRC functions?"

The slight amusement remained on his face. "Simple. Through national advertising, we canvas the United States for donations. We ship food, medicine, and supplies to disaster areas across the world.

And we do it more efficiently than any other relief organization. Which results in us continuing to get a bigger share of every charity dollar."

"How much?" Paige realized John's amusement arose from her sudden switch to detached questioner. It surprised her, too, and she wondered where this determination came from. Through twelve years of marriage, her role had been much more passive.

"How much? Last year alone, $275 million. Not including another $120 million in goods and services donated from the corporate sector. We also receive some government assistance, hitching rides whenever possible through peacetime military actions."

Paige wondered how to ask her next questions without raising suspicion. She was floundering, and she knew it. She sensed Darby's death had resulted from money—he was an accountant, after all, and in his last conversation had mentioned corporations—but how could she struggle through a maze of money questions when she knew so little about finances, and how could she hope to maneuver around John Hammond, so obviously expert and comfortable with large-scale finances?

"Could . . . could donations come in and not be recorded?" she finally asked.

"Impossible," John replied, "All donations are public knowledge. All expenses are public knowledge. We cannot afford to leave one penny unaccounted for. Not only that, but the system was set up—by Darby—to make any discrepancies impossible."

You get paid a half-million a year? she heard the raspy voice. And Darby's reply. *For my time and expertise. Not for my conscience.*

As she kept a smile on her face and returned John Hammond's gaze, Paige screamed inside against the conclusion she did not want to draw. If Darby had set up the system, Darby could also beat it.

One hour had passed since midnight. Both guards had two hours remaining on their shifts. Yet neither yawned or blinked as the hallway clock delivered magnified ticks in the silence. Neither shifted weight in restlessness. Neither spoke. At Bethesda Medical Research Center, on this high-security wing, undeviated attention to duty was the only duty.

A muted bell announced the arrival of a visitor. To this, both guards shifted slightly, more a honing of attention than actual movement.

Seconds later, the elevator doors released a single man. He approached the armed guards with confidence. He carried nothing in his hands. His dress, casual—a black golf shirt and khaki trousers. The bright hallway lights bounced off a smooth, middle-aged face, and he smiled acknowledgment as he reached the guards.

"Jack Tansworth. General Prowse is expecting me."

The first guard consulted a clipboard. "Tansworth. TechnoGen, Inc. The general expected you by 10 P.M."

"I, too, expected to be here by 10 P.M." An unruffled smile. "I suggest you consult with General Prowse. Chances are he won't be asleep."

The guards remained silent.

"Think this through, gentlemen. I'd be surprised if more than three other names have been cleared to visit the general. That in itself should indicate the importance of my visit. What's a bigger mistake? Disturbing the general? Or sending me away?"

The first guard grunted, an impressive noise from someone young, solid, and brush-cut fit. He turned without consulting his partner. During the wait, Tansworth and the second guard watched each other without expression.

"He's cleared," the first guard announced on his return.

Tansworth made to step forward.

The second guard gripped Tansworth's bicep. "Identification." Tansworth turned his head to glance at the guard. A hardness transformed the middle-aged smooth face into something forceful enough for the guard to add a single word. "Sir."

Tansworth patted his back pocket, came out with a wallet, and handed his driver's license to the second guard. The first guard patted searching hands up and down Tansworth's body.

"Take him in," the first guard said.

Tansworth followed the second guard around a corner of the corridor.

The first resumed his watch of the silent hallway.

"Privacy," the general croaked.

The guard beside Tansworth hesitated.

"I will not explain an order. Privacy. Now. Close the door behind you as you leave."

"Yes sir." The guard saluted and spun on his heel.

General Prowse closed his eyes. The show of will power had drained him. He was a sagging, wrinkled rag doll with a long nose and a thatch of gray hair. The hospital sheets clung to his body like a shroud. He looked eighty but was at least fifteen years younger.

The man in the black golf shirt stared down, hardly hiding his scorn. What a fragile package of protein and neurons. The general's only remaining worth was the power of his reputation and his signature on whatever documents Van Klees requested during infrequent visits as Jack Tansworth, a man fond of casual dress and a driving force behind the corporation called TechnoGen.

"Good evening, General." Josef Van Klees nodded slightly at the man in the bed. "I shall sit, if you don't mind."

Van Klees pulled a chair up to the bed without waiting for permission.

"Tansworth, you do take liberties." General Prowse raised his upper body and rested on his elbows as he spoke to Van Klees. "That's a bloody golf shirt you're wearing. And I'll bet it's been thirty years since anybody was late for a meeting with me and forgot to apologize."

Van Klees smiled. "I didn't forget."

The general's face arranged itself into a grimace. Or maybe a smile. Van Klees couldn't tell. Nor really care. Not with the secrets they shared together.

"You can relax," Van Klees said. "At the latest, your liver will be here by the weekend."

"Too bloody long to wait. And I shouldn't have to wait, not with what I've given you over the years."

Van Klees leaned forward. "I can answer your comment in one of two ways. The first way, I'll describe to you in great detail the logistical difficulties of finding a qualified surgeon who will agree to perform the operation, then arranging to deliver him to the site, and finally of shuffling the papers it will take to explain the wonderful coincidence of a donor's liver that conveniently matches your blood type when a thousand fatal car accidents haven't been able to do the same."

Van Klees moved his face to within inches of the general's. "The second way, I simply remind you of the mutual blackmail material we have pointed at each other like nuclear bombs. And of the no-win destruction of unleashing those bombs."

General Prowse didn't flinch. "Go easy on an old man, Tansworth. No need to bring out the big artillery. I'm just crotchety at the best of times, and more so without a liver."

Van Klees leaned back, satisfied that the general had bared enough throat to the leader of the pack. Van Klees enjoyed pushing the general. Enjoyed the power of knowing that should either this general or his stiff-backed crony, General Stanley, call his bluff, they would only discover their blackmail bombs exploding harmlessly against the illusion called Jack Tansworth. How could they destroy the life of a man who didn't exist?

"Rwanda," Van Klees said. "Relief troops are finally moving in. I'd like you to arrange one cargo flight for me."

"Hellfire, boy! Wasn't Bosnia enough?"

"I don't tell you how to run the military."

"No, you don't." The general groaned. "Still, every run you get just ups the odds that some paper shuffler will ask the wrong question. With me here, Stanley will have to make the arrangements, and he'll scream bloody murder. Can't you hold off?"

Van Klees leaned forward again. "I can answer your comment

in one of two ways, General. The first way, I'll describe to you in great detail how and why we set all of this up. The second way, I'll remind you of the packets of information I can release to the *Washington Post* at any time."

"Boy, there are times, like now, I'd like to put a bullet in your head."

"Which would be the fastest way possible to have those packets released. General, with all due respect, my schedule leaves me less than four hours of sleep a night. I don't have time to argue with you over details."

General Prowse waved weakly. "You'll have the bloody cargo flight. Leave the particulars in the usual way. Just get me my liver by the weekend."

"Certainly." Van Klees bestowed the general a magnificent smile. "Isn't that what much of this is all about?"

Five

Saturday, May 18

"WITH ALL DUE RESPECT, do we have to go through the usual cloak-and-dagger stuff? Every time I get home, I've got bruises you wouldn't believe. And in places you wouldn't believe. Try explaining *that* to a girlfriend.

"What kind of transport do you use any—"

Henry L. Mosse snapped his mouth shut as Zwaan directed a steely stare at him. Satisfied with the results, Zwaan diverted his attention again to the crazed California drivers around him on Interstate 5.

For several minutes, as he pretended interest in the passing hills barely visible through the locked-in smog of an inversion, Mosse kneaded his hands together, something he didn't realize he did as a subconscious warmup to major surgery. He also sniffed frequently as he restlessly kneaded his hands, another habit he failed to notice, because noticing would require he admit to himself that his cocaine use had skyrocketed beyond his control.

It had been a snort of cocaine just minutes before stepping into the car, in fact, that had fueled his courage to allow him for the first time to actually question the freak behind the steering wheel. In a less altered state of consciousness, Henry L. Mosse prided himself on his practicality and, coldly sober at five feet three inches, never saw a percentage in antagonizing anybody, let alone a bald freak-show monster. Coked up, however, he had a whole new attitude, and it took Henry L. Mosse less than five miles of air-conditioned luxury rental car comfort to break his self-imposed silence.

"I mean, it's not like I'm going to spill my guts to *Time* magazine or anything," Mosse said. "I wouldn't kill the golden goose, if you get my drift. Besides, why would I want to put myself behind bars?"

Zwaan didn't glance over this time. Something about the glossy edge to Mosse's voice told him nothing would stop the babble. Repugnant as it was, to enforce silence Zwaan would actually have to touch the greasy little man in his trendy designer blue jeans and silk shirt to enforce silence. At least he would have the pleasure of inflicting pain.

"You are an excellent reason to vote against public medicine," Zwaan said. He slid his hand over and gripped Henry L. Mosse's thigh directly above his knee. Zwaan began to squeeze. As Henry yowled, Zwaan brought his own leg up to press his knee against the steering wheel, allowing him to guide the car hands-free. He kept his attention on the road, changing lanes to miss a slow truck as he used his left hand to adjust the radio volume to correspond with the rising pitch of Mosse's protests. Sadly, at full volume, the radio didn't quite drown him out.

Zwaan sighed at the inefficiency of the sound system. Mosse's squealing would deliver a headache long before Zwaan could work his fingers down to the bone beneath the man's flabby thigh muscle.

Zwaan released his grip.

Henry L. Mosse could only gasp for breath. He'd never felt such tearing pain, never believed a man could be so strong. Mosse had frantically pulled at Zwaan's iron wrist with both of his hands. He had almost bucked his way out of the passenger seat and through the front window, yet the pressure had continued to go deeper and deeper, and Zwaan had idly kept watch on traffic.

Mosse wiped at his nose with the back of a silk sleeve. Then he nearly giggled. *What a rush*, he thought, *when the guy finally let go and ended the blinding center of pain. Wow, if you could get a street lab to bottle that kind of relief...*

Calmly navigating the big car to an auto-body shop a half-mile off the interstate, Zwaan doubted the little man would protest a hypodermic now.

When he pulled behind the shop into the privacy of a walled-off dead end, Mosse proved Zwaan's guess right. Even before the car had finished rocking on its shocks, Mosse had his arm extended, his sleeve rolled back.

Zwaan wordlessly injected the man with a hypodermic needle he took from his vest pocket. As Mosse leaned back in the leathered luxury of the rental car, he closed his eyes.

Reaching over him to pop open the glove compartment, Zwaan hit the electric trunk switch. He stepped out of the car, retrieved a military-issue duffel bag, then walked around to the passenger side where he laid the five-foot-six-inch duffel bag on the ground. Aside from an olive-green jumpsuit, it was half-filled with rags. Zwaan pulled the jumpsuit over his vested pinstripe, counted to thirty, opened the passenger door, and pulled out his unconscious passenger. He laid Henry L. Mosse into the duffel bag and zipped it over the man's head.

Zwaan lifted the bag as casually as if held nothing more than rags, and dropped it into the trunk.

Half an hour later, he passed through the security gates of Miramar Naval Air Station. Another quarter-hour and he was stepping into the cargo hold of a C5A Galaxy military jet, the same military-issue duffel bag slung over his shoulder as easily as if it carried no more than clothes for a weekend pass.

Zwaan set the bag down beside a couple of wooden crates then moved to the front area of the jet and strapped himself in.

Zwaan allowed himself a smile of approval. Hitching rides on military flights was so much more efficient than traveling by any commercial jet. No check-in. No metal detectors. No baggage wait. With favorable winds, he could have Dr. Mosse at the Institute within two hours.

"What do ya think. Call him?" From the passenger side of a late-model gray car, Buddy McGoyle asked the question out of the side of his mouth. His eyes were intent on the blinding glare of a white two-story clapboard house across the street.

The sun was as high as it could get, almost straight up.

The recipient of Buddy's question, David Mariott, had sourly thought more than once in the last ten minutes that this side street—one of barely more than a dozen on the island of Cedar Key—offered less shade than a plucked chicken.

All the houses on this street had been converted to take advantage of the tourist trade. Antique shops, mediocre art galleries, and an ice cream store. In structure, the other buildings were almost identical; the only differences were the shades of paint, from faded to peeling to the white—just like a target, David thought—of the house across the street that served as an office to one of Cedar Key's few lawyers.

"So, like I said," Buddy broke the silence the same time as he broke wind, "what do ya think. Call him?"

On the driver's side, David tried to ignore his partner's vulgarity as he toyed with the stump of his left ear. Two years earlier, Mariott had lost the bottom of both his ears to a hedge clipper as punishment for picking the losing warlord in the Miami drug trade. The alternative to placing his ear in the hedge clipper had been much worse, and he'd developed the habit of rubbing the stumps himself as a way to remind him of how fortunate he'd been to be hired on by the winning drug lord, the same Cuban who had squeezed the clippers shut.

"Call him?" David repeated Buddy's question. He stopped pulling on his ear's stump long enough to stare at Buddy. Not that he enjoyed the sight. Buddy was short, and a couple dozen, sweaty, white-fleshed pounds overweight, an excess of flab that poked out from too-tight shirts and pants that were always sliding down. Buddy usually had a finger up his nose, and the rest of his personal hygiene followed the same philosophy, leading to smells that worsened considerably over the course of a stakeout in this Florida heat. But the money was good. It justified the twenty-four-hour-a-day watch they shared. And how often was all the electronic equipment supplied, let alone a brand-new car for the keeping and half the cash up front? The earphones and tracking device were on the backseat, almost buried now in the empty pizza boxes and hamburger wrappings that Buddy happily threw over his shoulder. But David would never complain. Buddy, a friend since boyhood, had chosen the correct side in that drug war and had been the one who talked the victorious Cuban drug lord into snipping only the bottoms of David's ears and not continuing on to the tip of his nose.

"Call him?" David asked. "This broad don't know the lawyer from Adam. She drives two hours north to meet him in this pimple of a hick town. He don't tell her over the phone why he wants to see her. And how many lawyers you know do regular business on Saturday? I'd say this is it."

"What do you think, then, call?"

David had looked back to the house but, by the slightly nasal tone of his partner's question, knew Buddy's nose was filled, probably knuckle deep.

"You're trying to get me to say it," David said. "You want me to say we should make the call. Am I right? You probably even want me to do the talking."

David made certain he kept his gaze on the house. He didn't want to see what Buddy might do with the results of his most recent nostril search.

"Hey," Buddy said. Sure enough the nasal quality was gone.

"I've never seen the guy, but he sounds spooky, like I wouldn't want him mad. Even the Cubans who sent us to him seemed scared. And I'm guessing for the money we're getting for this job, he don't go easy on mistakes."

David said nothing. Only because he had the same gut feeling about the mystery man who'd arranged for delivery of fifty grand in small bills and promised double for a package this broad was supposed to be getting.

David sighed. "It'd be more of a mistake not to call him. *You* know that too."

"So what do you think, call?"

David sighed. He knew what was coming next. Every time Buddy didn't want to do something, it was the same question.

"Come on, David. How much of your face you still got?"

David flashed back to the sensation of clippers slowly tightening on the gristle of his ears. "You're right, Buddy. Give me the phone."

Buddy contented himself to watch the tourists as David dialed the number on the cellular phone. A couple of them looked okay in halter tops, if only they didn't have stupid husbands at their sides as they gawked at window displays of junk they'd hate as soon as they got it home.

"Two, nine, eight, seven," David said into the phone. Stupid spy game, this repeating the last digits crap. "Our bird-watching took us to Cedar Key."

During the conversation, Buddy monitored his stomach for hunger. Stakeouts did that to him. As soon as he knew he couldn't get to a fridge easily, his stomach rumbled. Like getting an urge to sneeze at a funeral.

"There's a lawyer here," David said. "He got hold of her at the motel, says she needs to see him right way."

David listened, then spoke. "Naw, I don't know how he got her number."

David nodded. "Yup, we kept it all on tape. Just like everything else."

Brief silence.

"She's inside right now," David answered. "Been there maybe ten minutes."

Another brief silence.

"That's right, empty-handed. All she had when she went in was her purse."

David's silence lengthened.

Buddy glanced over. He watched David's eyebrows furrow in concentration as he listened to the cellular phone, soaking in instructions. Buddy admired David. Ever since they were kids, David had always been smarter. He'd helped Buddy every time he could during math tests, something Buddy hadn't forgotten when David needed help in front of the hedge clippers. Of course, David was only school smart. Otherwise, he wouldn't have picked the wrong Cuban in the first place.

A minute later, David said good-bye, folded the cellular phone, and handed it back to Buddy.

"Time to come out of the woodwork."

"Ice her?" Buddy asked. That was the thing he most liked about a good territorial drug feud. The body count.

David shook his head. "Our man figures she'll come out with a package. If it's sealed, we follow her. If she pulls over to open it, we snatch it there, take her purse, jewelry, make it look like a regular mugging. If she don't pull over, we snatch it in Clearwater, same thing, but better because it looks less connected to this visit here."

"So what if it's not sealed?" Buddy asked.

"He says if the package is open, it means she went through it in the lawyer's office."

"And?" Buddy knew there was more to the answer because David was starting to sweat. David didn't like body counts.

"And if the package is open, we ice her the first place we can along the highway, take the package, the purse, and all the other crap. But if she goes right to a pay phone, we do a drive-by shoot and run."

"That's it?" Buddy asked. On the open market you could get

someone stiffed for only a grand. Fifty was definitely overkill. The guy with the weird voice didn't have much of a head for business.

"That's not it," David said. "After she's done, we go back and do the lawyer too. Then burn the house."

"That don't give us time to plan or nothing," Buddy said. The nice thing about David was he sweated body counts so bad that he made sure the plans were solid-A, no mistakes. "We'll be lucky to get out of town. And in case you didn't notice, there's thirty miles back to the interstate and only one highway out."

David gave Buddy a shake of the head. "Hey, what do you expect for fifty grand up front?"

BB shots of sweat rolled off Slater's back and shoulders as he sawed through the last of the two-by-fours. At his feet lay a stack already cut, none longer than the width of his garage windows. He felt like he'd popped a few stitches during his efforts, and his head throbbed. To add to Slater's discomfort, the sawdust clung to his sweat and clogged his mouth as he drew deep breaths from the exertion. Much as he wanted to open the garage door for fresh air, however, he would not allow himself the luxury.

Nor did he have the luxury of sunlight. Slater had already cut garbage bags to the size of his windows and stapled the black plastic to the frames, reducing the sunlight inside to zero and forcing him to continue his work in the glare of a single 100-watt bulb.

After all, he was working with more than a couple of assumptions. Number one, that the kid was smart. Two, that the kid was nearby, constantly watching the cluster of cabins that formed Seven Springs. If the kid happened to notice this flurry of activity in the garage, no amount of bait would bring him in. It was risk enough that if the kid were around, he might suspect something just from the noise from Slater sawing wood and pounding nails, but Slater had that covered too. In the afternoon, he'd haul out a crudely built doghouse, as if that were the end result of all his time in the garage. Best part was, Slater had gone back into Los Alamos immediately after breakfast and, along with the other necessary supplies, bought two Labrador puppies to go with the doghouse.

Assumptions three and four were that no one else was looking for the kid and that Slater should be doing his best to find out what exactly was forcing the kid to live on the outskirts of this meager settlement like a half-wild dog.

Slater was working on a fifth assumption too. He'd have no chance at all of catching the kid on foot. It meant his trap would have to work perfectly, and work the first time. Once spooked, the kid would be impossible to tempt back again.

Slater had spent much of the previous evening and all of this morning's breakfast in concentrated thought on how best to capture a kid with the seemingly supernatural abilities he'd demonstrated a few nights earlier. He'd even wondered about using a dart gun, then laughed at himself for thinking through the complications of getting the gun, figuring out the right dosage, and waiting for hours in the night for the kid to appear.

Since he couldn't outrun the kid, it would have to be a self-activated trap. One that Slater didn't have to spend hours watching. One that Slater could check periodically. One that the neighbors wouldn't discover. One that couldn't hurt the kid. One that the kid couldn't see him build. And one, of course, the kid didn't suspect.

That left Slater few possibilities. He couldn't, for example, dig a primitive pit, cover the top, and use bait to bring the kid in.

Any new aboveground structure would also be suspicious. Slater pondered how to lure the kid into the house, then realized the boy could do too much damage, and there were too many ways of getting out. The garage, Slater had finally decided.

So on his return from town, in the late-morning heat, he had begun to barricade the inside of the garage. First the dark plastic for total privacy. Now the two-by-fours.

Slater used six-inch spikes to secure the wooden bars across the window frames, telling himself if the kid was able to pull those bars loose, it would be just as well he escaped.

The next part took less brawn but considerably more ingenuity. Slater stepped several paces in from the overhead door and screwed a J-hook waist high into the wall of one side of the garage. He attached a long piece of dark wire to the J-hook and strung the wire to a pulley at the same height on the other side of the garage. The wire then went up to another pulley, level with the tracks of the overhead door. From there, he strung the wire to the track itself, leaving Slater with a simple trip wire, set high so that a wandering raccoon or coyote would not set it off.

Slater then disconnected the thick springs that pulled the top of the overhead door to the back of the tracks. He estimated each panel of the door weighed fifty pounds, but decided he couldn't trust the combined weight to be enough. It took another half-hour for him to attach sandbags to the inside of the bottom panel, invisible to anyone outside of the garage.

At that point, Slater tried to lift the door.

He strained to raise it three inches and nearly broke his back at his efforts.

That brought a simultaneous chuckle and curse. A chuckle because the door would drop faster than a guillotine blade, and because if Slater couldn't budge it, neither could the kid, no matter how strong. A curse because he'd have to reattach the door springs to help him raise the door.

Twenty minutes later, when the garage door was partially raised, he inserted a small piece of wood into a gap in the track. It took another half-hour of experimenting to get the wood situated at a precarious wobble where its leverage was enough to hold the door yet wouldn't take too much pressure to release. During that twenty minutes of work, Slater hoped the kid wasn't looking into the half-open garage.

His final steps were to rig the trip wire to the wood and disconnect again—very slowly and carefully—the door springs that had help him raise the heavy door.

When Slater finished, only a couple of hours before dusk, the slightest tension on the wire would pull the wood block loose.

He checked the garage thoroughly for any tools that the kid might use to try to bust free and put them all into a locked toolbox, which he took with him to the house. Then he removed all the wood scraps and any other junk the kid might use in an attempt to free himself.

On his return, Slater carried a high-sided box that contained two sleeping Lab puppies. He hung the box in a hammock at the back of the garage—high and out of reach of coyotes—and stepped out the side door. Slater shut it and with a key, locked the bolt shut.

The trap was as complete as he could make it. Inside, the windows were barricaded. The side door was steel—the kid could kick all day and not dent it or knock it off its hinges. And the front overhead door was four feet off the ground—plenty of room for the kid to duck beneath on his way in. He wouldn't hit the trip wire until he was a couple steps inside, and by then the door would drop so fast not even a cat would be quick enough to race beneath it.

Slater wasn't worried that the kid wouldn't show.

Slater had two more assumptions. The kid would visit at night when he felt safer, when the trip wire was invisible. And the kid would definitely visit. If not this night, the next. Or the night after. When the puppies woke, they'd start mewling for attention. And what boy could resist puppies?

Paige Stephens looked across the burnished walnut desk at the man who had phoned her three hours earlier.

"I hope you'll forgive the delay," Franklin Hargrove said. He smiled and gestured at his wheelchair. "Even the simplest tasks become more complicated. Including, unfortunately, the call of nature."

Paige nodded. It had been a difficult fifteen minutes, sitting at the desk while waiting through his absence and fretting and wondering why he had called.

At his smile, however, she began to relax. The man across from her was a picture of southern gentility several decades misplaced. Distinguished gray hair, round spectacles, neatly trimmed goatee, black bow tie, starched white shirt. The office around her reflected that same feel of stepping onto a set for *Gone with the Wind*. The bookshelves, the straight-back chairs, the coffee table all matched the deep varnished luster of the expansive desk. The aroma of pipe tobacco filled the air, a smell that brought back pleasant memories of her grandfather rocking as he alternated between puffs and tall tales.

"I'm also sorry I couldn't say much over the telephone," the lawyer told her. "But I did have very explicit instructions."

"From who?" she asked, almost sharply.

"Your late husband."

Paige lowered her eyes. Although she could not escape the overwhelming subconscious awareness that Darby was gone, it still came like a blow to be reminded at any other level.

"Mrs. Stephens, please believe me when I tell you I wish there were another way to discuss this."

She lifted her eyes to his. "My husband shot himself. I don't understand why. If you can help answer any questions, it will do me much more good than sympathy."

He smiled again. "All right then."

He wheeled from his desk and turned to a wall safe where he began to turn the combination tumbler.

"Darby spoke to you?" Paige asked to his back. She could not recall Darby ever mentioning this small-town lawyer. "You knew him?"

"On both counts, I'm afraid not," Hargrove replied. His voice was muffled by his body. "The instructions were in the letter taped to the package."

"But why . . ."

"Why me?"

Paige nodded yes, then realized Hargrove could not see her, so she repeated her answer aloud.

"Good question," Hargrove said. The last tumbler clicked into place. He sighed with satisfaction, leaned forward, and fumbled inside the safe, then straightened. When he wheeled back to the desk, she saw the package on his lap. A heavily taped thick manila envelope with a smaller white envelope attached to the outside.

"A manuscript?" she guessed.

"I don't know. I haven't opened it." He placed it on the desk between them. Paige's hands quivered in her lap, but she did not reach for it.

"Let me read you the letter," Hargrove said. He paused to polish his glasses with a plain white handkerchief he pulled from a desk drawer. Spectacles back on his nose, he reached for the package, pulled a letter from the smaller envelope, and read slowly with the manner of a bedside doctor.

"January 2—"

"Five months ago?" Paige interrupted.

"Yes."

Five months. Had he been planning his death for that long too?

"Franklin Hargrove, attorney-at-law, et cetera, et cetera. Dear Mr. Hargrove, three years back, I overheard a colleague, Bill Morely, mention your name. I remembered it because Morely was impressed with your honest evaluation against a house purchase in Cedar Key." Hargrove stopped and looked over his glasses at Paige. "Very minor, I can assure you. I had to search my files for Morely's name to discover what Darby meant. It was a recommendation against purchase that cost me a chance at title registration fees, and I'd waived the initial consulting."

He peered back at the letter and resumed. "...honest evaluation against a house purchase in Cedar Key, and I am trusting it reflects your integrity in all matters. For reasons too lengthy to mention, I cannot afford to deliver this package to any lawyer within my regular association of friends and can only direct this package to someone who cannot be traced."

Franklin Hargrove pointed at the postmark on the manila envelope. "He mailed this from New York. Was he afraid someone was watching him in Clearwater?"

"He was in New York last January." Paige slowly shook her head. "Except for that, all of this is new to me. And very troubling."

Franklin turned back to the letter. "You will find enclosed a retaining check of five thousand dollars. I wish for you to keep this package in trust, unopened. Should I die—and I would request you subscribe to the *Clearwater Times* to review the obituary column on a weekly basis—contact Paige Stephens at the voice-mail number enclosed and deliver this package in person. I presume the retainer will cover any inconveniences. Yours sincerely, Darby Stephens."

"I see," Paige said after some thought. She did not see. The list of questions she'd written on the motel stationery swirled through her mind. The mysterious nature of this package easily suggested it held many of the answers. But did she truly want them?

"I see," she repeated, slower, as if she were daydreaming.

Franklin filled the silence by reaching for his pipe. He tapped the old ashes into a large glass ashtray and filled the pipe bowl.

"I'm afraid I'm too set in my ways to ask if you mind whether I smoke," he said as he lit the pipe. "However, if the smoke bothers you, I invite you to open an office window."

Paige shook her head. The package. It was there in front of her. All she had to do was take it.

Franklin drew on his pipe. The aroma was cherry wood, and the smoke swirled around his face. He spoke with the stem clenched between his teeth. "Your husband did not know that my wheelchair made it next to impossible for me to deliver this to you. Other than that, I have followed his instructions as wished."

"Of course," Paige murmured. She stared at the package. It hadn't escaped her that five thousand dollars was an extremely large retainer. Some of the words of Darby's last conversation echoed in her mind. *You get paid, what, a half-million a year? That's for expertise. Not my conscience.* Five thousand was peanuts—no peanut shells—compared to five hundred thousand. What would she find out about her husband's secret life in this package? How much of her remaining love for him would survive?

"Perhaps I may help further," Franklin Hargrove was saying. "For whatever reason, it appears your husband went to great lengths to remove this package from his normal business and personal circles. I suggest you review the contents here. By asking for any legal advice here, you, too, will be staying out of those normal circles."

Paige was hardly capable of any decision at this point, so she nodded and reached for the package. "May I borrow scissors or a knife?"

Hargrove opened a drawer, found scissors, and pushed them across the desk.

Paige watched her fingers as she cut through the top of the package. It seemed her hands were working separately from the rest of her; she could have been watching a stranger open the envelope for her.

She pulled a sheaf of papers loose. A quick glance showed them to be laser printed on plain white paper. Numbers in columns on some sheets. Business report format on others. The top sheet, however, was filled with familiar handwriting. Darby's.

Paige set the pages on Hargrove's desk and rubbed her eyes with both hands. She fought for the strength to reach for the top sheet.

Hargrove studied her face. "Perhaps I should leave you alone for several minutes."

He wheeled himself away from the desk without waiting for her answer. The door shut quietly behind him, and the squeak of his tires continued down the hardwood floors of the hallway.

Finally, she reached for the handwritten letter.

Paige,

Pray there is no God who waits for me on the other side of death. Because as I write, I know you will only read this letter in the event of my death. I am afraid of death, especially with the price I have paid for my soul. Yet I am afraid of life, for each day the burden for me becomes more terrifying.

I ask myself, what should these, my final words to you, say? An apology for putting myself into a situation that has led to my murder? Or, as I daily wrestle with the thought of ending my life, an apology for removing myself from you and the world? How could any apology seem adequate?

Should I try to explain instead—to justify—the course of events leading me to this letter? But how does one justify the Institute? Let me only say it began with a small step, and that each following step led me to steeper and steeper slopes, so that now I feel as if I am plunging without control. The steps you will see on the following pages, for at one time I believed that keeping separate documentation on TechnoGen and the Institute would protect me.

I was wrong. Instead, I became prey for a psychopath who used each of my successive sins against me, until I became as helpless as any insect in a web.

I have imposed upon you my death. I have no right to impose upon you further. Yet I must.

The rest of this package is a printout of the information that will stop the monster and the Institute. If you need the disks, you can find them. They are not enclosed, for I want them as a backup for this package.

Both these sheets and the disks contain all I know, and all that I have guessed, about the operations.

I have thought of having this released to the FBI or the media, yet I could not unleash the storm upon you unawares. You, then, read through it first. You judge me, and you decide what to do with the package. After you have read it, you will understand what I am asking, for as my wife, you will be the one to face a public hell during trial by media. Yet I beg that you stop the Institute, an action I am ashamed to say I could not face for how it would crucify me.

Remember me not as the person you will see in the next pages, but remember the best of our love, especially our first honeymoon night together.

Paige laid her head down on her arms and wept on the desk. How long, she could not tell. When she raised her head again, Franklin Hargrove was across from her, holding out a fresh handkerchief.

"I can also offer you tea," he said, "or even a hand to hold, except I'm afraid in this political climate you might file a sexual harassment lawsuit."

She tried a brave smile at his attempted joke.

"I'll take the hanky now," she said. "No tea. And a rain check on hand holding."

"Legal advice?" he asked. "I can assure you it has been amply paid for."

"Not yet. I haven't been able to read beyond his letter."

"Later perhaps? You are welcome to this office for as long as you need."

"Not today," Paige said. She stood. "I don't know when I'll finish."

Hargrove wheeled to the side of his desk as she gathered the papers and weakly pushed them back into the envelope.

He followed her to the door of the office where Paige drew a deep breath and exhaled. "I may return."

"You are welcome any time." He paused as he looked at the envelope under her arm. "Wait a moment, will you?"

Paige nodded. He went to a filing cabinet, searched briefly, and returned with a large, unused envelope.

"A personal quirk," he said. "Ever since college and a history course that dealt with the war between the states."

Paige smiled politely.

"Yes," he said. "The story's probably apocryphal, but it has stayed with me. At a crucial part of the war, General Lee made a daring move—split his army into three and began to invade the north. Had he shown a decisive victory, many of the European powers would have backed the South for the rest of the war. One of Lee's couriers misplaced a few papers containing his orders for the upcoming battles. The battle-plan papers were passed along until they reached McClellan, the Union general, and Lee was forced into a stalemate."

Paige's question was plain on her face.

Franklin Hargrove chuckled. "Bear with me; it's one of my favorite stories and far too much time has passed since I was able to lecture a new assistant with it. You see, Mrs. Stephens, had the South won that battle and the substantial European resources it would have gained with victory, this would be an entirely different country. The South would have kept its independence, and we, no doubt, would be a pack of petty, squabbling nation-states all guarding small borders, not a unified major power."

He took the envelope from her arms and pulled the thick sheaf of papers loose. Then he placed the papers into the large envelope and sealed it. "There," he said. "Just like new."

He noticed her amusement.

"Yes. I'm fussy," he told her. "But think of it this way. One set of misplaced papers drastically changed the history of the modern world. If the United States hadn't risen to become a whole greater than the sum of its parts, World War II, for example, would have become Hitler's playground. No space race for the moon. I could give you dozens of examples."

He waved his forefinger at her in good-natured admonishment. "In short, Mrs. Stephens—and this is the heavy moral I always drew for my young legal assistants—you can never tell how important a piece of paper might be. To a country. Or to a client. Which is why I've made it a rule from the beginning never to let loose files or opened envelopes leave this office."

Franklin Hargrove handed the sealed package back to her. "Now I feel much better. Call me an outdated, stubborn old man, but you never know when an ounce of prevention saves you from a pound of cure."

Peter Zwaan and Henry L. Mosse could have been mistaken for a comedy team acting out a hospital skit. Zwaan wore ridiculously small green scrubs; his sleeves were so short each movement around the operating table showed six inches of his wrist. Standing as he was at the tray of surgical instruments, he dwarfed Mosse. It only added to the surreal quality for Zwaan to obediently hand Mosse a requested scalpel.

Had there been an audience, however, a zoomed-in shot of the dark-skinned patient on the operating table would have immediately dispelled any laughter. The gaping cavern in the woman's side was not a special effect, but real. As was the blood on Mosse's thin rubber gloves. As were the glistening organs beneath the operating lights.

Henry L. Mosse tried not to think about what he did on his hundred-thousand-dollar house calls, but when he did, as would inevitably happen during post-cocaine blues, he comforted himself by telling himself he was innocent, he had no choice, that Zwaan was completely to blame for all of this.

The first time Mosse had stepped into this room, Zwaan had pointed to a man on the same table, equally dark-skinned, face up, strapped to the table and obviously terrified.

"Your patient," Zwaan had said.

"The simple operation?" Mosse asked. "You told me I would be paid for a *simple* operation."

"Kidney removal."

Mosse had laughed, actually laughed out loud. Back then, of course, he did not understand Zwaan.

"Kidney removal? You're nuts. That would take a skilled team of doctors and nurses. A proven anesthetist. I can't do this alone."

"As you requested, we have every surgical instrument you might require."

"I said a skilled team. Years of combined experience. Kidney removal is not the simple operation you promised. I don't care what machinery you have in here, I can't do this alone. "

"You have me," Zwaan said. "I learn fast."

Henry L. Mosse laughed again. Normally, his lack of height prevented him from such arrogance, especially in the presence of such an eerie giant, but Mosse was in his element. He was the expert, Zwaan the layman, and Mosse had already squirreled the first half of his cash payment in a security box at a local bank. He could walk out now and still be tens of thousands of dollars ahead.

"You don't understand," Mosse told Zwaan. "Without a team, this patient will die."

Zwaan had smiled in a manner so chilling that Mosse had his

first insight into his precarious position. "No, Doctor, *you* don't understand. The patient is not expected to live."

Mosse gaped at Zwaan.

"Furthermore," Zwaan said, "you may notice the video camera so discreetly placed in the ceiling corner nearest you."

Mosse noticed.

"That camera will record the method you choose to end your patient's life before you remove his kidneys," Zwaan continued. "As a doctor, you should find it simple."

"I will not do it," Mosse said.

"Self-righteousness does not suit you. Not a doctor who on two different occasions bungled routine surgeries because of cocaine addiction. Not a doctor now in general practice because his partners threatened to initiate malpractice proceedings unless you swore never to return to the operating table. No, Dr. Mosse, it was not coincidence that I approached you."

"My medical background does not include deliberate murder. I am many things but I am—"

"—three times divorced, twice investigated for your private bedside manners with female patients, and willing to sell your soul for a week's worth of cocaine." Zwaan had allowed an emotion to creep into his rasping voice—contempt. "You are a weak, spineless excuse for a human being. You won't find it difficult to remove this man's kidney."

Mosse opened his mouth to protest.

"Neither, Doctor," Zwaan interrupted, "will you decline further invitations to our little Institute. I predict once you survive today's task, your queasiness will disappear."

"Survive?"

"Certainly, for today, you face a simple choice. Operate on this man, or have him operate on you. Either way, I'll have my kidney."

Zwaan smiled dreamily as if he were envisioning the switch. "Your patient does not speak English, but I will have an interpreter explain to him what must be done. From where he comes, it is very common to butcher cattle and pigs. Messy as it might be,

and inexperienced with humans as he might be, I'm sure he'll salvage at least one of your kidneys."

Zwaan broadened his smile. "Your patient, though, will have a
slightly more difficult task. For he will not have the luxury of working with an immobile body. If you refuse to operate, I will ensure
that you are alive when he operates on you."

At those quiet words, and seeing the demonic joy in Zwaan's
smile, Mosse fought to control his bladder.

During the first operation at the Institute, Mosse had kept his
head bowed, not necessarily from shame, but because it gave him
the illusion that he was safe from the eye of the camera.

Zwaan had been right about many things, including Mosse's
frequent returns to the Institute.

And Mosse did discover it possible for the queasiness to disappear as he cut out his own soul along with the organs of unwilling
donors. All it took to push back the hollowness was to pretend it
didn't exist and to feed it with more and more cocaine and the pursuit of another future ex-wife.

Six

Sunday, May 19

"YOU'RE SURE this is the entire list from Wednesday?"

"Del," Louise said, "you've asked twice already. What exactly's got you to the point where you let your omelet collect flies?"

Del frowned and absently waved at his plate. It was the only disadvantage of brunch on the veranda. Bugs. The sunshine, crisp air, and his twenty-mile view of brown-and-pink hues along the valley of the Rio Grande, however, more than made up for the flies. And it was only once every couple of weeks that their shifting schedules gave them the luxury of a shared Sunday morning. Usually at this point, Del and Louise had finished small talk. Louise would be buried in the *New York Times* she went into town early to get; Del would be pouring more coffee into a belly stuffed with ham, eggs, and corn pone and leafing through boat magazines, and when Louise asked, as she always did, about the practicality of looking at boats here in the middle of mountains and desert, he'd reply it made as much sense as reading about plays and operas on the East Coast, and they'd both grunt neutrally and get back to reading.

This brunch, however, had no such peace, not when beside Del's plate rested a sheet of paper with fifteen names neatly printed in Louise's handwriting. And not one of those names had a matching address close to the Seven Springs area. All but one were locals, and each of them checked out negative. Their jobs ranged from automotive mechanic to legal secretary, and none was likely to be connected in any way to spooksville. The nonlocal was a Slater Ellis, whose social security number and driver's license placed him on Fifth Street in Kalispell, Montana.

"All right then," Del said, "what about the other list?"

Louise looked Del square in the face.

"Sorry," he said when he caught the look, "that came out rougher than I meant."

"Sure. And your omelet's still gathering flies." Married to a ex-military man this big, Louise had learned early not to let him intimidate her. It helped that Del had a set of rules he followed like a code; part of the code was that no man ever hit or yelled at a woman.

She decided he looked more worried than angry. She stood, knowing he liked seeing her outlines in the red cashmere sweater. Louise Silverton, nee Bourne, had been a college cheerleader and had lost none of her brunette prettiness since. She moved around behind Del and leaned forward. She knew he liked that, too, when her hair fell over his face.

"Hon, I promise I'm working on the staff list. Trouble is it's longer, and my connection in the computer department doesn't feel comfortable printing it all out at once. Is Tuesday soon enough?"

Tuesday. Another delay, along with waiting for the feds to report back to him on the fingerprints he'd lifted from the pay phone and enlarged and faxed to the bureau.

Maybe in the meantime he'd run Slater Ellis through Montana's department of motor vehicles. Only because he hated doing nothing, not because he thought it was likely to help.

Coming from Montana, this Ellis as a tourist—even if he was

the one who'd reported the kid—was no doubt long gone and wouldn't be part of a local spooksville organization anyway. Add to that the admission records report: Ellis had a head wound, explained by the overindulgence of beer followed by careless walking. The report appeared honest—most people looked for any plausible excuse to *hide* the alcohol influence. Numbers, too, were against Ellis. Fifteen emergency cases on Wednesday morning, versus three hundred possible staff, any one of whom could have made the call before crossing the parking lot to the hospital.

Louise rubbed the bunched muscles of Del's shoulders. "Hon, are you sure all of this is as simple as you told me? I can feel a lot of stress here."

He considered—briefly—telling her. Everything. He'd begun the marriage determined to start a new life. Until the photographs had been placed in his lap to bring back his old life, he'd done a good job of being an honest husband. But to tell her would be to risk dragging her into spooksville, and although love was a word he used with reluctance—in thought or conversation—he loved her fiercely, and it would kill him to dirty her, let alone put her life in jeopardy.

The telephone rang, interrupting whatever thoughts each was not sharing with the other.

"I'm out of my chair anyway, hon. Let me get it."

Louise went inside, leaving Del with the faraway horizon and a noisy cricket beneath the veranda. Louise had made a point of answering all the phone calls lately. That bothered Del.

Seconds later, Louise reappeared, portable phone in her hand. "For you."

"Business?"

Louise nodded.

Del took the phone. "Yeah." He listened. "All right."

Del set the phone on the table beside his breakfast plate. He swigged the last of his coffee, rose, and hitched his pants.

"Gotta run," he said. "But you already figured that out."

"No problem. I'll be here when you get back."

"I don't know how long I'll be. Some hikers found a body in a tent. Probably a heart attack, but they want me out there just in case."

"Sure hon," she said. "Drive safe."

Minutes after the dust had settled in their driveway and the insects and birds had resumed their clatter in the wake of Del's departure, the phone rang again.

Louise set her coffee down and reached across the table for the portable.

"Hello," she said.

"Five, eight, three, four."

Louise's hand tightened over the receiver. Although Del had left the house, she couldn't shake the instant nervousness of conversing with the eerie, strained voice on the other end.

"Five, five, eight, eight, three, three, four, four," she said, doubling each number as she'd been instructed to confirm her identity.

"I want a full report," the voice said. The voice didn't ask if she could speak freely. It never did. Somehow, the calls only arrived when she was alone.

"Yes?" she said.

"I want everything you know he's done in the last week," the eerie voice continued, "even down to clipping his fingernails. And if you think that's too much to ask, just remember that file folder of photos."

Van Klees rarely lowered himself to simple tasks that any first-year science student could perform after a day's training. It was ludicrous, however, to allow any but a select few researchers on the sixth floor of the Institute. And this task, simple as it was, dared far too much and promised the same.

During these moments—as he had once noted in his daily journal—Van Klees reined in his far-ranging mind and focused solely on the concrete application of theory.

He wore jeans and a simple white T-shirt. Over that, a hip-length lab coat. It gave him great pleasure to think of the irony. He was casting stones into the waters of the future, and his ripples would change humankind forever. And, unlike foolish blundering scientists in the past, he knew full well the implications of his experiments even as he threw the stones. Why not dress down for the occasion?

The microscope he looked through—German-made and untouched in precision by any other—cost forty thousand dollars. Its magnification allowed him to bring a single cell into such clear focus that the nucleus of the cell appeared like a dark egg, suspended near the center of the cell itself, a larger, transparent two-dimensional egg.

To the right of the microscope was a small mechanical arm, the micromanipulator. It held a glass tube—the length and diameter of a pencil—in a viselike grip. The glass tube was nothing more than an elaborate needle, handmade here in the lab through a simple process in which the technician heated the center of a longer tube over a flame. When pulled apart, the molten center separated like a strand of taffy, leaving two shorter tubes. The taffy strands at the ends cooled to long, hollow needles narrower than human hairs.

No human hand could hold the tube steady enough to be in focus beneath the 1,000x magnification of the microscope lenses. The micromanipulator, then, was designed to hold and move the needle. One dial moved the needle horizontally, another vertically, and, much like the focus knobs on a microscope, made incredibly minute adjustments. Van Klees would have to spin the dial a dozen times for an infinitely small adjustment of the needle.

Mechanical assistance was provided in one other area: injections. The large end of the glass tube was attached to a small rubber hose linked to an electric pump that, once triggered, blew a tiny, measured, and regulated pulse of air, forcing the contents of the tube out through the hollow needle of the other end.

Microscope, mechanical arm, and air pump combined were worth perhaps fifty-thousand dollars. Van Klees needed no other equipment for his simple task.

He did, however, need strings of DNA.

Again, procurement of the strings took nothing more than the routine lab work of a technician or first-year science student. In fact, all of it was so elementary, he covered most of it in his introductory lectures at the university.

"DNA. Deoxyribonucleic acid, life's building block," he would begin as he strolled back and forth in front of the podium, confident—as he was of all subjects—without his lecture notes.

"Why life's building block?" he would continue. "Look at yourself in a mirror. You are the monumental task ahead of the single cell created when sperm meets egg to become the human embryo at the one-cell stage, a cell consisting of little more than a nucleus with chromosomes—tufts of DNA—and the food to sustain that cell." At that point, Van Klees would pause artfully, because he knew that the reproductive process always caught the attention of first-year students.

"Yes, you were once a single cell," he would then say, "the result of the primitive, inefficient fumblings of two much larger creatures." Invariably, his students would laugh at this, and, having established a sense of fun and cynicism, he had them for the rest of the lecture. And he would explain the rest.

The task of that first cell? To replicate a trillion times, the number of cells in an adult human, and, as one trillion was too abstract for lesser beings to comprehend, Van Klees let them understand that a trillion oranges would fill a box 250 miles long, 250 miles wide, and 250 miles high.

That got their attention.

Then he would instruct the students to consider how these trillion cells work together. Some grow hair, others teeth, some produce hormones, others hemoglobin. Some cells kick in at puberty, then cease to function after. Others begin or end at mid-life. Yet all these cells function in coordination as a single entity.

What caused them to replicate? What caused each to differentiate so precisely? What programed them to begin and cease activity at the prescheduled time in an organism that might live as long as one hundred years?

The answer: those very first tufts of DNA in that very first cell, half supplied by the sperm, half by the egg. As the cell divided and replicated, so did the chromosomes that contained the original DNA. The DNA of the first cell was exactly copied in each new cell. Thus, each of the trillion cells contained the entire and exact same genetic code of the original cell. Each cell triggers its specific portion of the DNA, so that hair cells, for example, do not become or attempt the work of blood cells.

The incredible beauty of it was in the simple structure of DNA.

"Imagine a ladder," he would tell his students. "Now twist your imaginary ladder so that it is spiraled. Like a staircase. You then have the double helix form of DNA.

"Each rung of this double helix contains one of two base pairs of nucleotides—a protein molecule called adenine opposite thymine, or guanine opposite cytosine. Those are the rungs: A-T or G-C.

"In a human, the DNA ladder in a single cell contains three billion rungs. At the scale size of a real ladder, those three billion rungs would circle the earth more than twice. Section after section of the ladder forms gene after gene—some genes as long as three thousand of the ladder-rung base pairs. Each gene has a specific task. A gene for baldness. A gene for hemoglobin manufacture. For bone marrow. Eye color. On and on and on. In short, this staggeringly long string of base pairs dictates all of the programming of the human species. Computer buffs can think of DNA as the software that commands the hardware formation of the almost infinite number of protein combinations.

"Because DNA is shaped in the double helix, it is able to replicate itself unerringly. As the cell divides, enzymes—specialized proteins—coax the DNA to unzip itself down its entire length. Since an A on one half always seeks to pair with a T on the other, and G always seeks C, the two sides of the unzipped ladder each recombine with appropriate opposite base pairs, and both new ladders are identical.

"What causes enzymes to initiate the unzipping of DNA? Coding within the DNA structure."

Or, as he would tell his students with a confident grin, an experimental scientist, cutting and pasting at will along the three billion rungs of an unbelievably complex molecule.

It was so simple now, he assured them. It had taken the discovery of molecular scissors—restriction enzymes—that would cut the DNA at a target-specific area. Scientists could then decide which part of the three billion rung ladder to unzip.

The second advance was a technique that allowed pieces of DNA to mindlessly replicate again and again and again. It gave scientists an easy supply of material to paste back into an unzipped portion of the ladder.

All of this was old hat. The structure of DNA had first been discovered in 1953 and techniques for cutting and pasting during the next thirty years. Experiments on viruses, bacteria, worms, frogs, and cattle had led to the bizarre, the wondrous, and the freakish in gene mutations.

At this point in his lecture, Van Klees would smile a knowing smile that some co-ed always chose to take as a special smile for her.

Her mistake. No woman could compete with the headiness of discovery and research that gave Van Klees the smile at thinking of his special task, the same smile he now graced upon the world as he bent over his microscope on the sixth floor of the Institute.

Beneath the lenses of the microscope, he guided the tip of the needle to the edge of the cell. The needle prodded, and the cell wall resisted, much like a balloon's skin indents to the push of a finger. Slowly and carefully, Van Klees moved the dials of the mechanical arm, forcing the needle tip farther into the wall, until the needle finally poked through the cell wall into the guts of the cell. He did not stop there but guided the needle now to the nucleus of the cell and violated it in the same manner.

Finally, with the needle inside the nucleus, he triggered the mechanical pump, which blew an infinitesimally soft breath into the glass tube. And the equally infinitesimal contents of the hollow glass tube gushed into the center of the nucleus.

Yes, any first-year science student, any lab technician, even a reasonably smart high-school student could perform the task Van Klees had just performed—injecting restriction enzymes to unzip the mother strand, along with the injection of foreign strands of DNA.

The entire process was so commonplace it was boring.

Yet no one in the world had ever chosen this DNA and this species of a single cell as recipient; no one in the world had reason to smile as Van Klees did.

After all, DNA truly was the immortal thread, slowly unwinding from generation to generation, so slowly that over tens of thousands of generations, humans had changed very little in structure. Because it replicated so faithfully, the coils of the double helix—the unbroken descent since the very first human, the very instructions for human life, the history of the human species—were preserved in every cell of every person.

Other scientists, even with the technology so readily available, might be cowards to challenge this immortal thread.

Not Van Klees. He had no God to tend, no superstitious fear of defying a power greater than he.

Yes, Van Klees always smiled when he lectured about the example of the human embryo because he was the only scientist with the courage and vision to challenge the embryo of the species *Homo sapiens*, the single cell that he was now prodding.

At his command, human evolution vaulted into the vast, exciting unknown.

Shortly before midnight, the slam of the garage door woke Slater Ellis from light sleep. Not until then—sitting upright in bed and rubbing his face—did Slater realize his trap had one major flaw.

Sure the kid was inside, unless by bad luck a coyote had jumped into the trip wire, but how was he going to get the kid out? Whack him across the head with a baseball bat?

Slater shook his head and mocked himself with a wry grin lost in the darkness of the bedroom. He'd been so focused on the perfect trap.

As he slipped into jeans and a cotton shirt, Slater made a list of what he knew about the kid. He didn't speak English. Had rejected Slater's first offers of help. Could run like a deer in darkness. Seemed to have supernatural strength. Had knocked Slater unconscious. Robbed the 4 x 4. Scavenged from the surrounding cabins. The kid wasn't exactly a candidate for Sunday school extra merits.

Slater considered the matter further as he walked down the hallway to find his boots.

What kind of mood would this kid be in? Trapped inside to discover some guy, the same guy who had chased him through the woods, is calling him to step outside with his hands up and be a good boy about it?

Yep, there's the basis for a good, trusting relationship, Slater told himself as he reached for his boots and shook his head in self-admonishment again. *If he doesn't speak English, it's not like I'm going to be able to explain myself.*

And, of course, there was the one major flaw in this entire setup. With the overhead door as heavy as it was, the only way in or out of the garage was through the locked side door. Given his previous behavior, the kid would probably attack as soon as Slater opened it. If the kid didn't immediately attack, did Slater dare step inside and lock the door behind him? Because once cornered, the kid would be sure to fight. Either way, Slater could expect a battle. Which led to one of two possibilities. The kid won. Or Slater won. If the kid won, he'd be gone again. If Slater won, the kid could be hurt, maybe badly, depending on how hard the fight went.

Slater laced up his boots, feeling his way from eyelet to eyelet. He hadn't turned on any lights in the house and had no intention to. At this point, he didn't want his neighbors—especially Josh and Joyce—to have any reason for curiosity.

At the back door, Slater took his flashlight from the ledge above the coat hooks. He still had no idea how he was going to deal with the boy.

He walked through the night to the garage.

The moon was not quite full, but here in the mountains, its light magnified as it passed through the clear air. The pines cast shadows, the ghostly white clearings between them were almost as visible as if it were an overcast day. With the moon at his back, Slater had no need for the flashlight he carried.

At the garage, he paused, straining to hear any clue as to what waited inside.

He rolled his eyeballs at another thought. Say it wasn't a kid, but some big predator animal in there—now that he thought about it, he'd heard stories about the occasional stray cougar that passed through these mountains—how much worse would it be to open the side door to that?

He leaned his hand against the garage wall to brace himself as he placed an ear against the side door. No sound helped him guess.

For a moment, he was tempted to get it over with. Put his key in the lock, open the bolt, and yank open the door. Then he remembered the overwhelming fear that had driven him to run through the woods.

He continued to strain for sound but heard nothing, not even the whining of the puppies in the hammock.

No sound in the woods around him either. It was something that had taken him weeks of adjustment. The total quiet that fell on the mountains when the wind was still. No distant rumble of traffic. No airplanes. Nothing but his own heartbeat.

He stepped away from the door.

Slater thought of calling the Los Alamos sheriff department for help. Then he imagined the conversation. *Yeah, I lured a kid into my garage and trapped him there. Only I've changed my mind about getting him out by myself. What's that? Am I the one who reported a naked kid just last Wednesday? That's right, officer. Same guy. Sure, officer, I'll wait here for you guys to show up.*

No way. Slater had been in this part of the state barely more than the winter. It looked like a good enough retreat to stay in at least a couple more years if he kept a low profile. Calling in the cops would end that chance right now.

What to do?

He stared at the door. *If I were Superman, I could use my x-ray vision.* That got Slater to thinking about being a kid again, when it was fun to wish Superman truly existed somewhere, when at the back of his comic books were all those neat things to order, like seeds that grew into fish, instructions on how to throw your voice, and x-ray glasses that all the guys in the neighborhood had been willing to bet would let you see through a girl's dress. Only when the glasses had actually shown up, they had been nothing more than darkened plastic and a waste of $1.49 plus postage.

Slater tightened his lips and pushed away his idle thoughts. He was using any excuse to delay action.

What to do?

Cut a hole in the door and run a hose into it from the truck's exhaust pipe? Then get the kid while he was groggy but before he died from carbon monoxide?

Right. *Hello, idiot,* Slater thought to himself.

Slater stared at the door. It would open outward. Maybe he could stand and wait with a huge net. He almost laughed, picturing that one. Better yet, get on the roof, pull the door open with a string, and when the kid stepped outside, throw the net down. Sure, if this were cartoon land, and besides, where do you find a net at Sunday midnight, twenty miles into the mountains?

There was something in the idea, though. It would be a lot easier if the kid was coming out of the door instead of Slater going into the garage.

Maybe wait with a burlap sack and throw it over the kid's head as he steps out? Nope, too chancy. Slightest mistiming and the kid was gone.

Slater continued to stare at the door.

An idea crept into his mind. He dismissed it. It returned. He searched for alternatives. Came up with none.

An hour later, Slater had implemented the idea.

It had taken him four slats of wood, two dozen screws, and a single bedsheet, ripped down the center.

On the lower half of the door, he had pressed a slat vertically along the edge of the bedsheet, then screwed the slat into the door, spacing the screws every four inches. He did the same on the upper half of the door with the other piece of bedsheet, leaving the lock accessible through a small gap between the two sheet halves. He tested the fabric, pulling as hard as possible to see if the material would rip loose from the slats. Satisfied, he then used the remaining slats to anchor the other ends of the sheets on the garage wall. Slater left a couple feet of slack in the sheets. The door would open until the slack tightened, but no more. The gap between the upper sheet and lower sheet would let him see the boy—or wild animal—but the sheets would act as a safety net to prevent escape. If it turned out Slater had actually trapped an animal, he'd push the door shut, cut the sheets and rig a way to open the door again, safely and from a distance. If it was the boy, well, Slater had a way to deal with that too.

As he'd been putting his crude netting into place, it occurred to Slater how ridiculous it was, all this effort in the middle of the night alone in the moonlit silence of the mountains, based on just a glimpse of the boy running across the road, and based on some guesses about the kid scavenging in the area. It occurred to Slater, too, to wonder why. He had no personal stake in this. It wasn't his kid. He didn't know whose it was. And there had been no headlines about a missing boy.

He wasn't doing it for revenge. His head was healing and his hair was even beginning to grow back, and the stolen groceries were easy enough to replace. The attack on the road hadn't happened because the kid was out to get him.

And Slater sure wasn't going to accuse himself of doing this for noble reasons, like some knight on a white horse. If that were the case, Slater could have found plenty of other windmills to tilt at in the last few years.

The answer Slater finally decided upon was much more selfish.

Capturing the kid and finding out why he was on his own and why no one was looking for him had given Slater a purpose. Short-lived or not, this was better than merely getting up each day to read another couple of books and monitor his stocks and bonds to ensure he had enough income to go through the motions of living.

Curiosity might kill cats, but Slater was also discovering it was a great tonic. He grinned as he checked the sheets across the door one last time.

All right, rodeo fans, he commentated to himself, *get ready for the eight-second ride.*

Slater unlocked the side door and pulled it until the anchored sheets were tight.

He braced against the door, waiting for an explosion of action to hit.

Here it is, fans, any second now . . .

Dead silence. Slater resisted an urge to laugh. After all this, nothing? It was like the chute being yanked open and the bronco refusing to buck onto the dirt floor of the arena.

A cloud passed in front of the moon.

Sure, he muttered to himself, might as well take away my light at the most crucial time.

He stepped back from the door and reached down for the flashlight he'd left on the ground.

Slater stood, motionless, flashlight in his hand but not switched on, and counted to sixty as he listened and watched the door in the new darkness around him. Slater counted to sixty again.

Another thought hit him, and he bit back laughter. What if the stupid door had simply fallen from its own weight? What if he'd put himself through all this tension, all this work, and nothing was in there but two sleeping puppies on a hammock? Wouldn't that be a story to tell—if he had someone to tell it to?

Slater took a deep breath. He'd waited long enough. Might as well find out exactly what had happened inside the garage.

He switched on his flashlight, edged his way to the partly open door. Standing as far back as possible from the gap between the sheets, he aimed the beam of the flashlight inside. First at the hammock.

The puppies have been moved.

He felt a brush of the supernatural fear that had filled him during the chase. Someone was inside. Someone canny enough to wait and wait and wait in silence, even as the door opened. As if that someone were trying to trap him.

Without realizing he'd done so, Slater shuffled backward a half-step. Every inch of skin tingling with adrenaline, he stood on his tiptoes and angled the beam to the center of the garage. The edge of the beam caught something white, and he centered the beam there.

The kid. Blinking, hand up to protect his eyes against the flashlight. Puppies in his lap.

Slater sagged with relief. After all of this, it was just a kid. Scared. Defenseless. And comical in ladies clothes far too large for him, the clothes he must have taken from Joyce Burns's clothesline.

Slater moved closer to the gap in the sheets. He aimed the beam lower so it didn't hit the kid in the face.

"Son, it's all right. Understand? No matter what it seems, I'm trying to help you."

The kid didn't respond.

"Come on, kid. Just let me know if you understand English. We'll go from there."

The kid just tightened his grip on the puppies.

Slater moved closer to the door. He rested his hand on the lower sheet.

"I'll give you the flashlight, all right? You won't have to be scared. I've got another in the truck."

No response.

Slater put his hand through the gap, extending the flashlight to the boy.

Screaming rage, the sound of monkeys gone insane, hit him like a physical blow. A tight, sudden horrible grip yanked on him arm, slamming him into the door, which crashed shut on his shoulder. The sensation of fangs repeatedly slashing at his arm.

Galvanized by pain, jerking and pulling as if he were clutching electrified wire inside the garage, Slater tried to tear lose. The savaging continued, relentless, violent. He braced his feet against the garage wall to take his weight from the door.

Again and again something slashed at his arm.

With a final heave, he yanked loose and kicked the door shut. With his good hand, he found the key in the lock and twisted it shut.

Frantic, hateful banging hit the inside of the door. Then abruptly stopped.

Slater found his breath. Cradled his arm against himself. Tasted blood from his nose.

The cloud drifted away from the moon, and ghostly light flooded Slater as he swayed against the pain.

The garage remained as silent as the moon.

Seven

Monday, May 20

"MA'AM, you all right?"

"Sure."

"I didn't want to bother, it's just …"

Paige accepted the offered napkin. "Allergies," she told the waitress. "Some people sneeze. Others break into a rash. Me? My eyes water something terrible."

Paige dabbed at the tears on her cheek. What had she come to, allowing herself to cry in a restaurant? She should have stayed three floors up. Sure, the brown carpet of a single-bed motel room was depressing, but she could sit on the balcony. Nothing changed the view of the gulf.

"Same thing happens with *my* allergies," her waitress said. She was pear-shaped, untidy, and middle-aged; resignation showed in the seams of her face.

Now she had a hand on her aproned hip and a sympathetic smile for Paige. "Course," she continued, "what I'm allergic to is having an old man who thinks work is a disease and seeing my oldest daughter living in a trailer park with someone who knocks her and her boy around pretty bad."

She watched Paige see her as a person, not a waitress.

The waitress's smile broadened in response. "So what's your allergy? Every morning the last few days, I've brung you two poached eggs, wheat toast no butter, and fresh-squeezed orange juice. And every morning when you go, I clear away two poached eggs, wheat toast no butter, a half a glass of fresh-squeezed orange juice, plus a tip as big as the breakfast bill. You can't blame a gal for wondering what's happening."

Paige smiled in return, but didn't feel it inside. She considered the resignation on the waitress's face. "If your husband left, would you miss him?"

"Not husband. Old man. Big difference. You divorce a husband, it might be worth something, depending what you'd be able to get judgment on. An old man, he just takes up space on a couch and makes sure your groceries don't go stale."

"Then why..."

"...why not get rid of him?" The waitress shook her head. "Hon, does it appear like I'm a woman who can afford to be fussy? You get to where I am in life, and you take what you can get."

Paige made no effort to hide her fascination. All the years with Darby, they'd never traveled circles where she'd be in conversation with people who did not understand that Perrier was *the* water then, or that Evian was in vogue now.

The waitress misunderstood Paige's open stare. She moved to the neighboring table, lifted up a coffeepot from where she'd set it, and busied herself by swiping a rag beneath it with her free hand.

"I wasn't trying to mind your business, ma'am." She paused, thought about what she'd just said. "No, I guess I was. But I wasn't trying to give offense. I usually keep to myself. I don't know what got over me, busting in like that. Maybe 'cause it's slow in here, just you and me and the coffeepot. I'm sorry."

"No, no," Paige said quickly. "I don't mind."

She didn't. This was conversation that didn't involve Darby or the International World Relief Committee or police reports.

"All right then, since I've already got one foot so far down my throat it's tickling my belly button," the waitress said, "I been watching you over the last days, and I wonder what it can be to get you so down. Give me your wardrobe, the money it takes to be able to tip as much as the meal, half your looks, and ten years less to put us in the same ballpark, I'd be singing my way through breakfast."

"I wish it were that easy. My husband's gone."

"Men are fools. Blind fools. Never know what they have until it's gone. I hope you soaked him good."

Paige managed a wry laugh, a pain that felt like she'd lanced a boil. "I *buried* him good. Funeral was yesterday."

Her waitress made the sign of the cross. "Bless his departed soul. I hope he didn't suffer."

Despite her brave attempt at humor, Paige felt the tears well again. "Another allergy attack," she said. "Forgive me."

Her waitress reached for a spare napkin from another table.

Paige accepted the napkin and regained her control.

"You got schooling?" the waitress asked.

"Two years of college," Paige said, "but I didn't finish."

"Enough money saved to tip this big rest of your life?"

"Does it matter?"

"What I'm working at," the waitress said, "is where you might be when you get to my age. See, I don't have much choice anymore. I stay with what I got, because it's there. My old man ain't much, but at least he stays on my couch and don't visit any others. This job swells my feet, but it's a job."

She rubbed her back as she spoke. "You still have choices. Get on or stay behind. No education, no money, either you find yourself a husband, or you end up at minimum wage and lousy tips. And don't kid yourself. I seen it happen to women you'd never believe. Year by year the hind end broadens, the chances go by, and if you don't look out for yourself, you'll be pouring coffee someday for someone pretty like you once was."

A couple of aging tourists—noisy in brightly mismatched beachwear—shuffled to a nearby table.

The waitress sighed. "Back to it, huh? You just remember what I been telling you."

She took a step toward the newcomers, then half-turned. "And do me a favor, hon. Finish at least half your breakfast today."

Paige paced her hotel room for nearly ten minutes as she battled with her indecision. Call? Or don't?

The waitress had been right. What was she going to do, hole up in this motel forever? Wait for a shooting star to flash instructions overhead?

You still have choices. Get on or stay behind.

She stopped and stared at the gray-blue waters of the gulf, sunshine so bright her eyes watered.

Get on or stay behind.

All right then, she told herself with sudden resolve, Darby had inflicted this on her after months of treating her coldly. It made her sad to discover it was easier to be bitter than bereaved. And should she cloister herself forever? This phone call wasn't being unfaithful to his memory anyway; it was only a phone call, and a necessary one. There was no one else she could turn to for advice on this. It had already cost her husband his life, led to a savaged home, and then an unbelievable daylight robbery that she'd felt lucky to survive.

Paige spun away from her view of the gulf, found her purse on the night table, and pulled from it a business card.

She sat beside the telephone and dialed for an outside line. When the operator answered, Paige dictated the number on the card.

A cheerful voice answered. "Hammond Developments. How may I direct your call?"

"To John Hammond, please."

"I'll put you through to his secretary."

Two more rings.

"John Hammond's office." This secretary sounded older, less cheerful.

"May I please speak with John Hammond?"

"I'm afraid he's not available," the secretary said without hesitation.

"Not available? But..." Paige hadn't expected this. She'd sorted through a half-dozen imaginary conversations, ranging from an invitation to New York to his irritation, but in screwing up her courage, she'd never considered the obvious, that a man as busy as John Hammond might not be in his office.

"Ma'am?"

"Where is he?" It was all she could think to ask. "Can I call back later?"

"He's out of town, ma'am. But he does check in for messages." The secretary's tone did not vary in tone from its professional coldness. "Would you like to leave your name and number?"

Paige took a breath. She could hang up now and not be a fool. What if she left her name, and he didn't bother to call back?

Go on or stay behind, she heard the voice.

So she uttered the words that would change her life.

"Could you tell him Paige Stephens called? He has my number."

"Yeah." Del didn't look up from the scattered paperwork on his desk. "Come in."

"This one bothers me, Del," Sol Hirshtein, the county coroner, said as he stepped through the office doorway. He and Del had shared a lot over the past years—decomposed bodies well gnawed by coyotes, traffic-accident dismemberments, and the one that had brought them both to tears, a three-year-old suffocated in a freezer whose forehead was swollen black from his attempts to head-butt his way to fresh air.

"I'd say something is up," Del leaned back in his chair, webbed his fingers behind his head. "Otherwise you'd have just faxed in the report. What is it?"

"First of all, it wasn't a heart attack. Like you figured, he'd been juiced by scorpions."

Del snorted. "Find a couple of crushed scorpions in his sleeping bag; says enough."

Sol shook his head. "That's where it gets interesting."

"Yeah?"

"Not so fast, Del. Just for kicks, tell me what you know."

By this time, Sol was sitting opposite Del's desk. Sol didn't look like he belonged in a chair. Skinny to the point of angular with dark eyes and beard just beginning to gray, he had a permanent stoop from his years over the autopsy table. Unlike Del, Sol leaned forward, anything but casual. The faint smell of formaldehyde filled the space between them.

"Well, his ID checks. Fellow by the name of Roberto Enrico. Dr. Roberto Enrico. From the address book in his gear, it didn't take much to track down his only living relative. An aunt. She lives in North Dakota. Says he's a research doctor. Wasn't exactly sure in what—something to do with worm's genes."

Sol lifted an inquiring eyebrow.

"Yeah, I wondered too. This old bat rambled a lot. Like she was glad for the excuse to talk to someone. By the time we got through all of this, I managed to decipher that Enrico had spent the last year in South America, researching at some university in Rio. One of his letters—and she was going to read each one word for word over the phone—mentioned something about a vacation in this area. It fits with the airline tickets we found in his knapsack."

"Hmmph."

"Hmmph?"

"I went over his body real close, Del. Once I got the hang of what I was looking for, they weren't difficult to spot."

"They?"

"Puncture wounds. Scorpion flicks its tail, jabs the stinger just below the skin. Near as I can tell, he'd rolled through an entire nest. And you only found two scorpions."

Del was silent for the several moments it took him to clue in to the significance of his colleague's statement. "What got you looking him over so close?"

Sol smiled. "Knew you'd pick up on that. I found abrasion marks on his wrists. Or what might have been abrasion marks. If someone *had* tied him, and I couldn't swear to it in court, it was someone who did his best to hide the fact. Maybe used wide strips of soft cloth." Sol paused. "One other thing. It may be insignificant. Two of Enrico's toes showed multiple fractures and fresh healing—like they'd been crushed in the last six months."

"Interesting," Del said.

"It's your call," Sol told him. "You'll see all of this in my report as speculation. It could have just as easily happened the way it seems. Maybe all those scorpions did nest in his sleeping bag. He crawls in at night, thrashes around, crushes a couple, and the rest escape. You'd have to first convince me scorpions travel in packs. I'm no expert, but I thought they were solitary creatures."

Del was reading through Sol's report—the odor of formaldehyde hadn't yet cleared the office—when his phone rang.

"Five, eight, three, four," the voice said.

Del straightened. The code was right. But the voice was wrong. Careful. Modulated. Not strained and hoarse. Del hesitated.

"Five, eight, three, four," the new voice repeated. "Confirm immediately."

Del spoke the last four digits of his phone number.

"Good. What have you to report since the last sighting?"

"Nothing." Del had been prepared to give this answer. It helped that the hospital list truly had given him nothing.

"If something arises, you will keep the media away."

What gives? Del wondered. He'd already been through this with the freak. Had spooksville's chain of command been compromised?

Sudden sweat.

If something had happened to the first spook, where were the photographs that hung over Del's head like a piano from a thread?

"Have the instructions changed?" Del asked.

"No. Definitely not."

"Then the media will be kept away. All other steps will be followed." Del took what satisfaction he could from the insolence he could project.

A long silence followed. So long Del wondered if he'd pushed too far. Or if the connection had been broken. There was no hiss to betray a cellular phone on the other end.

"Your department may find a dead tourist in the desert," the voice finally said. "There was no foul play. You do understand."

"I've already been given official paperwork that says otherwise."

"Too bad for you," the precise voice said. "You will find a way to shuffle it out of sight."

"It's not that easy," Del said. He noticed he was arguing, something he'd never dared with the freak.

"It will be easier than dealing with certain other files. Or photographs. Remember that."

The phone went dead.

Del set the receiver down very carefully.

He loathed this situation. Not only did he have to find a way to waive a murder investigation, but this also clearly showed that spooksville was behind it.

If he could pull himself away from the blackmail . . .

He picked up the receiver and punched in a number.

"Silverton here," he barked. "It's been three hours. Don't you have anything yet on Slater Ellis from Montana DMV?"

Zwaan didn't like heat. Or clamoring noise. Or dust. Or people. Or sickness and disease. The African refugee camp had it all.

He felt punished by jet lag. His trip had begun with two hours from Los Alamos back to San Diego to rid himself of the doctor. Well over five hours from there to D.C., babysitting the general's iced liver. Zwaan had then hitched a ride on a military flight from D.C. to a U.S. Air Force base in Germany, then on to Goma here in Zaire.

Little more than a hundred yards away, confiscated guns, grenades, and ammunition—taken from Rwandan government soldiers as they fled into Zaire—lay stacked in piles at the border crossing. Within the border, in all directions, fly-ridden bodies were bunched in small mounds, as if there was some comfort in shared death. Some had died from thirst and exhaustion. Others had fallen to mortar shells lobbed from the Rwanda side only hours earlier or had died in the ensuing stampedes. All of the bodies had been pushed aside to clear paths through the refugee camp.

Zwaan walked past dazed survivors, kicking through the remnants of their meager belongings, hoping little dirt would collect in the cuffs of his pants. Around him, refugees picked through the debris for anything of use. Spilled beans from a broken pot. High-top shoes from a twisted, dead body. A dented canteen.

Distant, sporadic rifle shots broke through the wailing, screaming, crying, and begging—U.S. troops could not be everywhere, and away from them, Zairian soldiers and police were methodically robbing the more prosperous refugees at gunpoint, firing into the air to intimidate.

During any chaos and discomfort, Zwaan would gingerly reach into his mind, as he did now, for the one fantasy he occasionally permitted himself. Someday, his face would be unblemished, his vocal cords replaced. How would it feel, then, to sit among people and not feel like an object of horror or pity or disgust? To look in a mirror and not feel the urge to turn away? He needed to be whole in appearance, and that would only happen with Van Klees's help. So he would drive himself to help Van Klees in return, even if it meant subjecting himself to this squalor.

Two U.S. soldiers trailed Zwaan. Neither was more than a teenager, barely out of boot camp. Rwanda was a peacekeeping gig. While they did watch carefully for Zairian soldiers, neither expected trouble from the people who reached out for them, clawing air with arms and fingers reduced to bones covered with loose skin. They did, however, keep an instinctive uneasy distance from

Zwaan. Unlike them, he was not carrying a .45 caliber M3 machine gun, yet each soldier, if forced to admit it, felt edgy around the monster.

Later, out of his earshot, they'd trade comments and nervous laughter, but for now, they would do as he requested. Not only did they have verbal orders from their commanding officer to help him, but the frightening man was also part of the International World Relief Committee. In their first days here, they'd seen and learned enough about human pain and hopelessness to age them a dozen years. Helping the monster, futile as it might be in the face of tens of thousands of refugees, still provided them a salve.

Ahead of them, a Red Cross jeep swerved to stop beside a bleeding boy. A relief worker—gray-faced with fatigue—lurched from the backseat, bent over the boy, then lifted him into the jeep.

Zwaan ignored the vehicle and pointed past it at a woman wrapped in a once-colorful sarong.

"Her," Zwaan told the soldiers without looking back. "She will be the first. See if she speaks English. If not, I still want her."

The boy soldiers looked at each other and shrugged. They had their orders.

They moved to the woman, stepping around two small girls who clung to each other, so dehydrated their weeping was without tears.

"English?" the first soldier asked. The woman stared at him sightlessly. Nothing in her eyes or slack face showed hope. "Understand English?"

She didn't respond. Each soldier took one of the woman's elbows and gently guided her back to the rough road where Zwaan waited.

"Let go of her," Zwaan said. "If she cannot follow on her own, I don't want her."

He began to walk again. Another dozen steps and he pointed to a man who held a dead baby to his chest.

"Him too," Zwaan commanded with an expert eye for the man's resilience. "Force him to leave the baby behind."

Zwaan continued, taking a zigzag path as he wandered through the refugee camp. He chose judiciously. Each refugee added to the parade was healthy enough to walk unaided, despondent enough to follow the soldiers' motioned directions without resistance. Occasionally Zwaan pointed at a couple, but usually at single men or women, and all who joined the parade were young adults— "mature animals" Zwaan called them in his mind.

When Zwaan finished an hour later, he and the two soldiers had a chain of thirty-eight refugees—two of whom spoke English, all but three of them women—one refugee for each seat on the bus waiting for them near the relief tents.

By midnight local time, the bus had bounced through thirty miles of bush trail—held up once by a flat tire and another time by a belligerent bull elephant—to reach the only interior airport with a runway long enough to handle a heavy transport plane.

Under floodlights, Zwaan supervised the unloading process.

The refugees blinked against the harshness of the white glare, but none protested. All had been fed and watered; furthermore, the two who spoke English had served as satisfactory translators, yelling above the incessant grinding of bus gears to deliver Zwaan's promise of a new life in the United States as sponsored immigrants.

Unloading the bus was hampered only by the slow movement of the refugees. Save for Zwaan's briefcase, there was no luggage.

Minutes later, the bus roared into the black of night.

The refugees stood without movement, huddled against the chill. Hot as the days were, cloudless nights meant piercing cold.

They did not wait long.

The low buzzing of four propeller engines reached them, growing louder as the airplane approached. It circled twice, searching for flares.

Zwaan did nothing. He'd paid the pilot more than ample in black-market dollars. The pilot had chosen this landing spot, arranged for help to be waiting.

As if lightning had broken from a clear sky, flare after flare burst into sputtering pink halos. It would take more than a two-person crew to coordinate the sudden bursts. Zwaan looked for and saw the shadows of perhaps a dozen men scurrying back to the fields. He smiled at the certainty of how powerfully money spoke in countries like this. Over the years and across the continents, nothing had changed.

The plane swooped in, barely landing before the flares died. Timing, of course, was crucial. This was the most vulnerable part of the operation; away from the umbrella of official U.S. military, too much would be too difficult to explain to local authorities. Vulnerable as this link in the chain was, Zwaan would do it no other way. By choosing to separate International World Relief Committee action at the refugee camp from military involvement at a UN base two countries over, he effectively compartmented the actions on each end and stopped any personnel from understanding the entire sequence of events.

The plane rolled to a halt at the end of the runway but did not cut its engines.

"Tell them to move," Zwaan said to the emaciated refugee who had translated on the bus. "We must get on the plane."

The directions were passed on in hurried and muted tones.

Zwaan marched ahead of them and urged each onto the ladder that was leaned against the open cargo door. Zwaan was careful not to touch them, preferring instead to assist them upward with insistent half shouts barely heard above the spinning of the propellers.

Above him, they streamed into the plane. It was outlined against the stars, and as Zwaan's eyes adjusted to the night darkness, he saw workers scurrying back onto the airfield to haul away the burned-out flares.

Zwaan followed the last refugee onto the plane, careful to breathe through his mouth against the body odors that he imagined clung to the air around him.

Once into the airplane's body, he sucked air into his lungs with short, shallow gasps. Here, the stench was not his imagination.

The door was closed but not yet secured when the pitch of the propellers rose and the airplane began to move. There would only be one flare on the runway now—a beacon at the very end as the lumbering plane fought to gain momentum.

There was no light inside the airplane. As Zwaan had instructed, the pilot had not switched on the overheads. The only light for the next half-hour would be from the flashlight that Zwaan removed from his briefcase. He needed it to inject sedatives into his fellow passengers. After all, it would not do for them to see the coffins stacked at the rear of the huge transport bay.

About the same hour, eight time zones earlier, Slater Ellis faced the same task as Zwaan. However, where Zwaan used a carefully proportioned injection of chloral hydrate to send his charges into sleep of very specifically calculated duration, Slater Ellis made do with sleeping pills and could only guess at the results. Zwaan had the advantage of an easily verified head count; Slater had no such luxury.

Slater only knew for certain he had no intention of opening the Pandora's box of his garage unless the savageness inside had been dulled—by any manner.

He'd been set up the night before. The kid, sitting there, waiting, unresponsive, deliberately lulled him. Someone, something, had waited at the door, maybe expecting him to open it completely at the sight of a boy holding two puppies. Slater still had no idea what had attacked his arm. His sleeve had been torn, his skin bruised and twisted. It still sent surges of adrenaline through him each time he recalled the suddenness and thoroughness of the attack. And what if, instead of sticking his arm inside, he'd opened the door completely, welcoming the monster outside? He shuddered to think of those results.

He hadn't really slept through the night. Just sat on his porch in the darkness, staring at the silent garage, holding ice against his swollen nose.

In the morning, Slater had cleaned himself up, then returned to watch the garage as the mountains heated beneath a cloudless sky and wondered what besides the boy waited so patiently for him to unlock the door.

The heat had given him his idea, thinking at first if he were inside, thirst would be driving him nuts, then realizing, of course, the kid and his companion *were* inside, and must be dying for something to drink.

So at noon, he had doctored a quart bottle of cola with enough sleeping pills to send two adults into extreme drowsiness, figuring that while the dosage might be excessive for one boy, it would be shared with whatever else lurked inside. As the day's heat built, so would the temptation to drink.

Slater had screwed the bottle cap back on and tied the bottle to the end of a long pole. He'd opened the door, pushed the bottle inside as far as he could go without letting his hand enter the garage, lowered the bottle to the floor, and flipped the pole inside before closing and relocking the door.

Slater had decided to give it four hours. One hour, maybe two—if they had any suspicions—for the kid and his companion to finally succumb to the urge to drink the cola. Another hour for the sleeping pills to work, and one more hour as a safety margin.

From his chair on the porch, Slater set down a paperback that had barely held his interest during the previous hours. After gathering up a flashlight, a pair of scissors, and a small fire extinguisher pirated from his kitchen, he walked with grim resolution toward the garage. If whatever awaiting him still had some fight left, and if the CO_2 from the fire extinguisher wasn't enough of a deterrent, he could always start swinging it like a club.

At the side door of the garage, he set the fire extinguisher down at his feet and tucked the flashlight into his back pocket. With the scissors, he began to cut the bedsheet netting in two. Because this was it. Either his plan worked, or whatever was inside escaped. Slater had no intention of continuing this standoff much longer, and for that matter had wondered again and again about the sanity behind his determination to go as far as he already had to satisfy his curiosity.

He made no noise cutting the sheets; if the kid inside was still awake, Slater wanted to give as little notice as possible of his approach.

The halves of the sheets fell away. Now Slater could swing the door open wide.

Putting the scissors out of reach, he took a breath before silently inserting his key into the lock.

Show time.

In one movement, he twisted the key and yanked open the door. Then he scooped the fire extinguisher into his hands and jumped backward, aiming the nozzle at the open doorway.

Nothing hurtled out at him. No boogieman. No kid. No puppies. Nothing.

Slater allowed himself to breathe.

Had the sleeping pills worked?

Eyes intent on the doorway, he gripped the fire extinguisher with his right hand and felt with the other hand for his flashlight. He clicked it on and directed the beam ahead of him. He tingled with readiness—at the slightest movement, he'd be dropping the flashlight and working the extinguisher with both hands.

Still nothing.

Slater moved ahead, not committing himself to standing directly in front of the doorway.

Still nothing.

He forced himself to breathe again.

Closer to the garage, he swept the flashlight beam into the darkness.

At first, it seemed like a pile of blankets. Then it became crumpled figures in a heap in the center of the garage.

Another cautious step. He was almost to the frame of the doorway.

Suddenly, something moved in the darkness. He slammed the flashlight to the ground and whipped the fire extinguisher nozzle to readiness.

Slater snorted. It was only one of the puppies, wandering to the light of the doorway.

Slater didn't need the flashlight now. His eyes had adjusted to the dimness of the garage, lit by the cracks of light at the edges of the plastic on the windows. As he stepped inside, he saw that a corner of the plastic on the window facing away from his house had been peeled back. Not much, as if the kid had been too canny to want it known he'd done it.

Inside the garage, and as yet unattacked, Slater knew his doctored cola had done its work. Aside from the puppies, the crumpled figures ahead of him were the only occupants of the garage.

Now, almost to the figures, Slater gaped. His attacker last night hadn't been a boogieman, hadn't been a werewolf or some dark creature from a horror show. It had been two other boys.

Slater shook his head.

Three ordinary boys. At least it explained one thing—the apparent supernatural speed of the kid in the dark. If two other boys had been waiting in the bushes, circling him as he went in, naturally the small noises would seem terrifying when he assumed it was one kid moving at top speed.

Yet it begged another question. What had driven them to run away, naked and foodless? From where had they come? And why wasn't anyone looking for them?

One at a time, Slater carried each boy from the garage to the front room inside his house. Each snored softly against his shoulder as he walked. Each fell limp against the couch as he gently set the child down.

Each time it wasn't until he stepped into the sunlight that Slater got a clearer look at his hostages.

The first kid wore Slater's clothes, taken from him the night they had stripped his 4 x 4 of groceries. The clothing had been ripped to shorten the sleeves and pants legs, tied with short lengths of baler twine to keep them snug.

Slater had to chuckle when he got the second outside. The kid had stolen three checked shirts, all too large, and wore all of them, giving him a bulked-up appearance. His pants were men's shorts, baggy and reaching below his knees. His shoes consisted of a sneaker on one side, a woman's shoe without the high heel on the other.

The third kid, of course, was a fashion statement in the loot taken from Joyce Burns's clothesline. He wore two of her blouses and a skirt wrapped around the outside of both as if the skirt were a shawl. His pants consisted of men's shorts similar to the second kid's, and he wore floppy rubber boots for shoes.

Slater noted with a large grin that kid number three had found good use for a brassiere taken from Joyce Burns. He'd slung the straps over one shoulder, draping it diagonally across his body so that the massive cups dangled beneath his opposite armpit. Each of those cups was stuffed full with the bounty of their scavenging. A hunk of cheese, screwdriver, knife, hankies, and more packed beneath. Slater decided not only was it an ingenious way to jury-rig a backpack, but it was probably also less stressful on the bra than its original contents.

With kid number three on the couch beside the first two, Slater lost all of his good humor as he discovered something that bothered him very much.

He hadn't noticed their features that closely—he'd been more aware of the different clothing on their bodies. But side by side by side, he saw now what he'd missed before.

Each was identical to the other. Absolutely identical. Same straw-blond hair. Same upturned noses. Same arch in the eyebrows. Same foreheads. Same lips.

Triplets. Absolutely identical.

Yet no matter how strange it seemed to see three boys who could have been one, it was something he could handle as coincidence or the one-in-whatever odds it took to produce identical triplets.

What disturbed him most were the numbers tattooed on their foreheads.

Eight

Tuesday, May 21

JOSEF VAN KLEES, master of anything and everything within his grasp, began to fret within seconds of losing control of this situation.

Barry Manilow.

Van Klees sat—at 6:00 A.M. mountain time, 8:00 on the eastern seaboard—waiting, with the phone against his ear. Him, waiting. Him, the man certain some day to be recognized and proclaimed with all the due his genius deserved, the man brilliantly capable of juggling all the balls and playing all the roles it took to run the Institute, the man keenly aware that each passing second was a wasted second, the man who held so much power—yet he had no choice but to endure Barry Manilow's "I Write the Songs," made worse by an elevator-music rendition.

On hold, and with no recourse, threats, or punishment to mold the situation to his needs, Van Klees fought rising fury.

He counted the ticks of his wrist watch.

Three minutes and five seconds later—thirty-five seconds into a Beatles remake that made him wince—a voice answered.

"Hello. Thanks for waiting."

"Jack Tansworth here," Van Klees said, proud at how he kept his anger from his modulated voice. "I have an order to place."

"Tansworth. TechnoGen? Am I correct?"

"Excellent memory. Two points if you recall our address."

The woman on the other end giggled. "I'm afraid I lose. With so much happening and so many different clients..."

"I understand completely," Van Klees said. "And you have much more to worry about than details like mailing addresses. We're in Pittsburgh."

"Of course, of course," she said in a tone that meant the opposite.

Instead of taking offense, Van Klees was grateful that TechnoGen remained low-profile with the clinic. Although no investigative force in the world could follow the connection from TechnoGen to the Institute, let alone physically locate the Institute, it was much better to prevent any questions in the first place. Which was one of the reasons Van Klees was forced to rely on people like this on the other end of the phone.

"Your time is valuable," Van Klees said. "I won't waste it. We'd like two—in cryopreservation. Have them sent overnight to Pittsburgh. A certified check for twenty-five thousand dollars will be waiting for your courier on receipt of delivery."

"Certainly. I'm just pulling your account up on the screen. Um, how do you spell TechnoGen?"

Van Klees smiled hatred into the receiver as he complied. How he detested sloppiness.

Half an hour later, Van Klees finished his calls to fertility clinics up and down the Atlantic Coast. By tomorrow, he'd have two dozen more human eggs for his experiments—and just in time, for he was almost out of stock. It was time consuming to divide the orders among fifteen clinics, but he would do it no other way. Who knew what eyebrows might be raised if he placed a single order of such magnitude?

Van Klees wasn't even certain he liked this method. Compared to his alternatives, however, he welcomed it. Sure, he could have the eggs produced here at the Institute, but with too much risk.

Very early, he had decided to subcontract as much of the work as possible. The fewer staff within the Institute, the fewer headaches, and the fewer possibilities of a leak.

Compartmentalization. That was the key. Separate the tasks. Separate the workers. Ensure no information crossed horizontally. Let no one person even begin to guess at the overall purpose of the Institute.

The ultimate in compartmentalization, then, was to purchase as much work and product as possible from outside.

His shipments of eggs, for example. Since 1978, scientists had been uniting human egg and sperm in petri dishes. Child's play, compared to how reproduction technology had evolved since then. New techniques made it possible to allow for fertilized eggs to be saved in a process called cryopreservation, which essentially froze the embryo for thawing and implanting in a womb when convenient.

Even though a mature women carried upward of 300,000 eggs, released one per month, Van Klees preferred to purchase eggs because—aside from needing extra and specialized staff to handle the harvesting—his own women were too valuable to risk. After all, a woman needed to be shot with extra hormones to overstimulate the ovaries, then anesthetized and sucked clean of her eggs by a needle. It was too chancy, the risk of hemorrhage and infection, the growth of ovarian cysts. Let women out there sell their eggs for two or three grand to the medical centers who in turned charged another ten grand for the handling service; Van Klees found it easier to come up with more money for an available product than to find replacement women for the Institute.

Life became a lot more interesting, and the situation a lot more intriguing when the boys awakened, sitting on Slater's couch. Slater sat opposite, sipping coffee as he contemplated them and his options.

The boys were probably nine, ten years old, although Slater had not been around kids in a while and wouldn't have placed much of a wager on the correctness of his guess.

Barefoot and without clothing, they couldn't have traveled far. So what in the entire world, he wondered again and again, would put the three of them out here? What had been their dropoff point? Who had dropped them off? And why?

The kids woke within minutes of each other. Each one briefly tested his own bonds, then relaxed. It almost frightened Slater to see them stare at him, waiting with the patience of hunters.

"Boys, I'm a friend. Honest." Slater said to their stares.

They only stared more.

"Look, I'll let you call home."

Slater didn't expect a verbal response to his question, but he did offer his portable phone. No shake of the head from any of them, no affirmative nods.

Slater punched in zero and let the phone ring. He held the phone up to the first boy's head. The boy flinched. Slater pressed the phone into place against the boy's ear.

The answering operator's voice was muted but distinct to Slater. "This is Carol. How may I help you?"

At those words, the boy bucked as if juiced by a cattle prod. Slater pulled the phone away. The boy's eyes were on the phone, wide with surprise.

The kid started babbling to the other two, who in turn focused on the telephone.

"Interesting," Slater said.

He dialed a local number that gave the correct time. As the phone rang, he held it against the second boy's ear. Same results at a voice on the telephone, same wide-eyed stare, same babble.

"Come on, guys," Slater said. "You're not cavemen. This is a phone. As in reach out and touch someone."

Their stares lost disinterest and were now tinged with suspicion.

On sudden impulse, Slater spun away from them and grabbed the remote control to the television. He moved behind them, extended his arm so they could see him point the remote at the television.

He thumbed the power button.

Color and sound sprang to life on the screen.

The kids pushed back in surprise, actually scrabbled with their feet in their efforts to move the couch away from the sudden noise.

When it became apparent that the television offered no harm, they leaned forward to stare open-mouthed at the screen.

"Laxative commercial," Slater told them. "One of my favorites too."

He clicked the power off and walked around to face the boys again.

"I've got a bad feeling about you guys," Slater said.

And he did. It came back to him, the questions he'd had when inspecting his truck after they'd trashed it. They'd left a wallet with five hundred in cash. *It couldn't be, could it, that they didn't even understand the concept of money?* Yet they'd left the radar detector, the cellular phone, cassettes. Hungry enough to steal his bread and perishables from the grocery bags, they'd left the canned goods.

No way, Slater told himself, *everybody in the world knows about storing food in sealed cans.*

He stepped to the wall and flicked on the light switch. Flicked it off again. Did it a few more times to be sure they understood the correlation between the light switch and the light. Nothing in their faces registered interest.

"Call me a fool," Slater said to their blank stares. "I found it fun."

He retrieved a hair dryer from the bathroom, plugged it in near the couch, and switched it to high. The roaring startled the boys.

He blew hot air in their faces, and watched fear turn to interest. The middle kid almost smiled, but caught himself in time.

"Go figure," Slater said. "You know light bulbs, but not television, phones, canned goods, or hair dryers."

He put his hands on his hips. "It'd be nice, gentlemen, if we spoke the same language. I imagine you have as many questions as I do."

Half an hour later, Slater had decided his approach. Chances were, the boys wouldn't comprehend a tape recorder.

Slater fed them first, one by one. He held toast in front of their mouths until they'd grudgingly bitten and swallowed. He poured milk into their mouths straight from the cartoon.

Then he found his micro tape recorder—one he used occasionally to dictate stray thoughts and ideas for a book he might someday write in all his solitude. He set it to record and placed it on his coffee table in front of the couch and left the boys alone.

Half an hour later, he retrieved it.

Slater had been tempted to replay some of their words back to them, just because it was so comical to watch their eyes bulge in surprise at new technology. But he resisted the urge, instead taking the tape recorder to a far corner of the house where he could assure himself that he had indeed captured some of their conversation.

Even a blind dog can find a bone.

Crude, Van Klees thought, *but apt.*

Here he was, checking through the results of his previous day's work, and all it boiled down to was one simple, crude saying: Even a blind dog can find a bone. Keep nosing around, never give up, dig here, dig there, and eventually, the blind dog gets lucky.

In genetics too.

You never knew for certain how and where a new strand of DNA would patch in on the original. All you could do was try. And try again.

On occasions like this—as he slid one petri dish under the microscope and then another—Van Klees envied the lesser men who experimented with less complicated creatures.

The nematode worm, for example. Under a thousand cells when fully mature. Some scientists made a full-time living off research grants that let them try to map out the gene sequences on nematodes. You could brew up a batch of ten thousand of them, throw in some DNA strands, and count the mutants that formed.

It wasn't quite as simple with *Homo sapiens.* Not at the going rate of $12,500 dollars per egg.

Fortunately, Van Klees had a partial solution to that problem.

After he'd fertilized an egg, all it took was careful pruning. He'd let a single-cell embryo go to two cells, then four. No more than four, because once an embryo got to the eight-cell stage, each of the eight cells began to specialize, and cutting them apart simply ended the cell's life. But at the four-cell stage, any one of the cells pulled loose would simply and patiently divide itself to start the task over again. At that point, he'd get four individual cells from the original embryo. Each one of those four cells replicated through the two-cell stage to the four-cell stage. And once more Van Klees would interrupt development and divide each of those embryos into four separate cells. That gave him a total of sixteen one-cell embryos, all identical to the original embryo. He never allowed assistants to help him with this task, and on a good day he'd manage to interrupt enough of those sixteen embryos to get another dozen or so single-cell originals. Sometimes—when his reflexes were especially fast—he could separate an additional sixteen to thirty-two one-cell embryos. By that time, all the unattended others would be into the eight-cell stage, and he'd have to flush most of them down the sink.

Ideally, then, he would have a couple of eight-cell embryos— essentially the original embryo as it continued its nine-month journey—and maybe thirty one-cell embryos for experimenting. Another generation, so to speak, all identical to each other. He'd run countless generations by now, all of them painstakingly cloned in this manner.

Even a blind dog can find a bone.

Van Klees squinted into the microscope. So far, the results of Monday's work were disappointing him. The first two dozen injected embryos had already mutated so badly they were merely blobs of dead cell material, barely past a day's growth.

But what was this?

He refocused on the next petri dish.

Even a blind dog can find a bone.

Normal development to the sixty-four-cell stage Van Klees guesstimated.

Encouraging. Yes, very encouraging.

Give it two more days—about when he should try to implant it—and he might have something here.

He'd have to implant an original embryo too. There was no sense letting one grow without the other to have as a comparison.

Fortunately, Zwaan would be back by then.

Elated by his possible success, Van Klees found the motivation to return to the telephone and the humdrum administration calls that always took too much time away from the laboratory.

He first collected his messages from all areas. Aside from the university, most were ordinary business calls. There was one message, however, that brought Van Klees to full attention.

He cursed under his breath. Hadn't Zwaan taken care of all potential problems in that area?

Good thing, then, he himself had taken the extra effort to cultivate a safeguard.

Van Klees punched in the numbers. The phone was answered in two rings.

"Hello, Paige," Josef Van Klees said. "This is John Hammond. I just called into New York and got your message. I'm glad to be hearing from you so soon after our supper together. Is this a business call, or pleasure?"

Coming up with the excuse for his phone call was a lot easier for Slater than it had been for him to come up with the taped material for it.

"UCLA main reception," a bored male voice said.

Slater checked his watch. Eight forty Pacific time. With luck, he'd catch one of the professors before classes started.

"Good morning," Slater said. "Could you transfer me to the language department?"

"Romance languages? Mideast? Far East? Slavic? Can you be more specific?"

"Um…" Slater didn't have any idea. That's why he was calling. "Romance. That's French, Italian, right?"

"If you say so." The connection ended.

Ten rings later, someone else picked up the phone.

"Romance." The woman's voice sounded anything but.

"I'm wondering if I could speak to one of the professors in your department."

"Which one?"

"Whoever is available, if you don't mind."

"Regarding?"

Slater hadn't realized he'd need his story so soon. "Regarding a possible journalistic piece for the *L.A. Times Sunday Magazine*."

This connection ended as abruptly as the first had. *Stupid,* Slater thought, throwing in the word *possible,* just to keep the statement from being an outright lie. Like, after everything else, whether he told a meaningless lie mattered!

Slater listened to silence on the telephone as he waited. He was grateful for silence—except for the murmur of his television—outside his study as well. It meant the kids weren't fighting their situation.

"George Franklin here."

"Hello, Professor Franklin. I hope it won't be inconvenient to ask one minute's worth of questions."

"No, not really. I do leave for class in about ten minutes. This is for the *Times*?"

"It depends on how the article works out," Slater said. "This might be too weird even for L.A."

"Really?" Franklin's voice grew interested.

"I've been working with some kids who might be from the inner city. As you can imagine, it's been hairy."

"Are you kidding?" Franklin said. "I wouldn't drive into East L.A. in a Sherman tank."

"Exactly." Slater looked at the microrecorder in his palm. "Anyway, the short of it is that I managed to get some conversation on tape, except I have no idea what's being said."

"The kids were Hispanic, of course."

"You'd be surprised." Slater found himself irritated at the racist overtones of the man's assumption. He took a breath. "How about I try a clip of it over the phone?"

"Sure."

Slater moved the recorder to the mouthpiece of the telephone and pressed play. The excited babble he'd captured early this morning transmitted clearly.

"Was it too loud?" Slater asked as he resumed the conversation.

"No . . ." Franklin hesitated. "It sounded strange, but familiar. Play it again."

Slater did.

"And again," Franklin asked moments later.

Slater complied.

"Real interesting," Franklin finally said. "If I'm right, you shouldn't feel bad for not having a clue. And like you said, something weird is happening there."

"Yes?"

"I think it's Latin," Franklin told him. "But call over to Austad. Ben Austad. He's sharing an office in the Greek department. Let him listen."

"Great," Slater said. "You've been a big help."

"No problem," Franklin said. "And it's an 'i.' "

"I beg your pardon?"

"For your article. F-r-a-n-k-l-*i*-n. Not '*e*-n.'"

Before making another call to UCLA, Slater went back to the living room to check on the kids.

At his approach, they stopped their whispering and graced him with ferocious glares.

"Hey boys," he said, "how's the party? Comfy? Need more snacks? All you need to do is holler."

If they understood his wry humor, they did a good job of concealing it.

Slater grinned, walked behind the couch and leaned over it to gently pull their wrists into sight, allowing him to inspect the knots on their ropes.

He'd made a difficult decision the night before. These boys seemed wild. They'd attacked him, robbed his truck. They'd scavenged the neighborhood. They'd tried trapping him in his own garage.

It seemed to Slater he had few choices. He could let the kids go. Except he was more than a little intrigued at the situation, somewhat concerned about the kids, and happy to have a problem to preoccupy him, so he wasn't about to cast them into the woods again.

He could call the cops, turn the kids over to them. But aside from putting him in a spotlight of publicity—a bad enough problem—there was something strange about this. The way the cop had suddenly changed his attitude when Slater phoned about the kid. The lack of media coverage you'd expect with missing triplets. The weird language. And the tattoos on their heads. No, Slater wasn't in a hurry to bring in cops.

He'd keep the kids as he tried to puzzle this through. Short of building a prison, that meant tying them up to keep them from doing damage to him or the house. Slater had opted to bind their hands behind their backs. He'd given them as much freedom as he dared by hobbling each one separately, a short piece of rope attaching left ankle to right ankle.

The ropes tested fine. They were still securely bound.

"Latin, huh?" Slater asked.

Malevolent stares.

Slater grinned. "*Caveat emptor,* boys." It was nearly the extent of his Latin. Senseless, of course, in this situation, but he gave them the translation anyway. "Let the buyer beware. *Caveat emptor.*"

They blinked. Comprehension?

"How's this?" Slater discovered he was enjoying, after his long solitude, having company, no matter how sullen. "*Carpe diem,*" he shot at them.

Now puzzlement. They even exchanged glances, the first time they had allowed him to see any reaction.

Slater grinned again. He could imagine their thoughts. *Why is this guy telling us to seize the day?*

"I saved my best for last, guys. Ready?"

Slater gave them a drum roll, determined to break down their walls with unrelenting good humor.

"*Cogito ergo sum*," he announced proudly.

He walked back to the study. "I think, therefore I am." Let the little cusses ponder that.

"Dr. Austad, I'm calling on the advice of George Franklin. He suggested you might be interested in some consulting work."

"That was kind of him," a measured voice replied. "Specialists in Latin rarely have the opportunity."

Slater never believed much in trusting first impressions. Yet this man's voice was relaxed, almost contemplative. Slater decided against the journalistic approach he'd found useful with Franklin and, on an impulsive hunch, asked a question he hadn't planned on.

"Dr. Austad, do you like mysteries?"

"Life is a mystery, if you choose to enjoy it that way."

Again, unperturbed calm. Austad could have answered so many ways. Annoyance. Flippancy. Nervous laughter. Instead, this was a man whose waters seemed to run deep.

Slater felt safer. He also realized the anonymity of the telephone still protected him. He plunged ahead.

"Well, sir," Slater said, "Would you find it strange to hear about runaway triplets who speak only Latin?"

The telephone transmitted five seconds of silence from the campus across the six-hundred-odd miles to New Mexico.

When Ben Austad spoke next, his voice had lost none of its calm. "Runaway triplets who speak only Latin," he repeated. "I don't wish to be rude, but are you from Hollywood?"

Despite his impatience, Del forced himself to move slowly on this one. He couldn't risk assigning anyone else to the questions. It didn't even matter now that Louise hadn't yet delivered her promised list of hospital personnel.

Slater Ellis.

In his hospital report, the guy had listed himself as a resident of Montana. So why didn't the Montana DMV have any record of him? No driver's license. No speeding tickets. If Ellis lived in Montana, he got around on horseback when he was there.

Which wasn't often.

Because Slater Ellis lived in New Mexico.

After Montana had checked negative, Del had done the obvious. He ran Slater Ellis through New Mexico DMV. Sure enough—Del had discovered yesterday afternoon—Ellis had a state driver's license. Not only that, Ellis had moved three times within the state over the last four years.

Nothing made sense about the moves either. The guy hadn't been ducking bill collectors. That would have showed up on the credit report now hidden in the lower-left-hand drawer of Del's desk.

Thing was, the guy lived on a poverty-level income. Or if he did make more, it was on a cash-only basis. Del knew that for a fact. He'd called an ex-army buddy who had a low-level position in the FBI—the call had been made from a pay phone because Del often wondered if spooksville had tapped his office phone—and that buddy had called someone in the IRS, who'd called someone two levels up and gotten income information and social security printouts on Slater Ellis, which Del had copied down by hand two hours later from the same phone on his return call to the ex-army FBI man.

What Del expected was that someone at Slater's level of income would have plenty of bills. The credit check—arranged by a local bank manager who liked to fish with Del—showed not only zero debts but also zero loans. The guy hadn't had a chance to miss any payments because he simply didn't borrow money. Yet a cross-check on vehicle plates showed Slater drove a late-model 4 x 4. Like he'd paid cash?

When Del had finally noticed something about all the incoming information, much began to fall into place. Nothing—nowhere— was more than four years old. The guy didn't exist before he'd applied for his driver's license in Albuquerque.

Put that alongside the FBI fingerprint report that showed the prints from the pay phone at the hospital belonged to some guy who'd been on the run for four years after being charged with attempted murder.

Four years on the run. Four years on the new ID for Slater Ellis. And they were rock-solid papers, too, the kind of stuff you paid big bucks for on the black market. A birth certificate that matched some baby who'd died around the same time the guy was born. Social security that wouldn't raise any flags on the computer. Clean driver's license. Call it ten grand for all the new papers.

Four years on the run. Four years on the new ID Convenient. Pretty safe bet Slater Ellis was connected with spooksville. And there was one way to confirm Del's guess—straight from the horse's mouth, even if it meant strapping the horse into a chair and pulling teeth from his mouth with pliers.

Slater Ellis. Del didn't care who he'd been before. Del knew Slater lived nearby. If Slater Ellis had a telephone or utility account, he was within Del's grasp.

Barely away from the airport and onto Gibson Boulevard, the quiet dude with the bad face reached over and snapped the radio volume control to instant silence.

"What you doing, man?" Wally Williams said. "That's ZZ Top!"

This was his truck, Wally thought, and once onto the interstate they had seventy-five miles to go from Albuquerque to Sante Fe, probably another hour more to Los Alamos. He needed tunes.

Wally reached for the radio and blared the volume again. Outside the cab of the truck, he took flack from plenty of people. His old lady, the car-payment nag down at the bank, a Hitler boss man. But inside the cab, Wally Williams was king. Put him in the groove of the highway, and the road was his. Took a special breed to drive these semis, and, long hair or not, he was as cowboy as any of the breed.

The dude reached for the radio again, and Wally would have slapped his hand away, but some old bag in a big domestic car hit the brakes for a yellow light when any idiot would have cruised through, and Wally had to fight the truck to a shuddering stop.

ZZ Top died with a click.

Seconds later, with the cab of the truck shaking to the rhythm of a diesel motor idling not quite in tune, Wally looked down at the radio.

"Are you crazy, dude?" Wally screamed.

The dude with the bad face handed Wally the volume control knob, which he'd snapped from the radio.

"Wake me from my sleep," he said, his first words since meeting Wally at the truck, "and next I rip off your earring."

Whoaaa, dude, Wally thought, *bad vocals.*

Regardless of his thoughts, Wally Williams understood serious intimidation. He said nothing during the entire three-hour drive to a military compound outside Los Alamos.

The silence nearly killed Wally. He kept having to deal with the thoughts bouncing around his head, and that was a real bummer.

As soon as he had unloaded the wooden crates by forklift and set them on a dock outside the one-story building, he was gone, glad to be king in his own cab again, vowing to blow his brains on the stash of major weed waiting for him at the trailer park.

Zwaan watched the truck clear the security gates and pull away. There was always a risk some trucker might ask one question too many, and it helped to hire someone whose brains had been fried by chemicals. It didn't make the trip any easier, though, when all the sleep Zwaan had caught in the last two days had been naps in transit.

He drew a deep breath and forced energy into himself.

Ahead of him were the considerable complications of emptying the coffins, introducing the surviving refugees to their new world, and testing them for AIDS—one of the disadvantages of taking specimens from a part of the world with such a high concentration of the virus.

After all the administration, Zwaan still couldn't afford to sleep. Not until he'd spoken to Del Silverton. Then to Del's wife.

For it wouldn't do to have the mice playing in his absence.

The phone rang at 11:40.

Seated in front of his computer, Slater snatched the phone

from its cradle before the first ring ended. "Good morning, Dr. Austad."

"I apologize for the delay," Ben Austad began. "Two students stopped me in the hallway."

"You're the one doing me the favor. Let me call you right back so we're talking on my dime."

"It's the university's dime," Austad said. "I consider this research."

"Well," Slater told him, "I'm as interested in the results as you are." *Understatement,* Slater added to himself. The two hours waiting for the call had not been productive. The boys had done nothing except stare at him. He in return had been on-line at his computer, logged in as a guest user on the off chance some hacker was tracking him, going over his hidden money markets, but concentrating little on the numbers, glancing back occasionally at the burning stares from his houseguests.

They had communicated aloud once. Briefly. Then simultaneously released the contents of their bladders on the couch. This action had only underscored Slater's frustration. Without a common language—or lacking that, some degree of trust—he would make zero progress. The sheer logistics of keeping the boys would force him to either let them loose or turn them in to the authorities.

This phone call, however, might change his choices.

"I'll put us on speaker now. Any questions before we begin?"

"I don't believe so," Austad said. "You did a more than adequate job of explaining the situation earlier."

"All right then," Slater replied. "Here goes."

He punched the button on the phone and set the receiver in its cradle.

"Dr. Austad?"

"I'm still here."

Austad's voice held the trace of echo that always made hands-free telephone calls annoying. Yet it was loud enough and clear enough.

The boys on the couch tilted their heads at the unfamiliar voice.

"You've got their attention, Dr. Austad. In fact, you might find it amusing. A new and strange voice in the room and they have no idea how it's reaching them."

"Hard to believe they don't even understand telephones."

Slater opened his mouth to reply, but Austad had continued.

"Salutatio," Austad was saying. In Latin, he told them his name was Ben Austad.

Slater could have dropped a hornet's nest among them and seen less reaction. They kicked their legs as if bucking loose from the hobbles and shot startled glances at each other.

"You've got their attention, Doctor," Slater said softly. "Keep going."

In a slow, strong voice, he asked them to introduce themselves.

Momentary silence. Although Slater did not understand the Latin, he knew Austad was asking them for their names. Austad had agreed it was important to get them speaking, and they'd chosen it as the least threatening question possible.

The silence continued too long. Finally, one boy whispered to another. They debated quietly among themselves.

"Can you hear anything," Slater asked Austad.

"On this end, only a murmur."

The boy in the middle glared at Slater. Slater held his hands wide and shrugged a universal gesture of noncomprehension.

The middle boy had been elected as spokesman, for in Latin he answered that he was twenty-one and his companions were twelve and seventeen.

"Slater," Austad said. "You told me they were triplets."

"They are."

"I just asked them their names, and he gave me their ages. Twenty-one, twelve, and seventeen. Triplets generally share the same birth date."

"Austad, those are their names. The numbers tattooed on their forehead. Damn it, Austad, what are they, lab animals?"

The boys watched Slater intently during his interchange. He hardly noticed. He was hearing the question he'd just asked in sarcastic disbelief. *Lab animals? Impossible.*

Austad was speaking to the boys, words fast and unintelligible. The boy in the middle fired back, then the other two boys.

Lab animals. Impossible?

Slater searched his memory for anything that might contradict the dead weight of sadness and horror settling upon him.

Tattooed, naked, unaware of anything about the modern world except for light switches. Like they truly had been kept in cages.

Slater no longer found it amusing to see the boys looking upward and around them as they searched for the source of the voice that spoke to them in a language that had been dead for centuries, one that in today's world was only found in the realm of—Slater closed his eyes—*science*. Latin, for centuries, the voice of science.

Slater nearly jumped to his feet to shout interruption of the conversation. Anything, just to ease his mind and prove his thoughts wrong.

Yet the bond Austad was establishing with the boys was too fragile. An interruption might cost too much.

Slater walked to the front window blinds to gaze at the mountain trees. Austad would finish when he finished. Until then, Slater would force patience upon himself.

Barely a minute later—as an electric surge of adrenaline charged through him—he realized how fortunate he had been to remain outside of the conversation. If he hadn't gone to the window, he wouldn't have seen the police cruiser on its slow approach up the driveway. Inside the house, and with the telephone speaker at full volume, he wouldn't have had warning of a visitor until a knock at the door. At that point, opening the door would show all three boys, send the stench of urine into the visitor's face.

In Slater's world, all visitors were unexpected—and possibly dangerous. Much more so any cop.

Slater snapped the blinds shut.

"Austad!"

The boys froze.

"Dr. Austad, I have no choice but to step outside. If you need to hang up before I get back, I'll call you."

"Slater," Austad told him, grimness apparent over the telephone line. "I won't hang up. And you'd better get back as soon as possible."

Slater closed the door quietly behind him and walked toward the police cruiser.

The shack would easily go for a hundred and a half, Del thought. Two levels, loft probably, fireplace, windows everywhere. This was a luxury mountain retreat. With no mortgage? Slater Ellis *had* to be spooksville. Slater Ellis was the man.

Del grunted as he pushed himself out of the police cruiser. He was right; he knew by the anticipation in his stomach, the same anticipation he savored when a buck was about to walk into his sights.

He leaned back into the car to retrieve his hat. By the time he'd straightened and squared the hat on his head, the guy was walking down from the porch. Right into his sights.

"Howdy," the guy said.

Del squinted into the sun. Lucky accident the guy had maneuvered himself to put the sun at his back. Or maybe not. Del decided against moving into better position, just in case the guy was playing games.

"Howdy," Del said. Friendly even though he didn't feel it. "Nice place you got."

"I like it." Friendly in return.

Del had his own game he liked to play as a warmup to any serious discussion with suspects. He'd say nothing. Stand big and tall. Silently count real slow. It wasn't a question of who would break the silence; it boiled down to how long before the other guy spoke. Del had a rule of thumb to go with his game too. For each ten-count before the guy spoke, it would take half an hour of interrogation to break him. Once a guy lasted until Del had counted to fifty. Sure enough, after barely two and a half hours in the room back of the jail cells, Del had the answers he wanted.

So Del said nothing, waited for the guy to rattle.

It didn't happen.

Del was at sixty already. It had given him time to check out Slater Ellis. The guy looked compact, but that was an illusion when you realized he was plenty tall, just broad to go with his height. Probably ran, worked with iron—the smart way, high reps with lower weights. Late thirties, early forties. Had kept most his hair and showed a lot of calm in his face. Del had seen that look before—on a couple of guys in the army who'd wrestled death to the ground and survived, who came back with two simple rules: Don't sweat the small stuff; it's all small stuff.

Del got to eighty-five. A minute and a half had passed in silence. Two men appearing casual and relaxed and watching each other while jays squawked and the tops of the pines swayed in a light wind.

Del watched the guy turn, go back up the steps to the deck.

"Hey," Del said, it surprised him so much.

Halfway up the steps, the guy pivoted again, faced Del.

"Yes?"

Del almost grinned. First time he'd lost his little game.

"How's the head?" Del asked. Might as well launch into his excuse for visiting.

"Twenty-seven stitches," Ellis said. The sun wasn't quite behind him now. Small mercy. "But that isn't new to you."

"No," Del said slowly. This guy was sharp, figuring out quickly Del was here because of the hospital report, but also not showing off by explaining he'd guessed it that way.

"I'm here doing a routine check," Del said. "We had a hit-and-run last Tuesday night, the uh, fourteenth."

Del watched close. If this was the guy who'd called, he should at least flinch. Hadn't the transcript mentioned almost hitting a kid?

There it was. Slight. Real slight. A tightening of the small muscles around his eyes. But enough.

"I had a hit-and-run myself that night," Ellis said. He lightly touched his skull. "It's still tender."

"Like I said, this is just routine. We went through the hospital reports and saw your name and alcohol on the report. You drive a..."

"Chevy Blazer."

"This year's model," Del told him. "Metallic blue. I got all that from the state DMV."

Slater watched Del. Del knew Slater was thinking through the hospital report, telling himself he'd listed his address as one in Montana, wondering how Del had tracked him here and, more important, wondering why. Pressure was building, even if the guy wasn't showing it.

"The vehicle we're looking for is a Chevy half-ton, though," Del said. "That's why this is routine. I'd like to look in your garage."

There it was again. The extra tension around his eyes, hardly visible. If the sun had still been over the guy's shoulders, Del wouldn't be seeing it.

"No," the guy said.

Del waited for an explanation. It did not come.

"No?"

"No. Any other questions?"

Del almost liked this guy.

"Why not?" Del asked.

"Because I don't want you to." The guy wasn't upset or aggressive in saying it, but firm and calm.

Del sighed. But inside, he was happy, very happy. He'd come here knowing he needed something, anything to tell him he should risk questioning Slater Ellis.

Del could have come in plain clothes, not a uniform, but it didn't matter, not with what he had in mind. If he didn't take the guy in, it truly could appear just a routine check. But if he did take him in, the guy wouldn't ever return, because either way, once Del began to question Ellis—spooksville or not—Ellis was dead. Two reasons. If he was spooksville, Del couldn't afford to have him reporting back to the freak. If Slater Ellis *wasn't* spooksville, it's his bad luck Del had guessed wrong, but no way could Del rough him up, discover the guy was just a civilian, then apologize and send him on his way. One, to know Ellis wasn't lying, Del would have to rough him up bad. Two, if the guy started to throw lawsuits around, not only would Del see his career go down the tubes, but spooksville would also learn Del was doing side work.

Del sighed again. "You're right. I'd need a search warrant. Look, you mind if I use your john? It's a long drive back to Los Alamos."

"Duck behind a tree," Slater said.

Del hadn't thought the guy would go for it, but it had been worth a try. Along with deciding he wouldn't take Ellis unless he felt there was an 80 percent chance the guy was spooksville, Del had decided he wouldn't take him—especially in his police uni-form—until there was a 100 percent chance he could get away with it.

"This is a serious biological need," Del said, "not the kind you can take care of behind a tree. You can walk me right to the john; I won't be doing a search of the house."

"Nope," Ellis said. Again, not upset.

All Del wanted to know was whether there was anyone in the house. If not, he'd just throw Ellis into the cruiser and drive to a remote fishing site he knew, hike him down to some caves and ask questions at his leisure.

"I hardly ever ask anything more than once," Del said. "But my bowels are pushing me beyond pride."

"I like my privacy," Slater Ellis said.

Del figured that made it 90 percent sure the guy was spooksville. New decision, then. Del would cuff him in the back of cruiser then check the house at his leisure. If there were no witnesses inside, the guy was dead. Any witnesses, Del would either say it was routine questioning and let Slater go right away to take him later—or, if it's only one witness, he'd take Slater anyway and do the witness too. It had come down to that. Just like war, make your decision and don't let emotion make you weak about it.

"Asking one last time," Del said.

"I like my privacy."

Del got ready to pull his gun from the holster. It'd be kind of funny. This guy would think Del had to go so bad he'd shoot his way into the house.

But before Del dropped his hand to his holster, the crunch of gravel warned that another car was pulling into the long driveway.

They both watched and waited for it to round the tight bend. A station wagon appeared with a fat man and a fat woman filling most of the front seat.

"Afternoon, boys," Josh Burns said as he rolled down the window. "Hey, I ain't interrupting anything, am I?"

Nine

"TANSWORTH, to be frank, I'm having second thoughts about some aspects of the operation."

"Oh?" Van Klees should have felt at his confident best. He was in his territory—at brunch at an elegant K Street restaurant in the D.C. power corridors of the most powerful nation in the world. But General Stanley, unlike General Prowse, radiated the unpredictable power of a grizzly. He had a massive bald head, the build of a bull, and, even sitting, erect military posture that showed very little belly. The lines across his fifty-year-old face were so thin they could have been cut by razor blades. In full military uniform, he was an imposing man. Van Klees always felt slightly soft and weak in this general's presence.

"Are you afraid of a security leak?" Van Klees asked. Stanley hadn't gotten wind of the lost boys, had he?

"If this were about a security leak, I'd have already strangled you," Stanley said. "I gave you that county sheriff on a platter when

I pulled those photos, and I don't expect a whiff of trouble. You read me clearly, don't you?"

Van Klees did. With anyone but Stanley, Van Klees could sit back with detached superiority. Instead, Van Klees felt a trace of vulnerability despite the safeguard of his false identification as Jack Tansworth. Van Klees hated, really hated, any sense of loss of control. As a result, he also hated, really hated, the general sitting opposite him.

Van Klees let his face assume arrogance. "General, not only do we have the sheriff working for us, but we've got his wife reporting to us on him. No sense in wasting good photographs."

Stanley grunted approval. "What I've got second thoughts about," he then said, "is a lack of progress on your part. It's been, what, more than a dozen years?"

Van Klees did not want to deal with General Stanley the same way he always dealt with General Prowse—the threat of mutual blackmail. With Stanley, the threat would be counterproductive. Stanley was such a stubborn bull of a man he might actually call the bluff. And where would the Institute be then?

"General," Van Klees tried to soothe, "you haven't needed the Institute in the manner of our good friend, Herman Prowse. To you, then, progress would seem slower. Yet..."

"Yet give me time and *my* body will fall apart?" George Stanley snorted. General Stanley leaned forward, pushing aside the cap he'd set on the table. His piercing blue eyes lasered into Van Klees.

"It's like this, Tansworth. I don't want patchwork repairs. It's no mystery to me where you found a liver for Prowse. Refugees. Bosnia. Rwanda. Before that, Afghanistan. We're letting you scavenge the world. When my body goes to pieces, I don't want replacement parts from some refugee too slow and stupid to avoid roundup. What I want is the big payoff. And it's been more than twelve years now. How much longer?"

"One year." Van Klees held his hands open, palms up in a gesture of helplessness. "Maybe five. Science is not a certain—"

"And maybe ten years? Is that what I'm hearing?"

"Sir, you knew the odds when we went in," Van Klees said. He hated it when he called the general "sir." "My only promise was to expect it in your natural lifetime."

"But all these years! Do you realize how much funding has been funneled in your direction?"

Van Klees wanted to pull back from the intensity in the general's voice.

"Is it money out of your pocket, General? Remember, too, we've always considered the implications for the military. In the long run, you'll have helped not only yourself but also the future of this country."

"You don't understand," Gen. George Stanley said. The blaze of intensity grew in his eyes. "I really need to know when to expect results."

Van Klees, an expert at fear and weakness, wondered what the general was trying to hide with his anger. It gave Van Klees no small satisfaction to hear the reason as the general continued.

"I've got the big C," Stanley said to answer Van Klees's unspoken question. His voice held disbelief that a body as strong as his might engage in such terrible betrayal. "Cancer of the colon, Tansworth. I'm running out of time, and I no longer give a damn what's good for the country."

An hour later, two blocks north to M Street and easy walking distance in the direction of the Potomac, Van Klees stopped at a bus-stop shelter. He needed a place to sit. He pulled a page loose from a newspaper on the ground, and spread the page across the bench before sitting down.

He placed his briefcase on his lap and snapped open the locks.

"That paper uses cheap ink," a derelict in the opposite corner of the shelter said. "You'll get dirtier from it than from the bench."

"Hang yourself this evening," Van Klees suggested. He didn't look up as he transferred his wallet from his inside jacket pocket to a small compartment in the briefcase. "Try to die slowly."

Van Klees reached into another compartment and pulled out another wallet. He glanced at the credit cards inside to confirm that they carried the John Hammond name. Van Klees never made mistakes; part of his perfection was to always double and triple check. Satisfied with the wallet, he placed it in his jacket where seconds earlier Jack Tansworth's appropriate credit cards and driver's license had rested.

Van Klees stood.

He finally deigned to focus attention on the derelict.

How distasteful. Crusty gray grizzle over wattled jowls. Stringy hair. One eye turned inward. The epidermis showed evidence of a multitude of dysfunctional processes. What a miserable excuse for *Homo sapiens*. And this man had dared to offer advice? It might take a hundred years, but eventually scum like this would be weeded from the species, and the world would have Van Klees to thank for it.

Van Klees reached into his suit pocket and took out the John Hammond wallet. He pulled a fifty-dollar bill loose, and extended it to the derelict.

"Really?" the man quavered. He began to reach for the money, joy lighting his features.

"Hardly." Van Klees yanked the money away just as the man's yellowed fingers began to close over it. "Have a nice day."

Van Klees whistled as he walked toward his noon restaurant meeting with Paige Stephens.

"What I want to say is a cliché," Paige said. "But I guess they become clichés because they are so suitable."

"Try me," Van Klees said. He smiled. Because he knew she liked it from him. "I'm sure you'll add life to it."

"All right, then," she told him. "Really, you shouldn't have."

"Flown you to Washington?" Van Klees arched his eyebrows in mock surprise. "Trust me; you're doing me the favor. There was no way I could get down to Tampa. And from your phone call, I felt this was important enough to discuss in person."

Paige sipped from her water glass, already half-empty. Van Klees was happy to see her drinking the water so quickly. Dry mouths meant nervous mouths. Put a beautiful woman off balance and you had her.

"But it's not like catching a bus and crossing town," she said. "We're meeting for lunch and both of us flew hundreds of miles to get here."

"I must respectfully disagree." Van Klees briefly placed a hand across the table to pat hers. He left his hand on hers, warm and soft, just long enough for her to realize he had interest in her on a level beyond friendship. "Hundreds of executives commute across the country on a daily level. An airplane is no different from a bus to them. Once you make a shift and think of distance in terms of time, not miles, you'll understand the corporate mind-set."

She hadn't flinched at his touch. Good. *Pigeons were pigeons,* Van Klees thought, *regardless of their feathering.*

"Take my route, for example. Dallas to D.C.—a couple of hours. D.C. to New York—under an hour. New York to Chicago— a couple of hours. If I start early and encounter no flight delays, I can touch down for business in three major cities and still make it back to New York for a late supper. If I switch from commercial airlines to my own Lear jet—and I'm to the point where it might be a necessity—I could commute to five major centers in a day."

He pretended to be warming to his subject, a male peacock preening. "Not only that, Paige, my business class seat on the airplane becomes my office. Laptop computer, telephone in front of me, and no incoming calls—I can do more in an hour on the plane than I can in three hours at my New York office. Fact is, I spend so little time in New York, my secretaries only recognize me by my voice. I have to walk in talking to them on my cellular phone, or they don't let me into my office."

She smiled appreciatively.

Unspoken—and Van Klees had done it deliberately—was the implication that a man had to be important, and his business profitable, to spend a thousand dollars a day on airfare.

"The real luxury," he finished, "is being able to spend a few relaxing hours here in a situation like this. I only wish we didn't have such a trying subject."

She opened her mouth to speak.

He raised a forefinger first. Off balance, she should feel control from him. It made it all easier. "Why don't we order first?"

She chose broiled salmon. He ordered the chef's special salad.

"Not hungry?" she teased. "Another date earlier?"

"Only so you would look that much better by comparison." He waited for her laughter to end, then took control again. "Tell me about the robbery," he said. "From the beginning."

She explained how two men—one very fat and the other short with mutilated ears—had jumped her from a nearby car as she was parking in broad daylight at her motel. Van Klees nodded sympathy where appropriate and made sounds of disbelief on cue.

They were interrupted by the delivery of the meal.

"Right in the motel parking lot," he repeated as the waiter departed. "Crazy, what this world is coming to. They just bowled you over and made the snatch. Your purse, everything?"

"And a package," she said. "That's what I wanted to tell you about. It was a package from Darby."

Van Klees put his fork down and stared at her. This was so much fun, acting out his role as he listened to her side of the robbery. Zwaan, too, might appreciate similarities and differences between the victim's report and operative's report.

"Darby? You mean your husband. It was a package to you from him?"

Van Klees thought he definitely deserved an Oscar. He could have told her, after all, that the package contained a far too precise assessment of the Institute, and far too few—meaning none—of the backup computer disks. If anything was worrisome, it was that the disks had not yet been found.

She nodded. "It's difficult to talk about, but you should know Darby was running scared."

The spineless, unappreciative fool, Van Klees thought. *He should have known better than to defy Zwaan. The real shame is that he died too quickly.*

"Scared?" Van Klees said, instead of speaking his thoughts, adding a precisely measured dose of concern to his voice.

"Very scared, John," Paige said. She lowered her head. "The package explained why."

Her statement hit him like a dagger thrust bouncing off his ribs. *She couldn't have known unless she'd opened the package. But he'd been given assurances otherwise.*

He reacted by calmly picking up his salad fork. "You read through the package?"

Van Klees was so grateful to himself that he had bothered to keep in touch with this woman. Little did she know her life depended on her next few words.

"No," she said, "definitely not. I was only able to read his letter explaining the package. It hurt too much in the lawyer's office to read more."

She stared across the restaurant and thought out loud. "I've been trying to tell myself it was only a purse snatching. That maybe the thieves thought a sealed envelope might have something valuable in it."

"It wasn't open?" Van Klees needed to confirm that the woman hadn't browsed through its contents somewhere between the lawyer's and the moment of theft.

"The lawyer insisted on resealing it," Paige told him. "I was going to open it again when I found the courage."

"What did the letter say that gave you such fear?"

"Darby warned it was too terrible for him to live with, that it would be my decision to pass the information on to the FBI or the media."

"Nothing else? No other clues?"

"He just referred to something called the Institute. That's it. Nothing else. How can that be a clue?"

Little pigeon, you just saved your life.

Van Klees reached a hand across the table and, this time, left it on hers. "I'm sorry," he said. "Perhaps we should save this discussion for another day."

She rubbed her face. "John, I've got too many questions, and I don't know who might be able to help me."

"I'm here," he said. He gave her hand a gentle squeeze. "Any time you want, I'm here. Trust me."

Slater had private speculations about humans and God. At one time people had been selfless in their consciousness, not focused on their own greedy needs and, in that state of innocence, were open to His presence all the time. Then had come the snake and the apple—whether Eden was a symbol or reality, Ellis never argued because it was pointless to battle either side without proof, and how it had happened was irrelevant to the much more important fact that sometime, somewhere, humans as a species had chosen their own path, leading them to camp beneath clouds that hid their view of the divine love constantly shining above.

Prayer, Slater thought, was one way to attempt to push away the cloud, but how often was prayer just another series of requests, as if it'd be convenient for God to step in and help further with whatever selfish interests clouded His presence in the first place.

Slater hoped God listened and understood the gratitude and quiet joys taken whenever one of the species marveled at the beauty of His world.

Like now.

Here was the light of the sun, rising over California, strong behind the distant sharp edges of the San Bernardino range, and the entire valley spread in front, rich with folded land softly green. The sky, pale where it met the sun, deepened to cloudless pure blue, scrubbed clean by the wind above the stillness of the vast valley.

Slater stood in damp grass at the edge of the road, filling his lungs with the cool air and the peace all of this brought him, stretching wakefulness into his cramped body.

Interstate 15, several miles below and at this hour not too clogged with traffic, was a postcard ribbon he could trace with his eyes as it rose and fell the length of the valley.

It had been sixteen hours of hard driving to reach this point, and nearly worth it, simply to suspend himself from reality in this moment of lifting his eyes to look beyond himself for a tantalizing brief and vague sense of eternity.

Then came tapping from the window.

Slater grinned at the faces of three boys pressed against the fogged glass of the truck.

He wasn't the only one who needed to stretch after a few hours of uncomfortable sleep.

It had been too weird, the afternoon before, facing down the big sheriff from Los Alamos. Slater understood most of the tension he'd felt was a result of what he'd been hiding from the sheriff as they spoke.

But there'd been more.

Slater couldn't swear it, but something in the big man had become more menacing at the end of their conversation, and somehow the arrival of Josh Burns and his booming voice had been like cavalry cresting the hill.

And if the gut feeling hadn't been enough, there had been Ben Austad's urgency greeting Slater as he stepped into the house after watching both vehicles finally depart.

"Get the boys out of there," Austad told Slater over the conference phone. No hello again, no what happened to keep you out of the house, no guess what the boys have been telling me. But a pleading, forceful, and alarmed order.

"Get them out of the house?"

"Out of there. The mountains. Move them anywhere in the country. But get them out of there. Put them in a car, cover them with blankets, and move. Don't stop."

"What did they tell you?" Slater asked.

"You want to know, you call me when you've put three hundred miles between you and the mountains. Just leave. If you have people who won't understand, call back home later and make your excuses then. But go. You've got to go."

Gone was the assured calm. Austad's fear was more powerful, coming from a man Slater guessed rarely felt or showed fear.

"All right," Slater said. "How do I convince them to go with me? I can't even talk to them."

For a moment, Austad didn't reply.

Slater looked at the boys. Each still in the ridiculous attire they'd been wearing when captured. He didn't dare move them like that. Even if he could convince them he was a friend.

"I'll talk to them," Austad said. "I'll talk them through it as you untie the rope."

"Will they believe you?" Slater asked. "To them, you're just a voice from thin air."

More silence.

The boys seemed more subdued, less wary as they returned Slater's studying gaze.

"You'll have to prove to them you don't mean them harm," Austad said. "Any ideas?"

Slater hesitated. "Yeah," Slater said, his voice slow. "Ask them what it would take to trust me."

Austad spoke a brief flurry of Latin.

The boys in turn looked at each other. Then at Slater.

The middle boy answered Austad in a longer flurry.

Another silence.

More exchanged Latin.

"Yes?" Slater asked in the next silence.

"They want to meet me," Austad said. "And now that you've got me in this, I want to meet them. I've explained the only way it will happen is through you."

"I can drive to Los Angeles," Slater said.

"Good," Austad said. "Now convince them you're a friend. Show them a bit of trust too."

"Sure. How?"

"Cut them loose and give them each a knife."

Slater waited an hour past dawn to call Ben Austad. By then, they were well into the heavy four-lane traffic and urban sprawl of outlying Los Angeles. Around them, the seamless spread of commercial buildings, apartments, and truck stops and fast-food restaurants.

"Hello, Ben." Slater said. "We're on 10, just reaching Pomona."

"That's good time."

"I caught a catnap a couple hours past Vegas," Slater said. "Other than that, we only stopped for clothes for the boys and for fuel."

"How are they?"

Slater grinned. "At this moment, faces pressed to the windows, absolutely in awe. Imagine you haven't even seen a television before. Now picture your first impression of Los Angeles."

Austad laughed. "I was thirty-five when I first arrived. It was bad enough then."

"Did you dive under a blanket the first time a semi passed you on the freeway?"

"They didn't!"

"Yep. Though it didn't take them long to peek out again."

"Can I talk to one?"

"Sure."

Slater handed the phone back between the bucket seats. The middle kid took it, shyly. In the rearview mirror, Slater saw the kid hesitate, then slowly place the phone to his ear in imitation of Slater.

The kid's eyes widened as he listened to Austad. He tried a few tentative words, discovered Austad could hear him in return. It didn't take much longer until the kid had adapted completely to the conversation and had lost all fear of the plastic miracle pressed to his head.

Slater switched lanes to stay in the flow of traffic and hid another grin. At the very least, he'd enjoyed watching the kids during the entire drive from Seven Springs, even if he was nervous about the knife each had taken into the backseat.

They'd left within fifteen minutes of ending the phone conversation with Austad. Slater didn't have much to pack—jeans, a couple of shirts, toiletries, and his laptop computer. The 4 x 4 had been mostly full of fuel, and with a blanket to cover the boys in back, they'd driven away without ceremony. Their only delay was a brief stop to leave the puppies with Josh Burns, where Slater, having first made sure the kids were well hidden, had mumbled something about having to go out of town unexpectedly.

Driving west from Seven Springs, beyond the settlement on the portion of road so primitive it was closed in winter, they'd faced another dozen miles of deep gravel and sand to escape the Nacimento Mountains and reach the desert flats. Each of the few times Slater had earlier driven that stretch of road, he'd taken forty-five minutes to wind through the hills and out to pavement. On this trip, he'd slammed the truck into four-wheel drive and pushed hard enough to get to the desert in twenty minutes. From there, he'd driven to Gallup on the western edge of New Mexico, taking two-lane blacktop and keeping a constant watch in his rearview mirror. Traffic was scarce, and the sight of any vehicle filled him with adrenaline. Austad's fear had been that convincing.

To the boys out from under the blanket, however, the wide-open desert flats brought amazement. So did open windows. Slater had lowered his window on the driver's side and the rushing wind had given the boys their first clue of how fast they traveled, setting them buzzing and laughing for at least fifteen miles.

They hadn't any chance of seeing their first city, Gallup, because Slater had made them understand they had to remain beneath the blanket again.

In Gallup, Slater had stopped at a sports store to buy sweatpants, T-shirts, and running shoes. At a service station, he'd loaded up on soda and chocolate bars. And they'd hit the road again, taking interstate 40 west toward Flagstaff, Kingman, and Barstow.

The kids changed as he drove.

Not once did Slater see the knives they carried as talismans. After a while, he forgot about their two-edged weapons of trust, and eventually he forgot, too, to worry about vehicles approaching from behind. The cactus and sand and red-rock buttes flashed past, and he settled into the rhythm of the highway's hum.

The land rose again on the approach to the cool, high pines of Flagstaff, but this time, safely away from Seven Springs, the boys had remained perched on the backseat instead of beneath the blanket, staring out the windows, pointing and talking at each new sight.

For grins, Slater had plugged in an Eagles CD, snapped his fingers, and sung along with "Tequila Sunrise." He wasn't sure what had astounded them more, the music or his voice. They'd reached for the CD case, passing it between themselves and speculating in hushed voices as they examined it from all angles.

Sunset then dusk had hit, and Slater drove on through the night. Robbed of new sights, the boys had fallen asleep, not even waking during fuel stops or when Slater finally exited the interstate to find a safe spot to nap on the shoulder of a secondary road.

As Slater now watched them talking to Austad, he decided they'd obviously slept much better than he had. The animation in their faces as they drove into Los Angeles was contagious, and Slater again found himself taking joy in their reactions to a new world.

He maneuvered smoothly through the freeway traffic as each kid passed the phone to another, learning quickly how to speak to Austad.

He'd almost reached the shadows of downtown Los Angeles skyscrapers when the third kid passed the phone back to him.

"Slater, again," he said.

"We've got plenty to talk about," Austad told him. "I've called in sick to give us the rest of the day."

"Good," Slater said. "It's not like I don't have any questions."

"I commend your patience. Where are you now?"

Slater squinted to read a sign. "Santa Monica Freeway. Vermont Avenue exit."

"Another hour, then, at this time of day. You've still got my directions?"

"Yep."

"Good," Austad told him. "I'll have a tape recorder ready. What they've got to say is incredible."

As Slater cradled the phone into place, he glanced into the rearview mirror and froze.

The kid in the middle had pulled his knife and was reaching into the front between the bucket seats.

Slater stopped breathing, almost swerved to the shoulder.

The kid tossed the knife onto the floor of the passenger side, grinned, and patted Slater's shoulder.

Before they'd reached the next exit, two other knives had joined the first.

Waiting for the return of Slater Ellis reminded Del of Vietnam. Long hours of cramped muscles. Patience that stretched nerves thin. Here, however, beneath the low sweeping branches of a spruce tree, looking down on the house from the hill nearby, it was better and worse. Worse because Del carried sixty pounds more than he had during Nam, and his body was far too accustomed to soft mattresses and midnight raids to the refrigerator. Better because the air wasn't wet and rotten and clinging like a hot, dirty rag, and he'd hadn't breathed each breath wondering if Charlie would slip in from the dark like snakes dropping silently from trees.

War had not been crisp uniforms and the glamour of ribbons. It had been filth and fear and a dry mouth no matter how many swigs from the canteen. It had been cargo flights of air conditioners and TVs and fresh beef for the generals; beds of grass, and beans and frankfurters for the grunts. It had been a fight against an army supplied with rice and fish heads by bike and wheelbarrow. It had been a place where the most dangerous opponent was an eight-year-old with a soft drink in one hand and a grenade in the other.

It had also been shame.

Del didn't want to let his mind go there, but along with the softening of his body, he'd lost the need and ability to empty his mind for hours at a time.

Waiting again as if war had returned brought his mind back to the one memory he wished he didn't carry, to the photographs he cursed.

Lt. William Calley's slaughter at My Lai of more than a hundred women, old men, and children hadn't been the only war atrocity carried out by an American platoon. Del knew Calley's claim that he was being singled out for the commonplace was too close to the truth.

In Del's case, he had missed most of the first of it, taking a half-hour to cover their advance by planting pressure-detonated explosives in the middle of a cart-track road and camouflaging them as the rest of the platoon surged through tiny fields of sweet potatoes into the village ahead. By the time he'd caught up, most of the screams had ended.

The village was hardly more than ten conical huts with banana-leaf roofs in a beaten clearing. There were scattered grass mats, old soot-blackened aluminum pots, spilled rice, a couple of yellowed photographs of a woman and child in straw hats. The trash of poor peasants.

Del took those details in mechanically as his eyes were riveted on the five of them hanging upside down from a pole hastily suspended between two supporting trees. Three *papasans*, a small boy, and an old man. Two soldiers stood nearby, focusing a camera on the bodies.

Del didn't see his CO move up beside him.

"You got that look on your face, Dog-breath." The man's cheeks were hollowed by fatigue and camouflage paint.

"Sir?"

"The look like you ain't one of us."

"Us sir?"

"Us. You've been in this platoon a week; it's time you joined. You got your choice. Bayonet those bodies. Or go in the hut where a few of the boys have themselves a woman."

Del was shaking his head, confused. The CO pulled an automatic pistol and pointed it at Del's head.

"I don't want to shoot you. You're a good soldier and the platoon can use good soldiers. But don't fool yourself. I pull this trigger, and you're just another dog tag in an envelope headed stateside." The CO grinned, his hollow cheeks pulling tight. "See, all the rest of us, we're a unit. I'm sure you've heard the rumors. Black-market contraband. Brisk trade in pharmaceuticals. War's making some nice things possible for us. All of us. We can't afford to have someone we don't trust. And you get our trust by posing for some pictures. So what's it going to be? Dead bodies, or a live woman? Surely you ain't as dumb as you are big."

Del chose to attack the bodies on the pole. Never could he rid himself of the vision of the men's dangling bodies, an albatross hanging around him as surely as if they had been tied to his own neck instead that green sapling pole in the steaming jungle.

If he got Ellis, Del could free himself of the damning photographs that he'd discovered later were only part of a collection that the CO had been building to use for blackmail after Nam. But the CO had been killed sitting in a latrine, hit by an incoming VC rocket. And all the photos had somehow disappeared, until the spook with the puckered skull had dropped them into Del's lap.

He cursed the photos again. If only Slater Ellis would return to his mountain-resort house. That was the first step to reclaiming his freedom.

Del had been waiting beneath the tree since eight o'clock the evening before. He'd rented a car for this—afraid his own vehicles might have electronic tracers and wanting to be certain spooksville wouldn't know he'd made the move here—and hidden the rental well on a dirt track some hundred yards down the road.

Out of police uniform and wearing noiseless soft hunting clothes, he'd eased along the trees that shadowed Slater's driveway to this rise. He would watch the house from here, unseen, as long as it took to decide when to hit, then hit hard. That would give him the night and as much of tomorrow as he needed to break the guy.

Except the house had been empty.

Del had wanted badly to go inside, check around, learn more

about Ellis, see if he'd packed and run. But that was too risky. If Ellis returned, not alone, it wouldn't be a perfect grab. Anyway, Del had taken the next day off, anticipating a long, difficult interrogation. He'd told only Louise his destination, and he'd told her it might take all night. So he could afford to wait. If Slater didn't return by noon, then Del would check the house and from there begin tracking Slater's flight. If Slater did return, it would make the night beneath the spruce branches more than worthwhile.

Just past dawn, Del had slowly rolled away from the tree, and, lying on his side, had emptied his bladder before rolling back to cover beneath the tree. This was a combat situation, and he was going to play it that way. War brought down the unwary and the lazy, and Del refused to get sloppy in his vigilance.

The sun was hot now, and Del had been motionless for nearly four hours, long enough to add pressure to his bladder again. He was thirsty—hadn't planned on a full night here—and tired of the crawly sensation of needles from the low spruce boughs against the back of his neck. Twice he had let a spider crawl across his face. Once a squirrel had darted across his feet. Yet Del was too stubborn to deviate from what he'd learned in Nam. He would not move.

As his bladder reached the aching point again, the noise of an approaching vehicle rewarded his sore muscles and determination.

But it didn't sound like a 4 x 4 to Del. Nor like the beat-up station wagon of the idiot who had shown up the day before at exactly the wrong time. Instead, it was a much softer engine noise—a late-model American make.

When the vehicle broke into view below him, Del saw he'd guessed right. What caught his breath was the person who stepped out: the freak with the scarred face and puckered head.

Del closed his eyes. There was only one reason he'd told Louise his destination. And he'd desperately hoped she wouldn't fail his test. Now the snake of betrayal coiling through his guts told him she had.

Van Klees drove to the square, flat industrial building at the north end of town. At the security gate he nodded at the guard, then proceeded to the back of the building and parked in the stall reserved for Jack Tansworth.

Nothing about the building rated a second glance. It was set well back from the street. Except at the rear, where the paved lot was large enough to accommodate thirty vehicles, large maple trees shaded and hid most of the building. Its unassuming appearance had helped Van Klees to choose this location.

As he walked to the rear entrance, Van Klees took in the lines of the building with an indulgent smile, a habit of his on every approach to the TechnoGen corporate headquarters. He freely admitted his weakness of allowing himself this satisfaction in TechnoGen. After all, as with the New York real estate corporation belonging to his John Hammond identity, TechnoGen was merely the means to an end. Just a cog in the conglomerate that only Van Klees and Zwaan—now that Darby Stephens was dead—knew and understood to be the support base for the Institute.

Van Klees always forgave his weakness of satisfaction, however, by reminding himself that TechnoGen alone would be the life's work of a lesser person. And he took pride in knowing the same lesser person would still be hailed as a genius by the business world, should a company like TechnoGen ever allow some of its activities to reach a higher profile.

Yes, this was a public company, traded on the New York Stock Exchange, a move that had put ten million dollars into Van Klees's slush fund. TechnoGen was designed to withstand any scrutiny—from the Internal Revenue Service or any other government agency. But, legal as the company's activities were, Van Klees would never permit the least amount of media profile. Not with the source of its revenue base: fetal parts.

Van Klees had fifteen specialists on the road every day. Each one traveled a weekly regional route to local abortion clinics to scavenge for the remains of aborted fetuses. Just about any fetal part was valuable—from brain slivers to organ pieces, to a whole heart. These "specialists" paid the abortion clinics a service fee for the inconvenience caused by their searches; fetal-tissue users in turn paid TechnoGen a handling fee. Thus, based on service charges only, no government organization would be able to claim TechnoGen actually bought or sold human body parts.

In short, one of TechnoGen's roles was as tissue broker. With scientists and researchers proclaiming fetal transplantation as one of the most exciting areas of human biotechnology, business was booming. One tremendous advantage of human fetal parts was the legal simplicity. Fetal tissue wasn't taken from anything the supreme court recognized as human; scientists and researchers never had to worry about lawsuits. Almost as significant, fetal body parts grow far more easily than the biological materials of mature humans.

Van Klees often felt smug at how well he had recognized TechnoGen as not only a perfect tie-in to the Institute but also as a business opportunity. There were maybe a half-dozen other fetal harvesters in the country, certainly no more than a dozen. He had conceived—and he often smiled at that pun—and formed a thriving company in a virtual monopoly position. TechnoGen's service-charge revenue in the area of fetal parts had recently broken the five-million-dollar-a-year mark, with a net profit hovering at 30 percent.

Van Klees had not been slow to see another opportunity, directly linked to his supply source. Upon reading research papers on the subject, he'd immediately begun a smaller division to copy other researchers' success of creating humanized mice. The process was simple. The TechnoGen lab technicians took the thymus, liver, and lymph nodes from human fetuses, then implanted a piece of each organ under the kidneys of young mice. Within a few days, the blood vessels of the mice would begin to penetrate the human subparts, and these fetal organs would begin to grow, eventually producing human immune system cells within the mouse. These mice were ideal for experiments; injected with human leukemia-causing viruses or the human AIDS virus, they could be used to screen antiviral compounds for effectiveness. Each human mouse was worth five thousand dollars in resale but cost barely a hundred dollars to raise; TechnoGen produced generation after generation for sale to pharmaceutical companies, who in turn knew a billion-dollar pot at the end of the rainbow belonged to the first to find a cure for any one of dozens of diseases.

TechnoGen's same division was also experimenting with other injections. If mice could produce human immune cells, why not graft other fetal parts—human lungs, or intestines, pancreas, pituitary glands, skin or brain cells—into mice? After all, TechnoGen could pick and choose the best part samples from the hundreds of aborted fetuses it scavenged each week.

Because of this, Van Klees and TechnoGen had lately—with success—been putting pressure on physicians for better quality fetal parts. Van Klees knew better than to hope for the ideal—copying Swedish researchers who had harvested tissue from a live fetus in the mother's womb *before* it had been aborted. So he settled for second best. TechnoGen advertised—discretely, of course—and paid higher fees to doctors who used the dilation-and-evacuation technique on fetuses in the second trimester of pregnancy. At that age, the fetuses were large enough and distinctly formed enough to provide excellent organ parts. Van Klees was forced to pay the higher rates because squeamish doctors preferred other methods of abortion, which killed the fetus before labor. The extra payment was worth it, however, since dilation-and-evacuation sucked the fetus out of the anesthetized mother, and the TechnoGen specialists were often able to harvest the fetus still alive in the operating room.

If harvesting the unborn and implanting their parts into experimental animals were all that TechnoGen did, it would still be a remarkable company, Van Klees repeatedly noted.

But always, and from the beginning, there was the shadow behind it: the Institute.

Van Klees carried a bulky briefcase into the reception area of TechnoGen. Nothing about him or his unwrinkled clothing hinted that since dawn he'd flown from Sante Fe to Albuquerque and then to D.C., then later from D.C. to Pittsburgh.

A smiling redheaded secretary welcomed him.

"Mr. Tansworth, how nice to see you."

Van Klees forced a warm smile on his face. So tedious, the predictability of women like this, believing he would respond to the wrigglings of mere flesh, as if his mind would permit bodily functions to overrule and risk the larger visions he carried. These women only wanted to leech from him, hoping with intimacy to gain some of his greatness.

"Good afternoon, Tammy," Van Klees said. "I see you've done something new with your hair. It looks terrific."

She beamed.

Van Klees moved on. Loyalty took so little to acquire.

He stopped several steps later, paused and turned, the act of someone remembering something casual.

"Oh, Tammy," he called. "Did the shipments of eggs arrived as scheduled?"

"Yes sir," she said.

Van Klees knew she was admiring the broadness of his shoulders. He wanted to snarl at her.

"Wonderful," he said with a return smile. "And a courier picked them up again to redirect the shipment?"

"Yes, Mr. Tansworth."

He maintained his smile. The eggs would be awaiting him at the Institute the next day. Let the taxpayers complain, Van Klees thought, but the military can be extremely efficient transporters when motivated.

Five minutes later, Van Klees sat relaxed in the heavy leather chair opposite the desk of TechnoGen's director.

"Keith, you'll find the notes to be in excellent order." Van Klees did that as frequently as possible, calling people by their first names. Salesmanship.

Keith Edison looked up from the open briefcase on his desk. "Why would these be different from any of the others?"

No reason at all. Not a year's worth of Institute research neatly condensed into a stack of laser-printed reports.

"Read through them before you pass them on to the researchers," Van Klees said. "I'm sure you'll find some commercial application."

Van Klees gave a leering grin. "And I'm sure you'll find some use for the year-end bonus when those commercial applications add to our bottom line."

Keith Edison leered back. A short, wide man, his face was almost puce. He liked his food, he liked his booze, he liked his private airplane, and he liked the yacht he flew to every weekend in Atlantic City. He was the perfect director for TechnoGen because he asked very few questions as long as his yearly bonus remained intact.

"Year in, year out, boss," he said, "you wait until the end of the university school year and plunk down these genetic miracles ten years ahead of the rest of the pack. Tough life, huh, going from campus to campus?"

"There are a few creature comforts," Van Klees allowed. He kept his grin at a leer. The button to push with Edison was women. Let him think you chased them as much as he did.

"Long-legged twenty-year-olds. Nice of you to sacrifice for TechnoGen."

"We all have our roles to play." Van Klees gave a theatrical sigh. "I'll endure mine."

Keith nodded and smiled dreamily.

"By the way," Van Klees said. "Any updates on the demethylase enzyme?"

"It's costing us a ton of money."

Van Klees leaned forward. "Then make more."

Keith held up his hands in mock self-defense. "Don't kill me, boss man. You'll break the hearts of all my girlfriends."

Van Klees resumed his relaxed position. Inside, he fumed. Partly at Edison's irreverence, and partly at how he himself had slipped, betrayed too strong an interest.

"Until I get your girlfriends' phone numbers, I guess you're safe." Van Klees hated common banter, but if that's what it took, he'd do it. "I couldn't let you die without knowing where you kept your treasure."

"Then I'll keep my little black book out of sight," Edison said. "As for the demethylase, we did get one of the frogs slightly beyond the end of the tadpole stage. But that was it. And we can't seem to isolate what blocked the rest of the development."

Van Klees nodded. "Stay with it, all right?"

Edison shrugged. "Your company, boss man."

Boss man. So vulgar. Van Klees wondered if it would be worth more to lose Edison's services in exchange for the satisfaction of seeing him reduced to begging hamburger by Zwaan.

He stood up and shook Edison's hand.

"You're a good man, Keith. Keep it going. And get me a copy of your latest work on the tadpoles."

"Sure." Edison was standing too. "If it finally works, I think I'll clone myself. Just imagine. Then I could handle a dozen more broads."

Van Klees smiled. "Yes, Keith. Just imagine."

Ten

She nearly said, "Hello, John," when she picked up the phone because she half hoped it was Hammond returning her call from wherever he might be in the country. She didn't expect any other callers anyway, not during her cloistered retreat here.

Instead, Paige merely said, "Good morning." If it *was* John on the other end, she didn't want to appear eager.

"Good morning, Paige. It's Suzanne." Her realtor. Wife of a friend of Darby's. "I hope this isn't an inconvenient time to call."

Paige glanced at the clock radio. Ten thirty-five. She'd been up since dawn, sitting on the motel-room balcony, staring at the gulf waters with an unread *Vanity Fair* in her lap, wondering, always wondering, about Darby, trying to feel more grief, trying not to hate him for the stranger he'd become in death.

"I didn't expect to be looking at houses until the afternoon," Paige told Suzanne.

"It's not about *buying* a house, Paige. You've got an offer on yours. Full price."

"I accept," Paige said. She had no enthusiasm for the house deal or for the search for a new house. Both were simply necessities as she struggled to put her life together.

"There's a hitch," Suzanne said.

Paige waited.

"The gentleman made it conditional to speaking to you personally by noon today."

"Impossible." Paige was doing her best to remain hidden. Since the attack and the purse snatching, she'd switched motels along the gulf shore every second night, checking in under her maiden name.

"He wanted your number." Suzanne rushed on, anxious to exonerate herself. "I refused, of course, because of your instructions. But I didn't see the harm of dialing it myself and handing him the phone. After all, the market's been tight for a while and a full-price offer . . ."

"He's standing right beside you?"

"Sitting, actually. In my office. With a copy of the signed offer in his hand."

Paige felt an echo of the fear she'd been trying to push aside ever since the daylight purse snatching. Who would want to talk to her this badly? And also had the money to trace her like this? It couldn't be good.

"What does he look like?" Paige asked.

"As much as you could ask for." Suzanne laughed at her own clever double answer; the guy would assume they were still talking price. "I'd give you more details, Paige, but he *is* sitting right across from me in my office."

"No, that's not what I meant," Paige said, impatient at the misunderstanding. "Is he fat?"

"Hardly." Suzanne's tone showed she enjoyed keeping her side of the conversation ambiguous to her guest.

"Short? Any pieces missing from his ears?"

"Not at all. I didn't realize you had a checklist so, um, particular."

Paige was not in a bantering mood. Fat or short with snipped ears covered the guys who had attacked her.

"I'll speak to him, then," she said. "But do not give him my number or where I'm staying."

"Absolutely. That's why I did it this way."

Seconds later, Paige heard an unfamiliar voice.

"Thank you," the voice said. "My name is Slater Ellis."

"I'm afraid I don't recognize your name."

"I'd be surprised if you did, Mrs. Stephens. I flew in from Los Angeles this morning to introduce myself to you. We need your help."

"We?"

"Three lost boys."

"I don't understand," she said.

"Neither do I," he told her. "That's why I bought your house to reach you by telephone."

"I started to work the stock market in my late twenties," Slater told the redheaded woman with the watching eyes. "Whiz kid and all that stuff. Graduated to the high-end bonds and stock options. I was absolutely fearless. Turned out I simply didn't know enough to be scared. In the bond market that helps—not to understand what it means to risk losing a couple million dollars before you finish your next cup of coffee."

Slater was aware he was speaking quietly. He tried to decide why he was keeping his voice so soft, even as he spoke. "One by one the guys I started with dropped out. Ulcers. Heart attacks. Booze. Like combat, I guess, but without the weapons. Me, I lost my nerve. Started playing it cautious. Deadly mistake. Like walking a tightrope. Once you start to think about the fall . . ."

Paige Stephens wasn't saying anything to help him along in the conversation. She'd insisted on a restaurant overlooking the marina; she had emphasized—*before* introducing herself—that Suzanne the realtor was waiting in the parking lot, and from the first minute, she had made him carry the bulk of the conversation. So he'd begun by trying to explain why he was able to buy her house when he had no intention of moving into it.

"Anyway," he said, feeling lame but seeing no way out except to doggedly finish, "when I quit, I had enough to live on if I managed it properly. So I've spent the last few years doing just that. Managing it properly."

Slater stared beyond her at the forest of naked sail masts that filled the view. "And to tell you the truth, the worst part is I've basically felt useless during the entire time."

Why was he telling her as close to the truth as he'd told anyone in years?

He glanced at her and caught the trace of a smile. Then he understood why he'd been speaking so quietly.

This woman made him shy. Merely the trace of her smile bewitched him. What was going on? He wasn't a kid, wired hot by hormones. He'd learned enough the hard way to understand the big L didn't happen because you both liked the way the other looked.

Slater didn't like feeling the way he did—hands like blocks of wood, tongue like a sock, and each word from his mouth just another stupid sound. He'd been like this in his teens, before he'd discovered most of the mysteries about women, the way they moved during an embrace, what they expected to hear, how to make them laugh.

Right now, looking at her, he could probably make a good guess about the designer's label of her two-piece silk suit, name her perfume, and offer and make good on the offer to take her to Paris and any of a dozen restaurants he knew there from previous trips.

So why was he suddenly scared, a country bumpkin ready to knock over a water glass?

"I probably won't eat," she announced. "I'm only here because you mentioned my husband's name during our telephone conversation. And you needn't go on about the house. I have no intention of selling it to you under these conditions."

"There didn't seem to be any other way to find you," Slater said. He wasn't whining, was he? "Nobody at the International World Relief Committee could tell me how to contact you. I got your house address out of the phone book, and I drove by and saw the for sale sign in front with your realtor's number."

"I believe I said you needn't go on about the house." Although she smiled, he understood.

Slater shut his mouth, hard. Clunked teeth.

This one was cold. All right, he'd play it her way. Lots easier not caring what she thought.

"I'm guessing you have good reason for your privacy," Slater said as introduction to what he wanted to discuss. "Suzanne told me why you're selling your house; she told me about the break-in."

The redhead stiffened. "That's only part of it," she said. "And I'd rather not share the rest."

"But I knew about your husband before I flew out here. In fact, that's why I wanted to see you."

"I'm beginning to wonder about your sense of hearing. I said you'd find me reluctant to speak on the subject."

Slater waved away a hovering waiter. Not often—maybe once every couple of years—would he lose his temper. Now he was on the verge. He'd done nothing wrong to this woman, nothing to justify her attitude.

"Tell you what, lady," he said. His voice dropped to a whisper the way it did when he struggled to hold back rage. "You'll find me reluctant to speak on *this* subject."

Slater dropped onto the table a Montblanc fountain pen he'd been holding in his right hand.

He pushed his chair back and stood.

"I'll tell you something else. If you want me to speak to you again, ever, you'd better get off your ice throne before I manage to make it to my car."

He walked away. Before he'd passed two tables, he felt ridiculous for the tantrum he'd thrown. Like a wet-diapered one-year-old. Probably less because of her stubbornness and more because this woman wouldn't make eyes with him. Stung male pride. But he'd made his stand; no way could he turn around now. With the time he had left in Florida, risky as it might be, he'd have to track down some of Darby's business acquaintances.

She reached him in the parking lot as he fumbled for the keys to his rented car.

"I'm off my throne, Mr. Ellis," she said to his back. Her voice trembled. "Please tell me where you found my husband's pen."

It gave Slater little satisfaction to have won, however, for when he turned, her eyes brimmed with tears and the hand that held the pen shook.

"I'm sorry," he said. "I had no right to force you to—"

"Please tell me where you found my husband's pen. Please. Please just tell me."

It hurt Slater to watch her bite back the tears.

"Yes," he said. "I will."

They shared a bench near the pier. A light wind rattled cables on the aluminum masts of the moored sailboats. Two pelicans nearby stoically shared the top of the same wide, wooden post. Suzanne still waited in her car among the Mercedes and BMWs that overlooked the restaurant and marina.

"I gave it to him when he was promoted to head of his department," Paige told Slater. "At the time, a Montblanc was double what I could afford."

IWRC. To Darby. With love, Paige. Tiny, discreet engraved letters down the side of the gold casing of the fountain pen. It hadn't taken Slater much detective work to trace the pen to Clearwater, Florida.

"If it weren't for the pen," Slater said, "I doubt you'd have reason to believe me. As it is, I won't blame you if you decide against it anyway."

He was leaning forward, elbows on his knees, staring at a low island in the gulf. "I might have mentioned I retired to New Mexico, in the mountains just outside of Los Alamos. About a week ago, late at night as I drove home, I nearly ran over a boy..."

Slater explained everything. Waking up in his own blood and stripped of his clothing. The thefts around Seven Springs. How he'd set the trap, expecting to catch one boy, not three identical except for differing numbers tattooed on their foreheads. Their strange reactions to television, radio. How he'd discovered what language they spoke and the phone call with Ben Austad. The overnight cross-country drive to Santa Monica.

"You're right," she said as he paused for breath. "It does seem bizarre."

Slater snorted. "That's only the beginning. I wouldn't be here if it weren't for what I learned in Santa Monica."

Slater took his eyes off the island and briefly dared a glance at Paige. She sat stiffly upright on the bench, hands folded in her lap. She turned her head and didn't flinch as their eyes met. Her eyes had dried, traces of mascara smudged at their edges. Slater looked away first, telling himself not to be stupid about his adolescent surge of attraction.

"It took some time," he said, his focus back on the island against the horizon. "Ben's Latin was a little more formal than theirs. And it seemed there were a lot of cultural barriers. With half of his questions, he had to stop to clarify some of his references. I mean, how do you explain television or telephone to someone from the cave ages?"

He stole another glance. It seemed he couldn't get enough of just looking at her. He told himself to blame it on years of being a hermit.

"In short, what these kids described was a laboratory. Paige, it was all they knew. Big rooms, beds in a corner, a gymnasium set to play on. Someone raised them using a language that's been dead for centuries."

"How can that be?" Paige asked. "You can't keep kids hidden forever."

Slater shrugged. "You should have been there in Santa Monica. Ask them how old they are—they don't understand the concept of years. Then have them ask you about the fire up there."

"The fire up there?" Paige's voice held more life, more animation. Slater liked the sound of it.

"The fire up there," he repeated. "What would you answer?"

She thought about it. Slater admired her profile, the tiny beads of sweat on her forehead, the tone of her skin.

Her eyes widened with sudden comprehension. "You're not telling me they'd never been outside!"

"I'm telling you exactly that. Nine, maybe ten years old, and they didn't know what the sun was. Or moon. Cars? The night I nearly ran him down, the kid had been standing in the middle of the road, trying to figure out what the approaching lights and noise of my truck were. Paige, it's spooky."

She said nothing to his last remark. Probably wondering whether to believe him.

He continued. "The spookiest part was when one of the kids showed us your husband's pen."

"No."

"He'd clutched it the entire time he was on the run, naked, in the mountains, then he'd hidden it in his clothes. Finally he trusted us enough to show it."

"No."

"This is the strange part, Paige. He told us it came from a man they'd never seen before. A man who showed them how to escape."

"I cannot believe this," she said.

Slater wondered. She was a poor liar, if indeed she was lying.

"Near as we can figure, he let them understand the air-duct system could take them outside. We asked if he spoke Latin. They said no."

She was rigid now. Hands clenched.

"What is it, Paige?"

"Nothing," she said. *Another lie,* Slater thought. It had been the mention of the air ducts, if his guess was right.

"Unfortunately, the more answers Ben and I heard," he said, keeping his thoughts hidden, "the more questions we had. Who was the man, and why would he help them escape? Where was this laboratory? Why were the kids in there?"

The pelicans fell forward into flight and recovered just barely above the water to slowly wing across the harbor.

"Paige," he said. "I told you a bit about my background in the money markets, how I've lived my retirement by managing my own portfolio. I do it through a computer—home base or laptop. I plug into the nearest phone line, monitor my stocks, explore others. The details of the internet are boring, but the essence is that through the telephone, I can go on-line and tap into virtually any public information out there. That's why I'm here."

"IWRC on the pen," she said.

"Yes. International World Relief Committee. I tapped into the archives of business magazines and pulled up any articles with reference to IWRC. I saw Darby's name."

"Unexpected death?" she said. Bitterness or pain, Slater couldn't tell. "Or did they report it as suicide?"

"The latter," he told her. "Just a couple of paragraphs, most of it on the search for someone to replace him. You can understand why Ben and I decided to look into this. A pen with his name found in an unusual place and a suicide—I thought maybe you could help."

"This is difficult for me," she said.

"Someone has held three boys prisoners for their entire lives. I wish I didn't have these questions."

They shared silence for some time. Slater turned his face to the sun and closed his eyes, concentrated on the feeling of warmth.

"Go on," she finally said.

"So I got to thinking that maybe money is involved. IWRC is public. I pulled up their financial statements. One contributor caught my attention. TechnoGen. It—"

Slater stopped. Paige had flinched again, become rigid once more. He gave her time to say what was on her mind, but she only stared at the same island he'd earlier used as a distraction.

"TechnoGen also trades publicly," Slater said moments later. "I've thought of investing in it myself. It's on the genetics frontier. High-priced stock, but profitable. By then, after listening to the kids,

I was ready to clutch at any straw. Here they are, identical, tattoos on their foreheads, raised in a laboratory. I didn't want to reach the horrible conclusion. Except there's a pen—small as the link is—somehow connected to TechnoGen. Do you understand what I'm saying?"

Again, a long silence.

"The Institute," Paige finally told him. She sounded extremely detached. "Darby once wrote about something he called the Institute. In a letter I found after he died. And he mentioned TechnoGen."

She paused. So long that Slater couldn't help breaking in.

"What else?" he asked. Incredible. He had been playing this like some sort of game, barely able to believe it himself. Now she was confirming enough of it to let him understand the enormity of the situation.

She didn't answer.

"Come on," he said. "IWRC is in Florida, TechnoGen in Pennsylvania. I found those kids in the mountains of New Mexico. They didn't walk a thousand miles barefoot and naked. How about Darby's travel schedule? Was he ever out to New Mexico?"

Something about her body language had changed. Briefly, she'd been involved in the conversation, almost an ally. Now her hands were pressed tight together, her shoulders square.

"You know something, don't you?"

"Yes," she said, almost a sigh. "There are some things I can tell you."

She drew a breath, came to a decision. "I'd rather wait until tomorrow. Will I be able to call you then?"

"I'm flying back to Los Angeles tonight."

"Tomorrow." She was firm about it. "One way or another, I'll call you there. I owe you that."

Slater stood. He knew this conversation had ended.

"Certainly," he said. He wrote Ben Austad's name and phone number on Suzanne's realty business card. "You can reach me here. Will you pick a time?"

"Noon," she said, taking the card and placing it in her purse without looking at it. "Nine your time."

"I hope you can help," he finished. "Those three weren't the only kids in the lab."

Shaded by scrub oaks along the street, Zwaan waited in a parked rental car behind Del Silverton's patrol vehicle. If he were a man who enjoyed beauty—which he was not—he would have found the wait pleasant as he watched the county building, which overlooked Ashley Pond, a tranquil, tiny lake surrounded by grass and tall, stately trees. The sky was cloudless blue, the soft air filled with the muted songs of birds and insects.

Zwaan had been ignoring the peace of this late-spring day for half an hour already and expected to wait another five minutes. Del usually took lunch at noon, but Zwaan preferred to cover the unexpected, and if this happened to be an occasion when Del left early for any reason, Zwaan wasn't about to let him slip away from his death.

Zwaan smiled, a movement lost in the waxy, scarred half of his face.

Today was a day Zwaan had anticipated for some time. A showdown of sorts. Rarely was Zwaan challenged; most of his assignments had neither size nor combat skill. Del Silverton had both. Rarely was it a personal matter for Zwaan; he did as directed by Van Klees. But in this case, Del Silverton had not only defied the Institute, he'd done it with full intention of deceiving Zwaan as well.

Much as Zwaan wanted to think of this as a showdown, however, his only real challenge was to find the most efficient way to torture Del without sending him into lengthy unconsciousness or a quick death. He must be careful not to let emotion interfere with duty and must not be so stupid as to give Del the chance to fight or escape.

His plan was simple. As Del walked up to his patrol car, Zwaan would invite him into the rental. The passenger side of the car was already prepared. Del would sit on hypodermics, needles invisible where they protruded from the fabric. The pressure of sitting on them would force the plungers to release chloral hydrate. Four needles were three more than enough, but Zwaan liked to play it safe. Del would wake up in the Institute, sitting on a chair across from Zwaan, bound and ready for Zwaan's favorite game; the sledgehammer delivered the sweetest symphonies of pain.

As Zwaan contemplated combining work with pleasure, he replayed the music that had come with dealing with the two idiots in Florida. He'd put them in separate rooms and compared their stories about how they'd hoped to make extra money with Darby's TechnoGen documents. Once satisfied their stories compared, and that the Institute had not been compromised, and that the package had not contained the crucial missing computer disks, Zwaan had let the music in his head begin. He'd started by severing each man's hamstrings. The symphony, one of his sweetest, had lasted for more than an hour. Perhaps it was the fact that there were two. Or that the one with the snipped ears had been so fearful of further mutilation.

As Zwaan tried to decide the reason, his thoughts were interrupted by a call on his cellular phone.

He pulled it from his jacket pocket, clicked the on switch. He didn't greet his caller. Just listened.

"Get moving," he heard. "I don't care where you are, what you're doing. Head to the airport."

Zwaan raised his eyebrows. Van Klees rarely sounded this urgent.

"Not a good time," Zwaan said.

"Move. Now. If you're not in your car, get to it. If you're in the car, return to the base. If someone's with you, push him out." Van Klees spit the words out. "Get to the airport."

"Not a good time."

"Listen to me. I know where the boys are."

Zwaan reached for the ignition switch. "Talk as I drive."

Del was walking down the steps of the county building as Zwaan pulled away from the shade of the oaks.

"What do you know?" Zwaan asked as he turned his head to keep his face hidden from Del. Zwaan consoled himself that Del could die another day, soon. "And how?"

"The sow from Florida just called. You were right about Slater Ellis."

Zwaan didn't mention that it meant Del's wife had been right about Del's search. Instead Zwaan swung into the left lane to pass a slow truck and asked the obvious question.

"How would Florida know about Ellis?"

"He met her for lunch about an hour ago. She thinks he's running some kind of bluff, trying to pump her for information. She called to ask me for advice."

"Lunch?" Zwaan echoed. "In Florida? What would take him there?" This was not good. Always, Van Klees had kept a full grasp of all aspects of the operation. There had never been surprises. Not even minor surprises. This, however, was so unexpected, it smacked of monumental disaster. How badly had this gone out of control, and how had it happened so quickly?

"Remember Darby's visit? He left a souvenir behind. A monogrammed pen. Slater found the boys, and one of them had it. It linked the boys to IWRC. He followed that link to her."

Zwaan was now on Trinity Drive, heading east at precisely five miles an hour over the speed limit, the fastest he could go with total certainty of avoiding a speeding ticket.

"As if Darby didn't do enough damage," Zwaan said. He showed anger as rarely as Van Klees, but this warranted it. "If I could follow him into the grave—"

"It gets worse. This Slater Ellis took the boys to Los Angeles." *Which explained why Slater's house was empty.* "He managed to find a translator."

Zwaan now fully understood Van Klees's agitation. "I'm about five minutes from the airport."

"Good. Hire a helicopter to Sante Fe. There's a commercial flight to L.A. leaving within the hour. You should arrive a couple of hours before Ellis. When he shows up, get them all. The boys. The translator. Ellis. I don't want them dead. I want them at the Institute. We'll need to know who they've spoken to and what they've said."

"Details? Where do I find them?"

Van Klees read out a Santa Monica address to Zwaan. Zwaan filed the address in his memory. If needed, he could recall it any-time for years. "She told you all of this?" Zwaan asked.

"I convinced her that if Ellis was legitimate, he would have turned the boys over to authorities. Told her he probably stole the pen from Darby's desk and was running a scam on her. Obviously my previous investment of time in her was worth it."

"What does she know about the Institute?" Zwaan asked.

Silence greeted his question. Zwaan saw the turnoff for the air-port ahead and started to slow the car.

"I said, what does she—"

"I heard you," Van Klees said. "I didn't like being reminded."

Zwaan's hand tightened on the cellular phone.

"She can link IWRC to TechnoGen, Zwaan. Ellis asked her about it. She said hearing TechnoGen jogged her memory. Darby had mentioned it is his letter. If she'd told me that during our Washington meeting, she'd already be at the Institute and Ellis wouldn't have reached her."

"Not good."

"She'll pay," Van Klees said. "We'll have everything mopped up by tomorrow."

"You want me to go to Florida after L.A.?" Zwaan was nearly at the terminal parking lot.

"No," Van Klees said. "That's where I'm headed now. To mop up. As John Hammond, I'll take her out for another supper. After all, it'd be a shame to let a prime specimen like her go to waste."

Slater found Ben Austad and the three boys dipping nets for goldfish. Over a span of years, Austad had carefully cultivated his hillside backyard into an Asian rock garden, complete with pools, miniature waterfalls, and miniature pine trees. Sunlight, softened by evening's approach, lit the scene into a Rockwell painting.

Austad set his dipping net down as Slater greeted them.

"About a half-hour ago, I found them here in the backyard, staring into the water," Austad said. "The boys were incredulous, discovering little things that wriggled away from their fingers but didn't drown in water. I can't imagine how they'd react to a zoo."

Slater hunkered beside the boys and watched the glints of silver and gold as the fish darted away from their nets. The world was a fascinating place, Slater decided, if you kept the vision of a child.

"Trouble is, when I tell them I caught a fish this big—" Austad stretched his hands apart in the classic fisherman's pose, "they look at me as if I'm an idiot."

Slater grinned at Austad's enthusiasm. "Is there a Latin term for the one that got away?"

"Really," Austad insisted. "A coho salmon. On a fishing trip near Vancouver Island."

He frowned slightly. The lines on Austad's face showed it was not a customary movement. Sixty something, he could have been a decade younger. Most of the creases on his face showed peaceful good humor, and his appearance matched what Slater had expected from the voice over the telephone—relaxed lean face, trim build, graying hair.

Austad was two years from retiring and planned to build a sailboat as soon as he left the university.

Slater raised an eyebrow at the frown. "Yes, Ben?"

"I didn't expect you back until later," Ben said. "I hope this doesn't meant it went badly."

"Just the opposite. We had lunch. I was able to catch an earlier flight here."

Ben nodded. "And..."

"And lots. She said her husband mentioned TechnoGen in a letter. Plus something she called the Institute. She had more to tell me, but wanted to wait until tomorrow."

Slater shrugged. "So I guess I wait. What about your day? Learn anything from your friend in the genetics department?"

"Yup. That to suggest human beings have been cloned is a believable concept but totally impossible."

"Interesting start," Slater said, "if this is how you lecture, I'll bet you never face an empty classroom. Believable but impossible?"

"Believable because worms and frogs have been cloned in experiments for decades."

"So any day they'll have the technology to clone more complex species."

"Technology's already there. It's now routine to clone cattle."

"Why not humans then?" Slater stood and stretched his legs. "I mean in principle."

Austad stood with him. They left the three boys at the edge of the pond and moved to a group of boulders arranged as a bench.

"I asked the same question, Slater. And I was asked a question in return, the same one I'll ask you." Ben smiled to take away any offense. "How long can an embryo grow in a test tube?"

"Good point," Slater said after some thought. "Very good point. You need mothers who would agree to bring the embryos to term. Where would you get all the mothers and doctors, and even if you did, how could you expect something like that to remain a secret for long?"

Slater thought again. "Maybe you implant the duplicated embryos in women across the country. Let them have the babies and if none of them ever saw the other babies, they'd never know each was a clone..."

He stopped himself. "Not a good theory. Sure the clone is secret from each of the other mothers and doctors, but how do you explain the Latin and the laboratory the kids told you about? Kidnap all of the babies at birth?"

Slater watched the three boys for several moments. "I don't want to hear that maybe these three were embryos transplanted into the wombs of apes."

"Terrible thought," Austad said. "Fortunately I can dispel that idea with two words. Umbilical cord. As they develop in the womb, babies share blood with their mother. Ape blood and human blood don't mix."

Austad sighed. "Only human mothers can nurture human embryos. You'd have to have a place to engage in large-scale experimenting in humans. No way could you have a place that big, involving that many people, and expect it to remain secret. Human nature dictates someone would eventually talk about it. And where would anyone find the funding? Something that big would take major money. You can't keep major money secret either."

"Military?" Slater asked. "Remember Los Alamos and the atomic bomb? Until 1957, the entire town was a closed base."

Austad frowned. "That's the wrinkle that bothers me. A major portion of the Human Genome Project is based in Los Alamos."

He answered the question before Slater could ask. "A five-billion-dollar project to map out the entire sequence of the human genetic code."

"They wouldn't run experiments on kids!"

"My source said no," Austad answered. "It's legitimate. High public profile. But still, you have to wonder."

"Maybe we'll learn something from Paige's phone call tomorrow," Slater said.

"And if somehow our guess is right, what then? These are kids, Slater; they deserve to live as kids. Not as medical freaks."

Slater sighed as loudly as Austad had. "You're right. For starters, they should be dressed like kids. What say we take them shopping tonight?"

"I'd like to, but I can't," Austad said. "I'm expecting a master's student to stop by with questions on her thesis. Should you be taking them public without me around as a translator?"

"How about if I take just one?" Ellis suggested. "Whatever I buy to fit him will fit the others."

"Good idea. Take Caesar."

At that name, the kid on the end looked back at Austad. Austad spoke quickly to him in Latin, and the kid want back to dipping his net.

"You've named them?" Slater asked with a half-chuckle.

"Better than numbers, don't you think? And they like the concept too. I chose names that meant something to them."

"Marcellus?" Austad said. The middle kid looked up, beamed. He held his net triumphantly in the air to show a trophy, flopping around in frantic pain against the air, throwing tiny beads of water all around.

Austad spoke gently to him in Latin and he put the net back in the water, not lowering it enough for the fish to escape.

"Pontius?" Austad said.

The third kid paused. "Ben!" he said, pointing at the professor.

Ben grinned and waved. He turned his attention back to Slater.

"See? Quick studies. Makes me wish all over again my wife and I could have had kids before she died."

He looked sharply at Slater. "How about you? Wife? Kids? I noticed you asked plenty about me last night but avoided the subject of yourself."

Slater made a noncommittal grunt.

"You've got to know I have questions," Austad said. "Someone who can leave New Mexico like you did on a half-hour's notice probably doesn't have a job or family. On the other hand, you were able to pay full fare to Florida and back."

"How about I just say I did have a wife? In another lifetime."

Austad kept watching Slater, then relaxed with a grin. "Dumb of me to ask. After all, this is California." Austad gave Slater a brief salute. "See you when you get back from shopping."

"You're fine with the other two? I mean, having an appointment and all."

Ben waved him away. "Of course I'm fine. What could happen while you're gone?"

Josef Van Klees and Paige Stephens stood beneath the sleek belly of a private jet. They'd walked a hundred yards to the jet from where Van Klees had instructed the limo driver to stop at the side of an airplane hangar. This corner of the runway was nearly abandoned. The relative darkness showed Tampa Bay's lights bouncing pale yellow off clouds that had moved in from the gulf and piled low in the night sky.

Van Klees was careful not to show it, but inside, he seethed. *Sow. Sow. Sow.*

He didn't castigate himself for indulging in raw emotion. In all the secret, careful, diligent years of building, he had not once faced a single threat—minor or major—that might unravel the structure of the Institute. Yes, each of the foundation corners had faced occasional and various perils. Even then, there had been no danger to the Institute. One corner or other of the foundation might fall—none had, of course, thanks to his brilliant tactics—but Van Klees had structured it so that at all times the Institute would remain hidden and untouched by the loss of any one of the cornerstones.

Until this stupid woman.

Without her, Slater Ellis could have done what he wanted with the boys, and that matter, damaging as it might now become, would have been a mystery, soon forgotten as the media moved to the next issue of the day. Without her, Darby's death would have sealed off that dangerous tunneling into another corner of the foundation.

With her, the connections could occur, the Institute might come to light.

Raging inside, he smiled for her the Van Klees womanizing smile, a hint of danger combined with boyish recklessness.

Almost a mile away, the commercial runways rumbled with the roars and high-decibel whining of incoming turbine engines. Van Klees raised his voice to be heard.

"For you," he said, sweeping his arm grandly to show the lines of the private jet. "The surprise you've patiently indulged me to present to you tonight."

"John, there's only one problem," she said, "I don't have my pilot's license." She laughed, throwing her hair back, probably taking pleasure from something as mundane as cool silky air brought in ahead of a gulf storm.

Oh yes, Van Klees reminded himself. *She has attempted a joke.*

He laughed with her. Deep and rich.

"You might recall I mentioned a need for a corporate jet during our get-together in D.C. It got me thinking, why not? What better excuse, I asked myself, than another chance to see you—without the hassle of commercial airlines."

She looked at him, looked back at the gleaming silver of the jet's body.

"A Challenger 604," he told her, "flies at mach .74. Or if you insist on crude measurements, 490 miles per hour. Our pilot's up front, waiting."

"Waiting?"

"I promised you dinner tonight," he said. "I just didn't say where. How about Mexico City? We can be there by nine. If not Mexico City, then Chicago. We'd be there by nine-thirty."

She laughed again. "You're not serious."

"Yes, I am," he said, injecting grave dignity. "I . . . I . . ."

Proper amount of hesitation now. Let her see the confident John Hammond suddenly becoming shy, awkward, fumbling.

"I . . . this . . . it . . . well . . . not much time has passed since your husband . . . since Darby . . ." He knotted his hands. "I'm sorry. I'm making a mess of this. What I'm trying to tell you is that I think of you often. No, that's a lie. I think of you constantly."

She was motionless.

Had he overacted?

"If I've insulted you . . . ," he began.

"No," Paige told him. "The opposite. I'm overwhelmed."

"Mexico then?" Giving her a grin of unabashed hope designed to make her laugh.

She did. But stopped.

"John, not this soon. I want to get to know you more, but . . ." She searched for words. "There's not only my feelings for Darby, but I also think I need to learn more about myself.

You're a powerful man. In your shadow, I don't know that I'll have that chance."

"New York," he said. "You'll be home by two tonight."

"I'm tempted. And I can't believe I'm asking for a rain check, but...a rain check?"

"I understand," Van Klees said moments later. "We're on the runway. Lower the steps."

A door in the body of the jet opened.

"John," Paige said, "really. Another night."

He shook his head no.

The steps reached the runway.

"Look behind you," he told her. "You'll notice the limo has departed."

It had.

She turned to him again, and faced the barrel of a small revolver in his right hand.

"Why?" she asked.

"You'll find out and wish you hadn't," he said, comfortable in a wide leather chair, revolver hidden again in his suit. "In the meantime, tell me everything you discussed with this Slater Ellis."

"I will not," she said from her chair opposite the aisle. She was ramrod stiff with anger. "Kidnapping is a federal offense. No matter how much money you have—"

"Don't be tedious. You've hidden yourself for a week, moving from hotel to hotel. You've cut yourself off from friends, acquaintances. Who's to know you've left Florida?"

"My realtor. We have an appointment at nine tomorrow morning."

He laughed, not deep and rich, but the laugh he felt and wanted to show. The grating sound of it widened her eyes. "You are a terrible liar. And even if it were true, nine o'clock is far too late. Didn't I earlier inform you this jet flies almost five hundred miles every hour? By then, you will be halfway across the world. Untraceable."

Paige clutched the armrests of the chair as the jet began to taxi down the runway. The interior was padded luxury, holding a full couch at one end, a large-screen television at the other, a bar area, and a work desk with a telephone. A door led to the cockpit—she hadn't once seen the pilot. Van Klees had given him instructions by intercom.

"Untraceable?" Her voice was higher now, strained. As the jet accelerated, the realization came that she truly was a prisoner. "Flight plans. My realtor knows you're the only one who could reach me. They'll get around to investigating the wealthy John Hammond and discover he flew in and out of Tampa Bay the same night I disappeared."

His laughter, longer and louder, frightened her into silence. Van Klees coughed and sputtered to recover his breath.

"John Hammond? He's only a shell. I flew in as Jack Tansworth, president of TechnoGen. And Tansworth is only another shell. My dear, you have no idea who sits before you."

Anger replaced fear, and the color began to return to her face. "You're wrong. I have a good idea of who you are. A low-life piece of—"

"Tsk. Tsk. I'm the one who funded much of your good life. You do remember a man named Darby?"

Darby's name shocked her into silence.

"Your late husband, I must admit, was very good at what he did. Few could work numbers and juggle books better."

"He did not. He was an honest man."

The jet was in the air now, banking above the city lights.

"I hear doubt in your voice," Van Klees said. "I'll even bet I can read your mind. You're thinking of the last words you heard Darby speak. Remember? Over the extension the night he decided there was only one way to escape from me?"

Her body lost its ramrod stiffness, sagged, as if she were collapsing into herself. "You can't know about that," she whispered. "I never told you. Never told anyone what I'd heard."

"Fool." Van Klees laughed. He glanced at his watch. "Let me

indulge you. It's not often I'm able to allow the light of my genius to reach the world."

Paige stared at him. "If you knew about the call, you've been part of this from the beginning."

"As John Hammond, I recruited Darby," Van Klees said. "Early. He could bend a few tax rules for me or lose his new promotion at IWRC. And I convinced him the rules, of course, were silly. Anyone would have done the same. It progressed until he had found ways for me to connect my other companies into IWRC and to move money in and out that no tax man could find. Later I brought him into the fold."

"TechnoGen and the Institute," she said, barley audible about the rushing noise of the jet as it gained altitude. "Slater was right."

"Slater is probably in Zwaan's care by now," he said flatly. "Right did him no good at all."

She closed her eyes.

"IWRC is perfect," her told her, "and you'll notice I said is, not was. For with you and Slater gone, life will continue as normal in all my corporations."

He stood and stretched. "Would you care for a glass of port?"

"With anyone but you."

"False bravado," he said. He moved to the bar and took his time pouring a glass for himself.

"A toast," he proclaimed. "To me, genius incarnate. John Hammond of Hammond Developments, Jack Tansworth of TechnoGen, and whoever else I choose to be. Money, after all, gives freedom."

He sipped on the port, and, still standing, continued his conversation.

"It is convenient that the world is filled with fools who believe in the force of good. When I first wondered how best to serve my Institute, I needed a way to hide money. A charitable organization made the perfect cloak to hide my magic from the work of fools. Then I realized I could form one that also served other needs. By the time Darby realized how IWRC truly aided the Institute, he couldn't back out."

"He did back out," she spat. For the first time, she was almost proud of Darby's final act. "And he did his best to stop you."

"I'll admit he disappointed me." Van Klees smiled. This was a smile that made his face almost skeletal in its evil. "For a while, I hoped to recruit him more fully. That was my mistake, of course, showing him the Institute. But I believed at the time my promises could overcome whatever qualms he had left."

Van Klees sipped more port and studied her. "Come, come. Ask. What promises?"

Her lips were pressed tight.

"He was fine with everything until he saw the children. I believe he had a weak spot for children. You had, after all, been trying for one of your own for years?"

No answer.

"Of course you had," Van Klees continued. "That was one of my promises. That the Institute would help him let your fertile womb produce an heir for him."

Van Klees set his empty port glass down on the bar. He turned his back on her briefly and reached for an object hidden in a cabinet.

"This will taste bitter," he said, taking a pill from the small case he had retrieved. "Don't be silly and resist. I'd rather avoid the barbarism of holding you down to force it into your mouth. Besides, you will wake up. You're much more valuable to me alive." He leered. "After all, didn't I promise Darby you would bear children?"

Zwaan left the television set on—a rerun of *M*A*S*H* playing the suicide-is-painless theme song. Kitchen lights were on too. Whatever it took to lull Slater Ellis into believing he should step inside Austad's house with the third kid in tow.

Zwaan stood hunched in the darkness of the front entry closet, occasionally peering through the slats at the television screen to confirm his bearings. The other two kids and Austad were safely stowed in the back of a used van now hidden in the garage.

During the flight to LAX, Zwaan had given great thought—in his own way, he was as meticulous as Van Klees—to the best short-notice method of kidnapping and transporting five people some thousand-odd miles.

He quickly discarded commercial airlines as a ridiculous method. You don't prop five drugged people on a push cart and move them through check-in; nor do you stow them in the unpressurized luggage compartment.

Zwaan had also dismissed hitching a ride on a military flight. He'd need to find trunks large enough to carry the bodies, and there'd be a trail, slight as it was, for some paper pusher to record.

So with cash and a false name, Zwaan had purchased a utility van, unmarked, not new, but not so old as to be unreliable. The drive back to the Institute would take barely more than the night; he'd gone farther on less sleep many times before. The only hitches had been Slater's earlier-than-expected arrival and his shopping excursion—both facts reluctantly given by Ben Austad in response to a knife held to number seventeen's throat.

Zwaan lifted his left wrist close to his face and pressed the watch button to give it light.

Two minutes past nine. *M*A*S*H*'s helicopter had flown into television's netherland, top-of-the-hour deodorant ads had ended, and a brainless sitcom began to the applause of canned laughter. According to Austad, Slater had already been gone for two hours. He'd be back anytime, shopping bags in hand, helpless to ward off attack.

Zwaan had rehearsed it in his mind. When the door opened, he would open the plastic bag in his left hand to pull out the chloroform rag, jump from the closet, and muffle Slater's face. Slater first because odds were he'd be tougher to handle than number twenty-one.

Zwaan heard the doorknob turn. He unzipped the plastic seal, careful to keep the bag as low as possible. Stupid move, to breathe the chloroform in these cramped quarters.

The light through the slats showed the door opening. Zwaan didn't hesitate. In a coordinated sweeping of body, shoulders, and arms, he burst through the closed door, pulling the rag loose and charging into the entryway.

His eyes and mind registered his mistake. Not dark-haired, male features and shopping bags. But a woman, blonde, wide-eyed, blue jeans and sweater, clutching a small knapsack.

She began to scream. Zwaan was faster, and he'd already committed himself. The rag was up and over her mouth before she could finish drawing breath.

Within seconds, she slumped.

Zwaan let go of her head and neck and she fell to the throw rug on the hardwood floor, her body blocking the path of the door. He stuffed the rag back into the plastic bag and bent forward to grab her ankles.

As he began to drag her backward into the house—a crouched hyena pulling its prey away from the firelight and into the darkness—he glanced through the open door and down the sidewalk.

And cursed.

Five seconds more, he'd have closed the door, set the trap anew.

Instead, the man was leaning into the back of a 4 x 4, reaching through the tailgate window for shopping bags. The kid was halfway up the sidewalk, face shadowed by the streetlight behind, frozen by fear.

Zwaan reacted without hesitation.

He sprinted forward.

"Slater!" the kid screamed.

Zwaan saw it all clearly. The man straightening, the kid pivoting to burst back toward the truck.

Both pounded down the sidewalk, the kid losing ground.

Zwaan hoped the man would stop, try to protect the kid.

It didn't happen.

Slater spun toward the driver's side.

All Zwaan needed was another few seconds. But California

suburb living defeated him, for the yard was too big, the distance from the house to the truck too far.

Slater was behind the wheel now, stretching across to pop the door open for the kid. The kid tumbled inside.

Zwaan's hands were out, clutching for an arm, a leg, anything to drag the kid loose.

And the heavy door shut.

Zwaan heard the crunch of metal and bone before he felt it.

He looked at his betraying hand in disbelief. The door had slammed to latch shut, a gap between it and the frame trapped his index and second fingers.

The look of disbelief cost him a precious two seconds, seconds he could have used to grab the door handle with his free hand. Instead, as he stared downward at his crushed fingers, the electric door lock snapped down.

Then the pain hit.

Zwaan embraced the pain. Smiled.

The kid inside leaned away in terror. The man fumbled with keys.

Still smiling, Zwaan drew his other arm back and smashed his elbow and forearm into the passenger window. Shards of glass exploded inward.

Zwaan reached for the kid, but he scrambled away, diving through the gap of the bucket seat to the safety of the rear.

Zwaan stood on the running board of the truck, his shoulder and arm inside, stretching to reach the man at the wheel.

And the engine roared into accelerated life.

Zwaan grabbed the edge of the steering wheel. He yanked it toward him as the truck leaped forward, causing it to jump the curb, onto the grass. The truck was moving fast, but Zwaan kept his balance on the running board by gripping the steering wheel.

The man tried yanking the wheel back.

Zwaan smiled. Not against his strength.

The truck kept plunging away from the street, into the yard.

The man would have to stop soon, and only then would Zwaan

let go of the steering wheel, then reach below himself to yank the passenger door handle and pop the door open to release his crushed fingers.

As the truck slowed, Zwaan strained to hold the steering wheel, strained against the man and his efforts to yank it away, when incredibly, the man gave in and spun the wheel in Zwaan's direction, accelerating at the same time.

It was a good move, almost throwing Zwaan one-armed, like a bronco rider flailing from his saddle. But Zwaan recovered, somehow maintaining his grip on the steering wheel. Then he saw the reason for Slater's move.

A tree. Scraping down the side of the truck. Slamming the outside mirror and pounding into the side of Zwaan's body.

It knocked him off the running board, knocked his feet onto the ground. He would have been spun away from the truck except his fingers were still stuck in the closed door, pulling Zwaan along.

He had no choice but to run with the truck as Slater turned toward the street again. Zwaan tried to jump back onto the running board, but the truck was bouncing and he couldn't climb on.

Five steps. Ten steps. The street was approaching in a blinding blur.

Zwaan did the only thing he could.

He dove away from the truck. The momentum of his massive body tore his fingers at the knuckles, and he landed, rolling, tumbling, stopping inches short of the curb.

He stared at the disappearing taillights of the truck. Not long. Zwaan understood when to quit the fight and move on. He still had two of the kids and the translator. That would do. For now.

As Zwaan walked back to the house, he held the torn stumps of this fingers up to minimize the blood loss, the gore dripping down his wrist. Inside, he'd find a towel, wrap it. Then he'd drive the van from the garage and find an emergency medical clinic far enough from here to be safe. It only took one hand to drive, and he could be in New Mexico early tomorrow.

Van Klees was waiting for him.

Eleven

Friday, May 24

PAIGE WOKE to a black mask. She couldn't scream. She didn't have the energy.

The black mask transformed itself into a face as Paige slowly focused. The face smiled broadly.

Paige managed to nod. The face disappeared. Paige closed her eyes, too tired to move, too tired to wonder where she was.

She woke again—unable to measure how much time had passed—to cool wetness. The same black woman with the wide face was gently wiping her forehead.

Paige tried to speak. "Hello," she croaked.

"How is it you do today?"

Paige tried to place the accent but couldn't. Not musical enough to be Jamaican. Not lofty enough for British. A strange, lilted and broken cant to the black woman's words.

"I don't know how it is I do," Paige said, her voice returning with wakefulness. "I don't know where it is I do either."

"You are in the Room of Joy," she said. "When it is you have a return of good spirits, I will tell you more." She set her wet cloth aside. With one strong hand she lifted Paige's head. With her other hand, she brought a glass forward to Paige's mouth. "For now, take this water into your body and rest further. All of us must be prepared for the miracle when it arrives."

"Miracle?" Paige asked after gulping down the water.

"Yes, lovely one. Miracle. An angel may deliver to you, too, a child conceived without the grunting efforts of a man. A child we pray you might be able to bear to term and deliver and present to the lord with joy."

Paige struggled to sit upright.

Her bed was one of a couple dozen in a large, windowless ward, pleasantly lit by recessed lights. Some of the beds held sleeping women. Others did not.

Women, most of them of African descent, moved slowly throughout the ward, speaking to each other in muted voices. Paige saw that many of them walked with bellies huge with child.

Past the last row of beds was a large open area. Stove, cupboards, and sinks were arranged in one corner. Dining tables in the center. Couches and a fireplace in the far corner. On the other side of the open area, the ward continued. Curtains blocked Paige's view of what that area of the ward held or how far it extended. Sounds, however, gave her a clue: crying babies.

The Room of Joy.

She woke next to the cold stare of the man who had called himself John Hammond. He was holding her wrist, his forefinger and second finger pressed to feel her heartbeat.

Paige pulled her hand away.

His cold stare continued.

She felt revulsion at how bare of humanity his face was. She loathed her feeling of nakedness as she lay vulnerable beneath that stare, and she swung her legs away from him, out of the bed. The effort brought her nausea, but she swallowed hard and kept moving.

As she prepared to stand, she discovered she was wearing only a thin hospital gown. She pulled the bed cover with her as she stoodand wrapped herself in it. Then she sat on the next bed over and hoped she had hidden her trembling.

"Are you coherent?" he asked. His eyes passed over her as if she were a specimen at the zoo. "I have no desire to waste time repeating myself to you later."

"Who are you." She said it as a statement.

He glanced at his watch. "Someone who cares little for idle conversation. Think of me as John Hammond. I return to his identity often enough to make it true."

She wanted to scream at him but had no urge to give him satisfaction. Or drive him away. She had too many questions.

"Where is this?" she said. "Can you at least tell me that?"

He shrugged. "Think of it as an institute for the advancement of the human species."

"I don't understand."

"You will soon enough, even without my explanation. One of my greatest needs has been to nourish and grow embryos. Test tubes, I'm afraid, only have value at the conception stage."

Against her will, she gasped.

"Yes," he told her, "there is no substitute for a mother's womb. As you can imagine, under normal circumstances, growth and harvest presents difficulties. Here, however..."

He pointed around her. "You will find women in here who would be dead unless the Institute had rescued them from situations of war or famine. They lead a pleasant enough life, often better than the village lives they had before in Third World countries."

She struggled to comprehend his words. Growth and harvest? Surely this was a savage and mad dream, brought on by the drugs he had used to slide her into unconsciousness.

"You, too, would be dead," he was saying, "unless the Institute had found a purpose for you."

"You are monstrous." Paige felt her fingers ball into fists of hatred. "Release me."

"Hardly." He glanced at his watch again. "Listen carefully. You cannot escape from this room. You are welcome to try. Indeed, you will find your attempts a distracting way to pass time. Don't, however, try to organize the women around you into something as gauche as rebellion. One, you will only succeed in setting yourself apart from them, as most are very content here. Two, you will need them as friends, for you will see no one else in your daily living. Three, Velma—you met her earlier—will report your efforts to me. Keep in mind she is much better as a friend than as a jailer."

Paige found herself swallowing with a dry throat. Delivered so casually, his words seemed horrifyingly true. Madman or not, her disbelief or not, she was beginning to understand the implications. This was not a ward, but a prison.

"Neither is suicide an option," he told her.

Suicide? How bad was this going to be, that he foresaw suicide as a way to escape?

"Velma counts the knives carefully before and after each meal. As for any other means of ending your life, you will not have the privacy."

He stood. "That is all."

"All," she repeated.

"Certainly. I have much more pressing things to do."

His arrogance infuriated her. She lashed out the only way she could. "Slater Ellis knows about this. He'll come looking."

He snorted derision. "I'm not the only one who enjoys the convenience of assumed identities. Slater Ellis? In his previous life, he is wanted for attempted murder. And he ran out on his wife."

He watched her face and snorted more derision. "Not only that, he'll be dead by this weekend."

He took a half step, then turned and studied her one more time.

"Much as you have caused me trouble," he said. "I will admit I do like your spirit."

He smiled, and to Paige it felt like he was caressing her with a scalpel. "Yes, you are definitely a suitable mother for my son."

Slater had hardly slept. He sat fully clothed on top of the bed sheets, his back propped by pillows leaned against the headboard. Beside him, the boy was sleeping beneath the sheets. One of his small arms was thrown over Slater's leg, as if he needed to know at all times that he wasn't alone. The boy's obvious pain and loneliness tore at Slater's heart and was all the worse because of his helplessness. How do you comfort someone when you don't share language or culture?

Slater had chosen to hole up in a cheap Santa Monica hotel— its chief advantage the rusty pre-Depression fire escapes that led from each room down the outside walls to the alley below. With the chain lock in place, a bureau blocking the door, and a chair wedged between the bureau and a closet to complete the barricade, he'd been fairly certain he and the boy would have time to jump out the window and down the fire escape if the nightmare man started to break his way into the room.

But Slater was only fairly certain.

He'd never shake the memory of a face mottled with scar and shadow, the puckered skin of that massive skull. And the man's smile, this while the heavy door of the truck had two of the man's fingers crushed to pulp and bone.

Nor would Slater forget the terror of pulling with all his might against the steering wheel, and losing the battle with two good arms against the monster's one.

Illogical as it was, Slater couldn't shake visions of a zombie, slowly but with unwavering steps, tracking him down, following his trail, and simply walking through the door.

Every creak of the hallway steps, every voice in the hallway, every flush of another toilet had brought Ellis from sleep during the night. And with each of Slater's successive flinches, the boy huddled beside him had moaned and turned in his own nightmares. One of those, no doubt, could be blamed on Slater's earlier carelessness. At their first stop following the escape, Slater had walked around to the passenger door and opened it to let the kid out. Slater himself had nearly vomited when he saw the crushed fingers land on the street; he hadn't been quick enough to keep the sight from the boy's eyes.

How could a man endure such pain and still silently, grimly try to take the kid?

Slater was convinced the man was superhuman. Convinced enough that not even the pistol and pepper mace he'd purchased at a twenty-four-hour pawn shop gave him any degree of confidence. The pistol was beneath his pillow; the small plastic canister of pepper mace would be a backup weapon tucked in his sock. Armed or not, listening for sounds in the hotel all night, Slater had half-expected the sound of twisting steel outside his window, a signal the nightmare man had chosen an alley approach, jumping and pulling down the lowest rungs of the fire escape before climbing up to the window.

Instead, all that arrived through the window was sunlight, increasing in gradient shades that Slater watched as dawn approached.

He was grateful for the three-hour time difference between Santa Monica and Florida. It meant he could call Paige Stephens's realtor almost immediately.

Yesterday Paige had promised to call at noon her time, nine his. Last night had changed things, however. For starts, she wouldn't be able to reach him at Ben Austad's number. Slater didn't dare return there again, not after the police had entered the situation.

Slater had driven back to Austad's house less than an hour after the attack, trying to decide how best to go back in and look for Austad and the other two boys. From blocks away, however, he'd spotted the flashing blue-and-red lights of patrol cars and had turned two intersections early. A pay-phone call to Austad a half-hour later had been answered by a neutral male voice; Ellis had hung up without identifying himself.

The presence of police—probably called by neighbors following the 4 x 4's roaring on the grass, or perhaps by the woman he'd seen dragged into the house—gave some degree of assurance to Slater. If Austad and the boys had survived the nightmarish attack, they were now safe. But if they had been taken away, Slater could do nothing until he spoke to Paige.

During his hours of sleeplessness, Slater had thought through as much as possible. He would call her and offer her the boy in exchange for money.

After all, the obvious possibility was that she had betrayed him. He'd told her about the boys; within hours an attacker had appeared on Austad's doorstep. Slater could not accept the attack as just another random Los Angeles crime. The monster had run from the house to chase the boy—what would any ordinary criminal hope to gain from such action?

If Paige Stephens had betrayed him, was she tied in to the evil her husband had helped the boys escape? Her reaction to Slater's offer of the boy would tip him. If she accepted, she would, of course, never see the boy or hear from Slater again.

On the other hand, he wanted to believe she was innocent, that the attacker had somehow found him and Austad through another source. Through traced phone calls between Seven Springs and Santa Monica, perhaps. Or maybe through someone at the university. In that case, Slater desperately needed Paige Stephens's help, and he prayed she would show no interest in taking the boy for herself.

The light in the room was barely more than gray when Slater dialed the Florida realtor. The boy beside him stirred slightly as Slater spoke.

"Suzanne," he said. "Slater Ellis. I'm glad you're in. More glad than you can know."

He visualized the realtor on the other end and was glad he'd thought to pay her a consulting fee for her time and effort the day before. It made it that much easier to expect she'd do her best to help now, even if it didn't involve a possible commission on a house sale.

"It's extremely urgent I speak to Paige," Slater continued after her reply of greeting. "Could I give you my number and have you pass it on to her?"

He gave her the information and tried to relax after hanging up the telephone.

It surprised him when the phone rang. Somehow he'd drifted into sleep.

"Yes," he said.

"This is not Paige," he heard. "But Suzanne again. And I'm worried. She's not at the hotel. And she expected me about now for a house viewing."

"Maybe she's having breakfast," Slater said.

"No. I'm at the hotel right now. She's not in her room or the restaurant." The realtor paused. "What's really got me scared is that her car is still in the parking lot."

"She stayed the night with a friend?" Slater suggested. And hoped, with irrational jealousy, she had not.

"You'd have to know her," Suzanne said. "She wasn't ever the type. Especially not now with her husband so recently passed on."

The third possibility hit Slater. Paige hadn't betrayed him. Nor had the attacker found Austad through another source. No, somehow, all the way across the country to the other coast, she'd been taken because she knew too much.

"How about you keep looking for her," Slater said. He felt even more paranoid now and wanted to be on the move. "I'll call in later and hope for the best."

"Only two?" Van Klees said. "If you only have two of the boys, tell me the third one is dead."

Zwaan drew a breath. He considered complaining. To get the van here to the loading dock within the Institute, he'd endured an all-night drive, chewing aspirin like candy in a vain effort to dull the pain of his savaged hand. Yet Van Klees found only fault.

"The third one is not dead," Zwaan said. "And you are permitted to help me unload this van." He pulled his hand from his jacket pocket and showed the bandaged stumps of his fingers. "When we're finished, I'll tell you about this."

Van Klees glanced at the blood-stained bandages. He tried not to show surprise. Zwaan's voice held irritation—he wouldn't appreciate extra attention to what was obviously a mistake on his part. "Of course I'll help you," Van Klees said. "We'll take them down to the sixth floor. I don't imagine they'll be awake for several hours."

Zwaan grunted assent.

Beneath the cold fluorescent lights of an enclosed loading dock the size of a small warehouse, they spent a few minutes in silence moving Austad and the two boys from the van onto stretchers.

When they finished, Zwaan asked, "This van? Do you have any use for it?"

Van Klees studied the plain white body of the vehicle and the California plates. "It's clean, isn't it?"

"Don't talk to me as if I am mentally deficient. False name, false papers."

Van Klees pretended he had not heard the increased irritation. "Perhaps, then," Van Klees said, "you will find it convenient to transport one other person." He paused and smiled. "Your friend Del Silverton. The Institute will find his services useful in another manner now."

Zwaan nodded.

"After a rest, however. Take him then." Van Klees said. He definitely wanted oil on these troubled waters. "Your drive must have been punishing."

Zwaan shrugged agreement.

"Slater Ellis?" Van Klees probed.

The stretchers stood between them. Here at the first level of the Institute, it was hot and, despite the thin air of the mountains, muggy from the exhaust fans that pulled air from the lower levels into this bay.

There was room for three semi-trailers to back into the docks here, protected from the elements and prying eyes. Aside from the weekly visit from a wholesale grocer based in Sante Fe, it was rare, however, for any other trailer to enter the building.

Zwaan stared down at the dark tire marks on the smooth concrete dock floor. Then he lifted his damaged hand again.

"Slater Ellis is a lucky man," he said, rotating his wrist and staring at his bandaged stumps in wonder that a mere mortal could have accomplished the damage. Zwaan's whisper was magnified in the echoing emptiness around them.

Zwaan explained the premature visitor who had given Ellis and the boy warning.

"We'll find him," Van Klees said. "I'll alert General Stanley to push whatever buttons he needs to at military intelligence. Slater will use a credit card. Or move some stocks. That's all it will take for a trail we can follow."

"In the meantime . . ."

"What's there to worry about?" Van Klees said. "He can't find us. If he didn't go public when he first found the boys, he certainly won't go now that he's down to one and responsible for losing the other two."

Zwaan nodded.

Van Klees smiled arrogance. "Yes, my friend, for a few days there, we did have some worries. Chemicals make interrogation a wonderful convenience, however, and I have confirmed that the Florida sow told no one about Ellis. Neither does she have the computer disks or know where Darby hid them. When this professor wakes, we'll use the same prescription to see how much he knows or told. You'll bring Silverton in and we'll dispose of him. And when we do get Ellis—soon of course—all possible leaks will have been plugged. I believe, in fact, it will be back to business as usual."

Zwaan had frowned at the mention of Silverton.

"By the way," Van Klees added, ever quick to sense opportunity to manipulate, "with your friend Silverton, you are permitted to show him the operating room. I know how much you will enjoy letting him taste the fear of knowing his fate."

Twelve

"TWO BREAKFAST SANDWICHES and..." From behind the wheel of the compact rental, Slater looked across at Caesar in the passenger seat. A human vacuum cleaner. Until the kids, Slater had forgotten how much boys eat. He turned his voice toward the speaker outside the car. "Make it *four* breakfast sandwiches, two hash browns, two orange juices, coffee, and whatever the gadget of the week is."

The kid looked back at Slater and grinned. Shy, but more at ease. He'd obviously appointed Slater as his guardian. He watched every move Slater made. He followed close behind, so close that when Slater stopped, the kid often bumped into him. When he wasn't watching Slater, he was soaking in all the sights and sounds of the world.

Which was why Slater wanted whatever plastic gadget would arrive with their breakfast. Just to enjoy the expression on the kid's face as he explored it.

It'd be nice if they could talk.

Slater would have given a grand to be able to understand Caesar's low, excited babble as the 727 had left LAX. At first, the roar of the jets had scared him, and he'd closed his eyes and put his hand in Slater's. As the jet had burst forward on the runway, the kid had peeked. And then the Christmas morning expression on his face as they'd left the concrete and risen into the air.

"...have your money ready at the first window, sir."

Slater brought himself back into the present. Which consisted of a drive-through just off the interstate. They'd eat on the move—Slater didn't want to chance sitting in a restaurant and having some kindly mother stop to chat, followed by the awkward explanations when the kid didn't respond to English.

They were going back to Los Alamos because Slater did not know what else to do.

In Santa Monica, Austad and the boys were gone—Slater had not been able to reach Austad at home all day and could only assume the worst. In Clearwater, Paige Stephens had yet to return Suzanne's messages. Slater couldn't even consider quitting now with the stakes increased. If he wasn't looking for Austad, Stephens, and the other two boys, who was?

Here in Los Alamos, where it had all started, Slater figured he had two choices. Take the kid on a hike and hope he might show Slater where the three boys began their trek away from their prison. Or trace that prison through the big cop who had appeared at his Seven Springs home.

The cop had visited for more than he'd let on—Slater felt sure enough of that to risk wasting a day or two following him. If the cop was tied into this, he just might lead Slater to where the boys had been held. From there, Slater could only pray he'd figure a way inside. By himself. Because if the cop was involved, there was no way to trust anyone up here in the mountains. And once inside, he could only pray he'd find Austad or Paige or both.

It was hell for Slater, with worry churning his guts the way it did. He felt like a blind man groping for marbles in a forest and was all too conscious of the pressure of time.

"Sir?"

The cheery voice of a fifteen-year-old girl at the drive-through window brought him to the present.

"Sorry," Slater said. "Daydreaming."

Slater leaned over to take his wallet out of his rear pocket. He noticed Caesar staring at the paper bills with open curiosity as he watched the exchange of money for the bag of food.

"Kid, you know as much about this green stuff as our national economists, don't you?"

The feeble joke was wasted as the smell of food overpowered the kid's attention.

"Dig in," Slater said as he accelerated into the flow of street traffic. He dropped the bag onto the kid's lap. "But save one for me."

"Del," Rosie said, "a gutshot grizzly would show more cheer than you."

"Gutshot grizzlies don't work weekends when deputies call in sick." With his fork, Del pushed his scrambled eggs around his plate. The rising sun poured light through the cafe window, throwing sharp shadows from the plastic salt and pepper shakers resting at the edge of the table.

Rosie poured Del more coffee. As flat-footed as any city street cop, and equally comparable in bulk, she made up for age and plainness with saucy humor and indomitable cheer.

"Del, you've come in for a breakfast break from work on plenty of other weekends." She slapped the breakfast bill down in front of him. "None of them did you show a face as long as a Texan liars' contest. And this is the first time in years you haven't finished breakfast before your second cup of coffee."

Del shrugged. She was right on both points. Tough to carry an appetite, though, when he had two worrisome problems: the disappearance of Slater Ellis and the knowledge that Louise had been feeding information to spooksville.

The problems didn't give Del much to look forward to these days. At the office, he could shuffle paper and find ways to delay a murder investigation so plainly needed, thanks to the coroner's findings of scorpion stings on a dead scientist. At home, he could endure the barriers to affection that Louise had recently slammed into place as surely as if she'd stepped behind bars.

Like I'm fool enough to believe her excuse about a bad back and needing to sleep on a cot in the living room?

Rosie had moved on to the only other table in the cafe that held customers—two fishermen bragging about what they'd catch and release before the end of the day. It left Del plenty of room to bury himself in morose contemplation of his coffee.

When the bell at the cafe door jangled, Del didn't look up at first. A shadow, a large one, covered his booth, and Del had to stretch his neck to see the visitor's face.

The freak from spooksville. Not in a suit this time, but in jeans and a corduroy shirt, like he was slumming, and rolls of white bandage wrapped around one hand.

Del almost grinned. As Rosie had observed, Del was to the point of fist-throwing grizzly mean. Despite the photos that spooksville used as a ring in Del's nose, despite the chill of fear that the freak seemed to inspire, Del had a suicidal urge to vent his frustration with the physical release of pain delivered and taken. The guy was down to one good hand. If Del could get in the first punch or two, it might even become a fight he'd survive.

"I didn't think people like you made public appearances," Del said.

"Only when it doesn't matter," came the whispered reply.

The man didn't sit.

Del took a slug of coffee, trying to prove he wasn't rattled. "Because the operation is over?"

"We'll discuss it outside."

"After I finish my eggs," Del said, riding his mood to deeper anger.

The spook lifted the salt shaker. Because he couldn't grip it tightly through his bandages, he pressed it against his side and with his good hand unscrewed the cap. Seconds later, he dumped the salt onto Del's breakfast.

"You may consider that a direct insult," he said in that strained whisper. "One to discuss outside."

Del did, enjoying his flame of hatred. He pushed himself out of the booth. "Outside's fine with me. It's a real shame you've got those photos to hide behind, like calling me names from behind your mama's apron."

The freak said nothing, just turned and left the cafe.

Del threw some bills down. "See you, Rosie," he said.

"Sure." She grinned. "If that was the date you were expecting, I can see why you had a case of the sours."

Del grinned dutifully at the joke.

As he stepped onto the street, however, Del's grin faded. It occurred to him he should be worried. There was something strange about this guy, so unafraid in the open. There'd been three witnesses in the small cafe, and the guy's face would be more than easy to pick out of a lineup. Plus he had become personal. Not like the times before when it'd seemed like duty was a matter of bore-dom.

Unconsciously, Del's right hand caressed the top of his holster.

"Get in," the freak said, pointing at a white panel van parked alongside the sidewalk.

"Where to?" Del asked. "I'll follow in my own car."

"Not a chance." He was leering, holding up his damaged hand. "If you're afraid, keep your hand on your gun. What can I do to a trained officer of the law while I'm driving one handed?"

Del spat on the sidewalk. He didn't pause to consider that anger might be making him careless.

"Fine, then. I'll get in first," Del said. He planned to have the gun out and cradled in his lap before the guy got around the front of the van and behind the steering wheel.

"Suit yourself."

While the freak watched from the sidewalk, Del opened the passenger door and swung into the front of the van. Two things distracted him. One, he noticed the woman lying on the floor of the van and started to register that it was his wife. But as his brain grappled with that, he settled into the seat and the second distraction overloaded his sensory equipment.

"Son of a—!"

If felt like someone had peppered darts into his hips. Del yelped and tried to push out. He couldn't. The freak had slammed the door on him and was holding it shut.

Fury filled Del. What kind of stunt was this, a pin cushion in the seat of the car? He moved to pull his gun now, to shoot his way out. Especially knowing his wife was in the van.

All he could see through the door's window was a belt buckle and blue jeans. It went through Del's mind as he reached for his gun that he'd pump a round or two into the belt buckle, figure a legal reason for it later.

As he was thinking his way through the action, however, the window seemed to dim. At first like a thundercloud passing over the sun, but the dimming continued, and Del's circle of vision shrank. He wanted to reach out and rub the window with the palm of his hand, like smearing away shower fog on a bathroom window. Only he couldn't move his hand. The fog darkened, became a film over his eyes. The sun disappeared completely.

Slater prepared for cyberspace.

Barely an hour earlier, he and the kid had been parked a half-block down from the cafe, waiting for Del Silverton to finish breakfast after they'd followed him there from the county office. What a shock, twenty minutes later, to see the monster from Santa Monica step onto the sidewalk from a white van. Although they hadn't been seen, both Slater and the kid cringed and ducked, the kid whimpering as he did so.

For Slater, the adrenaline rush had been massive. Seeing the guy with bandages wrapped over one hand had not only brought reality to the Santa Monica nightmare but had also hammered home one simple fact. This was the center. If the monster had returned here, Austad and the boys were here. And likely Paige too. Unless they'd been killed.

Slater veered his mind away from those thoughts.

Cyberspace, he told himself, think cyberspace. Focus on the results of following the white van from the cafe.

Slater hadn't been surprised when the monster and Del got into the van, although he still couldn't figure why the monster had gone to Del's side first, as if he were a valet closing a door for Del. Because the van had stayed to the main roads from Los Alamos, Slater had been able to keep a couple of cars between his rental and the van.

Up into the mountains, however, it hadn't been so easy. If a truck hadn't slipped in front of Slater's rental, he wouldn't have had any cover. Instead, Slater had been able to hang back, confident because of his knowledge of the local highways that the white van could make no turn for miles.

Instead, almost immediately, the white van had taken the one narrow strip of pavement Slater could not—a road barricaded by military guard. Slater had lost his quarry almost before the chase began, with only the consolation that Slater knew exactly where they'd gone. A hastily purchased topography map from a local museum showed only one destination. The road ended ten miles northwest in the Sante Fe National Forest, close to Redondo Peak and its 11,254 foot summit. The Jemez Mountains Silo Base.

Despite the complete lack of any other building site along that road, Slater couldn't believe the three kids had escaped from the silo base. And because of his disbelief, Slater was now heading into cyberspace from their motel room in Los Alamos.

With the kid hovering behind his shoulder, Slater wondered how he would explain cyberspace. He'd have to start with the concept of a computer, which would be difficult even with the laptop and its backlit screen here in the motel room as tangible proof. After that, it would only get more convoluted.

Minutes earlier, the kid had watched closely as Slater had run a telephone cord from the computer into the room's wall jack. How could Slater explain modem, the transfer of electronic information from computer to computer over existing telephone lines?

From there, he'd have to explain the internet, the biggest arm of cyberspace, a network of on-line computers stretched into millions across the world. Most of the time, Slater could hardly believe the technological capacity to surf through endless channels of information himself.

But Slater was no stranger to the internet. He managed his investment portfolio on a daily basis through modem. Because of it, when earlier in the week he'd begun the process of tracking down IWRC and the mysterious Darby through financial reports and business news, targeting his information search had almost been simple. Slater knew as thoroughly as anyone his internet niche.

In new territory, however . . .

"All right, Caesar," Slater said. "Here goes."

Slater typed a bit and hit the return key on his computer. Less than a minute later, password verification included, Slater and his computer were on-line.

"Now watch this," Slater told the boy. It didn't matter the kid couldn't understand anything Slater said. Slater had discovered he simply enjoyed the attention of words focused on him, and today, after seeing and following the monster man here in Los Alamos, the kid needed as much soothing as possible.

"First we find someone interested in a chat," Slater continued.

Slater clicked a few on-screen buttons, narrowing his search from all departments to Lifestyles and Interests. Opening that up, he browsed through the special-interests list: Astronomy Club, Aviation Club, Baby Boomers, Business Strategies, and so on. He searched the list until he reached the Ms. "Got it," Slater announced to the kid as he opened a new computer file. "Where else but Military City?"

Within Military City, he had a choice of electronic bulletin boards arranged into further subdivisions or a conference room. He chose the conference room. The screen came alive with the electronic conversation of people scattered across the country, all bonded by modem.

"Hey, Caesar," Slater said, pointing at the screen. "Six surfers in this one. Slow day. Sometimes a couple dozen sit around and gab."

Slater watched for a few moments. Caesar stared at the patters of type that leaped on the screen as the electronic conversations unfolded.

"Only rookies just jump into conversation," he told the kid. "You need to watch for a while, get the flow."

The conversation unfolded on the screen:

Hexon2: Does anyone know how to use this to go overseas? My wife's stepdad has a boy in Aviano. USAF. And they . . .

Hexon2: . . . want to use something faster than snailmail.

Lpst102: Hey, Hex, I have a son in Aviano.

S3810: Hexon, yes e-mail can be delivered via internet, even to ships at sea.

Slater scanned each new sentence. The screen gave the speaker's chosen screen name — Slater's own was simply Ellis — and the message each chose to send. Because it took several seconds to read a question, and several more to type and send a reply, often conversations seemed stilted. Hexon2's question was broken because any one message could only contain so many characters. Lpst102 had managed to throw in some idle chitchat before S3810 fired in his reply to Hexon2 about electronic mail.

Slater saw it as a good time to break in. He typed a brief message and hit return to send it. A heartbeat later, it showed up on his screen, as it did on the various screens across the country.

Ellis: Hello, all. Got a question of my own.

S3810: Hexon, go to departments. The key word is INTERNET. You'll be able to search info and find out more.

Slater waited, understanding S3810's reply was still part of the earlier conversation fragment. Soon enough, he saw the first reply to his greeting.

MikeGOO6: Hey, Ell. What's shaking?

Hexon2: Thanks, S38. Hello, back, Ellis.

Ellis: Looking for silo base info. Nuclear warheads. Any of you surfed internet enough to know where to send me?

There was a ten-second pause. Slater found the new quiet unnerving. When the next message came up, he understood why.

Hexon2: Are you a journalist?

S3810: Hope you're asking about unclassified stuff...

"Talking about establishing yourself as an instant outsider," Slater said. He hit his keys, hoping to recover.

Ellis: Background stuff. Wondering about setting a book there, not that there's much of a difference between journalism and fiction.

Hexon2: Good one, Ellis.

MikeGOO6: Give him a break, guys. Why assume journalists are always after the worst?

S3810: Good one, Mike. Does good news ever make headlines?

Ellis: S38,I wouldn't expect to find classified material. And if I were chasing that stuff, I wouldn't be on an open board.

Hexon2: Try Depart of Energy. I think it's in their jurisdic.

S3810: Good point, Ell.

Ellis: Thanks.

S3810:   No longer DOE, Hex. Now operated by Nuclear Facilities Safety Board.

Hexon2:   I stand, no, I sit, corrected.

Ellis: Any of you heard anything about the Jemez Mountains Silo Base near Los Alamos?

Within seconds, a new name leaped onto the screen. A silent observer—one who had been watching the screen much like Ellis had before jumping in—had decided to speak up.

Amscray: Los Alamos? You might have to put your novel characters into radiation suits.

S3810:   Ell, the safety board info is definitely public, nonclassified.

Ellis: Radiation, Am?

Ellis: Thanks, S38.

Amscray: Big accident, maybe 14, 15 years ago. Military did usual hush-up.

Hexon2:   My transfer to San Diego happened that year. I remember feeling sorry for anyone ...

Ellis: Am, accident sounds intriguing. Perfect for a novel. Anyone hurt? Did it reopen?

Hexon2:   ... who had to go to New Mexico that year.

Amscray: No one was hurt, Ell. Base is essentially closed. Skeleton staff to guard it for security purposes.

S3810:   You hardly hear about the base now. I don't know anybody who knows anybody who works there.

MikeG006:   Hey, Ellis, make a note of all our names. We want in on royalties.

Slater smiled at the screen, typed in a reply, and included a

semicolon wink. He hit return to send the message to
MikeGoo6.

Ellis: Sure guys, I promise!!!

Slater wanted out of the conversation now. He'd learned a lot
quickly. And, more importantly, almost anonymously. Time to
track down information from another direction. The on-screen
conversation continued without him.

Hexon2: Speaking of novels, I was on-line when Clancy cruised
into this room.

Ellis: Thanks, guys. Got some gopherspace to check out.

S3810: Tom Clancy, Hex?

Amscray: Maybe that explains how he makes his stuff so good.
Anyone read Patriot Games?

Hexon2: I wouldn't lie to you S38.

S3810: Tom Clancy! No way!

"Velma," Paige said, "I have questions."

"Deliver them to me." Velma methodically rinsed a plate and
handed it to Paige. "For as you can see, life is good and gives us
much leisure for discussion."

As Paige did too plainly know, there was much leisure. Less
than two days into her imprisonment, she was to the point where
the act of drying dishes at the end of mealtime provided entertainment.

"How long have you been here?" Paige carefully set the plate
onto a stack on the counter.

"Without the seasons to measure time, it is hard to say." Velma
turned to Paige. "I do miss the seasons. However, I gladly pay the
price to assist here in the Room of Joy."

"You are able to speak English to me. To the others?"

"Most are from my homeland. The others, no. We speak through example."

"Your homeland. Where is that?"

"Some questions I do not answer."

"Because . . . ?"

"Because I encourage all of us here to live in the present. We have a great calling. Miracle births!"

Paige hid her frustration at Velma's ignorance, smiled in return, accepted another dripping plate, and rubbed it dry.

Miracle births. Just past lunch, the evidence of those births was hard to ignore. The curtain to the far end of the ward was open, showing cribs and beds and babies in various stages of content and discontent. Women moved slowly in the area, tending to the crying babies.

Paige debated—only briefly—trying to explain to Velma how easily a doctor could implant any womb with a fertilized egg. Hammond, or whatever the psycho's name was, had virtually told her that's what happened here. The raptured shine in Velma's eyes, however, warned Paige of the uselessness of such an attempt. Obviously uneducated, Velma would have difficulty understanding the concept, and more important, wanted to believe in miracles. By speaking against those miracles, Paige feared she might cut off her only source of conversation. It was a significant fear, for Paige had tried English without success with every other of the couple dozen women in the ward.

"Tell me more about the miracles," Paige said.

Velma paused in thought. When she lifted another plate from the sink, she had her answer ready. "If one could explain miracles, then how could they be considered as such?"

True enough, Paige thought with a trace of irony; *true enough*. She tried another tact.

"Do all the women here conceive?"

"Most. To be barren brings great sadness."

"Sadness?"

Velma lifted a soapy hand from the water and pointed at the

baby ward. "Look at their joy. Instead of meaningless empty days here, each woman has a purpose. Her child. And all of us know that the barren ones eventually depart."

"To where?"

Velma shrugged. "In the morning, we awake and they are gone."

"You have no desire to know?" Paige found herself adopting the formal language structure, falling into the strangely enjoyable lilting rhythm of Velma's speech pattern.

"Life is simple here," Velma said. "We ask no questions. We live for the joy of bringing life into the world. We face no famine, no disease, no warfare. Life is good."

"I see no children," Paige said. "Many babies, but no children."

Her statement was true. Their conversation had been punctuated frequently by the loud cries of babies, and the low hum of mothers singing. But no child was beyond toddler stage.

"When the time is right, the child is raised elsewhere, much like the prophet Samuel was given away by his mother. For the child was a gift, and we have no hold upon the gift."

Velma studied Paige's face.

"It is not anger you should feel at this," Velma said. "Many here have had the joy of raising three or four babies over the years. And while we carry the child, our time is not idle, for we assist the others with their babies. Much like in a village."

Three or four babies? Paige struggled to understand what it meant. What had Hammond told her at her bedside the day before? These women were brought in from Third World countries. In other words, each woman was a baby factory, held contented in this prison by ignorance and the bribe of peaceful life.

Paige hesitated as she struggled for a delicate way to phrase her question. "Velma, do you find it strange that the babies share little of their mothers' nature..."?

"You mean that each child is clearly white, when the mother is not?"

Paige nodded. Perhaps here, she could venture to explain egg implanting.

"It is strange," Velma said after some thought. "However, it clearly shows the no man could have planted the seed for the child."

Paige said nothing to this. She couldn't get the single thought from her head. *Baby factory.*

"You must pray you conceive as well," Velma was saying, handing Paige another wet dish to be dried. "And once that happens, all of us will pray that you carry it to full term. And once carried to full term, we will pray you bring forth the child alive."

Velma made the sign of the cross, uncaring of the soapy water that spilled onto her apron and the floor.

Paige must have gaped.

Velma dropped her voice to a conspiratorial level. "It is I, you see, who assists in the births. And I must warn you to seek holiness as you carry your child. For sometimes the mother is punished by the birth of a child that carries her sins."

"Yes?" Paige said. Velma had stopped, her face inscrutable.

"That is all I wish to say," Velma said. "You have no need to know the horrors I have seen."

Velma looked over Paige's shoulder. "We appear to be blessed with fortune. Another arrives."

Paige followed Velma's gaze. Fifty paces away from where she stood at the sink, the single door to the ward had opened. A man almost as big as the doorway pushed a stretcher into the ward.

Paige barely glanced at the stretcher. Across the distance, she was riveted not by the size of the man, but by the waxy scar that covered half of his face. Something about the stony way he moved gave her a chill of fear.

She only had a few seconds to observe him. He lifted his hands—one hand heavily bandaged—and turned and shut the door behind him.

Velma was already walking to the stretcher.

Paige followed.

When Paige reached the stretcher at Velma's side, she saw a woman who could not have arrived from a Third World country. Another Caucasian, brunette, lying face up and strapped in place, with smeared mascara and smudged lipstick, sure signals of non-refugee status.

The woman's eyes were open, blinking with fright at the sudden appearance of two new strangers.

Velma began to unstrap the woman.

"Where am I?" she pleaded.

"You are in the Room of Joy," Velma said. "When it is you have a return of good spirits, I will tell you more."

With the kid engrossed in the colored images that splashed across the screen of the motel television, Slater went back to the network and typed in the key word for internet. Here, he wouldn't be looking for conversation but information, using the "gopher" system to sort through millions of documents spread through thousands of mainframe computers across the world. The system had been developed at the University of Minnesota, where the campus mascot was the Golden Gopher, one of the bizarre twists that computer hacks loved: The system was used to "go fer" information.

Slater started at the main menu and followed into subsystems. It took him half an hour to find an archive with background information, an op-ed piece from the *Washington Post* already a few years old, relating to the accident years earlier.

He pulled the article up on the screen, an introduction to a special information section that examined the status and dangers of American nuclear weapons storage in the aftermath of the end of the cold war.

Epilogue to Near Disaster—The trucks, a long snaking convoy of supertankers led by the flashing lights of police escort, had arrived in San Ysidro, New Mexico (see insert map) barely hours ahead of national headlines—Nuclear

Leak Threatens Mountain Residents. Earlier, the trucks had roared in the darkness across the desert flats west of the mountains at 80 miles per hour, a speed easy to maintain unloaded with the powerful diesel engines pounding full rpms. The truck drivers acknowledged the resident populations of San Ysidro and remaining towns along Highway 4 only by slowing to 50 miles per hour as they passed through, a rumbling 18-wheel speed that still shook the buildings nearest the pavement. Ahead of them was the arduous climb into the Jemez Mountains of northwestern New Mexico and the contaminated soil of stored nuclear warheads gone bad.

At the missile site waited excavating equipment and mining conveyer belts to lift with military precision the first of tons of poisoned earth into huge tanker canisters that had been manufactured to carry petroleum, not this radiation-soaked soil from the depths of the earth.

The trucks did not leave in a convoy. Instead, each rolled away as soon as it was full and sealed, to pass through guarded barricades now in place at the main intersections at the east and west ends of Highway 4, barricades that also blocked access from Los Alamos, the closest major center.

Each truck continued out of the mountains, back along the desert flats to the center of a former nuclear testing site, where the super tanker canisters were abandoned to armed guards who had little appreciation of the irony of these fourth-generation nuclear weapons returned by proxy to their spawning grounds.

When, 73 days later, the trucks finished rumbling day and night along Highway 4, nearly 2,000 of these canisters filled 50 orderly and tightly pressed rows, presenting to the sun each morning a sea of shiny beetle backs of silver.

And the military, having deemed the evacuated base near the summit of Redondo Peak safe, continue to guard the damaged site again in relative obscurity.

After reading the article three times, Slater thought through its implications. He shifted at the cheap desk to pencil a list of reasons he should actually believe the entire situation was real.

His shorthand notes told him that he'd found three kids, he'd listened to a translator confirm they spoke Latin and that they'd escaped from some sort of institutional facility, he'd been the target of a kidnapping attempt, had seen the kidnapper here in Los Alamos, and had followed the kidnapper to an obscure military base hidden miles deep in the mountains.

Add to that one other factor. The same base had been evacuated, and under high-security conditions, tons upon tons of dirt were removed. Enough dirt to leave room for an underground institute?

What had he just learned about the base from the military hacks? *No one was hurt, Ell. Base is essentially closed. Skeleton staff to guard it for security purposes. And you hardly hear about the base now. I don't know anybody who knows anybody who works there.*

Worse, and too convincing to Slater, was the topography map. A straight line from the military base to his house in Seven Springs showed the path the kids might have taken through the mountains to appear in the headlights of his truck.

Last, Slater recalled Austad's information from a genetics professor. *Only human mothers can nurture human embryos. You'd have to have a place to engage in large-scale experimenting in humans. No way could you have a place that big, involving that many people, and expect it to remain secret. Human nature dictates someone would eventually talk about it. And where would anyone find the funding? Something that big would take major money. You can't keep major money secret either.*

Now it appeared Slater had found a real-life location for the secret. And who better to hide big money than the military?

Slater stared at his scrawled writing. He still couldn't trust himself to accept the wild conclusions he drew from what his five senses had plainly delivered to him during the past week. He wondered if this was how someone sitting in a plane going down felt—the overwhelming disbelief that it was actually happening. Slater faced an added factor. What if there was another, much more rational explanation for all of this and he was making himself the biggest fool in the world by plunging ahead? Like diving into a lake to save a drowning victim only to discover he was interrupting the filming of a movie scene. Except this situation was much bigger, much more frightening.

Slater shook his head at his dithering.

"Hey, kid," he said, "speak English, will you? Tell me I've got a hyperactive imagination."

Unfortunately, the kid only smiled after looking up briefly from the television set. And that quick glance showed Slater too clearly the tattooed number on the boy's forehead.

And Paige Stephens was still missing. He'd called Suzanne in Florida a half-dozen times already; she'd hadn't yet heard from Paige and was considering calling the police to report Paige as a missing person.

Add to all of this that Paige, too, had confirmed the strangeness of the situation with vague references to an Institute. Slater could not deny to himself the significance of a web of events that stretched as far as Florida.

He sighed.

All right, so he'd admit that by some ironic twist of God's humor it was him, Slater Ellis, thrown into the middle of all of this. As if God were pulling him from the whale's belly and telling him he could no longer hide from life. Couldn't he have been thrown into something much simpler? Why him, a regular guy? Why not some 007 agent trained in five languages, seven strains of marital arts, explosives, lock picking, and computer espionage?

That's who it would take, Slater told himself sourly. James Bond. Because normal guys just didn't bust into highly secret military bases and mop up all the evil thugs.

If this project was sanctioned by the military, didn't it somewhere, somehow, need government approval? Wouldn't it then be Slater breaking the law, making him the evil thug? Besides, who was Slater to be the one to declare human genetics experiments as beyond any government law?

It didn't take Slater long to realize he was looking for an excuse to bail out. But government project or not, the kidnapping attempt and his missing friends put this in a new realm. And didn't we-the-people have a right to know and decide what the government should allow at the edges of the new frontier of genetics technology?

Despite the realization, Slater winced at the thought of being a noble white knight riding forth to protect and save. He disliked left-wing journalists who self-righteously peddled their opinions under the same armored guise.

Slater stared at the depressing brown wave patterns on the depressing orange curtains of the motel room.

He had to do something. No way could he salvage any self-respect if he walked away from this.

But what could he do?

Time was the key element. Slater couldn't go to local authorities for help to expose a military project. Not in Los Alamos, the government town that had produced the first A-bomb in total secrecy. Not when, with his own eyes, Slater had seen the sheriff of Los Alamos meet with the kidnapper from Santa Monica. Going to the police for help was a laughable idea.

All right. Say, instead, Slater ran to the media, despite how much a high profile would cost him on a personal level. Say a major whistle-blowing scandal actually developed, that the military and government don't pull strings to hush it. Say Slater doesn't end up dead or kidnapped himself. That was the most success Slater could hope for, and successful or not, too much time would pass. The people inside would be able to move the boys and Austad and Paige—as they surely would to hide any evidence of wrongdoing. Once moved elsewhere, if not outright killed, how much chance would Slater have of finding them?

The alternative was to lone wolf it, make sure Austad and Paige and the boys were safe, then let Austad or Paige do the whistle-blowing act, keeping away from any floodlights of public scrutiny himself. Maybe at the same time, he'd leave behind a diary, maybe send copies to some newspapers in case he didn't get back out again.

Slater shook his head in disgust at the sense of melodrama he was creating.

Still, he shifted back to his computer to write a brief report he'd send to a friend in case anything happened to him. The kid was happy to be mesmerized by all the new information delivered via television, giving Slater time to write everything he could recall. Tonight he'd take the kid into the hills to look at the base. If the kid reacted like he'd been there, it would be proof Slater could not ignore, much as he might want to.

Del's throat burned. The bile of rage. Or the pressure of the noose. It didn't matter to his situation. The spooksville freak was behind him, with his undamaged right hand holding a long aluminum pole, as if carrying a flag at a 45 degree angle. Instead of unfurled cloth, however, the end of the pole held thin steel wire, an effective choke chain looped around Del's neck. As the freak pushed the pole, Del was forced to stumble down the well-lit hallway, barely able to draw breath because of the pressure. All the freak had to do was lift the pole a degree higher, and the steel wire would cut through the skin of Del's neck.

No way could Del make a rush on his captor either. Del had awoken helpless. Iron clasps around each wrist were connected by two feet of plastic-sheathed steel cord. His feet had been hobbled in the same manner. Another steel cord connected the wire of his hobbled hands to the wire of his hobbled feet. It gave him just enough freedom to shuffle, stooped to the point of pain as he tried to keep sufficient slack in the wire between his hands and feet.

They reached an elevator midway down the hall.

"This will be delicate, as inside the elevator I won't be able to maintain my pressure on your choke wire," the spooksville freak said. His whispered voice sounded like someone had a noose around his throat instead. "You might be tempted to do something foolish, like ram me into the wall. Please don't. It takes very little effort to pull a trigger, and I'd prefer to avoid an awkward mess."

Del stepped inside the elevator.

The threat of a gun had not been empty. The freak screwed the barrel into his kidneys with such enthusiasm that Del almost wished for the return of the noose's pressure.

They rode downward in silence. The man's breathing sounded as harsh as the ventilation fan. When the elevator door opened again, he pushed Del forward. Zwaan kept tight pressure on the noose as he went through the routine of the retina-sensor check and keypad entry code for the vault door to give them entry to the halls of the sixth floor.

When the vault door closed behind them, Zwaan commanded Del ahead and to the left, reinforcing the order with a jerk of the steel noose.

Del stumbled left.

"I hope you appreciate my ingenuity," Zwaan said. "I saw this method used on stubborn horses—rope though, not piano wire—and I hoped some day I'd have a chance to test its effectiveness for myself."

Del seethed hatred.

"In fact," the man mused aloud, "I think I could get you on your tiptoes..."

Del grunted agony as the steel wire bit into his skin. Pride made him fight the urge to rise onto his toes for as long as possible. Pride lasted less than three seconds. Pain lanced through the throbbing fogginess of Del's head.

"Good," the freak whispered as Del balanced on his toes. "I like cooperation. Now, ahead again."

Almost to the end of the hallway, the man jerked Del to a stop. Still holding the pole with his right hand, he fumbled at a door handle with his bandaged left hand until the door popped open.

"Meet your new roommate," the man said. He pulled Del backward, then pushed him into the room.

A gray-haired, elderly man, strained to exhaustion, sat on the edge of a bed on one side of the room. A matching steel-framed bed hugged the opposite wall. The man's wrists and ankles were bound in a similar manner to Del's. The only difference was the steel cord looped around the man's waist and attached to a ring bolted to the wall behind him.

"To the other bed," came the strained whisper.

Del saw an identical waist cord waiting there. It was a slack straight line, its free end consisting of a small unlocked hasp.

Del stood beside the bed.

"Face away from me," the orders continued.

The freak slid the pole in his hand to shorten the grip while keeping the pressure on the wire as he moved closer to Del's back.

"Take the end of the cord."

Del had just enough slack in his hobbled hands to obey. He lifted it from the bed.

"Around the front of your waist and give it to me."

If Del had any thoughts of resistance, the tightness of the wire around his neck kept him from the foolishness of action. The freak took the end of the cord and locked it around itself behind Del's back.

Finally, the noose slackened as the man lowered the pole and lifted the wire away from Del's head. Del was now a prisoner within the five-foot circle that the waist cord permitted him.

"Introduce yourselves," the scar-faced man whispered. "Become lifelong friends." He snorted amusement. "Which should last less than a week."

"All the comforts of home," the gray-haired man said. "You'll find a potty under the bed, and meals served three times a day."

Del ignored him with the silence he'd maintained for the ten minutes since the scarred man's departure.

"By the way," the man said, "my name is Ben Austad. I'd offer to shake your hand, but I don't think we can reach."

Del still ignored him. His head hurt from the lingering effects of the drugs that had zombied him; he was trying to absorb the information that the freak had delivered with such pleasure just before moving him to this cell; and he was frantically worried about Louise.

"You must be one of the good guys," Austad said. "Your police uniform."

Del finally looked over. "No such thing as good guys and bad guys. Just winners and losers. And we're not exactly odds-on favorites."

"Bad guys and good guys," Austad insisted with a grin. "We've got lots of time. I'd be happy to debate Judeo-Christian ethics."

Del grunted. He *knew* they didn't have time. Just before their trip down the hallways, the spooksville freak had taken tremendous pleasure in outlining to Del the organ-donation system they used here. It hadn't given Del much satisfaction to find out he was worth eighty grand dead through the sale of his body parts.

"I'd also be happy to trade stories," Austad said. His voice was oddly bright, as if he were fighting to keep the edge of sanity from slicing him apart. "I'm a Latin professor. From Santa Monica."

Del cast a disbelieving glance across the small room. "Latin?"

The man nodded. "I got this call out of the blue from a guy named Slater Ellis. He had some triplets who spoke a weird language..."

"Slater Ellis?" Del started to pay attention.

Del listened to the rest of the story with full attention. He didn't figure knowing the situation would do much good, but it took his mind off Louise and how limp and vulnerable she'd looked lying on the floor of the van.

The guy wrapped up his story by describing how the scarred man had taken him and two kids from his house in Santa Monica.

"Two?" Del said. "I thought you said triplets."

"Slater had the third. I hope he's all right."

Del felt his first real interest. "You're saying Slater is still out there?" *Weird,* Del thought, *going from a determination to kill the guy for information to cheering for him from a bleak set of sidelines.*

"I don't know," Austad said. "But they spent a lot of time questioning me about what he might have told people. Or about what I'd told. I'm pretty sure they used some drugs on me, because I was telling them everything, including the name of the first girl I kissed in seventh grade."

"Slater's out there?"

"He isn't here, and it seems like they stuck the good guys together." Austad frowned. Old as his face was, the intensity of the frown gave him innocence. "You are a good guy, aren't you? This isn't like the movie *Stalag 17*, is it, where they put an informer in the barracks?"

Del didn't feel like one of the good guys. Not only that, he'd just discovered how easily he could disappear. The spooksville freak had also taken delight in describing how they'd made it look like he and Louise had left on a sudden, extended second honeymoon, and how they already had a successor groomed to step into the county sheriff position, a successor less likely to give them trouble.

"Sure, I'm a good guy," Del said, knowing he was lying. He groaned and rubbed his face, too conscious of the shackles that followed his hands upward. "But don't expect no movie ending."

Del almost told him about the doctor's appointment he could expect but decided there was no sense in adding to the professor's misery.

"Look," Del said. "Does Slater have any idea where we are?"

"Do you?" Austad answered.

"Somewhere near Los Alamos," Del said. "Other than that..."

"Which is probably as close as Slater might guess. He'd said he found the boys nearby."

Del rubbed his face again. Why had he even begun to hope? What could a civilian like Ellis accomplish against spooksville?

Del settled back into his dark silence. Whenever his thoughts turned to worries about Louise, he speculated again on the doctor approaching him with a scalpel. It was less unpleasant to think about the horror of his own approaching death than to contemplate what might have happened to his wife because of his stupidity.

Zwaan found Van Klees wearing a white jacket over jeans in one of the laboratory rooms on the fourth floor of the Institute. Behind Van Klees, the counter was lined with test tubes of various colors and sizes, placed in a line of exact precision. Van Klees hated wasting time and had mixed two solutions while waiting for Zwaan.

The general and his forces managed to get us a trace on Slater Ellis," Van Klees announced. "So much as I dislike risking an appearance out there, as you suggested, it was worth my efforts."

Zwaan raised his damaged hand and stared at the bandages. "Good. Let me get him then. By tonight, he will have lost several of his own fingers. Which I will simply consider a good start."

"You are wrong, my friend," Van Klees said. His eyes glittered with what passed as amusement on his cold face. "Not tonight. Tomorrow morning. And you will have no need to search for him. He's coming to us."

Zwaan squinted puzzlement.

"Ellis stayed at a local motel. He billed some long-distance calls to his home number," Van Klees explained. "Only by the time I was alerted, he was no longer there. He'd checked out an hour earlier. With the boy."

"Then how—"

"Patience. Follow me to my office."

They walked the hall down to his office, a room large enough to appear uncramped despite the large leather couch at one end and a massive oak desk at the other. Two matching abstract prints— devoid of any warm hues of orange, red, or yellow—filled one wall. The desk was empty, save for a black telephone, a thick daytimer open to the current date, and a single sheet of paper.

Van Klees pointed at the sheet of paper. "Read it."

Zwaan lifted the sheet from the desk and studied the numbers listed in Van Klees's precise printing. "A dozen calls. Six I can guess by the area code—Florida. One, also out of state, but I don't know where. The first five have New Mexico area codes. I don't recognize them."

"Sante Fe numbers. All dialed from his motel room."

Zwaan scanned the sheet. "Traced them?"

"Of course. Wholesale grocers."

"What?"

"You might find it interesting to note there are at least a dozen wholesale grocers listed in Sante Fe."

"I might," Zwaan said in a voice that, with his scarred vocal cords, approximated a growl. "Especially if you'll quit with these games. I'm in no mood to play."

"Ask yourself why he stopped calling grocers at five. If he was price shopping, why not contact all of them? And ask yourself why he went as far as five. If he wasn't price shopping, no need to go past one."

"I am in no mood to play."

"The last Sante Fe phone number belongs to Winokur and Sons."

Zwaan's eyes widened. "Our supplier," he said with immediate comprehension of that significance. Zwaan set the paper back on the desk. "So Ellis called only until he found out which supplier delivered to the base. After he found Winokur and Sons, there was no reason to check further."

"Precisely."

"That's not good," Zwaan said. "He knows our location."

Van Klees shrugged. "Maybe he knew all along. After all, he did immediately fly back to this area."

Unaware of how the gesture acknowledged Slater, Zwaan cradled his stumped fingers in the palm of his right hand. He paced the office several times, mumbling under his breath.

"Why would he want to know who supplies us with food, you're asking yourself."

"You can guess?" Zwaan asked.

"Of course. His mind is a baby's compared to mine."

"And?"

"He's the one who first found the boys. He also knows you've got Austad. The Florida numbers show he was also trying to reach

Paige Stephens from his motel without success, and that has to tell him she's also gone. Still, he hasn't gone public. And he won't, not with his past. I believe he thinks he's Rambo, ready to take us on by himself."

"But why call a grocer?"

"He wants in, Zwaan. Can he ring the doorbell? Or plant dynamite? Think! What truck do we allow past the gates every Sunday?"

Zwaan nodded. "He finds a way to sneak into the trailer at Winokur's warehouse."

"Or bribes the driver to let him on. Tomorrow, he rides past our security gates and up to the loading dock. I can see him thinking he'll be able to find a way in from there."

"Our security is airtight."

"Have fun with this," Van Klees said. "Open up the security lid. Let Ellis inside. Give him hope and then slam the lid."

"A nice touch. But what about the boy?"

Van Klees smiled. Instead of answering, he consulted the list of phone numbers and dialed one. Van Klees listened for less than twenty seconds, and when he spoke next, his voice was official and warm.

"Mrs. Cassell," he said. "How is the weather up in Wisconsin today?"

Van Klees nodded as he listened, the consummate actor slipping into a new role. "Consider yourself fortunate, ma'am. Here in New Mexico, the sun has been merciless."

A pause. Van Klees grinned at the reaction on the other end.

"Yes ma'am, I did say New Mexico. I should let you know this is Agent Lifton from the Federal Bureau of Investigation, and I'm afraid I have to inform you that I know this is not the only call you've received from here in the last two days."

Van Klees held the telephone away from his ear so that Zwaan could share the loud response on the other end.

"Ma'am?" Van Klees cut in with firm politeness. "Ma'am, we know about your son. And we believe he's trying to involve you in another federal crime."

Zwaan was motionless now, intent on guessing through the side of the conversation he could hear.

"Ma'am, please admit you found it peculiar that he would call out of the blue after years on the run."

Van Klees gave her time to admit to the fact before continuing. "We happen to know he's been using an assumed name. And if our guess is right, he's asked you to shelter a boy."

Van Klees nodded at Zwaan as the answer came in.

"Yes ma'am. I'm afraid to say he's involved with a kidnapping, which is why the bureau was called in."

In the next silence, Van Klees rolled his eyeballs for Zwaan's benefit. He also lowered his voice to sympathetic concern as he spoke.

"Ma'am, he might have warned you that the kid doesn't speak English. It's part of a foreign embassy thing and it almost worked. Your son was expecting national security needs to work in his favor. I mean, our government would rather pay ransom than risk embarrassment, and if we hadn't traced him . . ."

Van Klees waited again.

"Ma'am, I appreciate the information. May I ask instead that you meet the boy yourself at the airport."

Brief pause.

"Yes. Go ahead as agreed. It's important to the case. And can you do me a personal favor?" Van Klees winked at Zwaan as he said it. "Be good to the kid. He's just a boy, probably scared, and can use all the help he gets. When it's wrapped up on this end, we'll send someone there to bring him back to his parents at the embassy in D.C."

Van Klees winked again at Zwaan. "And ma'am, it goes without saying that you must keep this extremely secure. In fact, we have a budget to reward you for your silence. If, after a month, it's obvious nothing has been leaked to the media, you'll receive a ten-thousand-dollar gift from the embassy. And remember, to keep it from the media, you shouldn't let this call go beyond you and me."

Van Klees listened to the response, then hung up the phone. "I am the master of everything, am I not?" He said it, naturally, as a rhetorical question. "Why else would he contact her except to find a safe place for the boy? She'll keep him for us until you can go up there and eliminate them both."

Then his face lost its warmth and became a mask of scorn. "I'd like to see Ellis when you get him. Afterward, damage Ellis all you want. But don't kill him. When the good doctor comes in to handle that oaf of a sheriff in your care, have him do the same to Ellis and Austad. A triple shipment of organs can begin to recompense us in a small way for the difficulties he's caused."

Van Klees straightened his arms and tugged on the sleeves of his lab jacket. Zwaan recognized it as a signal that Van Klees was impatient to get back to the laboratory.

"Tomorrow afternoon I fly to New York to deal with some tedious paperwork for the Hammond identity," Van Klees said as he inspected the creases of his lab coat. "Then back to Chicago to tend to some of the undergraduates at the university. I have some interesting research questions from here I'd like them to pursue."

He flashed a sinister grin at Zwaan. "On a theoretical level, of course. We'll save the practical applications for here, won't we?"

Thirteen

FROM THE HIGH, stiff-springed seats of a diesel cab, and with sunlight instead of a quarter moon providing light, the base looked much different to Slater than it had during the midnight visit with the kid.

"Like I said," the truck driver told Slater above the deep-voiced country lamentations that blared from the truck radio, "it usually takes us only half an hour to unload the pallets. You'd best be quick."

Slater nodded, not taking his eyes from the low, squat buildings ahead of them. If it hadn't been for the kid's panicked reaction to the base, Slater wouldn't be here. Instead, Saturday night's hike into the woods had proved what Slater didn't want to believe. The triplets had indeed fled from this base on their way to Seven Springs.

Not that it had been easy getting there to confirm. They'd checked out early from the motel to do most of the hiking during daylight. Slater had taken the topography map, a compass, and a light knapsack of food, and they'd driven as close as possible, then cut cross-country from the parked vehicle. Five hours of hard hiking had brought them to a compound fence that marked the northwestern perimeter of the government's land. By leaning a deadfall tree against the fence, both had been able to climb over the barbed-wire top. There they'd waited until dark, finally creeping the last half-mile into the base, guided by the moon and discreet use of flashlights. At their first glimpse of the bare pavement that surrounded the base's buildings, the kid had frantically pulled at Slater's sleeve, trying to keep him from going nearer.

That had been the confirmation Slater needed.

They'd retreated then, slowly moved back to the compound fence, found another rotting tree to push over as a convenient ladder, and begun the laborious job of retracing their way out again. Once Slater had deemed them safely away, he'd stopped to wait for dawn to keep traveling. From there, Slater had driven the kid to the Sante Fe airport. Their parting had been difficult—Slater didn't have the ability to explain why he wanted the kid to go alone on an airplane. Only the warm smile, and protecting arm who promised her help in making the necessary connections, of a stewardess convinced the kid to go with her. Slater only hoped his mother would be on time and equally compassionate. Explaining everything to her later would be hell because he'd have so much of his past to clean up while doing it. But Slater prayed he'd have a chance to face that hell. It would mean he had survived this crazy attempt to rescue the boy's brothers.

"One last time," the truck driver said as he began to gear the truck down to a stop, "you're keeping my name out of this, right?"

Again, Slater nodded.

Fear and greed were mingled in the man's eyes. He was short, with a gut that swayed inside his dull green work shirt and bounced against the steering wheel with every bump of the road.

"You're fine as long as we both stick to our stories," Slater said. "One of your guys called in sick. And I showed up to help just at the right time."

They both knew it had cost Slater five hundred dollars for the driver's helper to agree to be conveniently ill for the day. Slater had spent another five thousand on the truck driver, telling him it was part of a journalistic effort to see the extent of the security of the aging nuclear base. Slater's cover story wasn't exactly a lie; after taking the kid to the airport, Slater had spent two hours documenting everything on his laptop computer. The disk, and an explanatory note, was already in the mail to one of his former investment buddies. If Slater didn't return, he could only hope his efforts hadn't been wasted.

Now, as the driver began to back the trailer to the loading dock, Slater felt a fierce sense of joy. It surprised him—he'd expected fear and worry. He hadn't felt this alive in years. He realized the sense of joy came from adrenaline and the vigor of purpose. He also admitted much of this purpose came from a possibly misguided romantic notion of charging in to rescue the fair damsel, for Slater didn't have to think hard to recall Paige Stephens's effect on him.

A jolt sent a tremor through the cab of the truck. The trailer had bumped into the rubber of the dock's edging. The driver shut down his motor and looked at Slater.

"Good luck, pal," he said. "You paid enough for the chance. I hope it's worth your while."

Slater was hedging his bet, waiting as long as possible before committing himself to action without return.

He first helped the driver use a hand forklift to pull pallets from the echoing interior of the semi. Crates of fresh vegetables, boxes of frozen meat, heavy cartons of canned goods.

"If anything, the military eats good," the driver grunted as he maneuvered the forklift from the dock toward a double-wide door that led into the building. "Unless the cooks ruin it like I remember from my own time in the service."

"The order's always this big?" Slater asked as he pushed against the back side of the pallet.

"Yep."

From the outside, the main building of the base appeared to have only two stories. Slater had his own suspicions about the real location of the recipients of this food.

"Is there a service elevator?" he asked.

"It's where we're headed," the driver told him. "We usually just stack the food outside the doors."

Slater was about to give a casual reply when they entered the double-wide door of a smaller warehouse space. A white van was parked prominently near a garage door. The same white van that had taken Del from the cafe in Los Alamos.

Again, adrenaline surged through Slater's veins. This didn't seem real—maybe that's why he was going ahead, because it felt like it was happening to someone else.

They wheeled the forklift toward the service elevator's dull steel doors at the far side of the empty warehouse.

Slater felt his heart pound. He'd gambled that somehow he would be able to slip inside the building itself. If the service elevator was operated by a key, his obvious and best bet would fail him.

They moved closer, and Slater allowed himself to breathe again. Two clear plastic buttons were plainly visible outside the elevator—one with an arrow pointing down, the other with an arrow pointing up.

"How about leaving this pallet here for me to unstack?" Slater suggested. "You go back alone for the next one."

Slater winked elaborately at the truck driver. "Then when you don't see me, you assume I'm so lazy I fell asleep in the back of the cab. If I'm not back to the truck in half an hour, leave without me."

The truck driver gulped. This was the moment of commitment for both of them. Once the truck driver turned his back, he would be engaging in a federal violation of security and five thousand dollars richer. Once Slater stepped into the elevator, there were no guarantees he'd be able to get back to the truck.

The driver found his voice. "You know, I'm not so sure this is something I can do. I..."

"You don't think *I'm* scared?" Slater said. "What's keeping me going is the good of this country. If a guy like me can get inside, what's it say about security? And that's the point we'll both be making when I finish this story."

Before the truck driver could answer, Slater pushed the elevator button with the down arrow. Internal cables began to hum.

Slater smiled at the truck driver, who rubbed his hands nervously through his thinning hair.

The elevator doors slid open.

The truck driver shrugged.

Slater stepped inside and let the elevator doors close upon the safety of the outside world.

When the man with the scarred face arrived to escort Paige from the ward—silently beckoning her from the doorway with his unbandage hand—she did not provide resistance. Earlier, Louise Silverton, the new arrival to the ward, had been unsparing in her description of his strength, and Paige saw no reason to engage in a futile fight.

Dressed only in a thin hospital gown, she walked with dignity down the hallway alongside the monster with the scarred face, refusing to ask their destination, watching, ever watching, for a chance to bolt. As she walked the corridor in padded slippers beside the huge, ugly man, Paige was discovering something about herself. Toughness.

It had come as a surprise when she suddenly realized—after more than two days as prisoner—that she didn't feel the fear she thought she should at his silent, hulking presence. She was focused on survival, and because of it, she was watchful and waiting, ready for any chance to escape.

The toughness inside became something she regarded with amusement and pride. How many years had she been content to go with the flow, as long as the flow was comfortable? Now, with all pretense of contentment gone, and forced to rely on herself, she could actually do it. She needed no soap operas to distract her, no compliments from a husband to sustain her self-worth.

As for other men, Paige had realized unless she first trusted herself, she shouldn't be wishing for strong shoulders to lean on. Hammond had fooled her completely. Slater Ellis, too, had disappointed her. During their brief talk, she'd sensed, or thought she'd sensed, an honestness. And a connection. But Slater, too, would have been a disappointment. *On the run for attempted murder?* Again and again Paige had shaken her head to think about her gift for becoming interested in the wrong kind of man. Darby. Hammond. Ellis. Of course, as she wryly told herself, after Darby and Hammond, attempted murder didn't seem such a bad sin.

She'd been relearning prayer, too, something she'd lost over the years among the distractions of boat parties and weekends to Miami. There was real strength there. Enough strength that she didn't ask nervous questions as she followed the monster.

No chances for escape arrived, and he led her into a small room that appeared identical to a doctor's office. An examining table filled the center of the room. There was a disturbing difference to this table, however. Straps. For ankles, wrists, waist, and neck. It took little deductive reasoning for Paige to realize the table was designed to hold someone helpless on her back.

Paige shivered, partly from cold and partly with the certainty she would soon be on the table.

The man she knew as John Hammond did not keep her waiting long. He pushed a trolley ahead of him as he entered the office dressed in jeans, T-shirt, and a white lab coat. The monster with the scarred face nodded, then stepped outside, shutting the door behind him.

"Ready for motherhood?" he asked. With an arrogant smirk, he gestured at the catheter, test tubes, and a petri dish before him on the trolley. "Even if *you're* not, Papa here is."

The straps, the stirrups on the examining table. Paige understood immediately. Hadn't he said in a chilling whisper to end their previous visit, *you are definitely a suitable mother for my son.* He meant to implant a baby in her womb.

Paige spat in his face.

He wiped saliva from his cheek. "This is precisely why all the others are drugged before they enter this room. It saves so much bother.

"Zwaan," he called to the closed door, "you are needed."

The door opened and the monster hulked inside.

"Slap her please. But don't draw blood. I haven't the patience for messiness."

With incredible swiftness, the monster stepped forward and with a single fluid motion, struck Paige so hard she almost fell backward.

"Thank you. Wait outside, please."

Moments later, they were alone.

"I trust I need not demonstrate more."

Paige only stared as hard as she could, biting the inside of her cheek to keep from crying.

"Good. Get on the table."

"Why?" Paige asked. Not as a plea, but coldly and flatly, for she knew if she allowed any emotion in her voice, she would break into tears.

"Don't be ridiculous."

"All of them, carrying babies for you. Why?"

"I haven't the time for theatrical nonsense. On the table."

"Why? A black market in babies?"

"I see I'll have to call my friend in again."

Paige thought of the crazy story she'd heard from Slater Ellis. The story about three boys found naked.

"Are you a weirdo? Getting kicks from helpless kids?"

"You stupid sow," he said. "You will bear the fruits of my genius. Thank me for your life. And thank me for the chance to be involved in the greatest experiment in the history of mankind."

"I'll fight you until I die," Paige promised.

"And I'll keep you alive, baby after baby, until your womb goes dry."

She spat in his face again, amazed at how cold rage and hatred displaced her fear.

"Zwaan!"

The monster entered the room again. As he approached Paige, she lashed out to punch him. He caught her swing midway, and twisted her arm until she cried out.

"Get her on the table."

The monster grabbed her other arm and lifted her off the floor. She screamed, bucked, and kicked, heedless of her loss of dignity. His incredible strength bore her down. Moments later, she was helplessly strapped to the table, her only movement the heaving of her ribs as she drew gulping breaths.

"Excellent. Thank you for your help."

"I've received word that Ellis has arrived," the monster said in reply. Paige felt her stomach tighten at the horrid sound of his strained whisper. *This was the man she'd heard on the phone with Darby!*

"You know what to do. Bring him here. I won't be long with the sow."

"Remember," the scarred man whispered, holding up his bandaged hand, "you promised I could hurt him."

"Yes, of course. But later. Now go."

The huge man backed out of the office and shut the door again, leaving Paige with her captor and his trolley of medical instruments.

The elevator hummed as it dropped.

The fact that he'd guessed right—the bulk of the facility was underground—gave him little comfort.

What was ahead?

Slater had planned to go only as far as the situation would let him. He was going in blind, and he knew it. It was stupid, and he knew it. Yet he felt it was his only hope, going in and trying to adjust to what he might find. If, for example, he stepped off the elevator and discovered dozens of bustling people in various hallways and rooms, he would try to blend in and cautiously proceed until a security checkpoint or something similar stopped him. On the other hand, if the elevator door opened to armed guards, he would hold up his clipboard and apologize for making a mistake as a rookie delivery person. It eased his mind slightly—only slightly—to be carrying a pistol in his back pocket. He'd definitely keep it hidden unless things became so desperate it would justify pulling a gun on a military base.

The elevator stopped one floor down.

Slater tried to put a dumb, happy-go-lucky look on his face. He was dressed for the part of a warehouse employee—dirty jeans, wrinkled T-shirt, scuffed shoes. Would it fool a military guard, if indeed one waited on the other side of the doors?

Anticlimax disappointed him.

The elevator doors opened to show a door set into a recessed entry way. Slater stepped forward, keeping one foot behind him to wedge the elevator doors from shutting on him completely.

First, Slater looked up for a surveillance camera. Nothing. Then he reached forward—the recessed entry way wasn't very deep and he could easily reach the doorknob. It was locked. There was a keypad for a security code that Slater did not possess.

Slater stepped back into the elevator. He punched the next button down.

The floor below was identical. A recessed entry with a locked door.

Another floor lower, the same thing.

Having exhausted the down buttons, Slater tried the top floor and found the same setup.

Each floor was barred to him unless he could pick locks. But even with those abilities, he wouldn't have tried. No telling how the doors had been wired for security.

Slater felt beaten before the fight had begun, his pistol dead weight in his pocket.

He stared at the panels of the elevator's interior.

His feeling of defeat grew. He couldn't even penetrate the first layer of security. His only consolations were that he hadn't been arrested in discovering this, and, defeated or not, he still had plenty of time to return to the grocer's truck.

In a way, it relieved him.

He'd done all he could in trying to rescue Ben Austad and Paige Stephens. It meant he could return to Los Alamos, try a different approach. One, perhaps, that put them in greater danger because of the time element, but he could honestly tell himself it was the only option left.

Slater punched the button that would take him back to the loading dock and his duties of unloading groceries.

His heart lurched with the next movement of the elevator, for, unbelievably, it continued dropping well past the dock level.

The elevator door opened with a gush of air, showing Zwaan his expected visitor. Ellis stood, framed by the open doors, holding a clipboard in front of his chest.

"Tough day at the office, hon?" Zwaan said. His whisper made it sound like a threat. Zwaan lifted his damaged hand. "Come on in and let me make you comfortable."

Ellis reacted by pulling the clipboard aside to reveal the small automatic pistol in his right hand. "Sit on the floor," Ellis said. "Hands on top of your head."

"No."

"You've got to three. One..."

"Kill me and the woman dies. So does Austad." Zwaan stepped forward and extended his hand, palm upward. "Give me the gun."

"You're bluffing."

"Hardly. Video surveillance covers this hallway. I die, they die. You won't even get through the vault door behind me to reach them."

"How do I know they're still alive?"

"You only get one guarantee." Zwaan didn't lower his extended hand. "That they *will* be dead if you don't give me the gun."

Zwaan smiled as Slater lowered the pistol onto his palm. Zwaan transferred the pistol to his bandaged hand and gripped it awkwardly. With his good hand, he reached in a flash of movement to pin Slater by the neck against the rear of the elevator.

"You must weigh two hundred pounds," Zwaan said as he pressed forward. He didn't expect an answer, not with Slater's windpipe almost crushed in his iron grip. One-armed, Zwaan began to lift Slater. "How many men do you know with this kind of strength?"

Slater's face had purpled.

Zwaan heard faint music in his head. Less at the pain he was delivering and more at the thought of how much he must be scaring this man. Early intimidation softened them; it made the music sweeter later.

Zwaan continued to lift until Slater's feet were well off the ground, until Slater's eyes were on level with his. Slater clutched uselessly with both hands at the corded muscle of Zwaan's forearm.

Zwaan enjoyed the moment. "Try to kick me and I'll squeeze until your throat collapses."

He watched until Slater's eyeballs began to roll. When that happened. Zwaan abruptly let go. Slater fell to his knees and fought for air.

"Consider that a prelude," Zwaan whispered. He grabbed Slater by the back of his shirt and yanked him upward. "Until then, you have questions to answer."

Zwaan reached into his back pocket for handcuffs. He snapped them around the dazed man's wrists. Then Zwaan stepped briefly out of the elevator. Along the wall rested the aluminum pole with a wire noose. Using Slater's pistol as a threat to keep him motionless, Zwaan grabbed the pole and lowered the noose over Slater's head and pulled it tight around his neck.

"Trust me," Zwaan said as he led Slater to the security checkpoint at the vaultway door, "if you enjoy oxygen, you'll avoid any struggle."

"What a timely arrival," Van Klees said to Slater. "Your friend may not need to suffer after all."

Although the gesture was not necessary, Van Klees pointed at Paige Stephens strapped to the examining table. Paige's hair was matted with sweat, her face and neck flushed red with exertion. The hospital gown had twisted around her body, a small mercy that it still provided enough cover to keep her from complete humiliation in the presence of three men.

Slater made an involuntary step forward.

Zwaan released the pressure on the noose and swatted Slater's head, crashing him into the wall. Slater clawed the wall—hampered by his handcuffed wrists—to keep his balance. Zwaan used the pole and wire to jerk him back to facing Van Klees, using such force that a thin line of blood began to curl around the edges of the wire.

"Touching," Van Klees said. "The Lone Ranger riding in to save his woman."

Slater licked blood that dribbled from his nose.

"Valiant but extremely stupid," Van Klees continued. His smile mocked Slater. "You didn't think it strange we had no one up top? Nor that a driver bonded for military deliveries would risk his job for only five thousand?"

Slater's reaction, a flinch, broadened Van Klees's smile. "He'd been warned about you, told to accept whatever you offered, told to bring you in," Van Klees said. "It saved us much trouble, wouldn't you agree?"

"Paige," Slater said, "have these animals done—"

"Don't worry about me," she said quickly, her voice strained as much as his. "I wish you hadn't—"

"Shut up. Both of you." Van Klees moved to the trolley and picked up a scalpel. "We have business at hand."

Zwaan raised the pole again slightly, digging the wire into Slater's neck. "You'll watch," Zwaan instructed, "from here."

"Unless I find your answers suitable, I first cut a half moon across her cheekbone," Van Klees told Slater. Van Klees laid the edge of the scalpel on Paige's face. "Then I peel the skin back. It should make for an interesting flap when her face festers."

Slater exhaled a long breath, fighting the pain inflicted by Zwaan.

"Yes?" Van Klees asked, his voice silky.

Slater grunted a yes.

Zwaan eased the pressure.

"Have you reported the kids to anyone?" Van Klees asked.

"No." Slater's voice was uneven.

Van Klees twisted the scalpel slightly and applied pressure to Paige's cheek. A pinprick of blood swelled into a large drop. "No?"

"No!"

"I could carve an eyeball too," Van Klees said. "You'll notice the restraining straps that will lock her head into position. There's a hydrostatic pressure in an eyeball that gives a satisfying pop, almost like squeezing a grape until it bursts."

"There is a package in the mail," Slater said. "To a reporter friend of mine."

"His address?"

Slater supplied it.

"You're certain?" Van Klees nicked her skin again. "After the eyeballs, I can always slit her nostrils. None of these little pleasures will come close to killing her. Imagine the fun I'll have. And I'll still have the rest of her body as a playground."

"I'm certain." Slater's fists were clenched.

"The boy, of course, is with your mother."

"Yes."

Van Klees arched an eyebrow. "My, my," he said, "aren't you amazed at our thoroughness?"

Slater said nothing.

Zwaan jerked the wire upward again.

"Yes," Slater said mechanically, "I am amazed at your thoroughness."

"As I thought," Van Klees said. "Did you tell your mother anything?"

"Only to keep the boy until I showed up."

"You're certain? If I later discover you've lied, this sow will be back on the table. My scalpel, after all, is thirsty."

"I am certain." Slater's voice had become dull with defeat.

"Excellent," Van Klees said. He turned his next question toward Zwaan.

"Weapons?"

"A pistol," Zwaan said. "Very clumsily hidden. I'd have found it even without the metal detector."

Van Klees shook his head sadly. "Not much of a hero, is he?"

"He won't be much of anything," Zwaan said.

"True, true," Van Klees agreed absently. He looked at his watch. "Zwaan, I have a flight to catch. I trust you'll take care of the reporter and the mail?"

Zwaan nodded. "Tomorrow."

Van Klees shook his head for Slater's benefit. "How does it feel to sentence a friend to death?"

Slater merely closed his eyes. The blood on his upper lip had begun to cake. He was a man beaten.

"Zwaan," Van Klees said as he unstrapped Paige with brisk, efficient movements, "I'll be gone most of the week. It's nice to know we can both go back to business as usual. Yes?"

"Of course."

"Get up," Van Klees commanded Paige. "You're going back. Home to the ward."

Paige rolled off the table and stood. She ignored Van Klees, walked to Slater and wordlessly touched his bruised face.

Van Klees grabbed her elbow and pushed her ahead.

"Remember, Zwaan," he called as he led her through the door into the hallway, "Slater is yours, as long as you leave him alive for the good doctor."

Handcuffed, stumbling down the hallway ahead of the monster he now knew as Zwaan, wearing tight steel wire around his neck that directed each of his movements, Slater Ellis knew he was dead.

Until then, Slater had rarely given his own death any thought, except on airplanes where he'd often decided from his fragile perch above the clouds that there would be a special horror in having time to anticipate the exact moment of death's arrival. If the airplane began a nosedive in a sudden loss of power, you'd have two, three, maybe five minutes as the plane fell from thirty-three thousand feet—time measured in heartbeats until you and the rest of the passengers and the tons of steel and rubber shredded into unidentifiable pieces against unyielding granite. What would you think during that numbing plunge, your body still intact and unhurt, your mind still able to comprehend the event? The dive, with spilled coffee and flying briefcases and terrified screams, would not leave you enough time to prepare for death. Yet—cruelly—it would leave you with far too much time to wait for impact.

If you had to die healthy, you'd want it to be so sudden you had no comprehension of its arrival—a bullet from an unseen sniper or a sudden head-on highway collision in a fog.

Next worst after a plane crash, Slater decided, would be death by scheduled execution. You could look at your watch and see each second sweep you closer to the moment of unimaginable oblivion. You'd try to distract yourself by reliving memories and loves or by clutching at hatreds, but wouldn't your mind always return to the waiting noose, firing squad, or body-arching voltage of an electric chair?

And now Slater was in that situation.

Healthy, very much wanting to live, but certain of his impending death. And worse, knowing by the satisfied grunts of the monster behind him, understanding by the handcuffs and wire around his neck he was totally helpless, that his death would be far messier and infinitely slower than the crash of an airplane or the jerk of a neck snapping to the body's weight against a noose.

His thoughts during this slow, grotesque procession of two surprised Slater.

He was dimly aware of the ache of his windpipe, the ghost sensation of the monster's fingers crushing his throat. His head throbbed from where he'd slammed it against the wall. Blood still clung copper to his lips and tongue. Yet he wasn't protesting the inventory of his physical complaints.

Nor was he clammy with fear.

He was thinking of God. Of spirit. Of soul. He'd soon find out the answer to the biggest question to haunt his species. Life after death or not?

The chorus of a childhood Sunday school song began to ring through his head. *Jesus loves me, this I know, for the Bible tells me so.*

Another part of his mind found it almost amusing that the tune had begun to play. From what depths of subconsciousness had it found release? Hadn't Slater done his best to rely only on himself?

Yes, Jesus loves me. Yes, Jesus loves me...

Dying was an ancient process, Slater told himself. His own death would not be unique.

...the Bible tells me so.

But death would be unique to him, wouldn't it? The only experience he couldn't anticipate or understand by asking others who gone through it. Or research. Or practice for. Or hire someone else to do for him.

Or delay.

Each step was taking him closer. He walked with almost an anticipation of curiosity and dread.

Slater imagined a flood of light on the other end. A flood of love. He prayed it was that simple. And prayed he might be forgiven for taking so long to pray for it. And he prayed for Paige.

He found strength in it. He prayed during the couple of hundred steps it took for the monster behind him to lead him—with a twisting yank of the steel wire—into a room with well-lit glass aquariums on plain tables.

When Slater saw the snakes and spiders and scorpions in the various aquariums and understood the possible implications, he prayed to hold on to the song in his head.

Zwaan heard his own music as he felt a glow of pleasure. He'd enjoyed watching Slater's body become very still at the sight of the aquariums in the first room. He'd enjoyed explaining how Slater could expect to die if there was any resistance to the punishment he deserved for ripping away Zwaan's fingers. And he would enjoy telling Slater not to expect the mercy of death until a doctor appeared to relieve him of his vital organs.

Now they were in Zwaan's favorite room. The one with a sledgehammer in the corner and two chairs facing each other.

"Sit," Zwaan said. He lowered the aluminum pole slightly to give the wire slack. Slater sat.

Zwaan continued to lower the aluminum pole.

"You may take the wire from your neck now."

Slater reached awkwardly with both hands and raised the wire over his head. Zwaan set the pole in the corner. Beside the sledgehammer.

He enjoyed watching Slater's eyes focus on the sledgehammer. Violin strings now, the wonderful notes of French horns as the symphony in Zwaan's head began to harmonize.

Zwaan took the chair opposite Slater and leaned forward. Zwaan, of course, knew how much he would enjoy this part too.

"Just you and me," Zwaan said. "Rather intimate. But so is the sharing of pain. You created a bond when," Zwaan lifted his bandaged hand, "you brought me my pain. Now we shall deepen the intimacy."

"You want me to cut your other fingers off?" Slater asked in a conversational tone. "Although I should warn you, I've never been real big on kinkiness."

"My fingers?" Zwaan asked in disbelief. The music jarred out of tune. He lashed out in sudden rage across the short distance between the chairs. Rage at the man's insolence. Rage at the man's lack of fear. Rage that he hadn't broken the man's spirit.

Zwaan's blow knocked Slater and his chair backward. Zwaan stood and reached for the center of Slater's handcuffs, jerking the man to his feet. Still holding the handcuffs with his good hand, keeping Slater a stationary, helpless target, Zwaan raised his bandaged hand in threat. He struck, however, with his elbow instead of his stumped hand, delivering a blow that crunched across Slater's cheekbone and nose. Only Zwaan's one-handed grip on the handcuffs kept Slater upright. Zwaan struck twice more.

Slater sagged, unconscious.

Zwaan set the chair upright and propped Slater back into place. He sat himself and had to wait five minutes for Slater's eyelids to flicker. Another couple of minutes for the eyes to open. By then, the side of Slater's face had swollen angry purple.

Zwaan's anger had not faded. "Take off your left shoe," Zwaan ordered. "Then the sock. Now. Without question."

Slater blinked comprehension.

Zwaan felt some peace return and heard the faint sound of violins again as Slater acted without resistance. It took some time. Slater wobbled as he leaned forward. His handcuffs restricted his movement, but eventually he had one foot bare on the floor in front of them.

"Good," Zwaan said. He stood, and took the sledgehammer from the corner. "I am about to break your little toe."

Zwaan felt his smile broaden as he began to explain his favorite part. "There is a condition. If you pull your foot back as I swing, I will break another toe, one for each time you try to avoid your punishment. Understand?"

"What goes on here?" Slater asked. "Why the kids?"

Anger briefly tempted Zwaan again. Hadn't he done enough to generate fear in this man? Then Zwaan realized the man was merely trying to stall the swing of the hammer. Zwaan liked that.

He raised the sledgehammer and watched the man flinch. Why not toy with the mouse? Zwaan set the hammer down again.

"What goes on here is a remarkable setup," Zwaan said. "By donating organs, you will become another contributor."

Zwaan noticed the man's intake of breath at the word *organs*.

"You won't die this session," Zwaan said. "No freezer can preserve your organs as efficiently as you can by simply remaining alive until the doctor arrives. You look in reasonable shape. We should be able to get as high as ten grand for your heart. All told, I wouldn't be surprised if you bring us a hundred grand."

"The kids?" Slater asked. "Organ donors? This is a farm to raise humans for harvest?"

Zwaan brought the hammer down, correctly guessing where Slater might pull his foot. The edge of the hammer's head thunked across two toes, and Slater screamed a piercing cry of agony.

Zwaan waited until Slater's eyes were open again. Wonderful, how pain made the man gasp for air. Wonderful, the music that accompanied the gasp.

"Harvest is inconsequential," Zwaan said. "Just another source of funding. One that gives efficiency to the necessity of certain deaths here. Yours, for example."

"The boys?" Slater persisted. Tears streamed down his cheeks. "Why? What?"

"I'm tired of this game," Zwaan said. "Remember my fingers? I've decided, in return, to break all your toes. Then all your fingers."

He swung down, but this time missed Slater's involuntary jerk of his foot.

"Close your eyes," Zwaan said. He was warm again with his total control over the man. "If I swing and miss again, I'll break your kneecap."

The man closed his eyes.

Zwaan knew then he'd finally broken the man. The symphony was bringing him to rapture.

Zwaan broke Slater's middle two toes with his next swing. The following swing, however, he swung and deliberately missed. The hammer thumped the floor and the man cried out in fear. Excruciatingly joyful, this cat-and-mouse stuff.

"Don't pass out on me," Zwaan said, his voice almost gentle with love. "I'll only wait until you come to again."

The man didn't open his eyes.

Zwaan broke Slater's final toe on that foot.

"Open your eyes," Zwaan said.

The man's chest was heaving in his efforts to contain his agony.

Zwaan looked closely into the man's eyes, satisfying himself that he was extracting suitable payment for the stumps beneath his bandage. He was tempted to thank this man for providing such good music.

"Next foot," Zwaan said. Zwaan crouched in front of the man. Zwaan wanted to reach out and touch the man's face, wanted to absorb some of the pain, bring the intimate music back.

"Next foot," Zwaan repeated. "Remove the shoe and sock on your other foot."

The man stooped downward to fumble at his shoe. He removed it with great difficulty. Zwaan moved closer, hoping to take in the warmth of the man's sobbing breath. Zwaan wasn't worried about Slater's reach. The man's spirit was broken, he was feebled by pain, hobbled by handcuffs. Zwaan could swat aside any blow he attempted.

"Good, good," Zwaan urged as the man began to roll down his sock.

The man croaked something, but his mouth faced the floor and the sound from his swollen lips was lost.

Zwaan lifted the man's chin. Why not enjoy the sight of his battered face? Let the music rise again.

"Repeat yourself," Zwaan ordered.

The man struggled to work his tongue and lips into words.

Zwaan was smiling at those efforts when he noticed the man had stopped fumbling with his sock.

Zwaan looked down.

For a moment, he couldn't place the unfamiliar shape. A small gray plastic tube. Almost like a small bottle of hair spray, the size a woman might keep in her purse.

As the object registered in Zwaan's mind, the man brought his hands up and pointed it at Zwaan.

Mace. Plastic. Unnoticed by a metal detector.

Zwaan took in a breath of protest and disbelief as the spray hit his open eyes and face.

There was no delay of pain, not like when this man had slammed the door across his fingers. Zwaan took the fire into his nostrils and throat and eyes, and yelled torment at the knives of demons that choked him and sent him stumbling backward, clutching at his face and throat.

The man was on him. Zwaan's eyes didn't tell him that, not with the blinding streaks of white flames in his vision. But the man's weight was on his chest, and he was pumping more of the mace into Zwaan's mouth and throat as he sobbed for air.

Then, without warning, the man was off his chest again, and Zwaan was free to roll into the chairs, desperate to shake off the agony that filled his focus. The bouncing of the chairs registered vaguely as Zwaan roared and kicked liked a trussed man galvanized by electrical shock.

His roar was more than a man fighting the flashclap of unexpected shock and pain. Zwaan was falling back into the memory of another fire, one that had scorched his throat, ruined his vocal cords, melted the skin of his face into the wax horror he faced in the mirror each day—falling back into the nightmare that had defined his every waking moment since.

And this fire, like the first one, seemed like an eternity of hell until, unbelievably, a new source of pain reached him, one brighter and sharper than the agony in his lungs and throat and nose and eyes. The new pain circled his neck, cutting into his consciousness with the intensity of a laser.

Then he understood.

The man had dropped the steel wire over Zwaan's head and was raising the pole.

Zwaan whimpered as he felt himself falling into a deep, black void. He should not have wasted the air.

When she first heard the scratching of metal against metal, Paige sat huddled beneath a blanket, knees curled to her chest, staring as mindlessly as she could straight ahead.

She had this half of the ward and all of her misery to herself. Louise, who had recognized and respected Paige's mood, was in the middle kitchen area, helping to prepare vegetables for lunch. The other women, who never spoke to her anyway, were on the opposite side of the ward, past the kitchen area, tending to the children.

The scratching returned. It irritated Paige, took her away from her blankness. She turned her head to locate the source of the sound.

It came from the door handle.

A sliding scratch. Almost as if someone were searching for the right key to open the door.

The scratching quit.

She was just turning her head away from the door when she caught movement. Very slight movement. The door was opening, but slowly and cautiously.

The crack widened.

Paige lost some of her apathy and frowned in concentration. Was this another cruel game from the prison keepers?

Without warning, a hand and finger appeared. The finger beckoned her to the door, then quickly withdrew.

Paige almost laughed.

The finger appeared, beckoned her again, and disappeared again.

Paige furtively checked around her—which added to the comedy. For that reason, she felt the hint of a smile on her face as she set the blanket down and stepped into her slippers on the floor.

At the door, she heard a whispered voice.

"If it's clear, step outside."

The whisper gave her no clue to the speaker's identity. That, however, didn't matter. Her prison keepers would not stoop to these games, and the hallway was one step closer to freedom.

Her back to the door, Paige checked to make sure she wasn't observed. Still facing the ward, she pulled the door open and stepped backward into the hallway. Only when she was completely in the hallway with the door closed did she turn to the mystery person.

"Slater!"

Her low, startled cry was involuntary for two reasons. First, she hadn't expected to see Slater again, not when her last view of him had been in handcuffs with the steel noose around his neck.

Her second reason was the damage to his face. His nose was twisted and smeared with blood. His cheekbone dark and swollen.

Slater tried an awkward grin. "Usually I dress up for a date."

"What? How?" Paige stopped herself. She glanced up and down the hallway. "Will they find—"

"I think we're safe," Slater said. "For now. I haven't seen anyone in the hallways. At the other end is a laboratory, but if we stay away from it, we should be all right."

Paige let out a deep breath. Still, she couldn't fight the urge to look for a closet, anywhere to talk where they wouldn't be seen.

"The big one?" she asked. "He's not looking for you?"

With his sleeve, Slater wiped at a small line of blood running down his cheek. Paige noticed the entire sleeve was soaked dark red.

"No," he said. He grimaced. "I left him in another room. Hands and feet wired together. We should be fine."

"But how did you manage to take him?"

He shook his head. "Let me explain later, all right?"

She nodded.

"I want out of here," he said, "and I think I know how."

Slater pulled a small gadget from his pocket. It resembled a television remote control. "I took it from Zwaan's pocket. I'm pretty sure this will bring the elevator down to us."

"We can't go yet," Paige said. She pointed at the door to the ward. "We need to take another woman from in there. Her husband is the—"

"County sheriff," Slater finished.

"You spoke to her?"

"No. To the sheriff. I found him in another room. Long story, but we found out we were on the same side. He also asked about her, said he knew she'd been taken."

"He's *here?*"

Slater nodded.

"Louise didn't know," Paige said. "She kept praying he'd find us."

"He's here," Slater repeated. "Along with the professor." He took a hesitant half step.

"Will you come with me?" he asked. "I could use your help."

She appreciated that he hadn't taken her by the elbow to lead her. And she appreciated that he hadn't told her to follow.

She moved to his side. He clutched at her shoulder as he took his next step.

"Sorry," he said. "My foot's had better days."

That's when she saw his foot was bare, the toes bloody and swollen like obscene sausages. She glanced into his eyes to see if he would explain, and she saw his forehead, untouched by ugly bruises, was bone white and popping with sweat.

He didn't explain.

It made her want to trust him, but she couldn't shake what she knew about the attempted murder and his leaving his wife.

They moved down the hallway in tandem, with him leaning on her as he hobbled.

"I was looking for you," he explained, "when I found the professor and the sheriff. They're chained to the wall. We need to find something to bust them loose. Once we get them and the sheriff's wife and the boys..."

"The boys are in a ward," Paige said.

"Other boys too?"

"You wouldn't believe it if I told you. One place for babies. One for children."

"Guards inside?"

"No," Paige said.

"Good," he grunted as they made slow progress. She couldn't tell if it was a grunt of pain or of satisfaction. "Let's check some more rooms. To free Austad and the sheriff we need pliers, an ax. Anything to remove bolts or cut through steel wire."

"You're not afraid we'll get caught?"

"Definitely. I keep expecting soldiers behind every door I open. But this floor is a ghost town." He managed a chuckle. "Plus I took my gun back from the big—"

He stumbled and she had to take his full weight to keep him from falling.

"Put your arm over my shoulder," she said.

"Notice I kept the beat-up side of my face away from you," Slater said. "This way you can admire my better profile."

"With lines like that, I imagine you're fighting off women all the time."

"How do you think my face got hurt in the first place?"

It took another twenty slow, halting steps to reach the next door.

Slater fumbled with the keys in his right hand. "Another donation from the pockets of the big guy," he explained. "Only he wasn't awake to accept my thanks."

Paige wondered exactly what had happened but didn't ask.

Slater was already cautiously trying a key in the lock. It took four or five tries until he finally unlocked the door.

He opened this one the same manner as he'd opened the door to the ward. No light greeted them as the crack between door and door frame widened.

"No people," he whispered. "I keep hoping I'll run into a janitor's closet or something like that. Maybe we'll get lucky with this one."

He reached inside the door and felt around for a light switch.

Paige tensed. People or no, she didn't feel comfortable with this search of the unknown.

With a click, light flooded the room.

It took her several moments to absorb what she saw.

"The jars!" she gasped and turned her head away from Slater and retched.

The clear glass jars were arranged in ascending size on dozens of shelves. The smallest were labeled vials; the largest, at the far end of the room, were too large for shelves. Almost as big as water barrels, more than a dozen jars rested on the floor, the mouths of the jars almost as wide as the jars themselves.

Each was made of clear glass and filled with clear liquid. The effect, especially with the light passing through the curves of the larger jars, was to magnify the contents of each jar, much as thick lenses in a pair of glasses will present bulging eyes to the world.

And it was such eyes in each jar that drew Slater.

For a moment, he was oblivious to the throbbing pain of his toes, to the feeling of cold floor beneath his bare foot. He forgot the grating pain of a cheekbone probably broken, forgot the urgency to escape. Because the eyes drew him in the same way as the cold, winding slither of a snake draws a chill of total, fascinated attention.

The eyes belonged to agonized faces that screamed silently from the liquid that preserved the motionless, suspended bodies.

"My dear God," Paige whispered. She said it as a beseeching prayer. For her. For the children in each of the jars. Children, stooped so that their knees pushed against their chests, large enough to fill the huge barrel jars with their contorted limbs. Children no more than toddlers in medium jars. Babies in smaller jars. Children in various stages of fetal development in the tiny jars closest to the door.

Slater became aware of her hold on his arm. "Step outside," he said. "Step outside and wait. If you see anyone, knock twice."

She didn't move, frozen by horror. He gently pushed her toward the open door. Slater did not want to remain in the room, but he needed to understand its purpose, if only to comprehend what might be at the root of this demented evil.

She was beginning to shake as he left her.

Slater fought nausea and forced himself to walk to the far end of the room. He breathed shallowly and rapidly, trying to maintain his composure.

In a college biology laboratory, he'd seen jars of preserved specimens. Mice, cats, monkeys. The animals, fur matted and eyes squinted shut, appeared oblivious to death. In a suspended peace. Dead to injected poison before reaching their transparent tombs.

These faces had mouths open, expressions contorted as if they hadn't been granted the mercy of quick death. He told himself it was an illusion that they appeared to be trying to claw their way out of their eternal prisons. Only because these were human specimens, he forcefully resolved, was he letting his imagination run wild.

Ignore them, he commanded himself. *Check the labels. What did the labels read?*

He kneeled to examine the sparse, typewritten notations on the square white label of the jar in front of him. There were only two lines, centered neatly. The top line gave a number. The bottom line a date.

On one knee, and against his will, he raised his eyes to the boy within.

Slater heard a cry of surprise. Brief, high, keening. His.

The boy's face, his hair floating upward, was identical to the triplets. And a tattoo was plain across this boy's forehead.

Number 73. Matches the number on the label.

Slater bit his knuckle to regain his composure. He stood, walked down the line of jars on the shelf, hardly daring to look. Each brief glance confirmed the worst.

As the jars grew smaller, and so the boys inside, the face of each boy became a miniaturized version of the boy before him.

Numbered boys, identical to each other, killed at different stages of growth.

In silence, Slater began to cry when he reached the toddlers. Perfectly formed. Tiny fingernails on hands curled in futility. Ears and noses delicately sculpted to perfection. The open screaming mouths showed first teeth jutting through small gums. Each jar with a cold, heartless label.

Slater would have stopped there; he could not stomach an examination of the series of fetuses that progressed to a newborn baby, his umbilical cord still in place. But something about one fetus caught his eye.

Number 27. Slater was far from expert on the subject, but could guess this fetus to be halfway through its term. What caught his eye was the hands of the fetus. All three of them. The left arm completely normal. The right arm's wrist ended in two hands.

Slater was too stunned to react. He stared at the fetus, trying to accept what he saw. He could not.

He scanned the jars.

Number 25—and he hated himself for thinking of them as numbers—had a noseless face. Another had legs webbed together.

Slater tore his gaze away from the jars. His tears had stopped now. Cold, implacable rage filled him.

Slater began to think with his head instead of with his heart.

He moved in awkward hops to return to the barrel-sized jars. He needed a label but could not bear to take one from a smaller jar. If this was part of science, the label would correspond to notes somewhere. Whoever carried those notes would answer for this. On earth and in hell.

Slater kept his weight off his broken toes and kneeled again. He began to peel a corner of the label and noticed a streak of dullness on the side of the jar. He shifted to examine the streak at a different angle. With the new perspective, he saw the streak to be the residue of dried liquid.

It puzzled him.

He noticed several other streaks, as if tears had run down the jar the same way tears had run unchecked down his face.

Slater couldn't help his nature. Curiosity always made him question cause-and-effect. *What could have led to the rivulets?*

The boy's eyes gazed sightlessly at Slater.

Then Slater understood.

Overflow. The liquid inside had overflown the jar.

But why would someone so neat and precise as to order the jars in ascending size be so sloppy in adding the preservative liquid inside the jars?

Slater's rage grew with his horror.

The open eyes, the faces contorted by screams, the clawing hands. They weren't illusion.

Slater buried his face in his hands as the horror of each boy's death washed over him. When he raised his head again, he felt the strength of the rage within him overcome his pain.

These boys, forever blind in the clarity of their prisons, couldn't see him now. The last sight each boy had registered would have been the face of whoever forced them inside. He vowed the killer would be brought to light for other eyes, living eyes, to bear witness to the punishment paid for these dead boys.

For the liquid had not been added to the jars after the boys. No. The jars had already been filled, then the boys pushed inside. Alive. Head pushed under, liquid gushing over, and the lid of the jar screwed into place.

"We leave all of this the way we found it," Slater told Paige. He hadn't winced during his hobbled walk to meet her in the hallway. She knew the pain should have staggered him. It hadn't. "We break out quietly. Then send the television crews back. Today. Government or not, this *will* end."

His face blazed with determined anger. Paige was glad it wasn't directed at her.

She also noticed he didn't need her for support as they moved down the hallway. Nor did he cautiously open each new door. Almost as if he welcomed the possibility of a fight.

They tried five more doors. Ironically, when they found what they needed, it wasn't locked inside a room. It hung near the end of the hallway behind a sheet of glass, partially hidden by a coiled length of fire hose. A fire ax.

Slater grabbed the ax.

"Come meet Del," he said. He saw the puzzlement on her face. "Louise's husband. You'll be glad he's on our side."

All four of them were going back to the ward when Zwaan surprised them. He stepped from a doorway and grinned at them. The massive scar on his face twisted the grin horribly.

Paige and Slater stopped midstep. Behind them, Ben Austad and Del Silverton weren't completely free of the steel cable that had bound them to their beds. With massive swings of the ax, Slater had only been able to sever the centers of their hobbles. Pieces of cable, ends glinting silver from the ax cuts, still dangled from their wrists and ankles.

Del, carrying the fire ax, reacted instantly. He pushed between Paige and Slater.

"Drop the ax," Zwaan rasped. His horrible grin remained in place.

"Drop dead," Del told him. "And if you need help, I'll be glad to assist."

Del hefted the ax and shifted forward only a couple of inches. Armed or not, he knew he needed to respect Zwaan's capabilities.

"You *will* do as he says," a voice with a curious lilt said from behind the group. "Drop the ax, or I shoot the woman."

Del didn't take his eyes off Zwaan. "Slater?" Del asked.

"It's not a bluff," Slater replied. "She's got a gun."

Del dropped the ax at his own feet.

"She's from the ward," Paige added bitterly. "Her name is Velma. She must have noticed I was gone."

"Of course," Velma said. "It's so much easier to watch the prisoners when they do not realize the jailer is among them. Or when they think the jailer is stupid, nice. It gave me great joy to release my friend from his bonds."

Slater had turned his back on Del and Zwaan and, facing Velma, moved between her and Paige. Velma brought her gun up and pointed it steadily at Slater's forehead.

"It matters little to me whether I shoot you or the woman," Velma said.

"I'd rather it was me," Slater said as he backed into Paige's stomach, keeping his hands high. Paige couldn't believe Slater. Was he making a move on her, pressing against her so firmly?

"Just you and me," Del was saying to Zwaan at the other end of the group. "How about it, freak?"

"I'd like that, even with only one hand," Zwaan said. "You are just big enough to make it satisfying."

Slater continued to press back against Paige. Then she felt it. A hard lump against her stomach. It finally clicked. He'd tucked the pistol in the back of his pants.

Velma's gun hadn't wavered.

"However," Zwaan said to Del. "I'll take my satisfaction by watching the doctor remove your organs. Lie on the floor and put your hands behind your back."

Zwaan raised his voice. "Professor, find the gun in Slater's pockets. Then remove it slowly. Velma, if either man makes a false move, shoot."

He focused on Del. "Lie down. If you don't, Velma pulls the trigger."

Austad stepped with reluctance toward Slater. He reached out to pat his front pockets.

Paige, hardly believing this was happening, moved her hand in front of her and furtively plucked the pistol from Slater's belt. The grip was in her palm and she was asking herself how she could actually shoot another human being, when Zwaan noticed the movement of her arm.

"Velma!" Zwaan said with sharp urgency as he drew the right conclusion. "The woman! Watch the—"

For a month the year before, in her previous life as a doting wife and social climber, Paige had joined her trendy friends in shooting lessons invariably followed by catty café au lait sessions. She remembered enough not to panic. She pulled the gun clear and reached around Slater, shooting upward from his hip, trusting that the instructors hadn't lied about point-and-shoot from close range.

Velma's eyes widened as she tried to react, but Paige had already pulled the trigger. The pistol barked. Velma spun back as if kicked by an invisible horse.

Slater pushed off his good foot, diving for Velma's gun arm.

Del did the same in the opposite direction, ramming his bulk forward to wrap his arms around Zwaan's waist. Del's weight slammed Zwaan into the wall.

Slater had managed to land across Velma's arm, was reaching for the gun in her hand. But he found no resistance. The bullet had pulverized Velma's shoulder, shattering the arm socket.

Zwaan brought a giant fist down on the back of Del's neck.

Slater rolled to his feet, Velma's gun in his hand, his shirt soaked with her blood while Velma writhed in silent agony.

Roaring and straightening his knees, Del tried to lift Zwaan off the ground. Zwaan punched downward again.

The professor had managed to get the ax in his hands, but stared helplessly at the two giant gladiators. Paige, too, held her weapon, unable to pull the trigger on Zwaan.

Slater understood why. He hesitated with Velma's gun for the same reason.

The fighters were whirling, tumbling, shifting, and sliding, making Zwaan an impossible target.

"Del!" Slater yelled. "Back off! Back off!"

The blood lust of rage had taken both giants, and they fought and cursed, oblivious to their spectators. Zwaan managed to wrap his arms around Del. The bandage of Zwaan's injured hand was sodden with blood.

Slater joined Paige. He found himself panting with the adrenaline coursing through his body. "If he drops Del, don't hesitate. Fire to kill. Fire until he drops."

Zwaan tightened his bear hug on Del, then with a surge of linebacker power, churned his legs and kept charging. Del was fighting just to stay on his feet, and for a moment, was weightless. Zwaan's charge slammed Del back into a closed door, smashing the door off the hinges. They both fell into the room.

Slater tugged on Paige's arm, pulling her to the doorway.

Then he stopped.

Because the hallway was so institutionally unvarying, he hadn't recognized their location. At least not until he saw the inside of this room.

The glass aquariums.

"Del!" he shouted again. "Let go!"

Both giants were rising, still held together by rage. Neither could punch, and they wrestled and pulled, hoping to knock the other down. Del brought a massive arm around, catching Zwaan under the chin with a clothesline blow. Zwaan staggered back, almost caught his balance, then tripped against a table edge.

He fell backward on the table, with Del pouncing his full weight on top of him. The table tilted beneath them, sending them sliding down into the legs of the table beside it. Aquariums from both tables crashed to the ground, sending clouds of sand upward in soft mushrooms.

A furball of tarantulas from the first aquarium fell onto their bodies.

Both men roared insane fury.

Slater saw scurrying dark shapes and the pale flash of timber rattlesnakes.

Slater didn't hesitate. He backed Paige and the professor into the hallway.

Incredibly, the roaring inside grew in volume, a bellowing of bull elephants.

A scorpion skittered into the hallway. Slater crunched it dead with the heel of his shoe.

A rattlesnake moved toward them with sidewinding precision. Slater had barely begun to lift his gun when the snake's head disappeared in a spray of blood. He'd barely registered the connection between that sight and the sound of the pistol firing when Paige's voice penetrated his stunned fascination.

"I detest snakes," she said, her voice calm.

Before Slater could reply, Zwaan fell face forward through the doorway, his massive body covering the writhing rope of the headless snake. Del staggered into sight. He dropped to grind his knee into the back of Zwaan's neck.

With both hands, Del held a large rock from one of the glass aquariums above Zwaan's head. The edge of the rock already held a sheen of red.

Zwaan didn't move.

For a long moment, Del remained poised to slam his crude weapon downward. In the horrible silence, Del focused only on Zwaan, the two of them gladiators, sculpted in the final breath of battle.

Then Del realized Zwaan was dead. He let the rock roll from his fingers onto the floor.

Del swayed as he fought to get to his feet. He stumbled over the unconscious Velma, and his erratic movement took him to the far wall, where he fell, slumping down.

"You were with my wife?" he gasped to Paige.

Paige moved to join Del. She kneeled beside him, watched as his neck, blue-red, swelled visibly.

"Yes, I was with her."

She gently reached for Del's neck. He groaned and pushed her hand away. "I won't live," he said. "I know it. Critters were like a bee's nest. I been bit a dozen places."

His breathing grew shallower and faster.

"She alive?"

Paige nodded yes.

"Hurt?"

She shook her head no.

"I knew she was telling them everything I did," Del said. Now tears fell from his eyes. "A few times I told her things no one else could know, and spooksville was there. Like a test she failed."

His hands began to jerk spasmodically. Paige reached for one, pressed it between her hands. She curled her fingers around his giant hand. It was much harder to watch him die than it had been to pull the trigger on Velma.

"What I got to know is . . ." he coughed. "Why'd she do it?"

A scorpion crawled from his shirt pocket toward his opposite shoulder. Paige swallowed a scream. He wanted her attention, not her fear. The scorpion disappeared beneath his shirt collar. He neither noticed nor cared.

"Was it the photos?" His insistence was barely audible. "They show her what I did in Nam?"

Louise had frozen every time Paige had ventured into personal questions about her husband. The only thing she'd said was a bitter remark about marrying someone who'd turned out to be a stranger. Maybe she did know about Vietnam, whatever it was that had happened there.

"Come on," Del begged. He was squeezing her hands so hard it hurt. "She know about Nam?"

"No," Paige lied. "She told me they promised to kill you if she didn't help."

Del smiled with his eyes closed. "She took the heat for me."

His grip softened, then his hands fell away completely.

Fourteen

SLATER USED the rubber tip of his cane to press the cracked yellow plastic of the doorbell. Paige, beside him in the shade of the distinguished brick residence, stared straight at the door, composing herself.

Slater pressed twice more. Eventually, approaching footsteps from inside greeted his patience.

"He'll see us through the peephole," Paige whispered. "He won't open the door."

"I believe you're wrong. He'll be curious."

Twenty seconds later, the unlatching of a security chain proved Slater right. The door swung open.

"My, my. Both of you here in Chicago," Prof. Josef Van Klees said. "By the grim expressions on your faces you could pass for the caped avengers Batman and Robin Hood. I'm trembling with fear."

He smiled arrogance. "Of course, Mr. Ellis, *your* face is much worse than grim. Zwaan obviously managed to punish you a great deal before his inopportune death."

Slater pushed his way past Van Klees, limping badly as he leaned on his cane. Paige followed without hesitation.

"Oh, please," Van Klees mocked them. "Step inside. I'll just shut the door and make it nice and cozy for your elaborate plans for justice. Amuse me, will you, and begin with a phrase like 'the game's over.'"

Van Klees passed them and entered a Victorian-style sitting room.

"Brandy?" he called. "The dinner hour does approach."

Slater and Paige followed the sound of his voice. Slater didn't like it that Van Klees had taken control of the situation. When they arrived, Van Klees was already holding a large, bulbed glass in his palm, swirling the brandy to warm it.

"Well?" Van Klees arched his eyebrow. He'd framed himself between two dark-hued Dutch Master oil paintings. In his brown cashmere sweater and blue slacks every inch the elegant, composed gentleman.

Slater merely leaned on his cane and stared. Paige crossed her arms.

"You're probably disappointed I show so little surprise and fear," Van Klees said. "You wanted me to gasp and ask how you managed to find me."

"Why?" Slater asked. "All those kids. Why?"

Van Klees sipped at his brandy. "Don't be so crude. Play this out a little."

"I feel very crude," Slater said. "I'd like to kill you with my bare hands."

"Will something so Neanderthal impress you, Paige?" Van Klees's eyes glinted with amusement. "I thought you preferred to be fooled by Italian suits and obscenely large bank accounts."

"Obscene is an appropriate word to describe you," she said, voice even.

Van Klees sighed theatrically. It was obvious he enjoyed the scene. "I'll play it your way. How did you find me?"

"My husband's computer disks," Paige said. "South Carolina. We picked them up this morning."

"You knew where they were all along? I applaud you for your will power. My military connections assured me the chemicals I used during your interrogation—"

"I found them where Darby told me he'd left them."

"Really?"

"Slater asked me again about the letter I read before the package was stolen—that *was* your doing, wasn't it?"

Van Klees merely smiled.

"Darby had referred to our honeymoon," Paige said.

"How nice," Van Klees said without meaning it.

Silence.

"Come, come," Van Klees said after several more sips of brandy. "Don't you realize how this works? You tell me your secrets, I tell you my secrets, and we wrap it up with a showdown where I kill you both."

"Tell him, Paige," Slater said. "He's trying to pretend it doesn't matter, but it's driving him nuts that he didn't anticipate every detail."

"Slater thought it was a strange comment. So I told him about the first night of our honeymoon at a beach resort in South Carolina," Paige said in calm, precise tones. "And how we'd found an oak tree with a little hollow at the base of a branch. We each wrote a love letter and, without reading the other's, sealed them in plastic and placed the letters inside. We vowed to return on our twenty-fifth anniversary and open the letters and read them to each other over glasses of champagne."

"Touching, although, of course, Darby is much too dead to make his rendezvous," Van Klees said. He shrugged for Paige's benefit. "Don't worry, my dear, he disappointed me too. I'd almost begun to trust him as he helped me build my small conglomerate of corporations. But, Paige, he had you fooled for years, too, didn't he?"

Paige looked down at the floor.

"See if I miss anything," Slater said. "As John Hammond, you used the International World Relief Committee for legitimate access to Third World countries. You needed a way to steal women without having troublesome questions raised."

Van Klees poured himself another shot of brandy. "Simplicity is beauty, is it not? The confusion in refugee camps made it extremely easy. And who was around to complain, even if they could find someone to listen to their complaints?"

"As Jack Tansworth," Slater continued, "you ran an extremely profitable genetics corporation. It made some astounding break-throughs, based on some of your less public research in Los Alamos."

"It was a nice circle, actually," Van Klees said. "The better TechnoGen performed, the more money I could pour into my lit-tle Institute, and the more money I invested in the Institute, the better my returns from TechnoGen. That corporation also gave me a legitimate way to purchase some of the biological materials I needed."

"He's boasting, Paige," Slater said. "Like he's been keeping all of this so secret for so long, he's grateful to finally have an audience to appreciate it."

"My true genius was dealing with the military," Van Klees said. He reached with his free hand and patted himself on the back. "You have to understand the system. It's a setup where no one questions their superiors. The perfect pyramid. All I needed to do was reach a couple guys at the top. Do you have any idea how much money Washington wastes on projects it can only track through paperwork?"

"Fifty-five million a year in your direction," Slater said. "It's all in the disks."

"Roughly the amount the military spends each year on toilet paper. Get a couple of good old boys who see something in it for themselves, and with their connections they can siphon money any-where. Jack Tansworth promised them the perfect retirement. In return, they built me an underground Institute. The pyramid again. Everyone believes the guys at the top, right down to a faked radia-tion disaster. The generals never even had to show up. They didn't want to. They just wanted results. The soldiers had no idea what they were guarding. And if anyone checked really close, they'd find five levels of a legitimate top-secret genetics project had been funded. Only the sixth floor would never be suspected or found."

"The sixth floor. A place to raise babies and kill them."

Van Klees laughed. "Your moral outrage is amusing. Don't forget the organ harvesting. It was a wonderful little side venture I stumbled across as I looked for ways to dispose of some of the more troublesome women. Imagine my delight when I discovered the average refugee was worth so much in body parts. Ten refugees added a million dollars in gross revenue. There was some trouble in setting up a delivery network, of course, but the military was invaluable there. It helped that there already was an extensive black market across the world."

"Why?" Slater asked again. "All those kids. Why?"

"You poor man," Van Klees said with his arrogant smirk. "You could understand this if it boiled down to profit. Nothing more American than that, is there? But I'll wager the sight of my jarred specimens confused you greatly. As it did Darby Stephens. In it for profit, until the jars led him to do something stupid."

Van Klees drained the last of his brandy. His voice hardened. "Money? I couldn't think of anything less challenging than to accumulate money. Everything I did with real estate as John Hammond showed that. No, true genius lies in how you use money to achieve your goals."

He paused. Madness began to shine from his eyes as his voice grew stronger to match his sudden, terse pacing. "My goal? It so far exceeds any milestone in the history of mankind that in comparison, Christopher Columbus will be a boy who played on the beach and Neil Armstrong's first step on the moon will seem like a baby learning to walk."

He grinned, stretching the skin of his face tight across his bones. "Most delightful of all, I'll be around to enjoy my own legend and accolades."

He stopped his passionate monologue and frowned, as if unable to comprehend that Paige and Slater were not appreciative.

"Fools," he said, "my gift to myself and to mankind shall be nothing less than immortality."

"Even if immortality were possible," Slater said after an incredulous pause, "I'd like to point out it's a little late for your project. You might remember the television newscasts late yesterday and today? How every major network calls this the story of the century? All the headlines about an FBI search for the mystery man behind it?"

Van Klees furrowed his brow in a gentlemanly fashion and touched his chin thoughtfully with his index finger. "Which proves my point exactly about fools. Did you read the editorial in USA Today? The moron compared my genetics research to Icarus, with no concept at all of where I am headed."

"Were headed," Slater said. "It's over. Your wings are torched."

"I will admit you have delayed my goal somewhat," Van Klees said. "But immortality is still easily within my grasp."

He pointed at two wicker chairs. "Sit. I'm sure you'll want to know how."

Neither Paige nor Slater moved.

"You asked me why," Van Klees said with sudden impatience. "You've come this far; don't quit on me now. Become my audience, and I'll tell you why."

Slater shuffled to a chair. He waited until Paige was seated until he lowered himself.

"No brandy?" Van Klees asked, charming warmth in his voice again.

"Why the kids?" Slater asked.

"Paige," Van Klees said, "surely, you don't find someone this tedious to be attractive."

"He doesn't kill boys and store them in bottles," she replied. "I like that in a man."

Van Klees exhaled another theatrical sigh. He poured himself another brandy, admired the golden liquid briefly, sipped, and began to lecture them as if they were undergrads.

"DNA. Deoxyribonucleic acid. Strands of chromosomes that

program every cell in your body. You start as a one-celled embryo, and these strands replicate again and again as your cells divide and copy themselves into the trillions, each with the original blueprint. And we've long had the technology to cut and paste these chromosomes. Cross species? Goats with sheep heads is old news. Cloning? Frogs, cattle, it's been done. What was needed was someone with the vision and guts to apply this to humans."

Van Klees bowed. "You've probably guessed, of course, at the cloning in Los Alamos. I could start with a single embryo, let it divide, then separate the unspecialized cells. By repeating the process again and again, I would have dozens of identical embryos, which I would store frozen. Again, easily available technology. An embryo can last for years, with an excellent chance of revival.

"Once I had a supply of wombs to nurture the embryos, the setup was perfect. First, I had control specimens. Three embryos, untouched, brought to full-term. Identical triplets."

"The boys," Slater said.

Van Klees nodded. "Yes. Now nearly ten years old. Each additional embryo received a minor chromosome change, letting me compare the new results to the originals."

Van Klees shrugged. "Some embryos self-destructed almost immediately. Others lasted well into gestation. Still others survived birth. I was able to judge quite closely the sections of the chromosome that dictate size, and I believe in future experiments, I will be able to produce some specimens to grow to nine, maybe ten feet at maturity." He sipped more brandy. "One, a very interesting specimen, had extremely high adrenaline production. He was twice as strong as the control specimens. I may return to tweaking that section of the chromosome. Unfortunately, his temper literally killed him at the age of two when his heart exploded. I'll need to find a way to solve that."

"I can't believe I'm hearing this," Paige said.

"Don't be barbaric," Van Klees snorted. "Try to appreciate the difficulties I went through just to set up the logistics. Some scientists work on fruit flies. Much easier. Fruit flies replicate in far greater numbers, and their generations are measured in days. Human specimens gestate over nine months and take years to mature. I had to show extreme patience."

"Why?" Slater said. "How can you justify this?"

"That isn't obvious? For the good of the human species. Any genetic change you make in an embryo will be passed on to the next generation. I was laying the groundwork for future scientists to evolve us into superhumans. Hitler tried to do it by elimination of less desirable specimens. I'm doing it by producing superior specimens. Eventually, much like *Homo sapiens* took over the Neanderthals, *Homo supersapiens* will be a much better and dominant race. In the long run, we can mold the human species to our own vision."

"For that," Slater said through clenched teeth, "you drowned the boys."

Van Klees arched an eyebrow. "Very good deduction. When there was no longer any use for a specimen, I didn't care to risk any structural changes by injecting them with a poison before preserving them. Who knows how a contaminated specimen might compromise future research? And trust me, minute examination of each of those specimens would release realms of new data. My trouble was I simply didn't have the time for that grunt work myself."

"You are insane," Paige hissed.

"A trite cliché. But fear not, I don't expect better from you. Much closer to the truth is psychopath." He smiled. "I can't expect you to understand that such definitions are merely a way for the entire whining, snapping pack to try to impose their limitations on people such as me. And because packs can represent such danger, except for rare occasions like this, I hide my brilliance."

"Psychopath bereft of conscience fits. If you had a conscience, you wouldn't experiment on humans."

"Again, my dear. Trite. Very trite. You, in the manner of so many other pathetic creatures, stubbornly cling to the quaint belief that humans have souls."

"Love," Slater said quietly. "Explain love."

The question caught Van Klees off guard.

"There is no biological explanation for love," Slater said. "No gland that dispenses it. And you talk about trillions of cells. Where in the fabric of all that complex protein would love come from if not from an invisible soul, given the miracle of life?"

"I refuse to be derailed into a discussion of such nonsense."

Slater leaned forward. "Then I assume when you mentioned immortality, you meant an immortal body, that you are one of those too poor in spirit to understand an immortal soul."

"Who cares about an immortal soul when you can have immortality through genetics?" Van Klees immediately began to glow with fervor. "Yes, we can clone embryos. The next step? Cloning from an already-mature specimen. Think of it! Every cell in the body contains all of the genetic information of the original cell. Skin cells, blood cells, each cell has the blueprint potential for the entire body. Enzymes, however—methylase enzymes—force the new cells to specialize to their various tasks. If you could stop a cell from differentiating..."

Van Klees paused for breath. He was pacing again. "I've been finding ways to repress the differentiation. Not just me. Other scientists. They've worked on frogs. It's gone so far that TechnoGen can take a single cell from an adult frog and have it begin to develop all over again, now getting as far as the tadpole stage before breaking down."

He opened his hands expansively. "Then apply the demethylase research to humans! I've been able to fool one of my own testicle cells into thinking it was as unspecialized as the embryo I once was. When I first began, I was only able to grow it from one cell to sixty-four cells before it self-destructed. Later, cells grew to the point where I could successfully implant them into the womb. One of my greatest triumphs reached the seventh week of gestation."

Van Klees saw Slater shaking his head in disgust.

"Have you no vision?" Van Klees shouted. "Once I am able to

clone myself, I will be able to replicate every single body part I need. Modern surgery makes transplantation a risk only when the body rejects the new organ. How can my body reject a duplicate of itself? Heart, lungs, kidneys, bone marrow, even arms and legs. That alone will double my life span. And within fifty years, I'm sure we will be able to do brain transplants. Imagine that! The greatest men on earth—the ones who have proven it by accumulating wealth and power—will be able to use that wealth and power to keep themselves alive. The poor and the useless wouldn't ever be able to afford to clone themselves or the expensive transplants. Another way to raise the level of our species!"

"Is that what 'Jack Tansworth' promised to your military connections?" Slater asked. "Long life?"

"Of course. Retirement like none other in the history of the military. Or humankind. I would be able to raise clones for them. An eighty-year-old with the heart of a twelve-year-old would have little fear of death!"

"Have we heard enough, Paige?"

"Too much," she told Slater.

Slater stood and unbuttoned the front of his shirt. It showed the taped wires of a recording unit.

Van Klees laughed. "Simpletons. You think I didn't anticipate something like that?"

Van Klees reached into his back pocket. He pulled out a small plastic case, half the size of a garage-door opener. "Why do you think I hopped around the country using various identifications? Each identification was a safety parachute. Police stormed my New York office for John Hammond. They'll never find him. Military people in Washington can send out their best bloodhounds for Jack Tansworth. He's gone too. All along Josef Van Klees has been preparing for this day. Huge sums previously siphoned to Swiss banks. And this morning's television publicity gave me enough warning to move the bulk of Hammond's and Tansworth's remaining funds to the same place."

He pointed at his plastic control. "This is yet another fail-safe.

On the slim—and in retrospect very real—chance you or someone else might appear here in Chicago before I was ready to leave for Europe tonight."

He mocked them with another smile. "New identity there. Enough money to continue my research. You haven't stopped me."

Van Klees used his thumb to press a button on the plastic transmitter.

"Perhaps you noticed a van parked on the street? My round-the-clock surveillance crew. As I speak to you now, two men are running to my door from the van. Not-very-nice men who are accustomed to killing people for an appropriate sum of money."

Van Klees laughed again. "All right, boys and girls. Listen for the sound of the opening door. "

Five seconds later, the front door did indeed swing open. The sound of heavy boots on hardwood floor reached them all very clearly.

The man who stepped into the sitting room wore a full military uniform, ribbons and medals pinned regulation height on his broad chest. His cap covered a massive bald head. His scowl showed razor-sharp lines radiating from dark, intense eyes.

Van Klees dropped his brandy glass, splashing liquid against his trouser cuffs.

"Thank you, Mr. Ellis," Gen. George Stanley said.

"Yes sir." Slater used his cane to push himself upward.

"My aides have recorded everything. Mr. Ellis, as promised, the conversation will reach our president. You have my word that within the year, legal guidelines will be established and enforced for all genetics experiments."

"And you have my word," Slater replied, "that your involvement will not reach the media through us."

General Stanley nodded, then turned his attention to Van Klees. "Jack—or should I call you Josef?—you seem surprised to see me. Your hired guns wisely decided my soldiers outside weren't a good risk."

Van Klees, probably unaware of it, was biting his lower lip.

"Our mutual friend here, Slater Ellis, visited me around noon in D.C.," the general continued. "He showed me some computer disks with some interesting spreadsheets, bank account figures, and my name and my involvement. At the same time he asked me what I would do if I had three identities and two of those identities were wanted men, and how I might react knowing my third and much safer identity had access to millions of dollars in another part of the world. Funny thing is, I told him I'd probably make a run for it. What a coincidence. Seems you were thinking the same thing, Jack." The general waved his hand as if brushing away a fly. "Or John. Or Josef."

General Stanley unbuttoned his holster and withdrew his pistol. "Jack, Mr. Ellis didn't come to me to make any blackmail money, although he knows and I know he probably could have named his price. He came to me because he thought if I had any blame in what had happened, perhaps I would also like the chance to undo as much of it as I could."

With the pistol safely pointing at the floor, General Stanley slid back the bolt. "I'm dying of cancer, Jack. You know that, don't you? Money means nothing to me. I can now understand deathbed confessions, the urge to die with a good conscience. Even if my soul rots in hell along with yours, I wanted a chance at death with honor, Jack. So Mr. Ellis and I, we made a trade. He got what he wanted. Me? I'll get to try to salvage my honor."

General Stanley lifted the pistol and pointed it directly at Van Klees's head.

"Mr. Ellis, you have the necessary papers," Stanley said without taking his gaze away from Van Klees.

"I do, sir."

"Please hand them to the professorly looking type across the room who has just emptied his bladder in a very cowardly manner."

Slater extended a pen, too, to Van Klees. "Darby had a pretty good record of your bank accounts. I have some money background of my own, and it didn't take long to get these financial documents by fax. Sign at the Xs. This will discharge all the funds into my care. You should be happy knowing the money will be used to help all the women and children who survived your Los Alamos base."

Van Klees signed without protest.

General Stanley lowered the pistol.

"Good-bye, General," Slater said. He hobbled at Paige's side as they began to leave the two men alone in the sitting room.

"Those papers will be useless," Van Klees finally managed to say. "Any lawyer will prove they were signed under duress. I'll be using that money to fight my legal battles."

The general raised his gun again. Neither Slater nor Paige hesitated. They'd promised to give him privacy.

"Jack," the general said as they reached the hallway. "You are forgetting that all I have left is my honor. There won't be a legal battle. Not for you. Not for me."

Paige closed the door behind them. They hadn't reached the steps to the lawn before the first shot rang clear and loud behind them.

The second shot followed closely.

"Are you all right?" Slater asked her.

"I told you earlier," she said. "I detest snakes."

They were driving along Lake Shore Drive, the highrise apartments throwing long, evening shadows that almost reached the waters of Lake Michigan to their immediate left.

"That's that?" Slater finally said to break a long silence.

"That's that," she said.

More silence.

Slater figured maybe five more minutes before they reached the downtown loop and then the Eisenhower Expressway out to O'Hare. He figured on the expressway their departure would gain momentum, and she'd be out of his life.

"I've noticed a lot of women over thirty consider any guy who's single, straight, has a steady job, doesn't beat women, and keeps his fingernails clean a good catch."

She turned her stare out toward the white sails cutting the horizon of the darkening lake. "You saying I look desperate to find a man?"

"I'm trying to be funny. Blame it on nerves."

Finally she reacted. She turned away from the lake and gave him a smile. "You? Nerves?"

Slater braked for a traffic light. "In case you didn't notice," he said, "I'm throwing myself at your feet."

He said it dryly, hoping the contrast between his exaggeration and tone would amuse her.

Strangely, her face seemed to grow bitter as she considered him. "I may be pregnant."

He nodded and pursed his lips, like suddenly he understood. Although he didn't. "Maybe we should pull over somewhere, grab a coffee," he said.

The smile partially returned to her eyes. "I'm glad you said coffee," she said, "not latté or cappuccino."

"So, have you known the guy long?" Slater asked, fighting the sinking feeling in his heart.

"Which guy?" Paige hadn't touched her coffee. To Slater, she looked great, her hair highlighted by the sun shining through the restaurant window at a low angle across her face.

"Which guy? The, um, father."

"How can it matter? He's dead."

"Darby?"

Silence again. A tightness grew around her eyes. She stared directly at him and spoke without flinching. "No, not Darby. The guy the general just killed."

Slater tried to comprehend.

"You know," she said. "Hammond. Tansworth. Van Klees. Whatever name he decided to die under."

Slater now did comprehend and didn't like it. "You mean what he said about falling for Italian suits and obscene bank accounts...? You and he actually...?"

She giggled. "Slater, you should see the look on your face. Like you're swallowing a cactus and trying to pretend it doesn't hurt."

Just as suddenly as she had giggled, she became serious. "No," she said, "not like that. It was when he had me in the operating room. Remember? When he was going to cut up my face if you didn't tell him what he wanted."

"Yeah," he said. "I remember."

"It happened then, Slater."

His hands around his coffee cup tightened. She noticed and half smiled.

"Not like that," she said. "He did it like a doctor, implanting an embryo the way they do it in hospitals when a women gets...," Paige took a deep breath. She was not going to cry, "when a woman gets artificially inseminated."

They let restaurant chatter around them fill their next silence. The waiter came with refills, gave them a dirty look because they'd decided not to order any food.

"There's a moderate chance he was successful. If I'm pregnant, I'm going to keep it."

"Was it an embryo he experimented on?" Slater asked.

"From what he said, I don't think so," she answered. "But does that matter? The embryo is a baby. A human. Unless it develops in such a way that birth becomes impossible..."

Slater wisely just listened as she struggled with obviously powerful emotions.

"Look," she finally said, "I didn't really know I was going to keep it until I heard what you said today. I'd been telling myself I'm Christian and all that, but I thought this baby wouldn't be mine, it was like I was raped, and surely I could excuse myself for considering not keeping it."

"What did I say today?" Slater asked.

"Love. You said if you're looking for proof of soul, don't look further than love. And I realized ending this baby's life puts me in the same state of mind that lets a scientist begin to think of embryos as some protein with interesting experimental possibilities. I want to be on the other end of the spectrum. Where life is a gift, something sacred from God. Those cells inside me are not only duplicating, but creating the machinery for a soul to live a lifetime of chances at giving and absorbing love."

She was crying softly now.

Slater didn't patronize her tears. She had good reason to cry, and he wasn't going to trivialize it by patting her shoulder and telling her it would be all right.

When she finished, he had his next words ready. "I wouldn't be afraid to try to help you raise the baby."

She stared at him.

"I mean if we fit together the way I think we do." This woman *did* make him nervous. "I'm not proposing this second. I just don't want you flying out of my life in the next hour."

Paige softened and smiled.

"But I've got to tell you something first," he continued, less nervous after her smile. "About why I was in New Mexico. Think of it as part two of my retirement story."

She straightened.

"You get the short story, though. It's about the brother who joined me in my investment firm and found creative ways to spend our clients' money and make it look like my doing."

He shrugged. "You'll have to trust me on this one," Slater said. "Because his side of the same story paints me as the one with sticky fingers."

Slater looked her directly in the eyes and made sure he didn't flinch as he continued. "This is the same brother I found spending a distinctively unbrotherly weekend with my wife. We fought. Bad. I nearly killed him. About then I decided to bail out on everything—the divorce fight, the legal charges against me. I ran. I've been living on funds I'd shifted to Switzerland. I bought a false ID and started over as Slater Ellis. And I made sure I haven't once stopped feeling sorry for myself."

When she didn't comment, he added, "But these last few weeks have shown me bigger things to worry about."

"I knew about most of it," Paige said. "From Van Klees."

He hid his surprise.

"I needed to hear it from you though. Makes it easier to think about trusting you."

He grinned.

She did not. "I said *think*. Look. I need to see who Paige Stephens is, see if she's really got some of the toughness I was surprised to find in Los Alamos. After I'm convinced I can be my own person, maybe I'll be ready to think about someone else."

"Pick a place for sixty days from now," Slater said.

"What do you mean?"

"I've got my own stuff to go through. I'm going back to face what I should have faced four years ago. I've already talked to a lawyer, and it appears I'll have a good shot at leniency. Not only that, there's the triplets. I talked it over with Austad. The general arranged for us to get some of the Van Klees funds. Austad and I are going to find a way for the boys to get good schooling and good parenting. That's going to take time, too, even if my mother has already fallen in love with the one she's met. What I'm saying is, let's meet in two months for another cup of coffee."

Paige was studying him, her expressionless face giving him no way to judge how well he was pleading his case.

"You pick the place and time of day," Slater said. "I'll meet you there. No promises, no expectations, just a date. If that works out, we pick another time and place, try another date."

Paige suddenly stood. "I'm going to catch a cab."

"Why?"

"You're too contagious. I'm not sure I want someone in my life again."

"Sure," he said. He wasn't going to beg. Not yet.

He watched her walk between the tables. Watching her, he wasn't sure he could handle being alone anymore. Not when it felt so good to just be near her.

He watched her very closely, hoping she might change her mind. At the door, she turned around, caught his stare. She began to walk back to him.

He grinned, feeling it stretch to the point of hurt.

She ignored his grin and picked the bill off the table. "Nobody pays my way."

He stopped grinning.

"I definitely like that," she said. "You *can* be rattled. I'm tired of men who try to play Superman."

She reached down to lightly touch him on the shoulder. She let her fingertip rest there, a decision playing across her face. "London, England," she finally said. A small smile returned. "Five in the evening, local time. Not for coffee. Dinner and a show. My treat, not yours."

She straightened and lifted her head.

Slater fought the grin he felt inside, trying to be cool about his elation. "Could you be more specific? London's a big town."

"Westminster Abbey. I've always wanted to see it."

"I'll be there."

"Good." She touched his shoulder again. They locked eyes at the physical contact. Only briefly. Yet the touch and glance were enough of a promise. "Don't be late."

AFTERWORD

The Institute, TechnoGen, and the Jemez Mountains Silo Base
are fictional.

However, very little of the biotechnology presented in this book
is fictional speculation. One major exception is the existence of
humans cloned from the same embryo—genetic experts predict
this will be possible by the end of the decade. As for the fictional
Van Klees's goal to clone himself from one of his own cells, this too
is considered theoretically possible, and rapidly growing more possible on a practical level.

Currently in the United States, there are no legally defined eth-
ical guidelines for experimenting in human genetics.